RH

D0066235

Praise for *Go Away Home*

"*Go Away Home* is a tale of choices, dreams realized and rejected, and how values evolve.... Gently compelling and highly believable."
—D. Donovan, reviewer, Midwest Book Review

[*Go Away Home*] "skillfully blends the events of the wider world into the talk and gossip of small-town Iowa. The result is a memorable and warmly small-focus novel that repays rereading."
—Steve Donoghue, Historical Novel Society

"*Go Away Home* is the perfect story of coming home. Excellent characters and an extremely realistic plot made this a great book."
—Samantha Rivera, Readers' Favorite

# GO AWAY
# HOME

# Also by Carol Bodensteiner

*Growing Up Country: Memories of an Iowa Farm Girl*

# GO AWAY HOME

# Carol Bodensteiner

LAKE UNION
PUBLISHING

Text copyright © 2015 Carol Bodensteiner

Published by Lake Union Publishing, Seattle

www.apub.com

ISBN-13: 9781503944206
ISBN-10: 1503944204

Cover design by Elsie Lyons

Printed in the United States of America

*In memory of my grandparents,*
*Carl and Mary Elizabeth Jensen,*
*whose lives inspired this story*

# Chapter 1

## Iowa—1913

A fly buzzed against her cheek, and Liddie brushed it away with the back of her hand, leaving a streak of flour in the sweat trickling down her temple. When a train whistle sounded in the distance, it triggered dreams that were never far from her mind. She imagined standing on the platform, handing the porter her bag, stepping up into the car, and waving good-bye. The boldness of the idea thrilled her.

She sighed and turned her attention back to the bread dough. At sixteen, she dreamed of breaking away, of deciding her own future, of traveling, of doing *anything* but living on a farm. She wanted to see beyond the farthest rolling hill and start living her life. She hummed a wordless tune, matching her rhythm to the pulse of the train chugging by on the tracks.

Grabbing a handful of flour from the bin, she spread it across the breadboard. She lifted the heavy gray crockery bowl and turned a small mountain of sticky dough onto the floured surface. Enough to make six big loaves. Enough to last her family a week. After coating her hands with more flour, she dusted it across the dough. Then she grasped the outside edge of the dough and pulled it into the center, pushing the mass with the heels of her hands.

Outside to inside: Brown's Station to Chicago. Outside to inside: Chicago to New York.

Looking out the kitchen window, Liddie saw her mother and sister bent like question marks over their hoes. Amelia had inherited their mother's stocky build. From this distance, and with both of them wearing wrappers and straw hats, one could be mistaken for the other. The hems of their dresses snagged on vines as they moved down the long garden rows, clearing weeds and breaking up the black Iowa soil—ground so rich a seed need only fall on it to spring to life and make a crop. Just-picked radishes and peas filled a basket at the end of the row.

Liddie strained to make out what they were saying. The words eluded her, but she could detect a certain tension in the tone. Well, it was a hot day—unusually so for mid-June. She was glad to be inside making bread. Though it was close in the kitchen, at least she was out of the sun and an occasional breeze through the open door offered some relief.

She had begun mixing the lard, water, yeast, and flour as soon as the breakfast dishes were cleared, measuring the amounts automatically from long experience. Before she was ten, she'd learned to make bread. She was a competent cook—*the best way to a man's heart*, her mother so often said. Bread baking was the only household chore for which Liddie was solely responsible, and she took great pride in it.

Outside to inside. Outside to inside. The dough took shape. A lock of cinnamon-colored hair came loose from the twist she'd so carefully sculpted that morning. It was when she put up the pin-straight hair that came from their father's side that Liddie especially envied Amelia their mother's curls. She hooked the strand with her little finger, tucked it behind her ear, and continued kneading.

In her free time, she studied pictures in magazines and newspapers to see how city ladies fixed their hair and dressed. The latest fashion was hobble skirts. As she had considered making such a dress for herself, she had wondered how anyone negotiated such a narrow hem. So one morning, she'd looped a rope around her ankles to limit her stride just as a hobble skirt would. She practiced walking in her room, giggling as she inched around with short-ened steps. When she finally went downstairs, she found she could not move with ease and had to grab the table several times to keep from falling.

"What's the matter with you?" her mother asked as she set to folding the towels she'd upended out of a laundry basket onto the kitchen table. "Are you sick?"

Laughing, Liddie collapsed into a chair, pulled up the skirt of her cotton housedress, and displayed the ropes that had worked their way past the tops of her shoes and now snagged at her stockings.

"What on earth?" Her mother frowned.

"I was practicing how to walk in a hobble skirt." Liddie slipped the rope off one leg and ran to the bureau to get the picture of the dress she'd found in the *Ladies' Home Journal* her aunt Kate had brought during her last visit.

Her mother surveyed the picture. "That is the silliest thing I've ever seen," she said.

"It's beautiful. Look how the shape of the skirt makes her seem so tall and elegant."

"You couldn't do an honest bit of work in that." She pulled another shirt out of the clothes basket.

Liddie considered the picture. Women who lived in cities did not hoe weeds, gather eggs, or milk cows. How they did spend their days she could only imagine.

"And now you've torn your stockings," her mother had said. "Mend them before the holes get bigger."

Remembering that day made her giggle. She glanced at the table where her sewing basket waited. She enjoyed making bread, but not nearly as much as she enjoyed sewing. She picked up the pace of her kneading to get to the work in her basket more quickly. Only the monogram remained to complete the shirt she was making for Papa. Her future was in that shirt—it was part of the plan she and Aunt Kate had hatched to transform her from farm girl to city seamstress.

After spreading another bit of flour on the board, she continued to work the dough outside to inside, enjoying its transformation into a firm, elastic ball.

"How's the bread coming?"

Liddie jumped at the unexpected greeting. "Aunt Kate! I didn't hear you come downstairs." Holding her flour-covered hands in the air, she gave her aunt an awkward hug.

Kate kissed her niece's cheek and wiped away the flour smudge. "I didn't mean to scare you."

"I've survived worse." Liddie grinned. "It's ready to rise." She returned the ball of dough to the bowl, swiped fingers dipped in lard over it to keep the surface moist, draped a cotton towel across the top, and slid it to the back of the counter.

"Where's Margretta?" Kate asked.

"Mama's in the garden with Amelia. Did you talk to her again?" Liddie asked. "What did she say? What do you think Papa will say?"

Kate laughed as she looked out toward the garden. "Are you forgetting I just arrived last night? I have to work into these things." She opened the cookie jar and peered in, considering the contents before taking out three chewy molasses cookies. "It was good of you all to let me sleep in on my first day. But alas, I've missed breakfast."

"I thought maybe you talked after I went to bed." Liddie poured her aunt a cup of coffee, and they sat at the kitchen table.

Kate dipped a cookie in the coffee and chewed it slowly, a look of bliss on her face.

Liddie waited. It was pointless to rush her aunt when she was savoring a sweet. An abundance of pastries lent a plumpness to Kate that strained the seams of the dark tailored suit dresses she had favored since moving from classroom to administration.

"Yes, I talked with your mother. She still doesn't much like the idea of you living away from home so young . . ."

"I'll be seventeen in four months!"

"You're still her baby and she worries about you. And since you're dead set on not following in my footsteps into the classroom . . ." Kate's eyebrows arched in a familiar movement that often signaled the beginning of a lecture, most likely on the merits of teaching. Liddie kept her face impassive. "Your mother doesn't want you to be at loose ends."

"I don't mean it as a slight to you. Or Amelia. Amelia likes keeping a roomful of children corralled. I wouldn't."

"Teaching has its advantages. Like spending weeks each summer with you."

"That's true." Liddie enjoyed her aunt's visits. Each time she came, Kate brought with her a bit of the world Liddie longed to experience. Though her mother and aunt looked alike, the similarity ended there. While her aunt talked about suffrage and women's rights and the latest theories in pedagogy, her mother's days revolved around laundry and gardening and the next meal.

When she was thirteen, Liddie had spent a week with her aunt in Dubuque, where Kate worked as a school superintendent. Kate took her to a suffragette rally, where Liddie was entranced by the speakers who described so fervently the changes women would make when they had the right to vote.

Now Liddie leaned forward, willing to set aside her own interests for news of the suffragettes. "What have you heard about suffrage?"

Kate signaled dismay with a shake of her head. "I really thought with Illinois getting the ball rolling with their vote this year we'd see more fervor in Iowa. We have been distressingly quiet since the march in Boone. Five years ago already! There's a rally in Dubuque next month. Mrs. Carter—you heard her speak—hopes Mr. Roosevelt's enthusiasm will convince more women to join the cause and more men to support suffrage even though he didn't win the presidential election."

"Could I go? Would you take me?"

"Your mother wasn't happy with me the last time," Kate said. "She sent you away for a week, and you returned making placards and marching around the house."

Liddie slumped in her chair. "Every day I spend on the farm, I feel like the world is passing me by. I want more."

"More what?" Kate asked. "And please sit up. Ladies do not slouch."

Liddie pulled herself upright. Since the last time her aunt visited, Liddie had grown two inches and was now taller than her mother. She stretched tall and lean like her father and her brother, Vern. Excitement pulsed in her chest as she thought about her future, and she leaned forward, her face animated.

"Training to be a seamstress is a good start. From there, who knows? I might have a career. I could make dresses like the ones in the magazines." She hesitated. "Can women do that?"

"I don't see why not. Women surely know better than men what a woman would wear." Kate finished off the second cookie and bit into the third.

Liddie started to flop back in her chair but immediately thought better of it. "If I stay on the farm, Mama and Papa will push me to marry a farmer, like they're trying to do with Amelia."

Six years older than Liddie, Amelia was well into marrying age. And Amelia wanted to get married, as she said so often. But none of the men she liked survived their father's critical eye. Meanwhile, the local farm boys their parents suggested invariably arrived cloaked in the aroma of pig manure—and left, predictably, before it was dark.

"What do you mean?"

"Amelia was seeing a fellow. Fred Winslow. He came here from Indiana last summer."

"Was seeing?"

"Papa put his foot down last week. Said Fred was a no-account, not worth Amelia's time. Right after that, Fred left town. Papa said Fred leaving so quick only proved his point. Amelia's heartbroken."

"What did this Fred person do?"

"Not enough, Papa said. When he came to Iowa, Fred worked for the railroad, but he quit and hired on with a farmer over by Hurstville. Then he quit that and made deliveries for the mercantile."

"Hmm."

"He liked Amelia. He took her to picnics and dances, he sang and was a lot of fun. They'd sit on the porch at night until Papa made him go home." Liddie paused. "Mama and Papa say they want Amelia to get married, but they don't agree with the men she likes. It's been a row around here lately."

"Are you as determined not to marry a farmer as Amelia seems to be?"

"I don't plan to marry anyone! You know that." She shifted uneasily as she thought for a bit before asking something that had been on her mind for months. "Aunt Kate, does it bother you that people call you an . . . old maid?"

"My goodness! Why do you ask?"

"I overheard Mrs. Stevens say if Mama and Papa don't look out, Amelia will be an old maid. That made me wonder about you." Liddie furrowed her brow as she looked at her aunt. "You're successful and happy even though you never married. But she made being an old maid sound like the worst thing in the world."

"Many people think it is. And they have their reasons. But I believe no woman should get married just to be married. Thank heaven and the suffrage movement that girls have choices these days. That's what we've been fighting for." She saluted Liddie with what remained of the last cookie. "If I'm called an old maid because I made my own choice, well, my dear, then I wear the title proudly." She popped the cookie into her mouth.

"Liddie!"

Liddie heard her mother's voice and ran to the window. She saw her sister collapsed in the garden, and the hair rose on her arms. "Something's wrong with Amelia!"

She raced out the screen door and across the lawn, leaping over the vegetable rows, then dropped to her knees at Amelia's side. The sight of her sister's pasty-white face sent a chill up her back. "Is she dead?"

"Don't be silly." Her mother rubbed Amelia's cheeks. Margretta looked up at Kate, who'd arrived breathing heavily from the exertion. "She fainted."

"Amelia!" Liddie grasped her sister's hand and pressed it to her own cheek, the warmth assuring her, more than her mother's words, of her sister's well-being. "Amelia! Say something. Are you all right?"

Amelia's eyelids fluttered. She struggled to raise her head, but her eyes crossed and she fell back. The look on Amelia's face would have been comical if her face hadn't been so white.

Their mother grasped Amelia under the arm. "Let's get her to the house. Help me lift her, Kate." She motioned Liddie toward the pump. "Get some water."

"What happened, Margretta?" Kate asked as she took Amelia's other arm and helped to half walk, half drag Amelia out of the garden and into the shade on the porch steps.

Racing ahead to the pump, Liddie couldn't hear her mother's answer. With a few urgent strokes of the pump handle, she coaxed cold water up from the well into the bucket and grabbed the tin cup from the hook. She ran to the porch and thrust the cup into her mother's hands.

Margretta dipped water and held the cup to Amelia's lips.

"Your apron, Liddie." Kate held out her hand.

Liddie untied the strings and handed the apron to her aunt, who soaked it in the bucket and pressed it against Amelia's neck.

Liddie crouched at her sister's knees, relieved to see color returning to Amelia's cheeks. "What happened?"

Amelia didn't look up. "The heat."

"Don't fret your sister," Margretta said. "She's going to lie down a bit."

"It was the heat," Amelia insisted. She took the cloth from the back of her neck, dipped it in the bucket, and wiped it across her forehead. "See? I'm better now." As she pushed herself upright, she wobbled and had to grip the handrail to steady herself.

The three women watched in silence as Amelia made her way up the porch steps and into the house.

"What's wrong with her, Mama?" Liddie asked. She'd never known her sister to be ill, though lately she'd taken to bed with headaches.

Margretta shook her head. "I feared this," she muttered. She handed the cup to Liddie. "Put that back. Then get the basket from the garden. And take water to your father and the boys." She motioned for Kate to follow her up the porch steps, her shoulders bowed as though carrying a heavy weight.

Kate's lips creased in a tight line. "You better check on that bread, too, Liddie. It'll be ready to punch down soon."

Liddie frowned. She wanted to know about Amelia. She wanted to say she didn't need to be reminded about the bread. They were keeping something from her; that was certain. She felt shut out, but out of what, she didn't know.

# Chapter 2

Once she returned from taking water to the men and put the bread in the oven, Liddie settled herself on the porch swing, her sewing basket beside her, a shirt on her lap. Finally, she had time to finish the monogram. Her father's full name was George William Treadway, though everyone, even her mother, called him G. W. Liddie thought it a distinguished name. GWT—blue on blue, on the breast pocket. So subtle. He would know. She would know. But unless someone looked closely, it wouldn't be apparent to anyone else.

The first time she'd presented him a handkerchief she'd hemmed, he'd picked her up and twirled her around the parlor, planting a warm kiss on her forehead and whispering "Thank you, princess" in her ear when he landed her gently back on her feet. Though she'd outgrown being twirled around, she hadn't outgrown the enjoyment she felt from pleasing him with her sewing. She cut a length of embroidery floss, separated two strands, and threaded them through the eye of a fine needle.

Her mother had put fabric in Liddie's hands as soon as she could hold a needle. Even at five years old, Liddie had shown an unusual willingness to sit quietly and stitch. By the time she was ten, her stitching had far eclipsed Amelia's skills. The more her mother taught her, the more she wanted to learn. After making quick work of hems and tears and other everyday sewing tasks, she moved on to the fancier work she enjoyed.

Recently, she had taken to cutting blue printed fabric into an oak leaf and reel pattern, then appliquéing it onto muslin squares. Her aim was twenty eighteen-by-eighteen-inch squares. Enough for a quilt. Each time she picked up a square, the oak leaf and reel pattern reminded her of fall and how much she enjoyed walking in the hills, hearing the fallen leaves crunch under her boots. It had taken months to complete the first square, and she'd begun a second.

Liddie's sewing basket always held projects she was making for others. She embroidered the recipient's initials on a cuff or a pocket. Then she stitched her own initials in some hidden spot—the interior of the placket, the yoke just below the collar, a cuff. It took a little extra time, and although some—her brother, Vern, for instance, or their hired man, Joe—were unaware the initials were even there, she drew pleasure from putting some reminder of herself on each item she made.

She patterned doll dresses she sewed for friends after fancy designs she'd have no occasion to wear herself. Sometimes, she worked to duplicate the dresses she saw in Aunt Kate's magazines. Other times, she combined features from many dresses.

As the yeasty smell of baking bread wafted out to the porch, she tied off the embroidery thread and snipped the ends.

"There," she said, smoothing the front of the shirt. "Ready." She folded the shirt and went inside to set the table for supper.

"Are you all right?" she asked when Amelia came downstairs. "You really gave us a turn. In my life, I don't ever remember you being ill. Why don't you sit awhile yet. I can get supper ready."

"I'm fine." Amelia took the silverware out of Liddie's hands. "I'll set the table."

"Where are Mama and Aunt Kate?"

Amelia shrugged.

"I hope Aunt Kate is talking to her about me."

"I hope so, too," Amelia said.

Amelia's voice sounded so oddly hopeful that Liddie looked at her. Since Amelia didn't say more, she went on: "Do you think Papa will say yes?"

"I have no idea. Now don't be wasting time talking. Papa and the boys will be in soon."

Liddie drew back from her sister's sharp tone as if she'd been slapped. "What did I do?"

Amelia didn't answer. Instead, she dropped the silverware on the table with rattling force and ran out of the room.

For the second time that day, Liddie was left looking at someone's retreating back.

———

"You still planning to go into town tonight?" G. W. asked Joe over supper.

Joe nodded. "Catherine's making dessert."

Vern snickered.

"What?" Joe asked.

"I'm thinking you're sweeter on her than that cake she's making."

Joe elbowed him. "Maybe someday you'll be so lucky."

Joe had come to live with them four years ago after his father died, leaving him the only member of his family still in Iowa. G. W. had said he could use another hand, so Joe moved in.

Liddie had been twelve, and she remembered well those first days after Joe arrived. Her mother had sent her with sheets to fix a bed in the tack room for the new hired hand. She'd expected a man and had been surprised to find a thin boy sitting on the edge of the bunk.

"Hi," she'd said. "I'm Liddie."

He stood at once, extending a hand to shake hers. "I'm Josef—Joe—Bauer."

She shifted the bedding to her left arm and reached for his hand, a strong hand, rough with callouses. Hardly ever did anyone shake her hand. "I'm pleased to meet you, Josef."

"Joe." He reached for the bedding. "I'll take that."

"No bother. I'll do it." She slipped past him and began to unfold a sheet.

He caught the loose corners. "I'll help."

Between them, they flicked the sheet out so it billowed over the bed. Pulling it taut, he tucked the sheet around the mattress, deftly mitering the corners the way she'd learned to do it.

He straightened up when he saw her looking at him and raked thick, dark hair away from deep-set hazel eyes. "My ma taught me."

Liddie had liked him at once.

———

A month later, Joe had run off.

"Where is he?" Margretta had asked when Joe didn't come in for supper.

"Did he say anything, Vern?" G. W. asked. A tall man with even taller expectations, G. W. carried himself with the confidence of earned success. Investments in sound livestock—particularly the sows that sent a steady stream of pigs to market each year—had allowed him to retire the mortgage ahead of schedule and build a tidy savings. Though not a churchgoing man, he made regular contributions to the Union Methodist church because his wife attended and because he agreed with the church's values of hard work, honesty, and neighborliness. It was also his belief that both livestock and children benefited from a firm, gentle hand and clear expectations.

Vern simply shrugged. He forked potatoes into his mouth without looking up.

Liddie looked at him in surprise. On a regular day, Vern conserved words as though they were drops of rain in a drought, but she'd always known him to answer a direct question.

"Vern." Her father's tone made Liddie stiffen in her chair.

Vern went to set his fork on the edge of his plate, but his hand shook and the fork tipped, flipping peas around the table. As he grabbed for the fork, his hand knocked against his glass, splashing milk. Vern's neck flushed red as he clenched his hands in tight fists.

Liddie clapped a hand over her mouth to hide a laugh. At fifteen, Vern was as clumsy as a newborn calf.

"Did you boys get into it?" G. W. asked.

"Oh, Vern," Margretta said. "You didn't fight!"

G. W. lifted his hand and she fell quiet. "Tell me what happened, Vern."

"He acts like he knows everything." Vern's eyes darted between his parents and wound up focused on his plate. "Just because he could break that horse."

G. W. regarded his son. "Vern, every man has his own talents. Joe has a way with horses like you have a way with building things. It takes all of us to run this place."

"You act like he's so special," Vern muttered.

"He's had a hard time. We're blessed to have a great deal. The least we can do is share it." G. W. took his knife and cut into a pork chop. He looked at Vern before forking a bite into his mouth. "And be gracious about it."

It took a while before Vern was able to meet his father's eyes. "I don't know where he is, Pa. He headed south. Should I go after him?"

"I expect he has things to work out. I'm thinking he'll be back."

When Joe returned three days later, it looked as though he hadn't eaten or washed since he left. G. W. met him on the porch steps. Liddie followed, but he waved her back, so she watched from inside the doorway.

"I don't know as how I belong here," Joe said. He stood with his feet planted, shoulders squared. He clenched his hands into fists and then loosened them before finally shoving them into his back pockets. "I came back to get my things."

"Have we made you feel unwelcome?"

"You and Mrs. Treadway have been good to me. I appreciate it."

"So this is about you and Vern?"

Joe looked away. Liddie saw the muscles work in his cheeks and she wondered what he was fighting to say. Or not say. She strained to hear.

"It's just you aren't my family."

"Every family has its own ways. Every man does, too. You can't run off every time the going gets rough."

"I know, sir."

"You're a good boy, Joe. You'll be a man to make your folks proud." G. W. put his hand on Joe's shoulder. "We'd like you to stay."

"You'd let me?" Surprise showed on Joe's face.

"As long as you want. We don't abide fighting, though, so whatever's going on between you and Vern, you better work it out."

"Yes, sir."

"Another thing. You can't run off like this. It upsets Mama too much."

Joe flushed. "It won't happen again. I promise."

"All right, then. Get cleaned up and come in to eat. This afternoon, you and Vern go hunting. Mama has a hankering for rabbit stew."

Vern and Joe had come back later that day with a brace of rabbits.

Throughout that fall, Liddie had watched as the relationship between the two boys developed from tolerance to friendship. Farm chores like grubbing out tree stumps, making fences, and picking corn forced the two to work together. Beyond work, they discovered a common interest in card games—Joe had a mind for pinochle while Vern had the face for poker. Her father had been wise when he sent them out after rabbits that day. They both enjoyed the companionship of hunting.

In those first weeks, Liddie grew a crush on Joe that embarrassed her to think of now. She'd followed him around like a puppy, trying to get his attention, abashed when she did.

Her fascination began at a neighborhood barn party when he chose her as his partner for a square dance. With his arm around her waist during a promenade, she imagined herself a young woman with Joe as her beau.

But the crush lasted only for the better part of a month, ending when Joe dashed her hopes by taking a neighbor girl to a dance.

"I remember my first crush," Amelia had said when she found Liddie lying on the bed, a pillow flattened against her chest, girlish tears wetting her cheeks. Amelia curled up next to her, stroking Liddie's arm gently as she shared the story. "He was a hired man, too. Hank Thompson. Remember him?"

Liddie shook her head.

"He worked here one summer. He was so handsome." She made a face. "He never looked my way."

"What did you do?"

"Mooned around him like a sick calf." Amelia laughed. "He left at the end of the summer. Joe will be gone by the time you grow up, too. You'll get over it."

Another tear trickled down Liddie's cheek. She doubted that could ever be true.

But soon enough, Liddie's interests had begun to move in the direction of suffragettes and sewing and careers and travel. And over the years, the only boy she'd ever taken such a shine to became more like a brother. He encouraged her to join him and Vern in games of catch, teaching her to throw the ball when Vern only laughed at her feeble first attempts. Joe defended her when Vern's teasing brought tears to her eyes. Though she was so much younger, Joe told her of his dreams of having his own farm and listened with respect as she talked about her dreams of seeing the world.

Now she was happy for Joe and Catherine. She expected he'd be happy for her, too, when he learned she was going to Maquoketa.

As she thought again of Maquoketa, Liddie's attention returned to the supper table. She looked at her aunt, waiting with growing impatience for her to bring up the apprenticeship. Kate responded with an almost imperceptible shake of her head. Liddie mouthed, *What?* Kate tilted her head toward Liddie's mother. For the first time, Liddie noticed that her mother's eyes were red and that she'd barely touched the food on her plate.

"You got a good scald on the roast, Margretta," G. W. said.

Even the compliment didn't bring a smile to her mother's face. Anxiety gained traction in Liddie's stomach. Had her mother changed her mind about the apprenticeship?

"Pass the bread?" Joe asked.

"At least you didn't burn it this time." Vern pointed the tip of his knife at Liddie.

"No. I didn't burn it this time. Or the last six times." This was an old jibe, one Vern brought up too often. With heat radiating through her chest, Liddie gripped the edges of her chair and glared.

"Let it rest," Joe said to Vern. "That only happened once, and you know it."

"Aw, I was just joshing. Can't she take a joke?" Vern looked at Liddie with a satisfied grin. "Got you again, didn't I?"

"Some joke." Liddie frowned.

Amelia squeezed Liddie's hand under the table. Liddie tried to smile. Amelia supported her. With Amelia at home taking care of things, she could go to Maquoketa.

"I can't do this. Not tonight!" Margretta pushed back from the table, standing so abruptly the legs of her chair caught in the rug. The chair teetered and Kate reached out, grabbing it before it fell.

Raspy sobs erupted from behind Margretta's hankie as she ran out of the room.

"What the . . . ?" G. W. looked bewildered.

"I'll go." Kate left her napkin crumpled by her plate.

Liddie's mouth fell open. She turned to Amelia. "I didn't mean—" She stopped. Amelia was crying, too.

———

Later that night, Kate joined Liddie on the porch. Sinking heavily into the porch rocker, she spoke without preamble. "Your sister is pregnant."

"Pregnant!" Liddie felt the bottom drop out of her stomach. "Pregnant? How can Amelia be pregnant? She's not married."

"Ah, Liddie."

Kate's weary voice held disappointment, and Liddie realized just how naive her comment had been. The heat of embarrassment burned her cheeks.

"It does happen. Unfortunately. But there are places for girls who get themselves in trouble."

"She'll go away? But where? She can't be alone." A pang of fear for her sister pierced Liddie's chest.

Kate nodded. "In the morning, I'll call a colleague to make arrangements. There's a place in Des Moines where she can stay until it's her time."

"But . . ." Liddie saw immediately that if Amelia was gone, not just away teaching during the days but really gone, there was no chance her parents could do without her on the farm.

"It's necessary. She won't see anyone there who knows her or the family." Kate had been sitting still; now she set the chair to rocking. "It's a shame. She had such a promising future."

"Couldn't she teach? After?"

Kate shook her head. "Oh my, no. News like this has a way of getting around."

"But she'll come back here, won't she?"

"I suppose she will. But this will hang over her the rest of her life."

"But she has to be here. She has to stay on the farm." As the reality solidified in Liddie's mind, so did desperation. "So I can go."

"We'll have to see about that."

"But Mrs. Tinker needs an answer. You said so."

"It can't be helped. Your parents cannot be bothered with that decision now."

Liddie's eyes stung. "It's not fair."

"That can often be said of life, dear."

When Liddie went to bed, she had the bedroom she shared with her sister to herself. Amelia was still with their parents.

Sitting at the dressing table, she paid halfhearted attention to brushing her hair one hundred strokes as Amelia always said she should. Her eyes strayed around the room as her mind struggled to absorb a world that had gone topsy-turvy. The wallpaper covered with pink roses that made her feel as though she slept in a flower garden. The elaborately painted china teapot that had inspired bedtime stories when Liddie was little and then talks of dinner parties and guests as the girls grew older. The heavy, scrolled wrought iron headboard their father had painted white to appease his daughters' pleas.

As Liddie pulled her nightgown over her head, she imagined Amelia doing *that*—though she didn't exactly know what *that* was—with Fred. Bile rose in her throat, and she pulled the quilt up around herself, a protection from the idea of a man doing such things to her. Her thoughts turned to Maquoketa and sewing. As she saw her own future slipping away, disgust gave way to anger, embarrassment, and shame.

From Liddie's earliest memories, Amelia had been the one to bathe and dress her. Amelia had washed and braided Liddie's hair, taught her to put it up when she went from a child's short skirts to a woman's long dresses. Amelia was more than her sister; Amelia was her friend. Amelia was always there.

How this had happened was beyond her comprehension. She knew Amelia was disgraced. The family was disgraced. How could they look at their neighbors ever again without feeling shame?

She thought of how other farmers came to Papa for advice on crops and cattle. How the school directors got his approval on work to be done on the schoolhouse.

She thought of how much Mama enjoyed having the neighbor women over for quilting bees. She knew how proud Mama was that all of her children had finished eighth grade. When Amelia took over as teacher after she graduated, Mama had brought out her special cordial glasses. Even Liddie had a sip of corn wine.

No one had needed to explain to Liddie that her behavior—or the behavior of any of the children in the family—would be above reproach. How could it happen that her sister was pregnant? Out of wedlock?

When Amelia finally came to bed, Liddie pointedly rolled over onto her side, her back to her sister. She wanted Amelia to know that she was awake but that she was not going to speak with her. She pulled the covers over her ears and pretended not to hear her sister's muffled sobs.

# Chapter 3

Liddie set the breakfast table, making a point of not speaking to Amelia, who was in the kitchen frying eggs and sausages. Amelia looked as though she hadn't slept all night. Liddie didn't care.

When G. W. came to the table, his face turned red.

"Take that plate away, Liddie." He pointed at Amelia's place.

"G. W., please," Margretta said.

"She's still your daughter," Kate said.

"She will not eat at this table."

Liddie froze, her father's anger shocking her into sympathy for her sister.

Amelia stopped in the doorway. Her hands trembled, and Liddie thought she might drop the platter of eggs.

"Do as I said, Liddie. Vern, get rid of that chair."

"Pa . . ." Vern said.

"Not a word." G. W.'s voice filled the room, driving out every other sound as he slapped his palm flat on the table.

Liddie scooped up the plate and silverware and ran to the kitchen. Amelia followed, barely getting the platter set on the counter before she collapsed to the floor. For the first time that morning, Liddie met her sister's eyes.

"Take the eggs in, Liddie," Amelia said.

"But—"

"Do it. Go."

Liddie picked up the platter and stepped around her sister.

Her father pushed two eggs and four sausages onto his plate. He picked up his knife and fork but sat transfixed, staring at the wall above Margretta's head.

No one spoke a word through the whole meal. The only thing Liddie could think of was her sister on the kitchen floor. When G. W. left the table, the food on his plate was still untouched.

For the rest of the day, Liddie's skin prickled with the tension charging the air. Amelia sought refuge in the bedroom. Mama took to her bed with a headache. Papa and the boys went to the barn. Liddie eavesdropped as her aunt made the necessary phone call. It amazed her that Kate could make such a call with complete calm, saying nothing that allowed the operator or those listening on the party line to know about the tornado ripping apart their lives.

By the end of the day, arrangements were made. Amelia would leave on the 2:00 p.m. train two days hence.

———

Liddie grabbed the egg basket and headed for the barn. She was grateful for any task—even collecting eggs—that took her out of the house.

"Here, chick, chick," she called as she scattered handfuls of oats on the ground, and a dozen hens clucked at her feet. She'd hoped to entice all of the birds off their nests so she could gather eggs without a hassle. But the red hen wasn't there. Sure enough, when she went into the barn, Liddie found the old hen solidly in place.

Holding a corncob at arm's length, she poked at the hen. "Shoo." The hen pecked at the corncob and then abruptly pecked again, aiming for Liddie's hand.

"I hate you," she shouted. Tears slipped from the corners of her eyes.

"You'll never get the eggs that way."

Liddie spun around. Joe was leaning against the door, his arms crossed, watching her with ill-concealed amusement.

She scrubbed at her eyes with the heel of her hand. "I hate these chickens!"

"Are you all right?" His smile faded.

"Dust. That's all."

"I thought it might be something else."

"You know?"

He nodded.

So that was how it would be. Soon everyone would know. "Nothing's all right. Not anymore."

"I'm sad for her."

"Sad for her? Sad for her? I'm so mad at her—so mad I could just . . . spit!"

Joe raised an eyebrow. "Spit?"

"Are you laughing at me?"

"I understand being upset, but why are you mad?"

"Last night, Mama and Aunt Kate were going to convince Papa to let me work in Maquoketa. Now I'll never get out of here. She's ruined everything."

"I don't understand why you're so set on leaving."

"Why, to do things. See things. If I stay here"—Liddie's gesture took in the entire farm—"it never changes. Collect eggs. Make bread. Do laundry. Milk the cow. Take orders from everyone. Every day. Over and over and over."

"You think that's what your mama does? Take orders?"

Liddie scuffed her toe in the fine dirt of the barn floor. "No. Not really. But taking orders is what I do. It doesn't matter now, anyway. I'll be here forever." She looked up. "Don't you want to get away? See the world? Do other things?"

Joe didn't hesitate. "No. This is what I want. A place of my own. Right here. Friends. Family. Land."

"It's different for you. You're a man, you can get away any time you want, so you don't want to."

"You think that's it?" He snorted. "What I'm downright certain of is that Amelia didn't expect this to happen to her. And she didn't do it to spite you."

"I just don't understand how she could do this."

"Did you ask her?"

"I don't know if I'll ever talk to her again."

He eyed the corncob. "Whatever you do, you shouldn't take it out on the chicken."

Liddie flushed. "You wouldn't be laughing if you had to do this every day. The corncob usually makes her move. But she's not having any of it today."

Joe looked at the hen for a few seconds. Keeping eye contact with the bird, Joe clucked in soft tones as he walked up to the nest. He reached in above the wary hen and stroked her back with a light, firm hand. She didn't peck at him. Instead, after a few strokes, the old hen relaxed her neck until her head rested on her plump breast. Joe eased his hand under her and brought out two eggs.

"There you are." He laid the warm eggs carefully into Liddie's hands.

"Why did she let you do that?"

He shrugged. "If you want to go to Maquoketa, and your mama agrees, I expect G. W. will come around." Joe slapped his gloves against his leg, releasing a cloud of dust. "I better get a move on. The fence won't get made with me standing here."

She was out the barn door when she heard him call after her. "She's your sister, Liddie, and she's going away. She needs you."

———

Joe's words echoed in Liddie's ears as she stood outside the half-closed bedroom door, watching Amelia pack. She felt as though she were observing a stranger.

The previous night, as the girls changed into their night-gowns, Liddie had felt Amelia's eyes on her, but she had refused to acknowledge her. They slid between the sheets as always.

"Good night," Amelia whispered, leaning over to kiss Liddie on the cheek.

Liddie turned away. "Don't."

She was angry, but even more, she was embarrassed that what she thought she knew about Amelia, what she thought she shared with her, had been a sham. She thought she and Amelia talked about everything, that they didn't have any secrets.

From the time boys had begun to call on her, Amelia had assessed each one, pointing out to Liddie both his good qualities and why, ultimately, he would not be a good match. In retrospect, Liddie realized she might have guessed there was something special about Fred. After their first date, Amelia never said a word to Liddie about him. Not a word about what she was doing.

Now, as the hour approached to take Amelia to the train station, Liddie knew she should say something, yet each time she opened her mouth, her emotions boiled up and her jaw locked. She watched outside their bedroom door for a good five minutes before entering. When she did go in, the open dresser drawers, the stack of books, the picture frame holding their family portrait facedown on the bed hit her like a punch in the stomach.

Amelia tucked a nightgown into the corner of a brown leather grip and began to fold the bright-blue scarf Liddie had given her last Christmas. When her sister finally looked up, her face drained of color, Liddie's wall of anger crumbled.

"Stop!" She pulled the scarf from Amelia's hands. "I don't understand."

"You'll be better off when I'm gone."

Panic seized Liddie's throat as the imminent reality of losing her sister sank in. "You can't!" She clutched at her sister's hand.

Amelia pulled away, took the scarf from Liddie's hand, and folded it into the suitcase. "You'd best go," she said.

"How could you, Amelia? I don't understand. How could you have done this?"

"I loved him. I thought he loved me."

"But you're not married!"

"I don't need you to chastise me, too, Liddie." Amelia sank onto the edge of the bed, resting one hand on her still-flat stomach. "I've made a mess of things." Her voice cracked. "I broke Mama's heart. Papa will never forgive me."

Liddie forced herself to step closer, made herself sit beside her sister. She put her hand over Amelia's. A baby. It was so wonderful. And so shameful.

"You'll come back?"

"You're better off with me gone." Amelia rolled onto her side, her back to Liddie, and sobbed.

Liddie wanted to crawl up next to her sister, wrap her arms around her, and hold her, comforting Amelia as her sister had so often comforted her.

But angry words fought to cross her lips. *You made your bed. Now lie in it!*

In the end, she was neither that kind nor that cruel. She didn't comfort her sister, nor did she berate her. She simply walked away.

———

"If we're all there, doesn't it look like we're happy about what she did?" Liddie asked that morning when she cornered her mother in the kitchen. "Doesn't it say to everyone that what she did was all right?"

"We don't wash our dirty laundry in public," Margretta responded as she drew hot water from the cookstove tank. "Now go put on your good dress."

"I don't want to go."

Margretta looked at Liddie with red-rimmed eyes. "Not another word, Liddie. You're going."

Frustrated, she whirled on her heel and headed for the stairs. "Well, she's ruined everything. Everything," Liddie said, knowing her mother could hear her. She dressed in the lightweight worsted crepe dress she'd made for herself, a dress she had anticipated wearing on the first day of an apprenticeship that she knew was never going to happen.

Once Amelia said her good-byes to Kate and Joe, there was nothing else to say or do at home. Crowded shoulder to shoulder in the backseat of the buggy, Amelia, Vern, and Liddie covered the miles to the station in awkward silence. Margretta attempted conversation, a painful effort to re-create more pleasant times, but ultimately fell silent. They arrived more than an hour before the train was scheduled. After G. W. purchased the ticket, they all stood waiting for the train. The train that would remove their embarrassment from their midst, if not from their memory.

Liddie stood apart from her family, keeping her eyes focused on the worn planks of the depot platform, wishing herself invisible. Her mother stood with her hand in the crook of Amelia's elbow. Her father stared down the tracks as though he could will the train into existence. Only someone who knew him well would notice the twitch of his mustache and know it signaled a struggle to hold his emotions in check.

Vern stood a step behind their father. Physically like G. W., Vern was strong enough to work a team of horses all day long. However, he showed none of their father's social skills. He kept to the fringes at parties, steadfastly rejecting his sisters' efforts to get him to dance even a two-step. Vern would take over the farm someday and no doubt get married, though Liddie presumed he'd actually have to talk to a girl to make that happen.

Until recently, Amelia's life path had been similarly clear. She would teach until she married, and then she would settle down to care for her husband and raise children. On a farm. It was the path Liddie knew her parents wanted for her, a path she hoped to avoid. But not as Amelia had done. Never as Amelia had done.

The westbound train sounded its arrival with a blast of its whistle, and Liddie looked down the tracks. Not even a week ago, she had spent a blissful afternoon imagining her family gathered at the depot, laughing, chatting, wishing Liddie well as she prepared to board. So much could change so very quickly.

The train whistle shrieked again. Absorbed in her own thoughts, she didn't realize Amelia was standing beside her until she spoke.

"Please, Liddie." Amelia touched her arm. "I can't leave and not say good-bye."

Unable to meet her sister's eyes, Liddie stared at Amelia's hand. Her earlier anger had faded. Now she felt foolish and embarrassed at her outburst.

Amelia tried again. "I didn't mean to spoil things for you. I'm so sorry."

The sorrow in Amelia's voice ripped at Liddie's heart, and she finally looked up. Soon her sister would be gone. She swallowed hard on the lump growing in her throat and bit her cheek to keep from crying when she saw the tears pooling in Amelia's eyes.

The wheels screeched as the huge steam engine braked, bringing the passenger cars to a stop beside the platform. A porter jumped out, set a stool by the first car, and helped passengers step down. Farther along, men opened the freight cars and set to loading and unloading baggage and mailbags.

"It's time," G. W. said.

Amelia threw her arms around Liddie and hugged her tight. "I love you, Liddie. Please forgive me." Her voice cracked. Then she stepped away.

Liddie would remember that moment for the rest of her life. She'd remember to her own shame that she didn't hug her sister back or even say good-bye.

Amelia went to her father, lifting a hand to touch him. "Papa?"

He didn't acknowledge her presence, and her hand hung suspended in midair until she finally let it drop.

"Mrs. Taylor will meet you at the Des Moines station," Margretta said. "I wrote it all down." She slipped a paper into Amelia's handbag and gave her oldest child a brief, hard hug. "You'd best go now," she said, her voice rough.

Amelia kissed her mother on the cheek and picked up the travel bag. One last time, she gazed at her father's profile. As she passed Vern, Amelia touched the back of his hand with her fingertips. Liddie expected Vern to take no more note than their father, but as Amelia moved toward the train, Vern took the grip from her hand and walked with her, then handed the bag to the porter as she boarded. On the top step, Amelia half turned back toward them. She didn't smile. She didn't wave. She studied each of them, then continued into the car.

Amelia took a window seat in the middle of the car on the platform side. She focused her eyes straight ahead and did not look their way again.

G. W. took Margretta's arm and steered her toward the buggy. Vern followed.

Liddie continued to watch as the train began to move. Just before Amelia's car left Liddie's view, she saw a man sit down across from her sister.

As the caboose disappeared in the distance, she wondered, *Why couldn't it be me getting away?*

# Chapter 4

For days after, no one spoke Amelia's name. Her father's jaw seemed permanently clenched. Each morning, her mother's red eyes told Liddie she'd spent the night crying. Joe was cautious in his comments. Vern didn't speak at all.

Liddie had trouble sorting out her own emotions. Each night when she went to bed, she felt her sister's absence acutely. Yet with the daylight, she was reminded that the future she'd hoped for herself was further out of her reach than ever.

"Let it rest awhile," Kate advised before she returned to Dubuque. "Everyone needs time to adjust."

"Aunt Kate, Mrs. Tinker won't wait forever. She'll get another girl."

"That can't be helped."

"It's my life, too." Liddie stomped her foot.

"Yes, it is. Now what are you going to do with it?"

*What are you going to do with it?* Liddie considered her aunt's question as she appliquéd another oak leaf edge on a new quilt block. Keeping the stitches even was a challenge that calmed her. It had been nearly a month since Amelia left, and the high tension of the first days had eased. The rhythm of everyday life had returned, with Liddie replacing Amelia in the garden, in the kitchen, and at the washtub.

Twice, Liddie had tried to talk with her mother about Amelia. Both times, her mother began to cry, so she didn't try again. The men spent little time in the house. For that, Liddie didn't blame them. The forced quiet of purposefully not talking hurt her head.

A low rumble caused her to look up from her sewing. A bank of clouds loomed on the western horizon. She wasn't surprised. That morning, she'd stood on the porch beside her father after breakfast.

"Think it'll rain today?" he'd asked.

She glanced up at his face. It was the first time since Amelia left that he sounded like his old self. She stepped off the porch, stooping to drag her fingers through the grass. "No dew," she said, looking around the yard. "And the oak leaves are turned." Of course, her father knew it was likely to rain. He'd been teaching her about the weather as long as she could remember.

"The wind's picking up," G. W. said to Joe and Vern, who'd followed them out to the porch. "Liddie thinks it's going to rain. We better get that last hay in the barn, boys."

As the three men walked toward the barn, she'd heard them talking as they used to.

Thinking about it now, she considered that maybe Aunt Kate was right. Maybe it just took time.

A few more stitches used up the thread and she tied it off. As she folded the square and put it back in her basket, she looked at the shirt she'd made for her father. Perhaps a gift would lift his spirits. She'd give it to him today.

The clouds that had darkened the sky that afternoon let loose after supper. The steady rain washed the heat out of the air and sent a cool, cleansing breeze wafting through the house.

"We'll keep an eye on the heifer," Vern said after supper.

"Let me know when she's ready," G. W. said. "She's big boned, but it's her first calf. She might need help."

Vern and Joe stood on the porch watching the rain. Then, with grins and whoops, they took off running to the barn, galloping as though they could outrun the raindrops.

Liddie carried her sewing basket with the paper-wrapped shirt tucked inside and sat near her father.

"Shall I read to you?" he asked, picking up the *Sentinel*.

She nodded. As a little girl, she'd sat on his lap as he read the news. He still read articles aloud, and she enjoyed talking with him about local and world events. At first, she fiddled with her needle-work. Finally, she let her hands rest in her lap and listened.

After finishing an article on local elections, G. W. folded the paper and picked up his pipe. He tamped tobacco into the bowl, struck a match, and drew in deeply.

"What do you think, Liddie? Does suffrage have a chance without Roosevelt?" He leaned back in the maroon damask wing chair, smoke from the pipe curling above his head.

Because Roosevelt had been the only candidate in the 1912 election to support women's suffrage on a national basis, she'd watched the campaign with great interest. Her disappointment had run deep, mirroring the feelings of Aunt Kate and the other suffragettes she'd met, when Roosevelt's bid to win the presidency under the Progressive Party banner had failed.

"Aunt Kate says—"

"Kate has her ideas. I want to know what you think."

"It's discouraging. Mr. Wilson hasn't supported suffrage at all. Illinois passed their law, but I was dismayed to learn it only applied to some elections." She sighed. "Women have been working for the vote for so long. I wonder if I'll live to see it."

G. W. laughed. "You are young to be so pessimistic. Have a little faith!"

"What would it take for the president to change his mind, do you think?"

"Good question. I suppose he makes decisions like the rest of us, talking to people he trusts."

"What if he chooses wrong?"

"Then, also like us, he makes a new decision." G. W. tapped the pipe bowl against the ashtray. "Every choice we make becomes part of who we are. That's why you must take care."

As she considered her father's words, she couldn't help but wonder if he was thinking of Amelia, if this was a conversation he'd had, or maybe wished he'd had, with her.

"I have made one decision." Liddie reached for the shirt in her basket. "To give you this."

He unwrapped the paper. "A new shirt." He smiled at her and held the blue broadcloth by the shoulders as he examined it. "I suppose you hoped to convince me to let you work in Maquoketa?"

"Well, yes. But that was—before."

"This is well done, Liddie. You didn't need to make something new to convince me of your ability." He traced the embroidery on the pocket with his fingertip. "A nice touch."

"I was making it for you anyway."

"It is a big decision." He drew on his pipe and ran a finger back over the initials.

Her father's words ignited a tiny flicker of hope.

"G. W." Joe poked his head in the parlor door. "The heifer's straining. It looks like it'll be rough."

"I'm coming." G. W. handed the shirt back to Liddie. "Your mother thought the opportunity would be good for you."

"It would. It really would." Liddie edged forward in her chair. "I love to sew, and Mrs. Tinker has the finest shop. I could learn so much." Even though she could tell his mind was with the cow and calf, she pressed the point. "Papa, it would mean so much to me."

He stood. "I'd have considered it before, Liddie. But now your mother needs you here."

Though she had expected this, hearing him say it out loud extinguished her last ember of hope.

———

"Ma!" Vern shouted as he kicked the kitchen door open. "Pa's hurt."

Liddie dropped her sewing and ran to the kitchen. She gasped when she saw her father hanging limp between the boys, his head lolling to one side. Blood drenched his shirt and matted his hair. "What happened?"

"The cow kicked him," Vern said.

"When he fell back, he hit his head," Joe added.

"Oh—God help us!" Margretta pushed past Liddie. When she lifted G. W.'s face between her hands, his eyelids fluttered open for a second and then closed. "Bring him in the bedroom. Liddie, get towels. And water. Then call Dr. Milburn."

Liddie knew she should move, but she couldn't. Not her feet. Not her hands. His face was so white. Except for the blood. That was so red. Pinpoints of light flashed in her eyes and the kitchen tilted.

"Liddie." Joe's voice reached her. "Liddie. Get water. Do it."

She blinked and the kitchen righted itself. She filled a pan with hot water, grabbed towels from a drawer, and ran to the bedroom, terrified of what she would find.

————

"Will he be all right?" Margretta asked as the doctor washed his hands at the kitchen sink.

"That's a nasty head wound."

"He'll be all right," Liddie said, willing it to be true.

"He has a concussion. You need to watch him close for the next day or two. He'll be sore and no doubt have a headache."

Margretta sat with G. W. through the night. Liddie, Vern, and Joe took turns joining her.

"He's awake, Mama. Look," Liddie said when she saw her father open his eyes the next morning.

"Oh, G. W. Thank God." Margretta pressed her palm to his forehead.

G. W. blinked a few times and his eyes closed.

"Papa." Liddie stroked her father's cheek. "Papa. Please wake up."

G. W.'s eyes flickered open. "M . . . Amelia . . ."

"Papa. It's me, Liddie."

G. W. groaned as his eyes closed again.

"He thought you were her." Margretta's voice caught.

"The doctor said he might be confused. He's getting better, Mama. I'll tell the boys." Relief lifted Liddie's spirits. "I'll make breakfast. Then I'll sit with Papa so you can sleep."

G. W. woke throughout the day, each time for only a few minutes. Sometimes, he recognized one of them. Sometimes, he was confused. The doctor assured them this was not uncommon.

Margretta seldom left his side. By the third day, Liddie had taken over the household chores as though she'd been born to it, which she supposed she had.

Throughout the day, Liddie poked her head into her parents' bedroom to see if her mother needed anything. "Mrs. Howe dropped by with a pot of chicken noodle soup," Liddie reported. "We'll have it for supper. I wanted to tell you while she was here, but she said not to bother you."

"She's so thoughtful," Margretta said. "I'll write her a note this afternoon."

Liddie scrutinized her father's face for any sign of improvement. "Has he woken up?"

"For a few moments. He even mentioned getting up. I told him he should rest yet. He's been asleep ever since."

"You should rest awhile, too, Mama. I'll stay here in case he needs anything."

"I believe I will lie down." Margretta cupped Liddie's cheek in her hand. "You've been such a help. I'm proud of you."

After Margretta left, Liddie held her fingers to her cheek, savoring the memory of her mother's touch and the pleasure of being found useful.

While her mother napped, Liddie held her needlework on her lap, but rather than stitch, she studied her father's face. Color had not returned to his cheeks; even so, he looked peaceful enough. Not as though he were in pain. The wound had stopped bleeding, so the bandage around his head was clean. She didn't understand why he wasn't getting better. As she thought this, his eyes flickered open.

"You're here," he murmured. "I'm glad."

"Papa." She took his hand.

"You're here." He licked his lips and struggled to swallow.

"I've been here all along, Papa. Let me help you with a drink." She lifted his head, holding a glass to his lips. He swallowed and sank back on the pillow.

"I'm sorry, Amelia. I thought you were gone."

Liddie stared at her father. "Papa, it's me, Liddie. Don't you know me?"

"Sure, Liddie. I know you." His eyes darted around the room. "Is Amelia here, too?"

"Amelia's . . . gone. Don't you remember?"

"I don't . . . What happened?"

"You were helping a heifer with her calf. She kicked you."

He groaned as his fingers searched out the bandage, flinching when he came to the wound. "Hurts." His eyes drooped closed.

Fearing he would drift off, she took his hand and rubbed his wrist. "Papa," she said. "Papa!" He opened his eyes.

"Hey! Good to see you awake."

Liddie turned at the sound of Joe's voice. He and Vern stood shoulder to shoulder in the doorway. She looked back at her father. "He's . . . not clear yet."

"I'm getting up." G. W. pushed against the bedclothes. "Where's Amelia? I need to talk to her."

"Wait a bit," Liddie said. She looked at Joe and her brother, and saw her worry mirrored on their faces.

"How's the heifer?" G. W. asked.

"She's fine." Joe came to the bedside and rested a hand on G. W.'s shoulder. "Her calf was dead. Probably why she was having so much trouble."

"What about the heifer?"

"As soon as we got the calf out, she was fine," Vern repeated.

"I'm getting up." G. W. struggled to get his feet on the floor.

"I don't think you should, Pa," Vern said.

"I'm getting—" G. W. knocked Joe's hand away, bent forward, and vomited.

———

"He didn't know me," Liddie told the doctor. They'd all moved to the kitchen after Dr. Milburn finished examining G. W. "He didn't remember about the cow kicking him."

"Even after we told him things twice," Joe said.

While Margretta sat at the table and repeated what she'd told the doctor when he arrived, Vern kept a hand on her shoulder. "We got him back in bed. He fell back to sleep and hasn't opened his eyes since." Repeating these details anchored them somehow, reassured them they'd done everything they could to help.

"The concussion is causing that confusion," the doctor said.

Margretta asked, "Isn't there anything we can do?"

"Give it time. It hasn't been a week yet. A couple of weeks for a concussion to heal isn't uncommon." He picked up his black bag. "Call me if he gets worse," he said, and left.

Liddie stood looking out the door after the doctor's buggy disappeared down the lane. Vern and Joe had walked out with the doctor and gone on to the barn. "He thought I was Amelia," she said. "He was so happy to see her. I felt bad I wasn't her."

"It broke his heart, what she did." Margretta spoke quietly, almost to herself, holding a now-cold cup of coffee between her hands.

"It didn't do anything for the rest of us, either, Mama."

Her mother looked up, and Liddie thought she looked a little startled. Maybe she hadn't realized she'd spoken out loud.

Her mother said, "I told her to write. I go to the mailbox each day. Hoping."

"Does she know about Papa?"

"I wrote. I don't know if she has the letter yet."

"You'd tell me if she writes?"

"Would you want to know? You've been awful mad at her yourself."

"She said we'd be better off with her gone, but I'm not. I expect Mrs. Tinker already has another girl."

"Honey, you may feel you lost out, but no man can shut a door God has opened for you. You could look at it another way. You're here when your family needs you. You get to care for your father. She doesn't."

Liddie exhaled heavily. As far as she could see, God had closed all the doors in her house. She could not find it in herself to be grateful she'd missed out on being Mrs. Tinker's apprentice, even if she was able to help her parents. Nonetheless, she couldn't imagine being away from home just now. She sucked in her cheeks. "Yes," she admitted. "I'd want to know if she writes."

"When your father is better, we'll talk about Maquoketa. I thought it was a good idea. I still do."

"You do? Won't you need help around here?"

"I took care of things before you children were born. I can do it again."

The ember of hope in Liddie's chest sparked back to life.

Over the next several days, Liddie noticed small signs of improvement. Her father was awake more, he initiated small conversations, he took an interest in the farm. He still experienced moments of confusion, but that happened less and less often. They helped him out of bed for fifteen minutes in the morning and again in the afternoon, though he still lost his balance easily and grew dizzy if he sat up too long.

One morning, two weeks after the accident, Liddie looked in and found her father awake.

"Morning, Papa," she said. "How are you feeling today?"

"Improving. My head doesn't ache for once." G. W. freed his arms from the bedding and struggled to push himself to a sitting position. "Give me a hand. I'd like to sit up."

She helped him lean forward as she wedged the pillows behind him. "Better?"

He nodded. "I don't imagine you thought you'd be spending your summer playing nursemaid to your pa."

"I'd do anything for you, Papa."

"I appreciate it. I want you to know I do."

"Are you hungry enough for breakfast?"

"I could eat a horse."

"Hmm." Liddie frowned as though considering his request. "Unfortunately, all we have is sausage and eggs."

"That would have been my next choice."

"I'll bring some for you when the boys come in." She kissed him on the cheek.

"I'll be waiting."

Hearing her father speak clearly and with his old humor cheered her so that Liddie fairly skipped to the kitchen. "Papa's really good this morning, Mama," she said. "He wants breakfast."

"He slept well, too." Margretta pulled a pan off the burner. "I have oatmeal ready."

"He says he'd like sausage and eggs."

"He must feel better."

"Pa, what are you doing?"

The alarm in Vern's voice drew Liddie and her mother to the kitchen door, where they saw G. W. gripping the edge of the sideboard with one hand and holding on to the door frame with the other. Beads of sweat covered his forehead.

"Figured I'd join you for breakf—" G. W.'s face paled to an ashen gray. As he lost his grip on the sideboard, he reached out. His hand collided with a vase that rocked back and forth before finally tipping over and sailing on a long, slow path to the floor.

"Pa!" Vern grabbed at his father's elbow, but the nightshirt slipped through his fingers.

The vase shattered as G. W.'s knees hit the floor with a leaden thump.

"G. W." Margretta reached for him, though she was half a room away.

G. W. looked up, his eyes fixed in the middle distance, his mouth agape in a frozen smile.

The scene played before Liddie's eyes like a dream. She saw her mother kneeling on the floor, cradling her father's head in her lap. She saw Vern and Joe lift her father and carry him back to the bed. She knew without anyone saying it. Her father was dead.

# Chapter 5

"Do you remember the time G. W. came half out of the saddle during that race at the county fair?" asked one of the men. He helped himself to a sandwich. The dining room table was filled with food brought by neighbors to the funeral reception.

"He clung to that horse like a tick!" the other replied. "And still won! That man could ride."

"One of the best horsemen ever. I'll never forget that!" The two laughed.

Liddie could not imagine how they could laugh, how they could act as though they had not just buried her father. She drew her arms tighter around her waist. Everything felt out of control. If she didn't hold on, she feared she'd shatter like the vase.

"How are you doing?" Kate touched the back of Liddie's hand.

"They act like this is a party."

"They remember G. W. in happier times. That's what everyone wants at a funeral. To remember the happy times."

Liddie swallowed hard as tears trickled down her cheeks.

Kate handed her a fresh hankie. "Crying has its place, too." She comforted Liddie with a one-armed hug before moving off to talk to another neighbor.

Liddie closed her eyes and rested her head against the wall.

"I'm so sorry about your father, Liddie."

It took great energy, but Liddie opened her eyes. The woman in front of her attended church with her mother.

"Thank you, Mrs. Gaffy."

"G. W. was such a fine man. Taken in the prime of his life. God must have wanted him very badly." Mrs. Gaffy clucked in a way that made Liddie think of the red hen. "Your mother is lucky to have you children with her."

"Yes."

"How unfortunate that Amelia is away at this time. I had thought she might cut her travels short." Mrs. Gaffy fell silent, gazing at Liddie with an expression that invited sharing. When Liddie didn't respond, she probed. "What have you heard from your sister?"

Liddie licked her lips. Her mouth felt like cotton. They had received one letter from Amelia. The day after her father died.

She and Kate had watched Margretta's hands shake as she opened the envelope and unfolded a single piece of lined paper.

"What does it say?" Liddie urged.

A frown creased Margretta's forehead as she scanned the letter. "Mama?"

Margretta looked at Kate and then back at the letter. "She says, 'I'm sorry. Do not worry. We are well. This is the best way.'" Her voice trailed off.

"What else?" Liddie prompted.

"She signed her name."

Kate took the envelope. "The postmark is Lincoln, Nebraska."

"How . . . ?" Margretta looked at her sister pleadingly.

"We know she's all right. She wouldn't have written otherwise," Kate reassured Margretta. "I'll make a call."

With a discreetly placed call to her colleague in Dubuque, Kate learned that Amelia had been at the home until a week ago. Then one day she didn't return from a walk. The matron at the home learned Amelia had bought a train ticket for Cheyenne, Wyoming. A letter was on its way.

But Mrs. Gaffy did not need to know any of this.

"It is all so sad." Mrs. Gaffy patted Liddie's hand. "Well, at least your mother has one daughter at home. She will need you more than ever now."

Liddie stared at Mrs. Gaffy. What she said was true. Her mother would need her at home. For now. Forever. She saw another neighbor approaching, and she knew she had to get out. She had to get away.

"Liddie, I'm so—" the neighbor began.

"I'm sorry," Liddie muttered. "I have to go." She pushed past the woman and ran. Out of the parlor. Past mourners crowding the entryway. Out to the grove of cottonwood trees a hundred yards northwest of the house. As she ran, a wrenching sense of pain filled her chest. She had lost her sister. Then her father. And now her future. She abandoned hope of holding it all together any longer. She simply ran.

In the shelter of the trees, Liddie leaned against a massive trunk, gasping for breath. As she watched the cottonwood leaves ruffle in the breeze and the sunlight flicker as if reflected off a polished brass pan, she felt her heart slow.

Pushing away from the tree, Liddie ducked into the lean-to that had been her childhood playhouse. There she sat on the grass, her back against a wall, catching both the warmth of the sun and the cooling breeze.

A dozen years ago, when she'd first discovered the lean-to hidden amongst the trees that served as a windbreak for the house, it had been falling down, close to disappearing into the underbrush of the grove. After she convinced her father to rebuild it and replace the tattered roof of branches and bark strips, the lean-to became her retreat. She'd used it as a place to act out fairy tales, escape Vern's teasing, and play house. Sometimes, she'd even sleep there. She imagined no one knew where she was. As she grew older, the grove became a refuge where she could read or sew or exist with her own thoughts.

Within the circle of trees that had brought her so many hours of pleasure, Liddie realized with a painful jolt that everything she knew about the woods, the fields, the weather, she had learned from Papa. And now he was gone. She drew her knees up to her chest, buried her head in her arms, and wept.

"Are you all right?"

Startled, Liddie looked up to see Joe standing at the edge of the clearing. She lifted an arm to shield her eyes and dried her tears with her hankie. "You scared me."

"I saw you run out of the yard. I wanted to be sure you were okay." He looked around. "Mind if I join you?"

She shrugged. Realizing she must look a mess, she brought her knees down, curled her legs under her, and smoothed her skirt.

"This is a nice place," he said, taking in the clearing and then widening his gaze to include the surrounding countryside. "It's hidden, but you can still see a long ways." He stood as he often did, hands in his back pockets, elbows angled out. "Nearly to the property line."

"Papa said hunters chose this spot because of that." Talking with Joe about her father made her feel better.

She studied his silhouette against the sun. Wearing his suit from the funeral, Joe looked older. The stance no longer seemed defiant, as it had the first time she saw him thrust his hands in his pockets like that, the day he returned after running away. Now it was just him. The easy way he held his space. When he turned toward her, she looked away.

He crouched down on his heels outside the lean-to, picked up a leaf, and rolled the stem between his fingers. After a moment, he said, "I'm sorry about your pa, Liddie."

"I know." She stared at her hands. "I don't know how I'll get along without Papa."

"My ma died when I was ten, and I felt that way about her, too. I missed her every day, and it hurt. Then one day I realized I hurt less, and I thought of her most when I came upon things she liked. Like roses. She liked to see the wild roses outside her kitchen window."

Liddie wondered if Joe's mother had eyes like his, warm and full of sympathy. "She sounds nice."

"*Ja.* I could talk to her about anything."

"Like I could Papa."

Joe twirled the stem between his fingers. "*Er war ein guter Mann.*" He stopped twisting the leaf and translated for her. "Your pa was a good man."

"I understood," Liddie said. At least half the children in her school spoke German, and she'd heard it enough to pick up words and phrases. This was the first time it occurred to her how seldom Joe spoke German. "Your parents spoke German, didn't they?"

"To each other. Pa said I was born here, so I should only speak English." He stripped the leaf from the stem. "Ma said we should remember where we came from."

Joe fell silent, then he stood and walked back to the edge of the clearing. In the quiet, Liddie's mind returned to her father. Already she missed his voice. That morning, she'd been certain she heard him talking with her mother. Without thinking, she'd run into the kitchen only to find the voice she'd heard was Vern's. Loneliness washed over her. "I can't imagine not having either of my parents to talk with."

"I know. I wish Ma could have met Catherine. I always thought I'd have family at my wedding."

"Your wedding?" Liddie couldn't contain her surprise. "Joe, are you getting married?"

"That slipped out. I didn't mean to say anything. Especially now." He rubbed a hand across his face, but was unsuccessful at stopping a grin.

"That's good news. I'm glad you told me." She smiled her first real smile that week. "Who else knows?"

"I told your pa. I wanted his opinion before I asked her."

"What did he say?"

"He said if I liked her that was good enough for him."

"So when is the wedding?"

He bent over and picked up a twig that he immediately tossed into the brush. "I meant to ask her this week. Then G. W. died, and it didn't seem right."

"I'm sure she'll say yes."

"I'm counting on it." He looked around. "I better get back to the house." Before leaving, he reached into his pocket. "I have something you might want." He pulled out a small arrowhead and handed it to her. "Your pa found this one day when we were plowing. He spent most of that day telling us Indian stories. He knew more about most things than ten men."

Liddie cradled the arrowhead in her palm. Not much more than an inch long, chiseled out of chert, the arrowhead was perfect. The nearly black stone felt warm, and she could imagine her father telling his stories. "But it's yours." She lifted her hand to give it back.

"Now it's yours. From the land to your pa to me to you." He started to walk away, then looked back. "I'd as soon you didn't say anything about Catherine to anyone."

"You have my word." Liddie drew a cross on her chest and touched her finger to her lips. A double promise.

"You going to stay here?"

"Awhile longer."

Joe's smile lingered in her mind as she turned the little arrowhead over and over, tracing the sharp edges with her fingertips. She pressed the arrowhead against her cheek. The sadness she'd felt these last few days had lifted while they talked. With Joe gone, the heavy feeling returned. Papa. And Amelia. Joe and Catherine. So sad, and so happy. Was life always so?

# Chapter 6

The letter from the unwed mothers' home arrived a week after the funeral. The supervisor had finally gotten a roommate to confess that Amelia left with a man named Fred. They were headed west, but the girl didn't know where.

"What was she thinking?" Margretta asked. "She knew how G. W. felt about him."

"She's twenty-two. Old enough to decide," Kate said.

"But where are they going? Are they married? What about the baby?"

They had so many questions and no answers.

Liddie's mind flashed to the man she'd seen sit down by Amelia on the train. Had that been Fred? She thought about telling her mother, but what difference did it make now?

There was nothing any of them could do but wait. With no address, they could only hope for her to write again.

Margretta's gout flared up as bad as it had ever been. Unable to walk or stand comfortably, she spent hours sitting in G. W.'s chair, writing letters she often didn't finish, holding needlework but making few stitches.

Without fanfare, Vern took over the farm. He and Joe worked through the days, showed up at the house for meals, dropped into bed at night exhausted, only to rise and do it again the next day. Liddie supposed Vern missed Papa, though the two of them never spoke of it.

Cooking, laundry, and the garden fell to Liddie, with help from Kate, who decided to stay at the farm for a time—news Liddie greeted with relief and gratitude.

"What about your job?" she asked, trying to be brave in the face of a bushel basket of tomatoes and a never-ending harvest of beans, beets, and cucumbers.

"We'll figure it out. At least I don't have classroom responsibilities," Kate said as she tied on an apron. "I can do most of what needs doing right here."

In the evenings, after everyone else went to bed, Liddie often sat sewing, as she used to while her father read to her from the paper. From time to time, she'd look up, and for a brief second, believe she saw him sitting there, tapping out his pipe. Like always.

But then that image always gave way to one of him crumpling to the floor, his face frozen, Mama's name on his lips. When the memories threatened to suffocate, she would drop what she was doing and go outside. There, she would stand on the porch, gazing out at the hills, where the pattern of fields and fences reminded her of a nine-patch quilt and surrounded her with a quilt's warm comfort.

Weeks passed, Margretta's gout receded, and the family settled into a new rhythm. They still stumbled on moments of sadness, but not so often, and when they did, it did not take as long to get up.

Only once did Liddie bring up the apprenticeship to Aunt Kate. *Now is not the time*, her aunt had said. Liddie swallowed a rock of disappointment.

———

Liddie woke confused. She knew it was late at night. Shadows on her bedroom wall indicated the full moon was near to setting. Yet she heard voices drift through her open window. One loud and strident, the other low and even. She threw back the covers and went to the window.

"She just met him, for God's sake. A man she *just met*." Joe repeated the words as if trying to make sense of them. "Hell, she doesn't know anything about him, and she's going to California with him."

"I'm sorry, Joe," Vern replied quietly.

Joe's voice faded in and out. Liddie saw he was pacing; his white shirt reflected the light of the moon. Disbelief thickened into anger in his voice. "I shouldn't have waited. I should have asked her weeks ago."

Liddie sucked in her breath. Catherine. Catherine was going away with someone else.

"I loved her." The words came out strangled, raw. "I would have always loved her."

Liddie sank down on the edge of her bed, the sound of Joe's pain pulsing in her chest.

The next day, Joe was not at breakfast. Vern told them of Joe's rejection.

"Where is he?" Liddie asked.

"Leave him be," Vern warned.

"I'm not going to bother him. But where is he?"

"Liddie, don't push it. He don't want to see anyone."

"All right. All right." She nodded, her words in conflict with her heart.

After the breakfast dishes were cleared, Liddie went outside. She sat on the porch rocker and breathed in morning air redolent with the smell of new-cut hay. She could not imagine what Joe must be feeling, but she needed to be there for him, as he'd been there for her when her father died. She left the porch and walked the farmstead. She had almost given up searching when she thought to look in the cottonwood grove. She found him sitting on a log, his head in his hands, dejection in the curve of his back.

She spoke from the edge of the clearing. "I'm so sorry, Joe."

"Go away, Liddie." He didn't look at her.

She stayed.

When he raised his head, the grief etched on his face took her breath away. "I loved her."

"I know." She sat at the end of the log.

"I thought she felt the same about me. *Ich war ein Dummkopf.*" His voice was filled with hurt and something like self-loathing.

"Not a fool, Joe. We all thought you two would be together."

"I don't know how I can forget her."

"I doubt you ever will."

Joe groaned. "*That* is a wretched thought."

"No, it isn't. I never forget Papa, even though I thought I would die when he did." Liddie shook her head. "Look. I know it's not the same thing. But you had good times with her. I think we're supposed to remember the people we've loved."

"Every thought I had of my future included Catherine. Where's my future now?"

"You told me when Papa died it wouldn't hurt so much after a time. I suppose losing Catherine will be the same."

Liddie looked up at the sunlight glinting off the glossy cottonwood leaves. Being in the grove brought her such peace. She hoped it would for Joe, too. She stood to leave, then impulsively she knelt, putting her hands on his. "We all care for you. We all hurt for you." She leaned in and kissed him on the cheek.

As she walked back to the house, she wondered at that boldness.

# Chapter 7

Liddie fished another lamp chimney out of the dishpan. While some women let their chimneys get coated with soot, her mother considered it a sign of a poor housekeeper if lamp chimneys were not well and regularly cleaned. So Liddie washed their chimneys weekly. No one, she mused, could criticize her mother on the housecleaning front.

Margretta poked her head in the kitchen door. "When you're finished, come sit with us for a moment. Kate and I want to talk with you."

"I'll be right there, Mama." Curious, she dried her hands at once and joined her mother in the living room. The chimneys could wait.

Margretta sat in G. W.'s chair. Kate claimed a comfortable corner of the settee. "Sit down, dear," her mother said.

Something about the way the women looked at each other caused Liddie to perch nervously on the edge of the chair, her back straight, her feet crossed at the ankles, her hands folded in her lap. "Yes?"

"We've been talking. When your father died . . ." Margretta's eyes filled with tears. She shook her head and gestured to Kate.

Kate leaned over to squeeze her sister's hand, then took up the thread. "When your father died, it changed a lot of things. Among them, the plans for you to go to Maquoketa. That was unfortunate but unavoidable."

Liddie nodded. She knew she wasn't going. Why bring it up again?

"We haven't forgotten," Kate said. "And . . ."

"Kate has continued to press your case," her mother added.

"You are talented."

Liddie's skin prickled. Was it still possible? "I don't understand."

"Your father and I talked before his accident. We decided it was the right thing for you, but when he died . . ." Her voice cracked again. Kate moved to speak, but Margretta held up a hand. "I couldn't think about it then, but now . . . well, now there is no real reason not to."

Liddie couldn't believe her ears. "But Mrs. Tinker got another girl." She pressed a hand to her chest. Her heart was hammering. "You said so."

"Apparently, she did not work out," Kate interjected. "I spoke with Mrs. Tinker. She could take you immediately."

"But who will help you with the work, Mama? And what about the extra costs of me living in town?"

"We will manage. You needn't worry."

Liddie had held herself still on the edge of her chair, but as their words sank in, she could not contain herself. She leaped up and flung her arms first around her mother and then around her aunt. "Thank you. Thank you. Thank you!" She clasped her hands to her chest and beamed. "Thank you."

"You need to be there on Monday," Kate said.

"So soon?" The smile froze on Liddie's face.

"Have you changed your mind?" Kate looked amused.

"It's such a surprise." Liddie shook her head like a dazed puppy. "Of course I want to go. I'm going to pack now." She raced for the stairs. She would not let this chance slip from her hands again.

——

The table was set with her mother's Bavarian floral china and the good silver, place settings that saw the light of day on only the most important occasions. Christmas Day. Weddings. Baptisms. Beading on the handles of the heavy silver flatware framed shells that made Liddie think of far-off lands. The equally ornate china was decorated with silver lattice, grape clusters, and flowers around the edges and a bouquet of blossoms in the centers. When Liddie finished packing and came downstairs for supper, the sight brought her up short.

"Mama?" she asked.

"This is a big day." Margretta smiled as she moved around the table, straightening a utensil, repositioning a glass. "My daughter is going off to see the world." She held one of the crystal cordial glasses up to the light. "G. W. would have lifted a glass of wine to mark the occasion. We will do the same."

Liddie ran a finger around the rim of a glass. "Are you sure about me leaving, Mama? You'll be alone."

"Alone in a much smaller household."

Liddie's face fell.

"Don't be thinking of that. I've already talked to Mrs. Sutcliff. Her girls will come help when I need it."

"You're sure?"

"I'm sure. Have you packed everything?"

"Mama, honestly." Her mother had asked her that a dozen times through the day.

"You can't expect me to stop being your mother!"

Liddie pecked her mother on the cheek, a gesture that brought a smile to her mother's lips and tears to her eyes.

"Now stop dawdling." Margretta cleared the tears with rapid blinks. "The boys will be in soon. Go see if Kate needs help with the pancakes."

"Pancakes?" Liddie asked with genuine surprise. "On your china?"

"Well, they are your favorite. We can't have just any meal when we're celebrating." Margretta laughed.

A wild mix of emotions swirled through Liddie's chest. She had never spent one night away from family. Every day, she was surrounded by people she'd known her whole life. Her days were attuned to the rhythms of the farm, where even the changing seasons brought the same familiar tasks—planting the garden, canning produce, churning butter, baking bread, doing the laundry. She knew this story like the back of her hand.

Boarding in town, learning to be a seamstress, living on her own—those experiences were exotic. That's how she thought of it. Her new life would be like a book she had not read—an adventure to discover. Even though Maquoketa was only ten miles away, her mother and aunt had taken to planning her departure as though she were embarking on a grand European tour. She could walk the distance home if need be. But ten miles or ten thousand, it was all the same to her. She would be on her own!

When Vern and Joe came to the table, scrubbed until their cheeks were red, hair slicked back, and dressed in clean shirts, she burst out laughing.

"Look at you," she exclaimed. "All dressed up."

"May I help you with your chair, miss?" Vern came to her side.

"Why, Vern! Thank you." Liddie looked at him in astonishment.

"This is the way they do it in the city. Isn't it, Margretta?" Joe asked, holding her chair as she sat.

"Indeed. Everyone on finest manners."

"But only on the farm will you find a meal like this." Kate placed a platter heaped with pancakes in the middle of the table.

"Oh, I will miss this." Liddie breathed in the aroma of a large bowl of liver sausage.

"Before we eat, a toast. Vern? As the man of the house?" Margretta lifted her glass.

"Aw, Ma." Vern looked painfully uncomfortable, but he cleared his throat and tilted his glass toward Liddie. "God knows why you want to go, but we wish you the best. Don't go forgetting us."

"To Liddie!" everyone chimed in.

Liddie inclined her glass to each person at the table. She wanted to say something in response, but her throat felt too tight. She could manage only "Thank you."

"Enough talk. Let's eat," Kate said.

They had mopped up the syrup with the last bites of pancake and the sausage bowl was empty when Joe pushed his chair back from the supper table. "I hope I'm not spoiling a good celebration, but I have something to tell you," he said. "I'm going to Canada. To homestead."

Stunned, Liddie looked from Joe to the others at the table. The grim line of Vern's mouth told her he'd known; Mama and Kate were as surprised as she.

"Oh, Joe. Do you have to go so far away?" Margretta asked.

"I tried to change his mind," Vern said.

"A fellow in town told me claims are available," Joe said. "If the holders don't work their land, they lose the stake. I'll have my own land sooner than I ever could in Iowa."

Joe's words bespoke enthusiasm, but Liddie thought he sounded as though he were trying to convince himself.

"You can't plant now," Margretta said. "And where will you live? Why don't you wait until spring?"

"It's better I go now. Get the lay of the land before planting time. There's always work to be had. I could work a dray at the railroad. Make deliveries. Meet people. It'd help me settle in."

"It's a different way of farming," Vern said. "Shorter season. Droughts."

"If you work hard, you can make a living. Just like anywhere," Joe responded.

"You never shied away from hard work," Margretta said. "The Lord knows that."

"And land is cheap. In a few years, I could have a spread that would . . . support me."

Liddie knew he imagined a wife beside him, and her heart ached for him. He had been so happy with Catherine. She wanted that for him again.

"I won't leave you shorthanded," Joe said. "I'll find someone you can hire on before I leave."

"I'll talk to the Engle boys," Vern said. "They were good workers last harvest."

"You can take some of those plums we canned this summer," Kate offered. "And we'll pack up a box of blankets."

"I'm sure they have food in Canada." Joe laughed. "And blankets."

"No need to spend money if you don't have to," Kate said.

"I won't have family of mine going off without food to eat," Margretta insisted.

Joe threw up his hands. "I give up! I'll take any help I can get."

"This table is going to seem empty with Liddie gone, and now you." Margretta's eyes glistened.

"Oh, Mama, we'll be back. We won't be gone forever," Liddie said, looking to Joe for agreement.

Joe did not smile. "I don't know when I'll be back."

"Of course you'll come back. You're family," Liddie exclaimed. An image of Mama and Vern alone at the table flashed into her mind. She thought she might cry.

"Come now. Tonight is supposed to be a celebration," Margretta said. "We had a toast for Liddie. We'll have one for Joe, too."

Vern stared at his mother. "Two glasses of wine? I've never seen you drink two glasses in one sitting."

His words broke the tension and they laughed.

After the dishes were cleared, Liddie slipped out of the house and walked to the top of a hill where she could see for miles. The farm was changing. Papa gone. Amelia gone. Now Joe. She would be gone, too, but that was different. She was heading toward the future she'd always dreamed of.

# Chapter 8

Alone in her room at the boardinghouse, Liddie sat on the edge of the bed, hands clasped tightly in her lap. "I won't cry. I won't cry. I won't cry," she whispered. A single tear trickled from the corner of her eye. She rubbed it away with the heel of her hand.

Her eyes were drawn to the address book and notepaper lying on the dressing table. Her mother had given her the packet of writing materials along with Amelia's last letter. Liddie had not responded to the hope in her mother's voice when she suggested Liddie write to her sister.

It had been weeks before they had heard that Amelia and Fred were married. That they'd gone to Wyoming to homestead. Her feelings toward her sister were so tangled, she couldn't sort them out. She hadn't written to Amelia at least in part because she didn't know what to say.

When she had hugged her aunt good-bye that morning, she'd seen Joe watching them. He'd stood there, his hands stuffed in his back pockets, smiling at her. She felt herself blush and wound up fixing her eyes in the middle of his chest, where a button hung by a thread. Who would fix his clothes in Canada? When he asked her to write, she promised she would. As soon as she had his address. Another tear now trickled down her cheek.

Here she was alone for less than an hour, and she felt the rest of her life stretching out before her like an endless empty road. If she wrote to her mother, what would she say? That she was sitting here feeling sorry for herself after they'd given her exactly what she wanted?

*Doing something is better than doing nothing.* Papa's words popped into her head. I will do something, she thought.

She stood and looked around the room, hands firmly on her hips, her head tilted to one side. The room was similar in size to the one she and Amelia had shared, yet it felt so different. So sterile. Functional. Nothing more. The washstand held a plain white pitcher and basin. A white hand towel hung precisely in the middle of the dowel rod. Besides the bed, a straight-backed chair offered the only place in the room to sit. A kerosene lamp on the dressing table would light the room at night. A pine chest of drawers completed the furnishings. Even the wallpaper, with its pattern of washed-out green flowers and leaves against an ecru background, did nothing to liven the mood.

The faded bedcover unsettled Liddie the most, as it was such a contrast to the crazy quilt on her bed at home. A riot of shapes, colors, and fabrics, the quilt had been pieced together by her mother and aunt before Liddie was born. When she was supposed to be asleep, Liddie often told herself stories about the clothes each piece must have once been. She could smell her father in the wool, see her mother in the silk, hear the rustle of taffeta at a dance. In the dark, she would trace her fingertips along the feather stitches decorating each seam, each bit of cloth from her family.

A dizzying wave of homesickness washed over her. She pushed her knees into the edge of the bed, steadying herself until the queasiness passed.

Liddie forced herself into action. She pushed the dressing table into a corner where the mirror caught the light from the window. She maneuvered the washstand over to the wall by the door. Immediately, her mood improved.

Just then, she heard a rap on the door. Worried that the overly attentive landlady had heard her moving furniture, Liddie wondered if she might be thrown out before she spent her first night. Drawing a breath for courage, she opened the door and was relieved and surprised to see a girl with deep-blue eyes and dark, curly hair that fell to her shoulders.

"Hello!" The girl stuck out her hand. "My name is Minnie. Wilhelmina, actually. Everyone calls me Minnie. My last name is Holter. I have the room across the hall. What's your name? May I come in?"

Liddie was so taken aback at the girl's breathless speech that she stood aside and gestured her in.

"You just got here. I saw you and your mother with Mrs. Prescott. That was your mother, wasn't it? And was that your brother driving the buggy?" She didn't wait for responses. "I wanted to give you time to settle in before I came over. Then I heard you moving furniture and thought you might like help. What did you say your name is?"

"I didn't say. I didn't have time!" Liddie failed to stifle a laugh.

"I'm sorry." Minnie looked abashed. "When I'm nervous, everything rushes out like water over rapids."

"You're nervous? Why?" Liddie asked. "Oh, and my name is Lydia Mary Treadway. Please call me Liddie."

"I'm so pleased to meet you, Liddie," Minnie said. "You're the only person living here who's my age. I'm eighteen. I have been unutterably lonely. I thought perhaps we could be friends."

"Maybe we can be," Liddie agreed, thinking that someone who would be so forthright as to suggest friendship on first meeting, let alone use the word *unutterably* in everyday language, was an unusual person indeed, and someone she'd like to know. "I don't know anyone here in town. You're the first." She did not tell Minnie she had turned seventeen only a week ago.

Liddie looked around, at a loss for what to do with her visitor. At home, Mama invited guests to sit in the parlor and offered them something to eat. She had no experience as a hostess and nothing she could offer for refreshments.

"Would you like to sit?" she asked. "I only have one chair. You're welcome to it."

"Thank you." Minnie sat.

Liddie had no choice but to sit on the bed. She had just been sitting in this very spot, near tears, and now here she was entertaining a guest. At least her guest wasn't a man. Mrs. Prescott had been adamant: *no men*. She giggled.

"What's so funny?" Minnie asked. "Did I do something?"

"No. Not at all." Liddie didn't want to talk about the landlady and grasped for another topic. "I'll be apprenticing with Mrs. Tinker. She's—"

"I know Mrs. Tinker," Minnie jumped in. "She comes into the store."

"Store?"

"Fisher's Dry Goods. 'Two stores, two floors,' you know. That's where I work. As a clerk. I keep my eyes open for lace and ribbon and notions she'll be interested in. Mrs. Tinker is lovely. You'll like her." Minnie's hair bounced as she nodded her head. Minnie popped up from her chair. "I'll tell you what. The weather's so nice, let's take a walk before dinner. We don't want to be late for meals, as I'm sure Mrs. Prescott told you. We can get a treat at Becker's Bakery. Have you been there? Mrs. Becker makes the best cakes. If you want to, that is."

"That would be nice." Liddie stood, too. "Vern drove us around before we came here, but it was quick."

Actually, Liddie had been intimidated as Vern turned the buggy up Main Street. The wide cobblestone street was crowded with buggies and automobiles; the sidewalks bustled with people on shopping or business errands. From Main Street, Margretta directed him to drive past Mrs. Tinker's home, which was in a residential area on the south side of town, and finally to the board-inghouse, which was on the north side of town.

Though she'd been to Maquoketa any number of times with her family, she'd never paid particular attention to what was where—beyond the dry goods store where they bought fabric. The town was the center of commerce and government for Jackson County and, as such, boasted a wide range of establishments in the two- and three-story red-brick buildings that lined Main Street: grocery, hardware, and furniture stores; an opera house and a picture theater; jewelry and drugstores; four bakeries, banks, billiard halls, the cigar store Liddie's father frequented, and tailors. Parallel streets were home to the Carnegie library, the courthouse, the jail, lumberyards, livery stables, and the undertaker.

As she thought about navigating all this on her own, Liddie had been momentarily fearful. She would welcome returning to Main Street with Minnie. She added, "By the time Mrs. Prescott showed us the room, Vern was ready to get back to the farm."

"Is Vern your beau?" Minnie asked. "I saw him help you from the buggy. And then you hugged him . . ." Minnie blushed. "I'm sorry. It sounds as though I was spying on you."

Liddie thought it amusing the girl was digging for information. "My beau? No, you were right the first time. He's my brother."

Minnie looked relieved. "I thought so. You bear a resem-blance. He's quite handsome. So tall. Like you. And he looks ever so strong."

Liddie didn't know how to respond to that. Vern was tall. He was strong. But handsome? She would never have said that of him any more than she would have thought herself beautiful. Her slen-der waist was her one feature of note. "So, a walk?"

"Yes." Minnie moved toward the door. "Oh, and you can fix the room up. Mine was like this when I moved in. It's ever so nice now. I even have a new quilt. Since you sew, you could do so many things. Pillow covers. A dresser scarf. Mrs. Prescott won't be offended."

"I thought of making a different quilt, too." Liddie threw her shawl over her shoulders as she surveyed the room. It was her room; these were her things; she was responsible for it all. She closed the door firmly behind her, locked it, and pocketed the key.

When Liddie returned to her room that evening after supper—"dinner," as Mrs. Prescott called it—she was glad to be in the solitude of her own room. Even though it felt bare, it was hers, as was this whole day. She'd soaked in the amber glow of the October afternoon, talked with Minnie as though she'd known her for her entire life, and met the other boarders over a passable supper. *Dinner.* She vowed to remember to call it that. She pulled the chair up to the dressing table and took out a piece of notepaper.

> *Dear Mama, Aunt Kate, and Vern,*
> *Thank you. Thank you. Thank you for letting me come*
> *to Maquoketa. I'm happy to report I've made a new friend.*

When she signed her name three pages later, she was surprised how much she had to share after only one day. She took one of the postage stamps her mother had tucked inside the address book and affixed it to the envelope. She'd post it on the way to work in the morning.

# Chapter 9

Ernestine Tinker had first begun taking in sewing projects as a way to occupy her days. Her husband, Jack, an accountant at First National Bank in Maquoketa, had encouraged her. As the years passed and children did not appear to be part of God's plan for them, Ernestine attracted more customers, and the sewing spilled out of the small back room and into the dining room. At mealtime, Ernestine pushed whatever dress or shirt or trousers she was working on at the moment to one end of the table, and she and Jack shared the happenings of the day while they ate. When a runaway horse tipped his buggy, throwing Jack into a ditch, breaking his neck, and ending his life, sewing became Ernestine's path to economic and social stability.

The back room off the dining room became a cozy dressing room with mirrors. A sturdy wooden box provided a raised platform for customers to stand on during fittings. The dining room evolved into a workroom with two new treadle sewing machines, each with its own worktable. Mrs. Tinker hired a series of girls to work at the second machine, preferring farm girls, who were used to working hard and who, once they survived the initial bouts of homesickness, settled in as responsible—if often unimaginative—help. At least until they each attracted the attention of a young man. Then they were gone.

Some of this Liddie had learned from conversations with her mother and aunt. The more dramatic details Minnie filled in based on gossip gleaned from the customers she served at Fisher's. Most relevant was that Mrs. Tinker's previous girl quit without notice, leaving the seamstress shorthanded as the holidays approached—and opening the position once again for Liddie.

On Liddie's first day, Mrs. Tinker welcomed her wearing the high-collared white blouse and gathered navy skirt that Liddie would learn was her standard work wear. With her graying hair pulled into a tight bun, she presented an image of efficiency that suited a tradeswoman.

Her home turned business was in a modest two-story frame house on a street lined with similar houses. Clumps of daisies and black-eyed Susans bordered a wood plank walkway that led from the street to the front door. When customers began coming to the house with some regularity, Mr. Tinker had installed a step at the curb to assist women descending from their buggies. Several of the houses along the tree-lined street, including the Tinkers', had picket fences.

Mrs. Tinker devoted the first floor of her home to sewing work. The parlor served as both a reception area and a relaxing space where customers could enjoy a cup of tea as they discussed clothing needs. A drop-leaf table near the front door was opened each day to accommodate transactions. In the kitchen, an ironing board stood at the ready. Dress forms, including one for larger women, stood like sentinels at one end of the dining room.

"With the holidays coming on, we have much to get done," Mrs. Tinker said as she moved purposefully through the rooms. "You'll have a lot to learn quickly." She pointed out a rack full of clothes needing alterations and a maple hutch full of clothes needing mending. A note pinned to each item described the work to be done and the promised completion date.

"Yes, ma'am." Liddie tried to convey confidence. "I'll do my best."

"Your best is all anyone can ask, dear," Mrs. Tinker said with a smile that included her gray eyes as well as her mouth.

Taking a measure of reassurance from the smile, Liddie began to relax, when the doorbell rang.

"That's Mrs. Jacobs." Mrs. Tinker moved toward the door. "Start on the rack clothes. Ask if you have questions."

As Mrs. Tinker greeted a harried-looking woman carrying a large bundle, Liddie stared after her, a bit stunned. Just like that? Wasn't there more to know? She turned to the rack, attempting to quell the anxiety in her stomach.

"Yes, Glenna left us," she heard Mrs. Tinker say. "Liddie Treadway started today." She beckoned for Liddie to join her. "This is Mrs. Jacobs."

"Ma'am." Liddie nodded.

"You're Margretta's daughter," the woman said. "My sympathy on your father's passing."

"Thank you." Liddie managed a tight smile. She hadn't expected to be reminded of her father and stood there in awkward silence.

"Mrs. Jacobs was one of my first customers." Mrs. Tinker gracefully changed the subject. "She encouraged me to start my business."

"It was one of the smarter suggestions I've ever made." Mrs. Jacobs smiled, obviously pleased to be recognized for her role.

"Why don't you start on that blue dress, Liddie?" Mrs. Tinker nodded toward the rack. "The one at the end."

"Give my regards to your mother, Liddie," Mrs. Jacobs said.

"I will. Thank you."

As Liddie returned to the workroom, she heard the woman titter. "I expect it is a little overwhelming. The first day." Then she lowered her voice. "I didn't realize the girl needed to work out."

"Let's take a look at your dress." Mrs. Tinker began to unwrap the package. "It will be Christmas before we know it!"

Although Mrs. Jacobs had lowered her voice, Liddie still heard her. *Needed* to work out? Is that what people thought? That she was here because their family needed the money? The back of her neck prickled with embarrassment, then anger.

She found the blue dress and lifted it off the rack. She stopped. This wasn't what she *needed* to do; this was what she *wanted* to do. She put the dress back and went into the parlor.

"Mrs. Jacobs?"

Mrs. Tinker looked up. "What is it, Liddie?"

Heat crept up Liddie's neck. Now that she was standing there, she wondered if saying something was wise.

"Yes?" Mrs. Tinker prompted.

"I'm not here because our family is poor. I'm here because I love to sew." Her eyes darted from Mrs. Tinker to Mrs. Jacobs and back again. "I—I wanted her to know that."

"Oh." Mrs. Jacobs's face went beet red. "I'm sorry."

Mrs. Tinker was no longer smiling. "Liddie. You have work you need to be doing."

Liddie blinked as though suddenly remembering why she was there. "Yes. Yes, ma'am. The blue dress." Her face hot with embarrassment, Liddie hurried to the rack.

"I'm sorry," Mrs. Jacobs said. "I didn't mean . . ."

"No, I'm sorry," Mrs. Tinker said. "Please forgive her. Would you like some tea while we talk?"

"No. I'll come back another time."

As Liddie took the blue dress to her sewing machine, she was acutely aware that Mrs. Jacobs hurriedly gathered up her bundle and left.

Mrs. Tinker closed the front door, planted her hands on her hips, and stared into space. Stealing furtive glances at her employer, Liddie feared this first hour of her career as a seamstress could be her last.

When Mrs. Tinker approached, Liddie laid the dress down and stood. "I'm sorry. I just . . ."

"Liddie, I wouldn't have thought it necessary to tell you that embarrassing a customer is never appropriate."

"But she—"

"But nothing. Mrs. Jacobs is my *customer*. Whether she did or did not understand your situation is irrelevant. Our customers are *always* treated with respect."

Embarrassment burned through Liddie's body.

"Your job here is to provide the best possible sewing work for my customers. That is all. Do you understand?" She spoke in a low, firm tone that left no doubt, yet at the same time was not unkind.

"Yes, ma'am." Liddie couldn't look Mrs. Tinker in the eyes. "I am so sorry."

"Very well, then. I'm going to chalk this whole thing up to youth and inexperience." Mrs. Tinker picked up the dress Liddie was supposed to be working on. "Tell me how you're going to do this."

Liddie looked at the front door. "Will she come back?"

"Mrs. Jacobs? Oh yes. And you'll do her sewing."

"Will she let me?"

"It's imperative that you do. You see, one of the reasons my business thrives is because Mrs. Jacobs talks freely with her friends. If you are to be successful, we need to replace this unfortunate first impression with a more positive one." She firmly pressed the dress into Liddie's hands, and a reassuring smile returned to her face. "Now. Let's put this awkwardness behind us and get to work."

Liddie settled in at the sewing machine and completed the work as well as she was able. Tidy rows of thread spools, folders of needles in all sizes, scissors hanging on pegs, all within easy reach—she had every tool she needed. She didn't have time to think another personal thought for the rest of the day.

Upon later reflection, Liddie realized she got off easy that first day because Mrs. Tinker was a kind and encouraging employer. Once a problem was addressed, Mrs. Tinker never brought it up again. And for her part, Liddie vowed to let her sewing speak for her in the future.

————

When her mother had commented that Ernestine Tinker did good business, Liddie hadn't really understood what that meant. In the following weeks, she learned firsthand. From the time she sat down at her worktable at seven thirty in the morning until she left at six in the evening, Liddie was seldom without a piece of work. Mending tears. Repairing buttonholes. Inserting padding. Making flat felled seams. Threading. Tacking. Basting. The tasks she might have done in a year of sewing at home passed through her hands each week.

Each morning, she and Mrs. Tinker reviewed the priorities among the garments on the alteration rack and in the hutch. They estimated what she could finish in the day, adjusting the order of tasks as necessary.

There was a sameness to the assigned work that reminded Liddie of life on the farm, yet because the people, the place, and the responsibilities were new, she looked to each day with a sense of anticipation. The fact that someone would pay her to do what she loved thrilled her.

Though it never came up again—at least not in her hearing— Mrs. Jacobs's comment about her having to work stuck with her, a simmering embarrassment. Her mother paid Mrs. Prescott for her food and lodging; Liddie herself was responsible for incidentals. Regardless of her family's help, if she was going to set her own future, she needed to be able to support herself.

She bought a ledger and kept meticulous records of what she earned and what she spent. She opened a savings account. Each week after Mrs. Tinker paid her, she went to the bank and deposited everything but a small allowance she set for herself. Her needs were few, and she was proud when she came to the end of a week without spending all she'd set aside for herself. Knowing she had this money in reserve gave her confidence and comfort, like a warm fire on a cold night.

With Christmas parties coming up, there was even more work than usual. Liddie knew girls in positions like hers were often invited to these parties, but Mrs. Tinker never said anything, and Liddie didn't dare ask. She presumed she was too new. She allowed herself to be blue for two days, then she and Minnie set to planning a party for everyone at the boardinghouse. Though it wouldn't be as fancy, they intended to make it every bit as much fun. It was Christmas. Of course it would be fun.

———

*November 15, 1913*

*Dear Joe,*

*How are you? I could not believe that your address is Forget, Saskatchewan. Does that explain why we didn't hear from you for six weeks? Did you "forget" us in Iowa?*

*We are all well. I am so happy here in Maquoketa. Mrs. Tinker is wonderful. I meet new people and see new things every single day. I also made a friend—Minnie. She rooms at the boardinghouse, too. She has a collection of animal figurines. Mostly little dogs. I don't know that I'd spend money that way, but she says it makes her happy to wake up to those puppies playing on her bureau. It must work, because she is the happiest, liveliest person I've ever met.*

*I hope you like your new home as well as I do mine. I am eager to hear about your trip and your work and where you live. Vern plans to shoot a turkey for Thanksgiving dinner. Shall we save a drumstick for you?*
   *Write soon.*
   *Your friend, Liddie*

# Chapter 10

"Tell me about your family," Minnie said. Propped up against the headboard of Liddie's bed, a throw over her legs, Minnie sat with the tin of Christmas candies on her lap. Slowly and deliberately she selected from the variety of sweet treasures Margretta had packed for them. Most recently, she'd chosen a piece of walnut fudge and nibbled at it with such tiny bites over such a long time that the chocolate melted on her fingertips.

"I've told you everything." Liddie was curled up on the end of the bed, her head resting on a needlepoint pillow. She propped herself up on one elbow. "Are you going to eat them all?"

"I'll trade the candy for more stories," Minnie said, nudging the tin across the bed. Raised by a distant and often disagreeable aunt from the time she was ten, Minnie never tired of hearing stories about Liddie's close-knit family. "You tell me about your mother and father. You tell me about Vern and Joe. You talk about your aunt all the time." She licked chocolate off her thumb. "But you don't talk about your sister. Why?"

"I don't want to talk about her."

"I don't understand. You shared a room. You had to be close."

Liddie swung off the bed, sat down at the dressing table, and began to pull the pins out of her hair. "I just don't."

"But why? It's almost as though you've erased her from your life."

Liddie felt Minnie staring at her. Waiting. She picked up her brush and began to pull it through her hair, straightening out the tangles, smoothing the thick locks over her shoulders. Like Amelia used to do. The memory brought tears that she quickly wiped away.

Minnie pushed the throw aside and slid over to the edge of the bed. "Are you crying?"

Liddie hunched her shoulders when Minnie touched her, as she felt her protective shield crumble.

"I'm sorry! I didn't mean to make you cry. You don't have to tell me anything."

Liddie had never said the words before. To anyone. Finally, holding the words in took more effort than letting them out. "She got into . . . trouble." She swallowed the word "trouble" as embarrassment and shame swept over her.

"She what?"

"She got . . . *pregnant.*"

When Minnie's hand dropped away, Liddie felt the rejection she'd expected.

"Oh."

The shock in Minnie's voice hung in the air. Liddie whirled around, defiant. "See? It was horrible. Then she ran away and got married without telling anyone. Mama was worried to death. She wasn't there for Papa. Or for any of us."

"Where is she?" Minnie asked, her voice low. "Do you hear from her?"

"She and Fred are in Wyoming." Liddie ignored Minnie's second question and returned to brushing her hair. The truth was, Amelia had written to her three times in the last two months. Liddie had not answered. It was not as though she was still angry. She wasn't. Not exactly. It was just that the longer she didn't write, the more awkward it became to do so. Each of Amelia's letters was shorter than the last. The last letter contained only three sentences:

*I want to hear from you, but I cannot make you write. It is
too painful to receive nothing in return. If I don't hear from
you, I will not write again.*

"What about her baby?" Minnie asked.

"She's due any time."

"It has to be hard for her. Being all by herself."

"She should have thought of that before she broke Mama's and Papa's hearts."

"Look, it's not good what she did. But I give her credit for making the best of a bad situation. She's married. She's keeping her baby. That took courage."

"People will never forget. She embarrassed us all."

"Listen to yourself, Liddie! You sound like she did it just to hurt you. I expect she'd take it back if she could. Besides, haven't you ever done something you wished you hadn't?"

"No," she insisted.

Minnie looked at Liddie, skepticism in the set of her mouth. "I know if she were my sister, I wouldn't be so willing to throw her away." She stood up. "You have family, so you don't know what it's like not to have anyone. You'd be sorry. I know that."

She stomped out of the room, closing the door with more force than necessary, leaving Liddie to remember, finally, that Minnie didn't have any family. No one at all.

Alone in the quiet room, Liddie stared out into the night. Up and down the street, light from houses reflected off the snow. It was never completely dark in town, not like on the farm. Amelia had written that she and Fred lived in a log house with no neighbors for miles. When Liddie read that, she'd imagined Amelia was enjoying an adventure. Now, with Minnie's comments needling at her, she wondered if Amelia was lonely.

Liddie realized how desperately she missed her sister. There was nothing Amelia could do to change things. But Liddie realized *she* had a choice. She could hold on to her stubborn sense of what life should have been like and lose her sister entirely. Or she could accept reality and have her sister back, even with the thousand miles between them.

She went to her dressing table and took out paper and a pencil. *Dear Amelia*, she wrote. *I miss you.* A half hour later, she signed her name at the bottom of the tear-stained sheet.

When she looked up from the desk, she saw the tin of candy still on the bed. She ate a piece of creamy-white, air-filled divinity. Then she took the tin across the hall and knocked on Minnie's door.

———

*January 1, 1914*
*Happy New Year, Joe!*
*I am glad you see humor in a town called Forget. I laughed out loud at your story about the lost dog that had to run away for three days before it was out of sight. Can the Canadian prairie really be so flat? I try to imagine what you see when you stand outside your door in the morning. I want you to tell me every detail.*

*Even though I am still in Iowa, my world has expanded. Aunt Kate said when women have the right to vote, we'll be able to do anything. One of Mrs. Tinker's customers implied that I have to work, as though that's a shameful thing. Her comment annoyed me. I want to work, and yet when some-one casts working in a negative light, I rebel. What do you think of that?*

*Mama probably wrote that Vern got a brace of rabbits. My mouth waters thinking of rabbit gravy and biscuits.*

*It snowed early, then it turned so cold. I spend my evenings doing needlework or playing whist with Minnie and other boarders. Have you made new friends?*

*Your friend, Liddie*

# Chapter 11

"You're Mrs. Tinker's new girl. Right?"

Startled by the disembodied male voice, Liddie looked up, her hand hovering above the Jane Austen books on the library shelf. Through the rack, she saw blue eyes peering at her out of a flushed face. "Pardon?" she said.

"You work for Mrs. Tinker, don't you?" He spoke louder.

"Yes. I do," she whispered, glancing toward the reference desk. The librarian, who brooked no loud talk, glared at her before returning to her work.

"You're new in town," he said.

She'd lived in Maquoketa for almost four months and had ceased to think of herself as new. "I've been here awhile."

"I've seen you coming out of Fisher's."

"Oh." He'd been watching her! She tugged *Pride and Prejudice* free of the books crowding it, opened to the first page, and tried to read. She could feel him still watching her. She flushed, mildly uncomfortable and strangely excited that a man had singled her out. She made a show of being engrossed in the book. No strange man had ever spoken to her before, and she didn't know quite what to do.

"I've seen you a few times," he added.

Liddie took a step back. The man—actually a boy, she saw now, probably no older than her—had come around the end of the stack and stood right in front of her. He was not quite as tall as she, sturdily built, with copper-colored hair that intensified his ruddy complexion.

"Shhh!"

Liddie glanced at the librarian, who frowned, her finger to her lips.

"What are you reading?" He took the book from her hands and glanced at the cover. "Jane Austen." He flipped through a few pages and snapped the book closed. "Never read her."

"I like her stories." She reached for the book.

Grinning, he held it up and away, beyond her reach. She'd once seen an older boy playing keep-away with a girl at school. The girl had laughed, seeming to enjoy the game, but it irked Liddie. She thought it childish and she let her hands drop to her sides.

A look of disappointment replaced the grin. "I'm Harley Ellers." He emphasized his last name as he put the book back on the shelf. "My dad runs the Decker House," he added, as though he expected Liddie to be impressed. "Would you like to have a soda, Liddie? We can go to the Decker."

He knew her name! He'd been watching her and asking about her. She guessed she ought to be flattered. She also thought it awfully bold of him to ask. She stalled. "How do you know my name?"

"I get around."

How brash. Did he think she was fool enough to walk off with someone she'd just met?

"Thank you," she said. "But I'm meeting someone." It seemed a safe thing to say. And appropriate.

"Oh really? Who?"

How cheeky. Now she was trapped. She'd come to the library that afternoon after work because she'd nothing else to do. She had promised herself she'd be back at the boardinghouse before dark but lost track of time as she wandered between the stacks, imagining herself in all the places she read about.

"I told Mrs. Prescott I'd help her set the table," Liddie blurted without thinking.

"The boardinghouse?" he asked. "I'll walk you there, then."

"That's kind of you to offer, but no." Liddie didn't want to appear rude, so she added, "Mrs. Prescott doesn't allow men."

"I could walk you to the door."

"Really. No."

"In the dark? Won't you be afraid?"

"I'm not afraid of the dark." She laughed. "Don't be silly."

The boy studied her. "All right. Another time."

"Perhaps."

He stuck out his hand. "It was nice to meet you." Before letting go of her hand, he added, "Be careful walking home. You never know in the dark." He sauntered away.

*Arrogant*, Liddie thought. She pulled out *Pride and Prejudice* again.

When she had checked out her book and the heavy library doors had closed behind her, she glanced up and down the street before descending the steps. A vague sense of unease troubled her. Even the gaslights along the street looked sinister. *Don't be silly*, she scolded herself. She'd never been uncomfortable before, walking alone in Maquoketa. Yet she hurried home, watching every bush and tree along the way.

"So he was clumsy," Minnie said when Liddie told her about Harley. "He wanted to meet you. That's all."

"Well, it felt funny. And now I feel uncomfortable."

"You might at least have a soda with him."

Liddie considered the idea as she buttoned the collar of her blouse. "You don't know that I'll ever see him again," she said.

"I think you will."

"I don't know. I didn't like him all that well."

"You didn't give him a chance. Not really. And you never know."

———

June 6, 1914

Dear Amelia,

I am glad to hear Hope has finally grown into the dress I made for her. I'm used to making dresses much bigger or much smaller than that one. I bet Fred was proud to take his two girls into Lusk! How fun that you and Fred are dancing again.

Mama says not to worry, many men don't take to babies. Babies and diapers are women's work. She says Papa wasn't at all disappointed he had a girl first, but many men think their oldest ought to be a boy. She says Fred will come around.

Have you decided who you will vote for in the election? Amelia, I just cannot believe that you get to vote! Aunt Kate and I are cheering you on. Maybe someday I will be able to mark a ballot, too.

I suppose you have your garden in. Do things grow in Wyoming as they do here? Write again soon.

Your sister, Liddie

# Chapter 12

Maquoketa was far from a society town, but as the county seat, it did have an active social scene that was most apparent during the holiday season. As early as midsummer, women began appearing at Mrs. Tinker's door with pages—torn from magazines, often sent by friends who lived in larger cities—showing dresses that were the latest fashion.

Ultimately, however, most women relied on Mrs. Tinker to suggest a style or fabric, knowing she would choose something flattering that no one else would be wearing.

Gladys Caither's husband, Ben, was president of First National Bank, and the couple hosted one of the best parties of the season. Mrs. Caither dressed meticulously with an excellent sense of style. When she arrived for her appointment the first Thursday in August, she brought her twelve-year-old daughter, Anna, with her.

"This is the first year Anna will be attending the party with the adults." Mrs. Caither briefly touched her daughter's shoulder.

"How wonderful!" Mrs. Tinker smiled. "Are you excited?"

"Yes, ma'am," Anna said. An attractive girl, Anna was slim like her mother, with honey-blond hair and soft brown eyes.

"Shall we have tea while we talk about what you have in mind?" Mrs. Tinker asked.

"That would be lovely."

Liddie brought in the tray of freshly brewed tea and biscuits. Gladys Caither invariably wanted tea, which was why her appointments were scheduled for midafternoon with nothing else afterward.

"Hello, Mrs. Caither. It's good to see you," Liddie said. She set the tray on the parlor table and began pouring tea in the delicate porcelain cups, which were painted with tiny red roses.

Liddie admired how regally Mrs. Caither sat in the wingback chair, and she knew a corset contributed to the effect. Girls as young as Anna wore corsets, and Liddie had once eagerly anticipated the time when her mother would let her wear one. But when Amelia let her try on one of hers, she found she could hardly breathe, let alone bend over. From that moment, in a move completely at odds with her interest in fashionable clothing, she had refused to put one on again.

"Would you like tea, Anna?" Liddie asked the girl sitting motionless on the edge of her chair.

"Yes, please?" Anna looked to her mother.

Given the way Mrs. Caither watched her daughter, Liddie wondered if this cup of tea was a first for the girl. Liddie took care to ensure the cup and saucer were steady in Anna's hands before she let go. She could not imagine coming to a seamstress with her mother to have a dress made just for her, just for a holiday party. But she could imagine being so young and trying to act so old.

"Look, Mama." Anna tugged her mother's sleeve and pointed. "Look at the doll dresses."

"It's not polite to point, dear." Mrs. Caither brought Anna's hand down as she looked to the workroom wall where the doll dresses hung. "Why, Ernestine," she said. "Have you broadened your services to include doll clothes?"

"That's Liddie's work. She does excellent needlework, and she's shown a talent for color and design," Mrs. Tinker responded. "Liddie, why don't you get the dresses and show them to Anna?"

"They aren't—" Liddie began to protest.

"I know Anna would like to see them," Mrs. Tinker interrupted. Though her voice was pleasant, a firm undertone reminded Liddie of the debacle on her first day.

"Yes, ma'am." Abashed, Liddie went to unpin the dresses she'd all but forgotten were there.

She'd been working at the shop for eight months when Mrs. Tinker engaged her in a discussion of her sewing interests. She was flattered when her employer suggested she might become a dressmaker if she were to continue to pursue sewing after her apprenticeship. It was then that Liddie told her about the doll dresses, and Mrs. Tinker insisted upon seeing them. When she placed the two little dresses on Mrs. Tinker's sewing table, Liddie felt as though she had laid her heart down with them.

Mrs. Tinker examined each dress inside and out, first at her worktable and then in the better light by the window. She was quiet for so long Liddie's skin began to itch. Then she basked in Mrs. Tinker's final words: "You should be proud."

At Mrs. Tinker's urging, Liddie put the doll dresses up on the corkboard, more pleased with them than she'd ever been before. She had returned to her work that day with a rush of energy.

Now, weeks later, instead of a rush of energy, she felt only embarrassment to be showing doll clothes that now seemed juvenile. And to an important client like Mrs. Caither. Reluctantly, she handed the dresses to the child.

Anna held them up. "Oh, Mama, aren't they beautiful? I wonder if they'd fit my doll?" Her attempts to appear older disappeared, and she gazed at her mother in a pleading way that Liddie imagined secured countless gifts.

Mrs. Caither asked Liddie, "Would you sell them?"

"I made them for a neighbor and only borrowed them to show Mrs. Tinker. I promised to give them back."

As Anna's face fell, Mrs. Tinker jumped in. "I have an idea. If your mother agrees, Anna, Liddie could make your holiday dress.

And then, if she has time, she could make a copy of your dress for your doll. What do you think of that?"

Anna's face lit up.

Liddie opened her mouth and then closed it. Had she heard correctly? She would make Anna's holiday dress?

Gladys Caither looked as though she had swallowed a plum pit.

Mrs. Tinker laid a hand on Mrs. Caither's arm as she said, "Liddie, why don't you take Anna into the workroom and have her tell you what she has in mind for a holiday dress? Show her some of the new fabric bolts."

As Liddie led Anna into the workroom, she saw Mrs. Tinker refill Mrs. Caither's teacup and engage her in deep conversation.

———

Liddie pushed through the glass doors at Fisher's a few minutes before Minnie's quitting time. She was bursting to tell her about the afternoon with Mrs. Caither and about Anna's dress. She spotted her friend in front of the cabinet that held drawers of ladies' gloves, where an elderly woman was working a pair of above-the-elbow gloves up her arms. Liddie caught Minnie's eye and waved. Minnie nodded discreetly toward the woman.

Liddie rolled her eyes and mouthed, "I'll wait." She pointed toward the sewing notions aisle. Once there, she moved from buttons to scissors to lace, hardly seeing any of it.

When Minnie appeared at Liddie's elbow, she had her bag in hand. "Why are you so excited?" she asked.

"I have so much to tell you. This has been a most unbelievable day."

Liddie's words tumbled out so fast that Minnie laughed out loud. "You sound like me! Let's get outside before someone wants something from me."

Out on the street, Liddie grabbed Minnie's hands. "I'm going to make a holiday dress." She beamed.

Minnie looked puzzled. "You sew dresses all the time."

"Yes, I sew what Mrs. Tinker tells me to. For this dress, I'll do everything. Design it. Choose the fabric. Sew it. Do the fittings. Everything, Minnie, *ev-er-y-thing.*" Liddie's eyes flashed as she dragged the syllables out. "And it's for Anna Caither, for their big party."

"A dress for Anna *Caither*? For the Caithers' *holiday* party?" Minnie pursed her lips in disbelief. Mrs. Caither's desire for the best was legendary. "And Mrs. Caither said *yes*?"

"Not at once. Mrs. Tinker had to do some convincing." Liddie shook her head in disbelief. "Minnie, I am stunned that she would even suggest such a thing."

"She really believes in you, Liddie. Ever since you finished your apprenticeship, she's been giving you more and more to do." Minnie clapped her hands. "I'm so excited for you."

Liddie wriggled with delight. "There's more. I'm going to Chicago."

"Really?" Minnie stepped back. "When? Why?"

"In two weeks. Mrs. Tinker was going anyway and says now that I'm doing dresses of my own, I need to see what's available in the cities." Liddie's face took on a dazed expression. "I can't believe this is happening to me."

"This deserves a celebration. Come on, I'm buying." Minnie pulled Liddie toward Becker's Bakery. "You have to start at the beginning and tell it all. And what do you mean by *dresses*?"

"Mrs. Tinker says I can go with her to the Caithers' party, so I need a dress, too."

———

*August 30, 1914*
*Dear Joe,*

*Mrs. Tinker and I are back from Chicago. Even in my dreams, I didn't imagine the city could be so glorious. We walked down streets where every store was full of fancy dresses. I felt like I was inside a magazine—or a dream. There were more dresses in those store windows than I thought could be in the whole world.*

*I also found soft flannel to make a dress for Amelia's baby. Mama says she has half a mind to get on the train and go visit. I doubt she'll go, but she is worried about Amelia being alone with little Hope. Fred hired on at a neighboring ranch and is gone for days.*

*It embarrasses me to admit it, but there was a time when I didn't write to Amelia. My silence hurt her, I'm sure, but I think I hurt myself more. You told me that Amelia needed me. I wish I'd listened to you.*

*I'm glad you've found new card partners. Vern doesn't get a game together nearly so much since you left. He is finding other things to occupy his time. He came to town just to see my friend Minnie. They sat on the porch swing at Mrs. Prescott's and talked for an hour. Can you imagine Vern talking for an hour? Oh, to have been a fly on the wall!*

*I'm glad you liked the towel. I was thinking of your mother when I embroidered the roses. Please use it. If it wears out, I'll make another.*

*Though Christmas is months away, I'll sleep with visions of sugarplums in my head. All because of those silly doll dresses. Please write again soon.*

*Your friend, Liddie*

Holding the letter closer to the kerosene lamp, Liddie reread the lines she'd dashed off in a rush. It pleased her that he'd put her towel on his table as a centerpiece. He had mentioned his neighbors visited. By now, he might have a girlfriend, too. A woman would notice such a touch. She began to think of what she might make him for a Christmas present. She wanted those women to know he had people who cared for him.

# Chapter 13

"Have you seen these photos?" Liddie directed Minnie's attention to the pictures displayed in the Littmann Studio window. Since the photography studio had opened in late October, the window had become a favorite addition to her morning walk. On the way to Mrs. Tinker's, she usually walked down Main Street, since it was less crowded in the early morning and she enjoyed seeing what was new in the window displays. At the end of the day, she returned to the boardinghouse on a route that took her by the library or down a residential street.

"I have," Minnie said. "They're different, aren't they? The ladies who come into the store can't seem to make up their minds whether they like them or not."

"Well, I like them," Liddie said. From the first time she'd seen them, she'd been drawn to the pictures, so different from the usual stiff portraits she associated with a photography studio. Children romping in a park, men fishing off a riverbank, a woman playing a piano while another woman stood at her side singing. The photos showed people in everyday life, acting so normally. That alone was enough to attract her.

The more she studied the images, though, the more she detected a symmetry that reminded her of formal photos.

As a little girl, Liddie had been fascinated by the only portrait of her family that existed, one taken before Liddie was born. Papa sat next to a small table, his legs crossed at the knees. With his dark hair and full mustache, Liddie thought him incredibly handsome. Mama stood behind him, her hand resting lightly on his shoulder, her hair in a neat bun. She wore her dark dress—a dress otherwise worn only for weddings and funerals—adorned with buttons that stretched diagonally from her left shoulder to her waist. Vern, still a baby, was wearing ruffled pantaloons and sitting atop the table. Four-year-old Amelia stood slightly apart from the group, her right arm on the table.

Whenever she looked at that portrait, she tried to imagine herself in the photograph. Without such an image to prove she was part of the family, how would people know? For the better part of her sixth year, she fretted about that problem. Later on, she worried because there were no photos of her and her father. As she looked at the images in the window of Littmann Studio, that ache that she'd never have such a photograph returned.

Eventually, she had realized the difference between the images in the window and formal photographs: she wanted to know the people in the candid photographs.

"Have you met the photographer?" Liddie asked.

"No. He apparently has no need of ladies' gloves," Minnie joked.

They kept walking down Main Street, enjoying the rare sunshine of the cool November day. They hadn't gone more than half a block when Liddie abruptly pushed open the door to the drugstore and stepped in, pulling Minnie along with her. Leaning against the door, she willed her heart to stop racing. She didn't think Harley had seen her. She hoped he had not.

"What are you doing?" Minnie asked.

"I thought of something I needed." Liddie peeked out the window from behind a display. It hadn't occurred to her that he'd be back in Maquoketa, but then again, it was almost Thanksgiving. He could be home from college.

"You didn't have to be so abrupt," Minnie huffed, straightening her coat. "What do you need?"

Liddie scanned the drugstore. "Notepaper." She strode to a shelf stocked with tablets like the ones she had used in school and picked up a thick pad.

Minnie looked at her in dismay. "They have paper that's much nicer. How about this?" She picked up a box of white sheets. "Or this?" She picked up another box with paper the color of pink roses.

Liddie pretended to assess each sample Minnie handed to her. She didn't really care. When she caught the glimpse of copper-red hair among a group of men down the street, she knew it was Harley.

The memory of the last time she saw him before he left for school in Illinois lingered like a festering wound, as ragged and sore as if she'd seen him yesterday instead of three months ago.

He'd sought her out a number of times after that first evening in the library, showing up to walk a few blocks with her on her way home from work and to invite her to watch him play at a ball game or to have an ice cream at a social. At Minnie's urging, she finally said yes.

"Why not?" Minnie had argued. "You'll have fun."

She prepared so carefully for that date. Her first date ever. She wore a dress she'd made of lightweight cotton trimmed with dotted swiss. She fashioned a band for her hair from the same fabric.

She felt pretty. Harley said she looked nice, and when he introduced her to his friends at the social, she was bashful yet pleased. At the end of the afternoon, when he walked her to Mrs. Prescott's door, he asked her out again. She said yes.

His primary interest appeared to be his own sports accomplishments. This wasn't a topic she had much interest in, but she continued to let him court her anyway. She didn't see the harm, and it was useful to have an escort.

"Harley!" she'd exclaimed, blushing when he stole a kiss on their third date. She had not stopped him when he kissed her again on their fourth date. Afterward—with her mother's admonitions about being "good" echoing in her head—she thought it was her fault, that she'd encouraged him.

As the end of the summer and his departure for college in Carbondale approached, he became more insistent. During what would be their last time together, they emerged from the theater into a humid August night.

"Soda or walk?" he asked.

She touched her fingers to the back of her neck. They came away damp with perspiration. "A soda would be nice, but it's too hot to go inside again. There's a little breeze. Let's walk."

"Walk it is." He put her hand in the crook of his elbow. "Chaplin was great."

"He was. I couldn't stop laughing." She searched for another topic. "I bet you're looking forward to college."

"I'd as soon stay here. With you." He squeezed her hand against his side. "But since I'm going to Southern Illinois, where Pa went, I'll play football this fall."

"You'll be good at it, I'm sure," Liddie said, noticing how quickly he switched from her to football. She didn't think she'd miss him.

They walked to the field where she often came to watch him play baseball.

"Want to sit down?" He motioned to a bench, then sat so close to her that when she edged away, she wound up balanced a couple inches off the end of the bench. He closed the distance, putting an arm behind her. "You're not going to make me go off to college without a kiss, are you, Liddie?"

She knew he would not want to stop at one kiss. Still, he was going away, and she had been seeing him for two months. "One kiss," she said.

"That's my girl." He wrapped his arm around her shoulders, leaned in, and found her lips with his.

Soon she was gasping for breath. "One kiss. One kiss!" She slid her hands between them, turning her head away as he tried to kiss her again.

"Come on, Liddie. It's not like we just met," he protested. "I'm going away and I don't know when I'll see you again."

He didn't wait for a response. As he kissed her again, she twisted and he found only half her mouth.

"Stop it, Harley." She spoke firmly as she struggled to wiggle out of his embrace.

"Aw, don't be a tease. You want to as much as I do. I know you do."

"I don't. Now stop it and let me go!"

She pushed against his chest. He didn't let go. When she heard the fabric of her dress tear, she scratched and bit. She tasted blood, and she didn't know if it was hers or his.

"What the hell, Liddie!" he growled, jerking back.

As soon as she felt his grip lessen, Liddie leaped to her feet and ran.

"Aw, come back, Liddie," he called after her. "It was just a kiss."

By some miracle, she had made it to her room without anyone at the boardinghouse seeing her. It had taken a half hour before her breathing returned to normal, before she stopped shaking. She could still hear him yelling, "It was just a kiss." Had it been? Had she overreacted? She had never told anyone about that night, not even Minnie. Instead, she had counted the days until he left for college. Only then did she breathe easy.

When she'd received a letter from him a couple of weeks later apologizing, telling her he hadn't meant to scare her, she'd wondered if it had all been her fault. She hadn't responded.

"How about this one?" Minnie handed her yet another box of stationery.

"This is nice." She took the pink paper.

"I thought that was you." The familiar voice interrupted them.

Liddie whirled around, a blush creeping up her neck as she fumbled to avoid dropping the box of paper. "Harley," she said.

"I thought I saw you, and then you were gone. I figured you might have come in here."

"I needed . . . some things." She noticed that he'd put on a little weight and wondered if he was playing football.

"Were you going to write to me?" He gestured to the paper she held.

She blushed fully.

"You didn't answer my letter," he said.

"Oh. Well. No." Liddie studied the box of notepaper, wishing he would leave.

"Say, I'm home until Sunday. Would you like to go to a movie this weekend?"

"I'm going home for the weekend," she mumbled. She felt Minnie's eyes on her wondering at the bald-faced lie. Liddie had never disabused Minnie of the belief that the only reason she was not still seeing Harley was that he'd gone off to college.

Harley shifted awkwardly, waiting for her to say something else. She didn't. He looked at Minnie, then back to Liddie. Finally, he said, "I guess I'll see you another time," and left.

"What was that about?" Minnie whispered as soon as he was out of earshot. "You didn't tell me he wrote. Why don't you want to go out with him?"

"He's not for me," Liddie said.

"I don't see why not. He's not bad looking. His family is well-off. And he seems to like you."

As Minnie ticked off what Liddie knew would also be her mother's checklist, Liddie looked for the clerk. "I'm getting this paper," she said. "Thanks for helping me pick it out."

# Chapter 14

"What do you think?" Liddie straightened the layers of crepe that formed the skirt of her dress.

"You look beautiful." Minnie clasped her hands to her chest. "Turn!" She twirled a hand in the air.

Liddie revolved slowly, stopping whenever Minnie exclaimed over some detail. She had wanted a dress stylish enough for the elegance of the Caithers' party; yet at the same time, this dress must serve for many occasions. Ultimately, she opted for a fitted bodice and slim skirt in a deep-blue crepe with only one peplum layer, though the year's fashion favored any number of circular flounces. Ivory lace framed her neckline and continued as an inset down the bodice to her waist. The same lace adorned cuffs on three-quarter-length sleeves. She hoped both the color and design made her look more mature.

"Choosing a dress design and this fabric was unimaginably difficult." Liddie pivoted back and forth to catch her reflection in the mirror. "Standing in the store, surrounded by bolts of fabric in all the colors of the rainbow, I was in awe. I'd never seen so much fabric."

"I'd think that would be fun!"

"I suppose it's silly, but it was almost too much. Mama always chose the fabric for my clothes. And if she asked my opinion, it was between one or two options. Not hundreds."

"Didn't Mrs. Tinker help you?"

"She answered my questions but let me decide. I think she wanted to see what I'd do."

"Was she happy with your choices?"

"She was," Liddie admitted. Along with the design and the fabric, Mrs. Tinker approved of her decision to forgo the rhinestones and glass beads they'd used on several fancier dresses. "She said, 'Fit in, but do not outshine. That is wise.'" Liddie searched Minnie's face. "You don't think it's too plain? You should see the dresses we're making. Some are Oriental with high collars and Mandarin sleeves. That's big in New York right now. Mrs. Tinker says we're lucky everyone wants to 'buy American.' Otherwise, women might order from overseas."

"This dress is perfect. You'll have all the men staring."

"That would make Mama happy," Liddie said dryly.

"And meeting the perfect fellow would make you unhappy?"

"I am not looking for anyone, though that seems to be what everyone cares about. And not just any man, but the 'right' man."

"Is that a crime?"

"It's not, I suppose. It's only that it seems so preordained. And confusing. I heard Mama and Aunt Kate talking one day. Mama wants me to get married, but I think one reason she agreed to let me come to Maquoketa was so I wouldn't get involved with Joe."

"Joe?" Minnie frowned. "You talk about him almost as though he's a brother. Why would your mother even think that?"

"I don't think she did until after Joe's girlfriend jilted him."

"But they like Joe. I'd have thought they'd think he was a good match."

"We all do. Like Joe, that is. But Mama said he doesn't have the money to take care of a wife. Like that's the most important thing. Even if I were thinking about Joe as a husband, which I wasn't."

"But now you are?"

"No, I'm not. I'm not thinking about anyone as a husband. I'm thinking about sewing. And becoming a dressmaker. Why does it all have to be about a husband?" Liddie stomped her foot.

"Don't be cross." Minnie twirled her in a circle. "Oh, Liddie, I cannot even imagine myself in a room with all those fancy people."

"Truthfully, I can't see myself there, either." Liddie felt a rush of anxiety. She liked the way she looked, but was it a charade? Did she really belong there?

"You'll be positively smashing. Besides, no one expects you to come out of the party married, for heaven's sake. Go. Have fun. That's all."

"Yes, you're right." Liddie scanned her reflection in the mirror.

Stepping up behind Liddie so she could see in the mirror, too, Minnie gave her a sly look. "And if you meet the man of your dreams, please don't turn away."

"You never stop!" Liddie laughed. "I wish you could come with me. What will I say to any of them?"

"Ask them about themselves. You won't have to do any more after that."

———

"Oh!" Liddie's breath formed a cloud that glittered like lace in the night air as she gazed up at the Caithers' house.

"Quite like a Christmas tree, lit up this way, isn't it?" Mrs. Tinker commented as she peered up at the house. The aigrette feathers adorning her new blue-gray hat fluttered in the chilly breeze. Dresses were her business, but Mrs. Tinker's preferred indulgence was elaborate hats. "They were the first in town to have electricity."

Every window of the massive brick house, one of the largest on Pleasant Street, was lit. Smoke coming from two huge chimneys spoke of multiple fireplaces. Unconsciously, Liddie put a hand to her throat and caressed her grandmother's cameo. Liddie had objected when her mother lent her the family heirloom she herself wore on special occasions. But Liddie was glad to have the cameo now, on the threshold of this new world.

"Shall we, my dear?" Mrs. Tinker took her arm as they climbed the steps to the oak and glass door.

"Welcome, welcome! Merry Christmas," Gladys Caither greeted them. "Ernestine, it's so good to see you. And Miss Treadway. Welcome. My, this weather did turn, didn't it?"

When Mrs. Caither handed their coats and gloves to a maid, Liddie couldn't help but stare. A maid!

"Merry Christmas, Ernestine. It's good to see you." Ben Caither shook Mrs. Tinker's hand and turned to Liddie. "Miss Treadway. I've heard so much about you."

"I'm pleased to meet you, sir. Merry Christmas."

Mr. Caither lowered his voice. "Miss Treadway, I want to say we were saddened by your father's death."

"Thank you, Mr. Caither. You knew my father?"

"We'd done business together. He was a man good to his word."

If Mr. Caither was acquainted with her father and thought well of him, then maybe she was not as out of place as she had thought.

"What a lovely dress." Mrs. Caither surveyed Liddie's gown. "Simple yet elegant."

"Thank you." Liddie smiled, though she was uncertain from Mrs. Caither's inflection whether she considered simplicity an asset or a deficiency.

"Liddie has shown talent—as she did for Anna's dress," Mrs. Tinker interjected, skillfully directing the conversation away from Liddie and back to her customer. "That style is right for a girl past childhood but not yet an adult, don't you think?"

"It's perfect," Mrs. Caither agreed, looking across the parlor to her daughter, who was surrounded by friends. "Anna insisted on trying on the dress every day since we brought it home. I feared she would wear it out before the party!"

As Liddie surveyed the dress she'd labored over so diligently, the satisfaction she felt during the final fitting returned. For the base fabric, she'd chosen a softer version of taffeta more often used as a lining. The fabric draped easily over Anna's slim figure. Borrowing from some of the popular elements of the women's dresses, Liddie had added a Mandarin collar and used a fine, lightweight brocade to bring a note of sophistication to the simple design.

Mrs. Caither turned her attention back to Liddie. "Thank you for replicating Anna's dress for her doll. It is truly precious."

Before she could say more, the front door opened and a gust of cold air carried another couple into the entry hall.

Mrs. Tinker steered Liddie into the parlor, which was already filled with guests. "Ah, there's Francine Goodman. We'll start there."

After introductions, Mrs. Goodman launched into a description of her plans for the annual charity dance, and Liddie surreptitiously scanned the room, surprised to realize she knew more of the women than she'd expected. The men she knew by name and reputation because of their wives. The mayor, the editor of the *Sentinel*, the owner of the lumberyard. Mrs. Tinker's shop truly was a gateway to the town's high society.

A burst of laughter drew her attention to a room she hadn't seen when she arrived. The laughter rose from a group of younger people standing near a piano. She scanned the group and her breath caught. At its center was Harley Ellers. A few of the girls Liddie knew because she'd helped make their dresses.

When she saw Harley in November, it had been such a surprise. Thinking about that encounter afterward, she'd wished she'd handled herself differently. She vacillated between various imagined responses that were courteous but not encouraging and blunt but not rude. Mostly, she felt that he had been too pushy, and that's what she thought he should know.

Despite all her imagined comebacks, she really did not want to talk to him, and fortunately, Mrs. Tinker kept her occupied chatting with the older women. People were more than willing to talk, and she could comfortably listen while sipping a cup of eggnog or enjoying a tidbit from the buffet laid out on the dining room table, a repast she wished Minnie could see. She didn't know what all the dishes were, only that one bite was as delicious as the next. And that the supply was never depleted, as fresh plates continuously materialized. "Canapés," someone called them. She rolled the new word around on her tongue, a word as delicious as the pastries.

At the buffet again, she had just picked up a small, flaky pastry filled with liver pâté when she felt someone at her elbow.

"Did you miss me, Liddie?"

At the sound of his voice, the hair rose on her arms. She steeled herself and turned to acknowledge him. His friends lounged close enough to hear while filling their plates.

"Harley!" She opened her eyes wide in surprise. "You've been gone?" She paused, then added with studied nonchalance, "The fall has been exceptionally full. I admit I hadn't noticed." She popped the pastry into her mouth.

"Ho! Good one!" One of the boys snickered.

It was a cut Liddie had not planned, but it seemed to strike home.

Harley stared at her, then twitched his shoulders. Gathering his confidence, he turned to his pals. "I thought she might like to join us." He smirked. "I guess she's too busy."

As the other boys drifted out of the dining room, Harley moved closer. "I said I was sorry," he muttered in a gravelly undertone.

"You were a boor," she said.

He backed away, his face flushed.

Liddie's heart raced as he walked away. Until the words came out of her mouth, she hadn't realized she'd say that. She picked up her eggnog, then took refuge near the bay window. She hadn't intended to be so bold, but now she felt exhilarated. She hadn't backed down, though it niggled a bit that Harley had apologized twice and she had not been gracious enough to accept. She wondered if Aunt Kate would approve of what she'd said. She was fairly certain her mother would not.

From her vantage point, she could view the front foyer, and she was relieved to see Harley and his friends depart. She felt no hurry to rejoin the party, but with him gone, she could relax. Conversations came to her in snatches. Among the men, the war in Europe was a major topic of conversation.

A portly older gentleman whose sideburns bristled like untamed shaving brushes challenged the newspaper editor. "Do you think it necessary to print an account of the war in every issue? It doesn't involve us, after all," he said.

"Obviously, I do, Mr. Adair," the editor responded. "Many readers have family there."

"Whether we have men in the action or not, the war does affect us," Ben Caither said. "Chemicals, metals, wheat. All being diverted to the front. We'll feel it here before long."

"It is difficult to absorb the loss of life." Another man shook his head. "The numbers you report killed in these battles is difficult to comprehend."

"We can only hope the war ends soon. And in the meantime, that it doesn't pull us in."

Liddie could imagine her father in a discussion like this.

"Should the French and Russians roll over? Wouldn't you fight?"

"I wasn't saying that. The line has to be drawn."

"Where's the line? Will the kaiser be satisfied unless he controls all of Europe?"

"That's the question, isn't it? President Wilson is determined to keep us out. I support him on that."

Some men nodded their agreement; others did not. A chill ran up her back at the idea of Vern or Joe going to war.

"Gentlemen." Mrs. Caither stepped into the group and laid a hand on her husband's arm. "This sounds quite serious for a holiday party. Might I encourage you to visit the buffet?"

"My wife is right as usual," Mr. Caither said. "We cannot solve the world's problems tonight, nor should we try."

"It's quite the party, isn't it?" A male voice spoke very near to Liddie's left ear.

She jerked in surprise. The eggnog sloshed and she thrust the cup away from her, praying nothing would splash on her dress.

"I'm sorry. I didn't mean to startle you." The man had been standing not half a foot away, but he stepped back even as he pulled a linen handkerchief from his pocket and offered it to her.

"No harm. The cup was not full." Liddie furtively attempted to survey her dress.

Relieved that she saw no stains, she turned her attention to an attractive man, slightly taller than she. She guessed him to be in his late twenties. Neatly trimmed brown hair framed a handsome face. A faint scar traced a thin line through his left eyebrow. But his eyes, deep brown, almost black, with gold flecks around the irises—that's where she found herself looking. Into eyes that focused on her so intently she felt herself begin to blush.

He reached for her cup. "May I get you another drink?"

"No. Truly. I've had enough." She set her cup on an occasional table and extended her hand. "I don't think we've met. I'm Liddie Treadway."

"Thomas Littmann," he responded, taking her hand more firmly than she expected. Littmann brought his heels together with a click and executed a formal bow. "My pleasure, Miss Treadway."

She had never seen such a bow. "Littmann? Of the photography studio on Main Street?"

"Yes." He cocked his head. "I'm surprised you know of me. I'm new to town."

"I pass your studio on my way to work. The photographs in your window attracted me. They're so . . ." She hesitated for fear of saying the wrong thing. "So unexpected."

He laughed. "Unexpected?"

"I hope you don't take that as an insult, Mr. Littmann."

"Not at all, Miss Treadway." The gold flecks twinkled. "That is a better reaction than many have given. I'd all but decided to take those photographs out of the window."

"Oh, I hope not! I would miss them."

"You would?" He considered her. "Then I shall leave them there."

Was he mocking her? Out of the corner of her eye, Liddie saw Mrs. Tinker approaching, and she exhaled in relief.

"Liddie," Mrs. Tinker said. "You have found the one person I have not had the pleasure of meeting. Will you introduce me?"

"Of course. Thomas Littmann, this is Mrs. Ernestine Tinker. Mr. Littmann has the photography studio on Main Street. Mrs. Tinker is the leading seamstress in Maquoketa. I am fortunate to work for her."

Mr. Littmann took Mrs. Tinker's hand and executed the same crisp bow he had made for Liddie.

"It's a pleasure, Mr. Littmann. Let me add my welcome to the many you've no doubt already received," Mrs. Tinker said. "How have you found our fair city so far?"

"Everyone has made me feel welcome. Mrs. Caither was most gracious to extend an invitation so late in the season."

"I understand you are related to the Marcorts near Andrew?"

"Somewhat distantly. A cousin twice removed on my mother's side."

Liddie watched this exchange with interest. So Mrs. Tinker knew of the man, even if she had not met him personally.

"I have passed your studio," Mrs. Tinker said. "The photographs in your window are refreshing."

"Refreshing. And Miss Treadway termed them unexpected." Mr. Littmann beamed. "I hope others will find them so."

"Miss Treadway has a good eye."

"So I am discovering." He looked at Liddie, holding her gaze until she felt obliged to look away.

"I must steal Miss Treadway to meet some other guests." Mrs. Tinker excused them with a gracious smile. "It's been a pleasure, Mr. Littmann. I trust we will see you again."

"I sincerely hope so." He bowed slightly to both women.

As Mrs. Tinker steered Liddie away, she whispered, "It does not do to spend too much time talking to any one person, particularly a man." Mrs. Tinker nodded pleasantly to a cluster of women gathered around the piano. "Some like to talk."

"But we *were* just talking."

"Yes. But we don't really know Mr. Littmann, and a woman cannot be too careful."

They joined a group Liddie had met earlier in the evening. Obviously, the excuse Mrs. Tinker gave the photographer was a ruse. After a respectable amount of time with them, Liddie moved on.

Later, she was drawn into a discussion with several boys and girls more her age. She'd worked on the dresses two of the girls wore, yet they acted as though they'd not met her before that night.

"That's a pretty cameo," one of the girls said.

"Thank you," Liddie responded, her fingers going automatically to the brooch at her throat.

"My mother has one much like it," the girl said. "I was so excited to get these pearls." She fingered a long strand. "Everyone's wearing them." She looked pointedly at her friend.

"Almost everyone," her friend replied. They both laughed.

Liddie flushed. She had noticed that virtually all the young women were wearing long ropes of pearls. She tilted her chin up and smiled evenly. "You look very nice in them. They have a wonderful slimming effect," she said.

As far as the boys were concerned, they appeared no more interested in her than she in them. At least she'd met enough seemingly eligible young men to satisfy Minnie's curiosity. And it would not be necessary even to mention Harley.

From time to time, she glanced up and found Mr. Littmann studying her, even as he engaged in conversation with others. Truthfully, she was observing him, too. He might be older than she'd first thought. His thick brown hair had begun to gray at the temples. He was one of those men—like her father—who stood out in a crowd. Well-fitting clothes, well built, easy to interact with. He had a charismatic air about him.

Each time their eyes met, he made a small gesture of acknowledgment, a barely perceptible dip of his head, a scarcely visible smile. Each time, she found herself wanting to turn again in his direction.

By the time she and Mrs. Tinker said their good-byes and stepped out into the brisk December night, Liddie had to admit that she hoped to see one particular man again.

———

*December 29, 1914*

*Dear Joe,*

*We had a nice Christmas at home. Mama was cheerful because Aunt Kate came for a long visit. Kate was enthusiastic about a suffrage amendment on the ballot in Ohio in November. It was defeated, but she is not deterred.*

*Another bright spot—Minnie also spent the holiday with us. She is so merry, and she plays the piano as Amelia used to. She is smitten with Vern!*

*The holiday party I attended was so wonderful it is hard to describe. Mrs. Caither had maids to serve the food. I did not think anyone did that. Not in Iowa. All the leading businessmen and their wives were there. And I talked to them as though I were one of them!*

*Did you find friends to celebrate Christmas with? I enjoy your stories about the people you deliver goods to from the train. Running a dray seems the perfect way to avoid the winter isolation.*

*It has been a year of change for all of us. My wish for you is that you receive everything you hope for in the new year.*

*Your friend, Liddie*

Liddie thought to write about Mr. Littmann but found herself conflicted and a little embarrassed. How could she admit she was so taken with someone she'd just met, especially when she did not want to be taken with anyone at all?

———

*January 23, 1915*
*Dear Amelia,*

*Happy New Year! We missed you at Christmas, but from your letter I could see your celebration as if I had been there. The tree Fred cut sounds perfect. The two of you stringing popcorn and cranberries sounds so homey. Next year, Hope can help.*

*The last Christmas in your first home together. I expect living closer to town will be nice since Fred will be away* some nights. Does he work for just one rancher or for several? Will you be close enough to still see your friend Gertie, who has helped you learn to live in the Wild West?

I met an interesting man at the holiday party I told you about. He's the new photographer in town. Judging from the way he looked at me, I think he thought I was interesting, too.

Did Mama tell you about Vern? He's sweet on my friend Minnie. She had a mountain to climb when she set her eye on him, but she just may make it!

We all send our love.

Liddie

# Chapter 15

Ever since Vern had invited them to go skating, Minnie had been praying for cold weather and a clear day. Those prayers were answered. Bright sunlight reflected off mounds of snow pushed to the banks of the river north of town.

Minnie and Vern had already taken to the ice. Meanwhile, Liddie dawdled with her laces, sitting on a log at the river's edge. She'd skated only a handful of times in her life when they'd visited cousins who lived near ponds. Back then, she'd struggled with skates several sizes too large, and her ankles had wobbled so precariously she could barely stand, let alone accomplish a smooth glide. She'd always been grateful when their mothers called them in for hot chocolate.

Skaters crowded the ice this morning. A young couple easily pulled a sled holding a bundled-up toddler, and two older women, linked arm in arm, moved in slow, sweeping curves, chatting leisurely. Others were as inexperienced and graceless as she knew herself to be, which gave her some comfort.

"Come on. Give it a go!" Minnie called from several yards away.

"In a minute. I almost have my laces done," Liddie replied, waving them off. "You two go on."

"All right, but don't sit too long. You'll get chilled."

Minnie held tight to Vern's hand as they skated farther out. Liddie could hardly comprehend the changes in her brother since he'd met Minnie. He smiled from time to time for no apparent reason. He talked more. Well, at least he talked some. Because of Minnie, Liddie was seeing a side of her brother she hadn't known existed.

She remained seated, marveling at how the relationship between her brother and friend had developed. From her first visit to the farm, Minnie had fit in as if she'd lived there her whole life. The hens seemed no more inclined to peck at Minnie than they had Joe, and Minnie had endeared herself to Margretta when she donned an apron and asked to learn how to make gravy.

Liddie held her hand above her eyes to shield them from the sun as Vern and Minnie circled back and slid to a stop in front of her. She clapped. "You're an expert, Vern."

"I have a good teacher." He tipped his hat to Minnie.

"Enough." Minnie spoke sternly. "You'll freeze if you sit there longer."

"C'mon, Liddie." Vern took her hand and pulled her up. "You'll get the hang of it."

"If you say so." Liddie remained doubtful.

With Minnie and Vern on either side, Liddie felt stable through her first tentative sliding moves. She was surprised at how much steadier she was with a well-fitting pair of skates. After a complete turn across the river and back, Minnie released her hand. Liddie wavered, her lips pinched in a tight line, her eyes never leaving the ice.

"I'll let you two skate a round, and then I'll show you a couple of turns," Minnie said. She was gone before either of them could object.

"It's not so hard when you get the hang of it," Vern said.

"Minnie's happy you asked her out. But ice skating? I could barely believe it when she told me."

"She likes to skate. I figured I could try."

Afraid to take her eyes off the ice for too long, Liddie hazarded a glance at Vern. He wore an uncharacteristic smile. "You're doing fine," she said. "Better than fine. I can tell Minnie thinks so, too."

"I'll never keep up with her." Vern motioned to Minnie, who was spinning on one skate at the center of the ice. "Have you seen anything like that?"

"She can certainly skate," Liddie agreed, though she didn't look up. Her breath came in short puffs. Her legs ached from the tension. "She was taken with the note you wrote."

"Did she show it to you?" Vern asked, his tone registering alarm.

"No. But when she got it, she was ecstatic and read a line or two to me." Liddie peeked at him. "Truthfully, Vern, it didn't sound like you."

The color in Vern's cold-reddened cheeks heightened. "I wrote Joe."

"You wrote Joe?" Astonished, she took her eyes off the ice. Of course, it made sense. They were friends, after all. Liddie squeezed his hand and trained her eyes back on the ice. "You said the right thing, that's for certain."

"Look how well you're doing," Minnie called.

Liddie tried to smile, but as she looked up, the tip of her blade caught on the ice and she lost her balance. Thrashing to right herself, she let go of Vern's hand, grasped for his arm, and missed.

The next thing she knew, she was on her back, the wind knocked out of her. She looked up at the concerned faces of Vern, Minnie, and a crowd of other skaters, including Thomas Littmann. She groaned.

"Are you all right?" Minnie knelt beside her.

"I'm fine."

"Miss Treadway, let me help you," Mr. Littmann said.

"I'm all right." Liddie tried to push herself upright. As she did, her hands slid on the ice and she banged her funny bone. "Ow!" She fell back, gripping her elbow.

"Together we can get her on her feet," Mr. Littmann said to Vern. "You take one arm, I'll take the other." He handed a camera to Minnie. "Hold that for me. Take care; it's fragile."

———

*February 20, 1915*
*Dear Joe,*

*We had fun skating on Saturday, thanks in no small part to you! Vern and Minnie got on so well. The best I can say for myself is that I didn't kill myself. Though I tried. I'm still sore from the fall I took. I spent the rest of the morning by the bonfire.*

*The Friday night dances sound like fun. I'm glad you eat a solid meal at least once a week at the potlucks.*

*Work is back to normal now that the holidays are over. Mrs. Tinker gives me more responsibilities all the time. Today, I measured a woman for alterations. Mrs. Tinker watched, of course, but she didn't make it seem like she was watching. I am proud she trusts me.*

*I'm sure hearing the wind blowing all the time does wear. Take heart, spring will be here soon. Sending warm thoughts your way.*

*Liddie*

# Chapter 16

In the weeks after the Caithers' party, Liddie had hoped to run into Mr. Littmann. Then, after she'd tumbled right in front of him while skating, she hoped never to see him again. But after her initial embarrassment faded, she returned to stopping by the studio window to see the new photos he displayed.

One day early in March, the snow had melted and Liddie could feel spring softening the edge of the cold morning. In the window of the photography studio, pictures of children skating on the river caught her attention, and she stopped to look. Those were the same children who'd been there when she'd been skating with Vern and Minnie.

"You've recovered from your fall?"

She jumped. Mr. Littmann stood just behind her right shoulder. She had not heard him walk up, but there he was, only inches away.

"I'm so sorry." He stepped back a pace. "I have startled you again."

"It's quite all right," Liddie said, even though she didn't think it was. He really didn't know her, and even if he did, it was rude for him to come up on her like that. She realized her hand had instinctively covered her heart, and she dropped it to her side. "Only my ego was bruised."

"I'm glad to hear it." He frowned. "Are you certain you're all right?"

"Yes." She forced herself to breathe evenly. "Believe it or not, I am almost used to being startled."

"Used to being startled?" He focused on her in the same intense way he had at the party.

Liddie averted her eyes. "When I'm concentrating on something, I hear little else. Because it was so easy, my brother delighted in tormenting me."

"That doesn't sound nice. How many siblings do you have?"

"One brother, one sister. I don't see them or my mother often now."

"When you talk about them, a shadow crosses your eyes."

"I do miss them. I only go home once a month. So I don't see them otherwise unless they come into town. And my sister lives in Wyoming now." Liddie stopped, finding herself saying more than she intended. "I'm sorry. I'm prattling on."

"You are not prattling. I enjoy knowing how families interact. That's what I attempt to show in my photographs."

"That's exactly what attracts me to them." Liddie brightened, thankful to move the discussion away from herself. "This child with his mother at the river." She pointed to a photograph at the center of the display. "He's looking at her with such a smile. They appear so happy together." Liddie glanced up. He was studying her instead of the photograph.

"If you like that photo at the river, I have others you might enjoy. Do you have five minutes? I could give you a quick tour of the studio."

She hesitated. Going into his studio alone—was that appropriate?

"I'm meeting Mrs. Davies," Mr. Littmann said. "Five minutes is all I have."

A blush warmed her cheeks. Had he read her concern? This was ridiculous. She could make her own decisions. She lifted her chin and stared directly into his eyes. "As long as I'm not late for work, I would enjoy a tour."

Mr. Littmann unlocked the studio door and swung it open.

———

Liddie arrived breathless at Mrs. Tinker's that morning, having run from the photography studio. The time had passed so quickly, she hadn't noticed when the promised five-minute tour turned into twenty.

"Why so out of breath?" Mrs. Tinker asked as Liddie unpinned her hat and checked her hair, then hung up her cloak and sat to wipe snow off her shoes.

"I'm sorry to be late. I thought I had plenty of time." She always made a point to be working on her first project of the morning by seven thirty, and here it was after eight.

"Is everything all right?"

"Oh yes." Liddie took a dress from the alterations rack and read the tag pinned to the shoulder as she settled in at her machine. "You'll never guess who I ran into this morning."

"Do tell."

"Mr. Littmann. The photographer from the Caithers' party. I walk by his window every few days to see his pictures. He's never been there before, but this time he was. And he gave me a tour of his studio!"

Mrs. Tinker raised both eyebrows. "Hmm?"

"He said it would only take five minutes, and it would have, except I asked so many questions." While she talked, Liddie tore out a seam and took the dress in along the chalk marks. "I had no idea there was so much work involved in taking photographs and printing them."

Liddie did not tell Mrs. Tinker about the pictures Mr. Littmann had taken that day at the river. Pictures that included Liddie skating and sitting by the bonfire. She had been completely taken aback at seeing herself. He explained that the light was right and the composition interesting. He hoped she didn't mind. She said she did not, but she couldn't get it out of her head that he'd been watching her, photographing her.

"I've heard he has done well with his studio," Mrs. Tinker said. "The party was an opportunity for him to meet people."

"That's what he said. He's had four appointments because of the party. He says he hardly has time to take care of everything." Liddie hadn't stopped talking since she sat down. Realizing this, she stilled her hands in her lap. She had been attentive to doing things perfectly since that first day. "I really am sorry I was late."

"Don't worry," Mrs. Tinker said. "You don't make a habit of it."

"I want you to know how much I appreciate . . . well, everything. I never imagined how much I'd like being here."

"You have talent, Liddie. For most girls, working as a seamstress is a stepping-stone to getting married. Seldom do I find someone who has both the capability and the interest to do more. You could become a real dressmaker."

"Oh, Mrs. Tinker." Liddie felt breathless and her voice squeaked. "Really?"

"The real design work is done in New York and Paris, of course. But a good dressmaker can offer creativity and value to her clients wherever she is."

Paris. New York. The names swam in Liddie's mind. She had never seriously thought of herself and those cities in the same sentence. It was beyond her imagination.

"You should think on it. Though I doubt this is what your mother had in mind when she approached me. Your Aunt Kate, maybe, but definitely not your mother."

"What do you mean?" She was surprised by the idea that her mother and aunt had discussed their expectations for her with Mrs. Tinker.

Mrs. Tinker walked to the window, where she looked out for some time before speaking again. Finally, she faced Liddie.

"Parents want to give their daughters opportunities—to see a bit of the world, to learn things—preferably to meet the right man. All without letting them get too far from home. So they seek out jobs like this." Mrs. Tinker waved her hand at the sewing room. "Girls stay with me for six months, maybe a year. They attend a party or two. They attract a suitable man, and they marry. They acquire sewing skills they'll use throughout their lives, but sewing is never the goal."

Mrs. Tinker continued. "Frankly, I feel lucky you stayed through your apprenticeship and continued working here after. I'm sure marriage is what your mother wants for you. She hopes to see you well cared for." Her eyes were gentle. "And what mother would not want that?"

"You mentioned my aunt. You think she has different ideas?"

"Kate is an uncommon woman. Her ideas ruffle some feathers. At least around here."

Liddie was not surprised to learn that Kate spoke her mind to others as she had with Liddie's father.

"She's chosen a nontraditional path for herself, and she may see you taking a different route, too."

"That would be good?" Liddie looked to Mrs. Tinker for agreement.

"It's not so much a matter of good or not good. It's a matter of knowing what you want to do."

Liddie surprised herself when she admitted, "I don't know what I want."

Mrs. Tinker laughed. "Some people just know. Others figure it out over time. If you don't know with certainty, don't act too hastily. That's the best I can tell you."

Mrs. Tinker went to the dress form and made a few tucks in the bodice of the dress hanging there. Then she stepped back and stood silently, tapping her thimble-clad finger on her chin. "In any case, it is wise to be prepared, and I just had an idea. If you think you might like to do more dressmaking, it would be useful to have examples of your work to show. Perhaps Mr. Littmann could take photos of dresses you make so you can build a portfolio."

"A portfolio?"

"Yes. A book of the work you've done to show potential customers."

"A portfolio," Liddie whispered in wonder. Then her heart sank. She'd spent her savings to buy fabric and notions to make Christmas presents and a spring dress for herself. "You're kind to think of it, but I . . . it's too early, don't you think?"

"Not at all. Your dresses have people interested. We want to encourage that interest."

"The photos cost a lot, don't they? I can't afford—"

"Oh my dear!" Mrs. Tinker exclaimed. "I didn't mean for you to pay for the photos. You are still working for me. The benefit would be mine, too. This is my business expense."

Liddie raced to the boardinghouse that night, eager to tell Minnie about her day. When she arrived, she found an envelope addressed to her on the hall table. In it was the picture Mr. Littmann had taken of her sitting on a log at the river's edge. She was laughing, her face upturned, the light on her cheeks. On the back of the photo, he'd written, *May you always be so happy— Thomas Littmann, photographer.*

# Chapter 17

When Mrs. Tinker decided on something, she did not dawdle. Within a week, she'd made an appointment for Mr. Littmann to photograph the dresses. She borrowed Anna Caither's dress with the promise that Anna could be there when the photos were taken. Liddie simply watched all the activity with amazement, unable to believe it was all about her and her portfolio.

On the appointed day, Mrs. Tinker had a dress form delivered to Mr. Littmann's studio along with the dresses, which were meticulously packed between layers of tissue paper. When she and Liddie arrived at the studio, Mrs. Caither and Anna were waiting.

"You brought your doll," Liddie greeted Anna.

"Do you think it's silly?" Anna's eyes darted to her mother.

"I am glad you like her dress so much," Liddie said, thinking about how often Vern kidded her about making doll clothes.

As he shook Liddie's hand, Mr. Littmann leaned in and added in a conspiratorial tone, "Lucky for me I came to work early that day, isn't it? Look at everyone you've brought in my door."

His comment flustered her. "It was Mrs. Tinker's idea," she said.

"Shall we start with Anna's dress?" Mrs. Tinker interjected.

"Quite right," Mr. Littmann said, holding Liddie's hand for an extra beat before releasing it. Then he led them to chairs against the wall. "You'll be able to see best sitting here," he said. "If you'll ensure the dress is well displayed, I'll adjust the lighting."

Liddie helped Mrs. Tinker position Anna's dress on the dress form. When she stepped back, the rose dress looked nondescript and a little forlorn. For the first time, Liddie wondered if the dress she'd worked so hard on was a bit plain. "Will such a pale dress show against this background?" she asked.

"It's all in the lighting," Mr. Littmann responded.

As he positioned silver panels on tripods, they caught light from the windows, and Liddie watched shadows appear and disappear, causing details to become more pronounced. In a matter of minutes, the dress looked like the gown Liddie remembered. "The light changes everything," she murmured.

"Even more so when you view it through the camera lens," he said, and Liddie yearned to see what he meant.

After photographing the dress, Mr. Littmann replaced the plate in the camera and stepped away. A frown carved wrinkles in his forehead. "It doesn't seem right," he said.

"What doesn't?" Mrs. Tinker asked.

"To take photos of the dress but not the young lady who wore it."

Anna grabbed her mother's elbow. "Oh, Mama, could I?"

"We are here as guests, dear. To watch. Remember?" Mrs. Caither placed the girl's hands firmly back in her own lap.

Mrs. Tinker hedged. "It may take more time than Mr. Littmann has available."

"I have blocked the entire morning for this sitting, so we have plenty of time." He lowered his voice so only Mrs. Tinker and Liddie could hear. "There would not be an additional fee."

Liddie observed that Mr. Littmann and Mrs. Tinker shared considerable skill in customer relations. Once he took photos of Anna, she expected there would be no way Mrs. Caither could resist buying prints.

While the Caithers were preparing for Anna's photo session in a little room down the hall, Mr. Littmann remarked, "We'll want to make photos of you in your dress as well, Miss Treadway."

Immediately, she imagined Mr. Littmann's piercing eyes regarding her through the camera lens. "No!" she exclaimed, blushing to the roots of her hair. "I mean, it's not necessary. We only need pictures of the dress."

"I leave it up to you, Liddie," Mrs. Tinker said. "It is an opportunity."

It was one thing to find out he'd been watching her at the pond. Quite another to *know* he would be observing her in that intense way.

"Think about it while we take Miss Caither's photos," he suggested.

Mr. Littmann brought in a small chair and a matching table, then directed Anna how to sit. Confident and efficient, he was masterful at helping the girl relax in front of the camera.

Liddie absorbed his every action. How he changed the film plates. How he talked with Anna. How he positioned her head and hands.

"Take a look, if you wish," he said to Liddie. He gestured to the camera as he stepped away to work with Anna.

Had he been reading her mind? Or her face? Self-consciously, she stepped up to the camera, standing as she'd seen him stand. She edged up to peek through the eyepiece. Everything was upside down. She peered around the camera and then through the lens again, marveling at how the camera reduced everything it focused on to a well-composed image. As she studied the effect, Mr. Littmann turned toward the camera and winked. He knew she was looking at him. Heat filled her chest and she pulled back. Avoiding his eyes, she retreated to stand by the wall.

"You have a budding fashion model, Mrs. Caither," Mr. Littmann said when he finished.

Gladys Caither beamed. "We are eager to see the pictures, Mr. Littmann. When will they be ready?"

"We'll check my calendar before you leave."

By the time he returned, Liddie had decided to model her dress for photos, too.

———

That night, as Liddie sat at her dressing table, the lamp casting an amber glow on the paper, she was eager to share with Joe the excitement that still rippled under her skin. When she put pencil to paper, she felt as though he were sitting across the table.

> . . . Though the studio is a big open room, the pictures look as though we're in someone's parlor because of the way he arranged his "props"—an elaborate high-backed chair and a small round table.
>
> When he let me look through the camera lens, I had the strangest feeling . . . as though I were somewhere apart, seeing something no one else could see, while no one could see me. There is a power I can't explain. A photographer saves a moment for the future. Or lets it pass by. If there is no photograph made, no one would ever know, but by making a picture, even an everyday event takes on importance.
>
> I don't think I told you that I first met Mr. Littmann at the Caithers' holiday party. He looked at me so intently that night it made me uncomfortable. Now I think he was looking at me as if he were looking through a camera lens—as though I couldn't see him. No doubt he looks at everyone that way.
>
> He was also at the river that day Vern took us skating. I wasn't aware of it, but he took photos of me there. He gave me one so I'll be able to remember the day I fell!
>
> Tell your postmaster friend I say hello.
>
> Liddie

In Joe's last letter, he'd told her the postmaster thought she must be either his mama or his girlfriend because she wrote so much. Joe hadn't set him straight. Instead, he said he'd had fun keeping their friendship to himself. Liddie laughed that someone would think of her and Joe that way. Joe obviously considered it a joke, too.

# Chapter 18

Mrs. Tinker ordered prints of Liddie and Anna wearing their dresses. These she framed and hung on the entryway wall where customers were certain to see them. They created quite a stir.

At first Liddie was abashed when someone drew attention to the photos. Gradually, she grew comfortable saying simply, "Thank you, I'm glad you like them."

Mrs. Tinker capitalized on this interest with questions that often led to an update of an existing dress or even a completely new garment. Two women for whom Mrs. Tinker designed dresses chose to have portraits made.

As a result, Liddie found herself at the photo studio from time to time to relay a request from Mrs. Tinker or pick up prints. If Mr. Littmann was not busy with a client, she grew brave enough to ask how a photo was taken or how a camera worked. He did not seem bothered by her queries. Indeed, quite the contrary. He seemed flattered.

One afternoon, Mrs. Tinker sent her out early to pick up notions from Fisher's and to return a photo proof to the studio. When Liddie arrived at the studio, Mr. Littmann was engaged with customers. When she caught his eye, she lifted the package slightly.

He excused himself from his customers with a polite smile. In the two steps it took him to reach Liddie, an impatient frown replaced the smile.

"I did not mean to interrupt," Liddie said. "Mrs. Tinker asked me to bring this by."

"I expected you later," he said, his tone clipped. "Come back in an hour." He looked at the clock. "Better yet, I'll meet you at the Decker House at four."

"The Decker House?"

"I'll buy you tea for your trouble."

"It is no trouble. Should I give you this package then?"

"No." He took the envelope and tossed it onto the disheveled desk. "I'll see you at four."

Outside the studio, Liddie looked in the direction of the Decker House. Why was she going there? She shook her head as she crossed the street. The more she thought about meeting Mr. Littmann, the more anxious she became. After she purchased the notions for Mrs. Tinker, she sought out Minnie in the ladies' department and confided her fears.

"Oh, Liddie. Don't be silly." Minnie giggled. "You are meeting him for tea. You and I have been there for tea a dozen times. Besides, you talk to him all the time."

"We've been there for tea exactly three times. But I have never been to tea with a man. I've never been anywhere, really, with a man."

"What about Harley?"

"Harley was a boy."

"And Joe. You told me you've gone places with Joe."

"Joe doesn't count."

"Really?" Minnie cocked an eyebrow. "I think he counts."

"Be serious, Minnie. What will I talk about?"

"I've told you, ask questions." Minnie shrugged. "People like to talk about themselves. Especially men." She glanced around at the other customers. "I have to get back to work."

Liddie gave Minnie a quick hug and turned to walk away. Then she whirled around and came back. "But what does he want?"

"He wants to meet you for tea." A mischievous grin played on Minnie's face. "And for all one knows, you'll tell me tonight that you have a beau."

"Oh, Minnie." Liddie dismissed the idea. But she wondered. Was he interested in her in that way? And if he was, would she really mind?

———

Liddie arrived at the Decker House at exactly five minutes to four. She paused, held her breath for a moment, and then exhaled to calm her nerves before stepping through the lobby doors. Forcing herself to assume the most casual of attitudes, she scanned the room. Mr. Littmann was not there, so she made her way to a small corner table. She thought to remove her gloves but decided against it. Instead, she folded her hands on top of her handbag and attempted to appear as though she belonged there.

Though the lobby was full of people, she didn't make eye contact with anyone. She studied the pattern in the rug, scanned the headlines of a newspaper someone had left on a nearby chair, tucked away a loose thread in her cuff. The fifteen minutes she sat there felt like an eternity. Had she misunderstood? Had he meant for her to come back to the studio? As she considered leaving, all of a sudden he was standing over her.

"Miss Treadway." He bowed. "I am so sorry to leave you sitting here like this. It is unconscionable."

"Mr. Littmann." The tension in her chest eased.

"My last appointment took longer than I anticipated." He set a satchel by the table and sat facing her. A waitress appeared.

He looked at the empty table and then at Liddie. "You didn't order?"

"I didn't know that I should." Her cheeks flamed.

"Tea and biscuits," he said to the waitress. "And hurry, or we may both expire." He smiled at Liddie. "Thank you for waiting so patiently. I hope I haven't gotten us off on the wrong foot."

"No. Of course not. I enjoyed watching the travelers come and go," she said. A polite lie.

Once the waitress delivered the cookies and a steaming porcelain teapot, Liddie focused on sipping tea, hoping to calm her stomach as she scrambled to think of something to say. Her mind was blank.

"This is quite the hub of activity," Mr. Littmann observed, nodding toward a group surrounded by luggage. "I understand you traveled to Chicago last summer."

"Yes. Mrs. Tinker took me with her to buy fabric. I've never seen so many people in my life!" Liddie said.

"Did you visit the Art Institute?"

"No. What's the Art Institute?"

"One of the finest art collections in the world, though it doesn't compare to New York. You haven't seen anything until you've seen New York."

Mr. Littmann leaned in, enthusiasm making his eyes dance. Liddie's eyes lingered on the scar on his eyebrow. It spoke of adventure and mystery. She had to agree with Minnie—he was handsome.

"Day or night, there's something going on. During my last visit, I met Alfred Stieglitz at his Gallery 291. Stieglitz and I talked for ten minutes." He paused, looking at her as though he expected her to say something. When she said nothing, he asked, "Are you familiar with his photography?"

Liddie shook her head and saw disappointment in his eyes. His questions made her feel woefully inadequate, but what should she be expected to know? She was only a farm girl.

"Many photographers—Stieglitz is one—want to create the same compositions and moods accomplished in paintings," Mr.

Littmann said. "It's the composition I'm working to attain, even in a candid photograph." He was gazing out the window. "Maquoketa has a quaint charm. And some surprises." He looked back to Liddie. "You, for instance. To find another soul with such an interest in photography is unexpected."

She had once described his photographs as unexpected. Liddie now wondered if he'd used that word intentionally. She took another sip of tea and said, "At the studio, when you let me look through your camera lens . . ." Again she hesitated for fear he'd think her foolish.

"Go on."

"I don't know how to describe it. It felt as though there was power in the camera. While I looked through the lens, I felt that no one knew I was there. Do you ever feel that?"

"A remarkable observation." He nodded. "Yes, I do feel that. But for me, the real power is in the darkroom when I print the pictures."

"I'd like to see that sometime," Liddie blurted, before it occurred to her that she'd just suggested a desire to be alone with him in a dark room. Heat crept up her neck. She lowered her eyes to the crumbs on her plate. Unconsciously, she fingered the high collar of her dress.

If Mr. Littmann noticed her embarrassment, he didn't let on. "I must say, Miss Treadway, meeting you has been a boon to my business. In fact, it is because business has been thriving that I invited you to meet me today."

Now she looked up.

"I'd like you to work for me a few hours a week." He sipped his tea without ever taking his eyes off her.

She blinked. "I couldn't. Mrs. Tinker . . ."

"Your commitment to Mrs. Tinker is weekdays. Correct? If you spend Saturdays at the studio, it would be perfect."

"A job?"

"I need someone to handle clerical duties, greet customers, prepare packages for clients. I'll pay a fair wage."

It took some moments for Liddie to digest the thought. But now that the possibility of a job was in front of her, she thought it was quite a brilliant solution. Though Mrs. Tinker had been paying her more since she completed her year of apprenticeship, she still did not earn enough to cover all her expenses herself. She wanted very much to prove to herself and her family that she could be self-sufficient. So why not take another job?

An idea began to form in Liddie's mind. "I am delighted you asked me. I'd like to work for you." The idea took root and she plunged ahead. "If it is not too bold to ask, as part of the arrangement, would you teach me more about photography?"

"It would be my honest pleasure." Mr. Littmann relaxed in his chair.

A swell of confidence caused Liddie to sit up straighter. "Then I accept."

He took her hand. "Yes. It would be my honest pleasure, Miss Treadway."

She felt sweat form on her palms. She slid her hand out of his grip and folded her hands on her handbag. "I do sometimes work for Mrs. Tinker on weekends."

"We need to agree on terms, then."

She nodded.

When they parted company in front of the hotel, Liddie walked quietly for one full block until she was out of sight of the Decker House. Then she broke into a skip, cavorting like a child until she was within a block of the boardinghouse.

Minnie would never guess the news, and Liddie could not wait to tell her.

# Chapter 19

"Good morning, Mrs. Tinker. Isn't it a beautiful day?" Still giddy from the previous evening, Liddie hung her shawl and hat on the hall tree. She put the box of pastries she had picked up at Becker's that morning in the kitchen. "For later," she explained.

"The sun is pretty in May," Mrs. Tinker agreed. "It's a little chilly in here, though, don't you think?"

"Maybe a little."

"This stove is so touchy. If I can get it going, it will take the edge off." As Mrs. Tinker puttered with the stove, she asked, "Did you get the notions?"

"Yes, everything you asked for." As Liddie sorted and stored the supplies, she thought about telling Mrs. Tinker her news right then. But the idea of announcing her new job over lunch tickled her. She imagined Mrs. Tinker would be delighted at her good fortune.

"Liddie?" Mrs. Tinker spoke over her shoulder. "Mrs. Ellers told me her son Harley saw you at the Decker House with Mr. Littmann. I thought it unlikely."

Harley! Liddie felt the color drain from her face. It hadn't crossed her mind that he might be there. She hadn't seen him since the holiday party. Now the memory of what she'd said that night and how he'd looked so stunned came rushing back.

"Well, yes. I did see Mr. Littmann. At the Decker House."

"Hmm?"

"When I got to the studio, Mr. Littmann was busy with a client. He took the proofs and asked me to meet him later."

"He asked you to meet him there?"

Liddie heard disapproval in the rising inflection of Mrs. Tinker's voice, and she began to feel as though she'd been caught in a misdeed. Though she hadn't done anything wrong, had she? "I didn't know what he wanted."

"You could have asked."

Liddie flushed. "He was busy with clients. Besides, we were seated where everyone could see us."

"I expected better sense from him." A frown creased Mrs. Tinker's forehead as she faced Liddie, her hands on her hips.

"I thought . . ."

"What did you think?"

Liddie's cheeks flamed. "That he might be"—she felt unbelievably foolish—"interested in me. But it wasn't that at all."

"It wasn't? What was it, then?"

"He wants me to work for him."

"Work for him? Indeed! Harley also told his mother you and Mr. Littmann were holding hands."

"Mr. Littmann says business has been so good he needs clerical help. Partly because of your customers wanting portraits. He thought of me because I'm so interested in photography." She rushed to explain. "I told him I couldn't because I work for you. Then he said only Saturdays. And I'd get to learn about photography. And the extra money will help pay my room and board. Minnie plays piano at Fisher's when she's not working her regular job."

"And what about holding hands?"

"He did take my hand for a moment. He was pleased I said I'd take the job. I took my hand right back. It didn't mean anything. Truly!" Liddie fought to control her anxiety. "I could only see good from accepting his offer. Did I do the wrong thing?" She hiccuped, and to her own dismay, dissolved into tears.

"Oh, Liddie." Mrs. Tinker tsked. "Come, sit here." She guided Liddie to the settee, where she sat with her arm around Liddie's thin shoulders. "I'm going to get us a cup of tea."

"The sewing . . ." Flustered by her tears, Liddie retreated to her responsibilities. "There's so much to do . . ."

"The sewing will get done in time." She headed to the kitchen, slipping the "Closed" sign in the front window as she passed by. Soon she returned with two cups of freshly brewed tea and the teapot. "Now drink this and let's talk. Start at the beginning."

When Liddie finished, Mrs. Tinker said, "I'm relieved. I don't hold with gossip, but Mrs. Ellers is generally reliable. I would not expect something inappropriate from Mr. Littmann. Still, one can never be certain."

"Then you're not angry?"

"I was never angry, my dear. I was concerned. Something that may be quite innocent can be so easily misconstrued. You cannot be too careful with your reputation." Mrs. Tinker refilled Liddie's teacup. "Now. Is this job something you are really interested in?"

"Very much."

"Then it is your decision."

———

After talking with Mrs. Tinker, Liddie no longer assumed her mother would be happy about this new job. She went home that weekend.

When her mother suggested they sit in the parlor, Liddie glanced around. Each time she returned, the spaces she'd grown up in and known so well seemed smaller. Nothing had actually changed—the furniture was arranged as always; the knickknacks held their traditional places—yet it felt different. She had come to realize it was she who had changed, not her old home. If she stayed for a few days, she knew the proportions would return to normal and she would feel as comfortable as always.

As she told her mother about the job, she explained, "I thought the money I earned would help. Then Vern wouldn't have to worry about how much it costs for me to live in town."

Her mother put a hand over her mouth and coughed. Her eyes started to water.

"Mama! Are you all right?"

Margretta held up her hand. "Yes . . . yes. I'm fine." She wiped at her eyes. "Liddie, I'm glad you're thinking about how you can take care of yourself. Your father would be proud. But don't be overly concerned about the cost. We want you to have this opportunity." She lifted knitting needles and a skein of yarn out of her basket, and knit several stitches before she continued.

Liddie had noted that after her mother's grief at G. W.'s death passed, she returned to sitting in her own small rocker.

"Now, what makes you think Vern is worried about the cost?" her mother asked.

"He didn't want me to go. And Aunt Kate said—"

Margretta inclined her head in curiosity. "What did my sister say?"

"She told me that after Papa died, Vern had a lot more responsibility. That he worried about how much it all cost."

"Your brother does have more responsibility. And the cost of things is always an issue. But your father was a good businessman."

Liddie hoped her mother would say more about Papa. She glanced at her father's chair, thought of him sitting there with his pipe, and wondered how he would view her life now.

Margretta knit half a row before she spoke. "Did it occur to you that Vern didn't want to lose you? After Papa and Amelia?"

"Vern? I never thought—"

"I keep telling you he cares about you."

"Maybe." Liddie had to admit her brother had been different since he'd been courting Minnie. Still, she had a hard time erasing the critical figure from her childhood.

Margretta completed a row and began to knit her way back. "Now tell me about Mr. Littmann. And this job."

"Then you're not saying no?"

"Not from what Ernestine says."

"You talked with Mrs. Tinker? How?"

"That is why they invented telephones, dear."

"Then everyone will know . . ." Party lines spread news faster than the Maquoketa grapevine.

"What people will know is that you have shown such talent that you will now be learning photography under the tutelage of the esteemed Thomas Littmann, as well as expanding your expertise as a designer and seamstress." Her mother paused to let the news sink in. "Mrs. Tinker has not achieved her success by being indiscreet."

"Mama, I will only be a secretary. A clerk."

"I've no doubt you'll also learn about photography."

"Then you're not angry I took the job?"

Margretta put the knitting needles down and patted Liddie's hand. "I'd have preferred you talked with me before accepting. I know you want to be grown up. But even adults can benefit from getting another opinion." She picked up her needles. "Try to remember that we're here for you, Liddie. You don't have to do it alone."

———

*May 12, 1915*
*Hello, Joe!*
    *Guess what! I have a new job in the photography studio.*
*I'll continue to work with Mrs. Tinker during the week and*

*spend Saturdays as a clerk in the studio. I am telling you before someone else does.*

*Mrs. Tinker was in a dither that my reputation would be tarnished because I met with Mr. Littmann. Yes, I met with him. In broad daylight. In the company of a whole lobby of people. To talk about the job.*

*I am excited to have a job I came to myself. Though I love the sewing, Mama and Aunt Kate arranged that. This job is all mine.*

*I expect fieldwork is keeping you busy. I think of you turning the soil and remember when you, Vern, and Papa worked our fields in the spring. Seeing the little plants push through the ground fills me with hope. Do you feel that way?*

*I'm surprised you were able to continue as a drayman once the fieldwork started, but with all the Canadian boys going off to the war, I imagine there are many jobs that need to be done. More money to be made, as you say.*

*Now we will both be working two jobs. I couldn't be happier.*

*Yours truly, Liddie*

# Chapter 20

"What do you think after one day, Miss Treadway?" Mr. Littmann asked as he locked the studio door.

Liddie looked up in surprise. Her first day had passed in a blink. "I think it went well." She began to clear the desk. "I do have some questions, if you have a few minutes." In fact, her list of questions filled a full page.

"Of course." He pulled up a chair beside her desk. Before sitting down, he took off his suit coat, brought the shoulder seams precisely together, smoothed both sleeves flat, then draped the garment over a chair.

Liddie had never seen him in anything but a full suit. She noticed that his white shirt fit well across his shoulders. The seeming intimacy of this caused her cheeks to flush. She lowered her eyes and busied herself, centering her list of questions on the desk in front of her.

"It certainly helped to have you out here entertaining customers until I could get to them," Mr. Littmann said.

His comment forced Liddie to look at him. He sat leaning back, legs crossed, his gaze as open and casual as his posture. Did he really think she'd only been entertaining customers?

She cleared her throat. In her discomfort, she read the first thing off the list. "How do you handle the proofs?"

He laughed out loud. "So eager to learn the business? Already?"

"Yes. I mean, no." Liddie was flummoxed. "I thought if I knew more about where things are and what you do, I could answer some customer questions without interrupting you." She sighed, forcing herself to admit, "There were times today when I thought I was more a bother than a help."

"A bother?" He laughed again. "You were no bother. You have no idea what a relief it was not to have to answer the door and deal with people when I was working with a client." He checked his pocket watch. "It's nearly two thirty. I don't want to impose on your time."

"I don't have other plans, and really, I'd like to know more."

"Let's have at it, then." He slid his chair next to hers. "Let's see your list."

He was so close she saw the blond stubble of whiskers on his chin, smelled the last cigar he smoked. He had just locked the door, and she was alone with him. In exactly the type of situation both her mother and Mrs. Tinker had cautioned her about. She rubbed her palms hard on her skirt. *This is my job*, she thought. *Nothing more.*

She continued checking questions off her list. His answers were thorough and helpful, though his manner kept her off guard. When she looked up from taking notes, she often found him staring at her, his head tilted slightly toward her. She chose to believe he was simply waiting for the next question, though she was never quite sure. When he showed her the filing drawers, she felt him standing so close to her shoulder as she leafed through the folders that she flushed and stepped back, telling him she'd seen enough for the moment.

She walked out of the studio two hours later with the understanding that the office was hers to manage as she saw fit. While he was meticulous with anything that involved taking or printing photos, Mr. Littmann had no interest in the paperwork of the business. Any system she came up with would be fine, wonderful, excellent, he said. She did not see how six hours on Saturdays were enough to stay ahead of the paperwork, but Mr. Littmann did not seem concerned. "You can see why I've gotten so far behind." He shrugged.

She was also left feeling unsure about the photographer's intentions toward her.

In the following weeks, Liddie delved into office management. The jumble of paperwork related to photo orders, payments, and receipts suddenly fell into place when she found a Kodak organizing system, including a cashbook and register cards, that Mr. Littmann had apparently bought and shelved in the closet. When the Kodak dealer made his usual delivery the following week, he was happy to explain the whole system to Liddie, who was delighted with the orderliness of it all.

Though Liddie enjoyed discovering new ways to make things run smoothly, it didn't take her long to find the work mundane. The best part of the job was after the clock struck two, when her paid hours were over.

While Mr. Littmann expected a degree of formality when customers were present, he was relaxed and friendly when they were alone. After he locked the studio door, they would spend an hour or more reviewing the work of the week and studying proofs from the latest printing.

One Saturday, after she'd been working at the studio for more than a month, Mr. Littmann was bemoaning a family portrait sitting he had just finished.

"What was the problem?"

"Almost everything!" Mr. Littmann paced as he listed the challenges. "The three girls in white dresses, for one. White draws the eye. When I positioned them in different spots, my eyes bounced all over. Grouped together, they became one big snowball."

"What else?"

"The strong contrast of color. Dark colors on the parents, pure white on the girls. Made it hard to get the exposure right." He took out a cigar and lit it, then drew on it and blew out a cloud of smoke.

She shifted to avoid the smoke. Cigars were not as pleasant as her father's pipe. "There's a lot to think about, isn't there?"

"More than most realize." He stood staring at her intently. "Do you have a camera?"

"Me? No."

"You should. You'll learn faster if you get used to seeing the world through a lens." He turned abruptly, headed to the back of the studio, and brought back a compact folding camera. "You can use this one. I even have film."

"Oh, I couldn't. What if something happens to it?"

"It was my first camera. I haven't used it in years." Mr. Littmann opened the camera and peered through the lens. "It works fine. See what you think."

Reluctantly, Liddie took the camera. She regarded the device from one side and then the other, holding it away from her body as though it were a slightly dangerous animal. Finally, she admitted, "I don't know how to make it work."

"It's easy. Let me show you." As he took the camera, his fingers grazed the palm of her hand. A shiver rippled through her wrist.

While she listened to him explain how to load the film, how to open and close the lens, and how to frame pictures, the palm of her hand felt warm where he'd touched it. The feeling was delicious.

———

"He gave you a camera?" Mrs. Tinker's normally well-modulated voice escalated in pitch. "And you accepted it?"

"I didn't think . . ." Surprised at the intensity of Mrs. Tinker's response, Liddie stumbled on her words. "We were just talking, and he thought of it . . ."

"You did not think, and that is the problem," Mrs. Tinker interrupted. "Liddie, men bestow favors on women because they expect favors from them in return."

"It wasn't like that."

"You don't know what it's like. You must return it." Mrs. Tinker tapped a thimble-clad finger sharply on the worktable, punctuating each of her last four words with a metallic exclamation point.

"I can't." Liddie was frantic. "What would I say?"

Returning it would embarrass her. She would have to explain that as a woman, she could not take a gift from him, and the tension she had felt would be out in the open. What if he laughed at her? What if he was insulted and fired her? If she returned it, she could not take pictures, something she desperately wanted to do. Give the camera back? She could not. She just could not.

"You'll thank him but tell him you only want to do your job."

As soon as Mrs. Tinker mentioned doing her job, Liddie knew this was her answer.

"That's just it, Mrs. Tinker. Mr. Littmann wants me to learn photography so I can be more help in the studio." Liddie talked fast, convincing herself of the logic. "The camera wasn't a gift. It's a loan! So I can learn about the business."

Mrs. Tinker eyed her suspiciously. "How would having a camera help your work? He hired you for clerical support."

Liddie described the difficulties Mr. Littmann had outlined with the family portrait. "I'd have been able to help if I'd known about photography. It was then he suggested I have the camera. It really is for the job. Nothing else."

In the end, Mrs. Tinker agreed to let her keep the camera, but the discussion left Liddie wondering if Mr. Littmann had indeed given her the camera because he liked her. That idea rather appealed to her, too.

All that week, Liddie carried the camera with her everywhere. At first, she felt self-conscious, certain everyone was staring at her as she fumbled to open the camera, found subjects on which to center the lens, tried to remember everything Mr. Littmann had said. She felt like a pretender to some grand skill about which she knew virtually nothing.

Gradually, though, her mind focused on what she saw through the lens. The feeling of anonymity she'd experienced in the studio returned. She pointed the camera at her fellow boarders playing whist in the parlor. On Main Street, she enjoyed the contrast of a horse tied up next to an automobile. In the park, she trained the camera on children playing tag, a mother pushing a pram, a couple sitting on a picnic blanket, each time thinking of a story the picture told.

Each of the images she framed through the camera that week burned in her mind. Except she never pushed the lever to take an actual photo. Not even once.

# Chapter 21

"You didn't?" Mr. Littmann stared at her in disbelief.

It was a quarter after two the following Saturday. The camera now sat in the middle of his desk, a monument to her insecurity.

"I couldn't make myself do it," she said, unable to meet his eyes.

"Why not?"

"I was . . . I don't know . . . afraid, I guess." She struggled to explain. He'd done an indescribably generous thing by lending her the camera. She'd repaid his generosity by not taking a single picture. She was miserable.

"Afraid of what?"

"I'm not sure. That the pictures wouldn't be good? That I'd waste the film? Maybe that you'd laugh?" She shifted uncomfortably in her chair, her eyes riveted on her hands, which were clasped tightly in her lap.

His laughter filled the studio. "Oh, Liddie! You thought I'd laugh at you? You must have a mighty poor opinion of me."

"See. You are laughing," she pointed out.

"But not at you. At this situation. I felt the same way the first time I held a camera." He sat beside her. "Please look at me. I can't talk with you if I can't see your eyes."

She drew a breath and raised her head. The gold flecks surrounding his irises sparkled as he held her gaze. She managed a weak smile.

"Better. Now tell me what you were thinking."

"The cost. Film is so expensive."

He shook his head firmly. "I cannot dismiss the cost of film, but as any photographer will tell you, in the big picture, film is cheap." He let the idea sink in. "Think of it this way. If I set everything up for a family portrait and then only take two images to save on the cost of film, what happens if someone moves or closes their eyes? The cost of the sitting will have been a waste and the family will be disappointed—or angry. A scene is only there for a moment. It is bad business to miss it because you are saving on film."

"Explained that way, I see the point," she said. And she did. For a photographer, film is cheap. But it still seemed too precious for her.

"Okay, then. You were worried about what I'd think?"

She nodded.

"It's true. When you do something creative, you wear your heart on your sleeve. You do the best you can, knowing not everyone will like it." He went to the front window and looked down at the photos displayed there, speaking almost to himself. "But there's a balance. To make a living, I have to take photos that people will buy. But if I only did that, it wouldn't make me happy as an artist. So sometimes, I slip in a bit of creativity they don't expect."

He returned to the desk. "Do you ever worry that someone won't like a dress you make?"

"All the time."

"Then do you make only what they ask for, or do you take chances, try new things? Something special to suit a particular woman?"

"Mrs. Tinker often convinces women to do something different than they thought they wanted. I admire how she does that."

"Exactly. You can't worry about what others will think of your work. You try things. Some work. Some don't. But don't be afraid to try. Okay?"

"Now I'm embarrassed I didn't try."

"Liddie! What am I going to do with you?" He frowned as he shook his head, but his eyes smiled.

It struck her that he'd called her by her given name. She liked the sound of her name coming from him.

"There's a whole new week starting this afternoon." He handed her the camera. "Fill this roll before you come in next Saturday. Then, if you're interested, I'll show you how to develop the film and print the pictures."

They talked on. She told him all the things she'd almost taken photos of. He brought out files of pictures he'd taken over the years, covering the desktop with pictures of people, buildings, and landscapes. They examined them together. As they stood side by side, his arm occasionally brushed against hers. Each time it happened, she peeked at him. He seemed completely oblivious, and she concluded the contact was accidental.

"Curses!" he exclaimed when he finally looked at his pocket watch. "I didn't realize the time. I'm late for a meeting." Mr. Littmann reached for his suit coat. "We'll continue this discussion. You'll catch on," he said, and was out the door.

She put the camera in her handbag, vowing to use every frame on the roll of film. As she walked back to the boardinghouse, she imagined Mr. Littmann standing beside her as she focused the camera, asking what she saw, suggesting something, and occasionally, just occasionally, brushing his arm against hers.

———

True to her word, Liddie took photos. Each time she brought in a roll of exposed film, Mr. Littmann gave her a new roll. He developed and printed the film. It delighted her to see the images she'd viewed through the camera appear as photographs. Mr. Littmann used every frame—even those that were blurred or dark—to teach her how to make better images. The thrill of seeing the photos far exceeded the excitement she felt when she completed a dress.

Two months passed, and he did not offer to show her how to develop film and print pictures; she was too shy to ask.

———

Liddie could feel the pain in her sister's brief letter. Since their son, Melvin, had been born with a harelip, Fred refused to hold him. Amelia asked Liddie not to tell their mother and not to say anything negative in the letters she wrote, lest Fred read them. It took a week for Liddie to figure out what to say without saying what she really wanted to.

> *July 6, 1915*
> *Dearest sister,*
> *We are so excited to hear that you and Fred have a baby boy, just as you both had hoped. Mama and I wish we could be there to help you. You must be incredibly busy with two wonderful babies. I'm glad Gertie's daughter is staying with you.*
> *Have you been on more picnics? It makes me smile to think of you and Gertie loading all the children in the buckboard and heading to the river for a day. Then loading them up again like cords of wood to sleep as you go home.*
> *I can't tell you how thrilled I am to be working with Mr. Littmann and learning the photography business. Recently, he loaned me a camera so I can take my own pictures. This is a whole new world to me, Amelia. Wouldn't it be something if I could take pictures of you and your babies?*
> *Thinking of you often and wishing all of you every happiness.*
> *Love to all, Liddie*

———

Even with improvements in how Mr. Littmann's office ran, she sometimes took work home to complete at night or came in on weekday evenings to complete her tasks. She did not ask to be paid for this extra time, and Mr. Littmann didn't offer.

One afternoon in late August, Mr. Littmann announced, "This isn't working out."

"Pardon?" She looked up from the filing drawer.

He stood in the doorway, arms folded across his chest, a perturbed frown on his face. "No matter what we do, we're behind."

"Is it the calendar? I've been trying—"

"No," he interrupted. "It's not the calendar. It's the amount of work. All good, don't get me wrong. But it's not enough with you here only on Saturdays."

It flashed through her mind that he intended to let her go. "I'm doing the best—"

He cut her off again. "There's too much to do. I want you here full time."

"But I have a job," she blurted.

"Quit."

"I can't. I'm working on two new dresses. And there's a rack full of alterations. How would Mrs. Tinker manage?"

"She'd get another girl." He grabbed a chair. When he sat down only a foot away from her, his tone was beguiling. "To me, you're unique, Liddie. She can always find someone to run a sewing machine. I'll never find someone who understands my work the way you do."

She blushed. "Oh, I'm sure you could, Mr. Littmann."

"Call me Thomas. We're colleagues."

Flattered as she was by the compliment, she felt a needle-like prick at how easily he dismissed her work for Mrs. Tinker.

He continued unabated. "My work has increased. You deserve some credit for that. With the systems you've set up, I can do more

sittings, and people don't have to wait as long for proofs and photos." He put his hand on hers. "If you were here full time, we could
do even more. And you could learn printing and retouching."

Liddie felt as though the air were being sucked out of her
lungs. "I appreciate . . . It's just that . . . Mrs. Tinker." Locked in the
intensity of his gaze, with his hand on hers, she could not form a
clear thought.

"The truth is, Liddie, I've enjoyed finding someone who likes
photography as much as I do and who wants to learn more." He
squeezed her hand.

She found herself powerless to say anything.

He continued. "We're in agreement, then! Tell Mrs. Tinker and
let me know when you can start. The sooner the better." He stood.

As soon as his hand left hers, she started to breathe. In agreement? Had she actually said yes? She didn't think so.

# Chapter 22

Liddie and Minnie sat side by side in the porch swing at the board-inghouse, waiting for Vern to pick them up. Not a breath of breeze stirred the humid August air as Liddie shared the conversation she'd had with Mr. Littmann, leaving out the part about him hold-ing her hand.

"What do I do, Minnie?"

"What do you want to do?"

Liddie spread her hands. "I want to do both."

"You've been doing both. Why can't you continue?"

"It sounded as though if I can't do the job full time, he'll find someone who can." She chewed at her lip. "He said Mrs. Tinker could always find someone to run a sewing machine."

Minnie's forehead wrinkled. "I don't understand why he'd say that about your work with Mrs. Tinker. He knows how much you like sewing. And how much Mrs. Tinker values you."

"At first it stung, but I don't think he meant anything by it. I think he's so busy, and he probably didn't think it would sound like it did."

"Maybe."

Liddie prodded. "Maybe what?"

"I don't like it when someone makes himself better by running someone else down." She touched her toe to the porch floor and gave the swing a little shove.

"I really don't think he meant to do that," Liddie insisted. "He says he likes having someone around who enjoys photography as much as he does. He said I'm unique." She looked sideways at Minnie, thinking she'd laugh.

Minnie did laugh. "Of course you're unique, you goose! Mrs. Tinker has been telling you that for months." Then she sobered. "But what about Mrs. Tinker? Don't you have an agreement with her?"

"My apprenticeship ended almost a year ago, so I don't have a particular obligation. But we're already working on holiday dresses." Liddie wiped perspiration off the back of her neck. On days like this, she found herself missing the breeze that blew almost constantly on the farm. In town, the still air and heat were suffocating. "How could I walk away from Mrs. Tinker? She opened my eyes to opportunities in dressmaking I never even knew to dream about. In fact . . . if it hadn't been for Mrs. Tinker, I'd never have seen the photos or met Thomas—Mr. Littmann."

"Oh, so it's 'Thomas' now?" Minnie smirked.

"He says I should call him Thomas, but that doesn't feel right. I think he'll always be Mr. Littmann to me."

Minnie raised an eyebrow.

Liddie ignored her.

"What appeals to you?" Minnie asked.

"Mainly, I suppose the appeal is having a chance to work with him. He's a walking library of art, photography, travel. I pinch myself to believe he's willing to spend his time with *me*."

"But he's hiring you for the job, and you say the job gets boring." Minnie pursed her lips. "Or are you taking the job to get the man?"

Liddie slapped at Minnie's hand and laughed. Could she separate the photography from the man? She realized that she wanted them both.

"Here's what I think," Minnie said. "If you want to do both sewing and photography, figure out a way."

The girls sat in silence, alternately touching a toe to the porch to keep the swing moving. After a few minutes, Minnie looked at Liddie, a smile spreading across her face.

"Besides," she said, "you can't quit sewing. Who will make my wedding dress?"

"Your wedding dress?" Liddie shrieked as she clasped her friend's hands. "Minnie, did he ask you?"

"Not yet, but I think he will. Soon." Minnie's eyes sparkled.

"My brother and my best friend—married." Liddie beamed with happiness.

"So will you make my dress?"

"Of course. We'll have such fun planning it."

"We have to wait a little bit. Mustn't count my chickens before they hatch." Just then, they saw Vern turn the buggy onto Maddison Street. Minnie gripped Liddie's hand. "Now don't say anything. Promise?"

"I promise."

Liddie talked to her mother about Mr. Littmann's offer. She talked to Mrs. Tinker. After several nights spent lying awake in bed, staring at the ceiling, she came to this: if Mr. Littmann and Mrs. Tinker both agreed, in September she would begin to work three days a week at the photography studio and three days with Mrs. Tinker.

Both agreed.

# Chapter 23

Liddie felt goose bumps rise on her arms as she followed Mr. Littmann into the small, windowless darkroom. With her mother's warnings echoing in her ears, she felt breathless being in such close proximity to a man—in the dark.

Mr. Littmann set to pulling out trays and bottles while her eyes adjusted to the dim light cast by a lamp cloaked in red film.

"Doesn't it have to be dark?" she asked.

He laughed. "Did you really think I work all those hours in complete darkness?"

She had thought exactly that. Her skin prickled in embarrassment at her own naïveté. She was grateful the light was so dim.

"Undeveloped film does have to be handled in total darkness." He showed her a black bag that was almost as big as a tent. "This bag is lightproof. I load unexposed film into the plates, and after I expose the film, I reload it for the developing tank. It is critical no light touches the film until it's developed or the image will fog. Even with this bag, I take the added precaution to only handle film in this windowless room. I put a blanket across the door to ensure no light leaks in."

"But how do you do all that if it's completely dark?" Liddie asked.

"It takes practice, but you learn to do it all by touch. Once the film is in this lightproof developing tank, we can turn on the light and finish the processing." He gestured to the light as he continued.

"But a red lamp like this is safe for the photo paper, and once the image is fixed, we can have a regular light."

"Fixed?" Liddie was overwhelmed. She felt as though the photographer were speaking Greek.

"I'll show you."

The darkroom was large enough for one person to move efficiently between the chemical trays. With two people, it was impossible not to touch from time to time. Liddie hoped—perhaps even expected—that he would try to steal a kiss. But Mr. Littmann was all business as he guided her step by step through the printing process, explaining which chemicals did what, how to mix them, how to expose the paper.

"Now watch this." He slid the exposed paper into the tray of developer. Standing at his elbow, Liddie was certain he'd hear her heart thumping.

Then, as the image rose up through the chemicals—a pale shadow growing more distinct by the second, revealing the faces of a man, a woman, and a child—Liddie lost all thought of the man beside her. "It's magic!" she exclaimed.

"That's how I feel."

He thrust tongs into her hand and hovered his hand above hers as he showed her how to swirl the chemicals and move the wet paper with its newly created picture from tray to tray. Liddie's anxiety evaporated, replaced by a fascination with making pictures.

When he clipped the last photo to a wire to dry, Liddie was surprised two hours had passed.

"That was incredible," she said. "I can't wait to do it again."

Over the next weeks, Mr. Littmann taught Liddie in meticulous detail how to mix the chemicals. Then he taught her printing techniques like dodging and burning. At first, she practiced printing from his negatives. As she shot more of her own film, she developed and printed her own pictures, relishing each moment of discovery and excitement.

*September 21, 1915*

*Dear Joe,*

*You must think me a poor pen pal. I hardly have time to write since I'm working six days.*

*I use half my spare time to work on Minnie's wedding dress. Half my spare time I spend in the darkroom making pictures. Half my spare time I save for writing letters. Since Amelia made sure I know my fractions, I'm aware this doesn't add up. Unfortunately, my letter writing suffers.*

*By the time you receive this, the threshers may have come through. I hope your wheat yielded as well as you expected. How will you spend the winter? Will you take up running a dray again?*

*I wanted you to have these pictures. The one of Minnie and Vern I took and printed myself! Don't you think she looks quite jaunty waving from the buggy? And doesn't Vern look proud? The other you may not want to keep. It's only me. Mr. Littmann took it on my camera, and I printed it.*

*I wish you could be here for the wedding. Minnie is eager to meet you, and the rest of us would be so happy to see you. If you're not doing the dray, could you take the time? At least think about coming back. I miss you!*

*With affection, Liddie*

———

"Is Maggie Driver's dress ready to pick up?" Mrs. Tinker asked after she checked the mail and scanned the job tickets from the last two days.

While Mrs. Tinker had been out of town visiting relatives, Liddie had been responsible for day-to-day client requests as well as for finishing the dress Mrs. Driver planned to wear at her daughter's wedding.

"I finished it this morning." Liddie's body felt as though it were filled with lead as she went to the rack and took down a dress of pale-blue watered silk with satin insets and crystal beading.

The dress had turned out beautifully. With one small exception. An exception so small Liddie hoped Mrs. Tinker would not notice. After all, this very small problem was in the back and on the hem.

After she had sewn the last seam and clipped loose threads, she'd set up the ironing board in the kitchen within easy reach of the irons heating on the stove. With any fabric, but particularly silk, Liddie tested the iron on a remnant. She also used a press cloth so the iron never touched the fabric. Then, ever so gently, she smoothed out wrinkles with an iron that was warm, not hot.

Though ironing wasn't her favorite thing to do, she enjoyed performing the task that day. For the first time in weeks, she was standing still, quietly doing one thing rather than rushing to complete a dozen different sewing tasks and an equal number of jobs at the photo studio.

As she finished ironing the front of the dress, she heard a knock at the door. She set the iron back on the stove and went to greet a customer. A short while later, back at the ironing board, she shifted the dress to iron the back left panel of the skirt and spread the press cloth over the silk. As soon as she placed the iron on the cloth, the smell of scorched material hit her nose, and Liddie jerked the iron away.

"Oh no." She sucked in her breath. A dark brown triangle marked the press cloth. She put the iron back on the stove, away from the heat, and peeled the press cloth off the silk.

"Oh no." She breathed again. The press cloth had protected the silk from burning, but the heat had drawn up the delicate threads in a crinkled triangle of little waves. She ran her fingers lightly over the silk, horrified to feel the ridges.

She sat down hard in a chair by the kitchen table.

For the rest of that afternoon, she tried everything she knew to smooth out the silk. But no matter what she tried, the arrow-like shape of the iron on the hem pointed accusingly at her. She felt nauseous.

Numb, she sat at her worktable trying to decide what to do. The mantel clock chimed six. She had to get to the studio. She'd promised to retouch a set of photos that night, and she needed to do it while the daylight was still good. She took the dress off the form and hung it on the rack, vainly hoping that the scorched fabric would relax in the night or look better in the morning.

Liddie had not been able to sleep that night for worrying. In the morning, she looked at the back of the dress again. The spot was definitely still visible, but she almost convinced herself it wasn't so awfully bad. She returned the dress to the rack, all the while trying to quell the anxiety ramming through her heart.

Now, as she positioned the dress on the form for Mrs. Tinker to review, her heart was in her mouth.

Mrs. Tinker surveyed the dress with her practiced eye. "It is *beautiful*, Liddie. Silk can be difficult, but you did a wonderful job. Maggie will be so pleased."

She walked around the dress, adjusting the shoulders, tracing a finger along the line of the waist. She stepped back, taking in the entire garment.

"Hmm. What is this?" She bent over and brushed her hand against the hem. She frowned, brushed at the spot again, and then knelt, picking up the edge of the dress. She looked up. "What is this, Liddie?"

Liddie sank into her chair. "I was ironing it. Mrs. Belham came in with some things. I left the iron on the stove, and when I came back, the iron was too hot. I ruined the press cloth, too. I'm so sorry. Do you think she'll notice?"

"Notice? Notice!" Mrs. Tinker was incredulous. "Of course she'll notice. She's paying a pretty penny for this dress. Even if she doesn't"—Mrs. Tinker riveted Liddie with a withering gaze—"I will know. You will know. You cannot honestly think we would let a damaged dress go out of this house."

"I'm sorry." Liddie cringed. Mrs. Tinker handled every challenge with equanimity, but this time she was truly angry.

"Why didn't you tell me? Did you think *I* wouldn't notice?"

Liddie didn't respond.

"Oh, Liddie." Mrs. Tinker shook her head.

"I'm so, so sorry," Liddie repeated. "Is there anything I can do?"

"This is serious business, Liddie. You are responsible for this dress." She stepped back from the dress, her eyes on the hem, her hands clenched on her hips.

"I can remake the panel. We have enough fabric."

"I planned to make another dress with the rest of the bolt." Mrs. Tinker's shoulders rose and fell as she absorbed the loss. She looked squarely at Liddie. "I can't believe you'd even think about selling an inferior dress." She breathed heavily. "You disappoint me."

Liddie blinked rapidly. She'd let Mrs. Tinker down. She'd let herself down. She knew her cheeks were red, but she would not let herself cry. "I'm truly sorry, Mrs. Tinker. I want to make it right. How can I do it?"

Mrs. Tinker averted her eyes as she thought, rubbing the back of her neck, tapping an impatient toe. When she spoke again, she'd regained her composure. "What I will do is tell her we need another day because I've been out of town. What you will do is fix this dress if it takes all night."

"I'll pay for it," said Liddie. She'd intended to use the money in her bank account to buy her own photo paper. Paying for the bolt of silk would require even more than she had saved. "I'll pay for it," she repeated.

"I think that is appropriate."

Liddie worked all that night to replace the damaged panel and ready the dress for Mrs. Driver the next morning. In the intervening hours, she had plenty of time to think about how—or whether—she could manage both of the jobs she enjoyed so much.

# Chapter 24

Mr. Littmann strode into the studio, tossed his hat at the peg near the door, and perched on the edge of Liddie's desk.

"Take a look at this!" He thrust a telegram in front of Liddie but did not leave it long enough for her to read it.

"Good news, I gather?" She settled back in her chair and waited. Mr. Littmann reveled in stringing out news a bit at a time.

"It most certainly is. Jon's coming." He studied the telegram as though trying to glean more from the few words it contained.

"Jon?"

"Jonathan Grey. Artist. World traveler. A Renaissance man." He smiled. "Jon's the best friend I've ever had."

That was a revelation. Liddie wasn't aware he had any friends. Mr. Littmann didn't talk about anything that had happened or anyone that he knew before he came to Maquoketa. When she asked about family, he was vague. If he went to see the cousins near Andrew, he never spoke of it.

"You'll like Jon. He's always involved in interesting things with fascinating people. Until recently, he was in Europe. He'll be able to tell us what's really going on with the war." Mr. Littmann began to pace.

"When will he arrive?"

"Next Thursday." He stopped midstep. "Not even a week! So much to do before then. Who do we have on the schedule?"

Mr. Littmann came to Liddie's side as she opened the calendar. Together they sorted through the appointments they could reschedule and those they could not, how much time he'd need in the darkroom, what he needed Liddie to complete.

As Mr. Littmann talked, Liddie sensed a thread of insecurity in his desire to show his widely traveled friend that he'd built a thriving photography business. She found insecurity in such an accomplished man charming.

Mr. Littmann worked into the night printing pictures that Liddie then framed to display in the studio window. At his direction, she removed most of the family portraits and replaced them with his experimental pictures, including the ones of everyday life that had first attracted her to his window. She also included a few character portraits Littmann had taken of local businessmen. Playing off the popularity of the portraits of women in their best dresses, he'd begun photographing businessmen, incorporating props such as canes, books, hats, overcoats—signature pieces that marked the man as someone of prestige, authority. Ben Caither was the first; other businessmen followed.

"Come with me to meet Jon," Mr. Littmann said after they'd rearranged the photos for the third time.

"Come with you?"

"Yes. I know you'll like him."

"Won't I be in the way? The two of you will want to catch up. Besides, I work at Mrs. Tinker's that day."

"This is important, Liddie." He moved one of the photos an inch to the left.

Liddie was torn. She didn't want to disappoint him, but her obligations to Mrs. Tinker were equally important, especially since the debacle with Mrs. Driver's dress—a defeat she'd never shared with Mr. Littmann.

"I'd like you with me, Liddie. Shall I make the request formal?" He drew himself upright, brought his heels together with a click, took her hand, and bowed. "Will you do me the honor?"

She had settled comfortably into her role at the studio. With this invitation, was he expecting her to step beyond her traditional role? She must have been silent for some time because he spoke again.

"If you don't wish to go . . ."

"No. I do. Wish to go. I'll talk to Mrs. Tinker."

———

As they waited at the depot, Liddie considered how lucky she was that Mrs. Tinker was flexible. Granted, July was not the busiest time of the year for the sewing business, but had she asked for time off from the studio, she doubted Mr. Littmann would have agreed so readily. Liddie had promised to complete the highest priority tasks on Sunday, not because Mrs. Tinker asked, but because she felt obligated.

The closer the train's arrival time drew, the more she noticed Mr. Littmann fidget. He straightened his tie, brushed at an imagined spot on his suit, ran his hand along his chin. Liddie was relieved for him when the train finally rolled into the station. As passengers stepped down onto the platform, she guessed immediately which one was Mr. Littmann's friend.

Jonathan Grey was a man you noticed. Even though he'd been traveling, he looked as refreshed as if he'd awakened in his own bed that morning. A dark felt fedora set at a jaunty angle partially hid wide-set eyes. His suit appeared to Liddie to be tailor-made, probably in Europe. She hadn't seen anything of that cut in any magazine. At the sight of Mr. Littmann, his eyes lit up.

"Jon! How are you?" Mr. Littmann shook his friend's hand.

"Never better, Tom." Mr. Grey grinned as he held Mr. Littmann at arm's length. "Seeing you makes the day a success!" He turned to Liddie. "And this lovely lady. You had not told me about a friend."

"Jonathan Grey, I am pleased to introduce Miss Liddie Treadway." He cupped a hand under Liddie's elbow, drawing her closer. "Miss Treadway is my assistant in the studio. You may want to be on your best behavior. I am letting her have the final say on you."

"Mr. Grey." Liddie smiled, relaxing at her introduction as Mr. Littmann's assistant. "It is a pleasure."

"The pleasure is mine." He took her hand and kissed it as he bowed. "Please call me Jon."

Liddie had never, ever had a man kiss her hand. She was enchanted.

"I've never had such a lovely chaperone, Tom," he said. "Well done."

Mr. Littmann nodded. "Shall we get your luggage?"

After Mr. Grey retrieved his bag, they headed for the Decker House. From the moment they sat in the lobby, the two men fell into a conversational rhythm, finishing each other's sentences and making vague references to past events the other remembered exactly; it reminded Liddie of the way she used to talk with Amelia. Watching the two men banter, she could not imagine why Mr. Littmann had been so anxious.

Mr. Littmann peppered Mr. Grey with questions about his travels. Liddie had imagined she might learn more about her employer from this conversation, but each time Mr. Grey asked about life in Iowa, Mr. Littmann deflected the inquiry with a question of his own.

At first, Liddie was comfortable sitting on the edge of the conversation. She had traveled so little, seen so little, done so little. Better to say nothing. But the longer she sat in silence, the more she wondered why Mr. Littmann had insisted she come along.

"In spite of the war, Montmartre teems with creativity," Mr. Grey said. "Charles took me to meet several of his friends—painters, musicians, actors. When you get to Paris, you must go there. Best to wait until after the war is over, though. Nasty business, that."

"Charles?" Mr. Littmann leaned in, arching an eyebrow.

"Charles Vildrac. A poet. Fascinating fellow. You'd find him"—Mr. Grey hesitated—"likeable, Tom." He sat back, hands clasped, elbows resting on the arms of his chair. "One night he asked me, 'Would you perceive that you are very happy if you had been happy longer than an hour?'"

Mr. Littmann considered the question. "What a thought."

Mr. Grey nodded. "Whatever he says sounds like poetry."

"It sounds sad!" Liddie interjected.

Mr. Grey turned to her with an amused smile. "I wasn't sure you could speak."

"There did not seem to be a particular need," Liddie responded archly.

"Touché." He saluted her. "Quiet but spunky. I can see why you like her," he said to Mr. Littmann. He shifted his attention back to Liddie. "So you think the idea is sad?"

"Why, yes. Can we not expect real happiness for longer than an hour? I certainly hope to look at my life and see I've had more than that."

"Charles's words made me consider what constitutes happiness. How many ever really experience it?"

"I imagine you must experience a great deal of happiness," Liddie said. "Traveling, meeting such interesting people. It sounds exciting to me."

"Exciting, no doubt. Happy? I venture they're not the same. Charles had a huge painting hanging in his apartment, all done with small dots of paint. Our conversation reminds me of it. Georges Seurat painted it—a crowd of people at a park. You'd think they were happy, but were they?" Mr. Grey rummaged in his satchel and pulled out a sketch. "This is a poor representation of that magnificent painting. Look at it and tell me what you see."

Liddie searched the scene. A man reclined on the grass. A couple held a monkey on a leash. Ladies, men, children. Sitting, standing, prim, stiff. No one was looking at or talking to anyone else.

"So many people," Liddie said at last. "Yet each looks alone."

"Exactly so. Does happiness depend on whom you're with?"

"What you're doing? Where you are?" Liddie continued the thought. She found herself enjoying the conversation. It reminded her of the relaxed way she could talk with Joe.

Yet she was suddenly aware that Mr. Littmann had remained silent throughout this exchange, staring out the window.

Mr. Grey tapped him on the sleeve. "What do you say, Tom? How do you define happiness?"

Drawn back into the conversation, Mr. Littmann bathed them in a smile. "Happiness? Happiness is being with the two of you! My oldest friend who knows me better than anyone and . . ." He laughed. "My newest friend, who may never want to know all that you do, Jon."

Liddie and Mr. Grey laughed, too, though she thought Mr. Littmann's laugh sounded forced.

"Now, Jon." Mr. Littmann abruptly switched the topic. "What do you hear of the war? We've seen some effect here. Chemicals for the darkroom aren't readily available anymore, and the cost of what we can get has gone sky-high. The paper here does a weekly column about the war, although I expect the coverage is woefully inadequate compared to what one would read in larger cities."

"They're using poison gas—both sides—no one is safe. Injuries and deaths number in the tens of thousands." Mr. Grey's voice deepened as he spoke, carrying the weight of the carnage he had seen firsthand. "It's a bad business. So many are disfigured. It's brutal."

"They say it'll be over soon," Liddie said.

"We can only hope. I thought to go to England after leaving France, but when Wilson declared the United States will remain neutral, it seemed that America was the better choice."

"It is sad," Liddie murmured. "We are right to stay out of it."

"You think we're 'out of it'?" Mr. Littmann scoffed. "Hardly. In a war, there's money to be made. My guess is there are plenty here with their hands in the pot. Why else have our chemical prices gone up?"

"I hadn't thought of that," she admitted.

"Have any of the men here—Germans, Italians, Brits—gone over?" Mr. Grey asked.

"Mrs. Tinker says there's talk," Liddie said, remembering that Mrs. Ellers had said Harley might go. Though she knew he was at college, she looked around when she thought of him, half expecting to see him at the desk pretending to check someone into the hotel while he spied on her. "Have you heard of anyone?" she asked Mr. Littmann.

"I've thought of it myself," he responded.

"Going to fight?" Liddie recoiled in shock.

"To be a war photographer."

"Did you not hear me?" Mr. Grey asked. "It's not safe. For anyone."

"Think of it, Jon. Being in the thick of it all. Shooting images that make a difference. Not one more farmer and his brood."

Mr. Grey looked at Liddie with alarm. "How long has he had this idea?"

"This is the first I've heard of it."

"That's a relief. We will change his mind." Mr. Grey laid a hand on Mr. Littmann's arm. "Look here, man. I came here to have fun, not dwell on the unpleasant. I'm eager to see your studio."

———

"Reminiscent of Mary Cassatt's paintings of mothers and babies," Mr. Grey mused as he stood on the sidewalk looking at one of the photos in the studio window. His arms were folded; one hand cupped his chin. "Don't you think so?"

Mr. Littmann cocked his head as though seeing the print for the first time. "Now that you mention it, there is a similarity. I guess there's nothing new under the sun."

"Mary Cassatt?" Liddie asked.

"An American painter in the impressionist style. Quite famous," Mr. Littmann explained. "Even in Iowa."

Liddie winced. Would she ever just know these things? Would she ever not feel . . . inferior? Mentally, Liddie added "Cassatt" to the list she kept in the studio desk drawer, a list she started because Mr. Littmann continually brought up people she'd never heard of. The library might have something on the painter.

"Not to worry, friend." Mr. Grey slapped Mr. Littmann on the shoulder. "The arrangements have your special touch. I can see women along Chicago's Gold Coast lining up to have you make photos like this of them and their young."

Mr. Littmann shrugged. "It's been a harder sell here. Though Liddie convinced some of her customers to give it a go."

"Customers?"

Liddie waited for Mr. Littmann to respond. When he said nothing, she explained her work with Mrs. Tinker.

"I am trying to rescue her from having her back and eyes ruined by sewing," Mr. Littmann joked. "Turn her talent in a better direction."

"A good eye can focus in many directions." Mr. Grey observed, returning none of his friend's humor. "Tell me about your work as a seamstress, Liddie."

"I photograph the dresses she designs," Mr. Littmann interjected. "I have copies in the file. Let's go inside. I'll give you a tour of the studio and find those pictures." He unlocked the door and led them in.

"Mrs. Tinker suggested we create a portfolio of my designs," Liddie added, feeling the familiar thrill the word engendered.

"Building a portfolio, eh? Well done," Mr. Grey said.

"Those photographs have led to a few sittings." Mr. Littmann opened a file and spread out the half-dozen photos. "You know women—whatever one has, another wants," he quipped.

"Lucky for you, I'd say," Mr. Grey said. "Lovely dresses, Miss Treadway." He picked up a photo of an older woman in a black velvet and satin dress. "I daresay I haven't seen anything more stylish in Paris."

Liddie blushed.

"It was the devil to photograph. Black on black. Good lord!"

"You were up to the task." Mr. Grey set the photo back on the desk. "I'd have expected nothing less."

"Put those away, Liddie, while I show Jonathan the rest of the studio. Then we'll have dinner."

While Mr. Littmann showed off his studio, Liddie lingered over the photos that made up her portfolio. It pleased her that Mr. Grey had taken the time to compliment both the dresses and her aspirations as a seamstress. She supposed it was natural that Mr. Littmann cared only for the photographs themselves, though it did rankle that he couldn't share the limelight—ever.

When they returned, Mr. Grey offered Liddie his arm. "I've never been to Iowa. Tell me what there is to see here."

"There are some caves north of town," she suggested.

"There are?" Mr. Littmann asked.

"Quite a warren."

"Sounds like fun," Mr. Grey said. "Would you be our guide?"

She looked to Mr. Littmann. "If you like, I could make a picnic?"

"Excellent," Mr. Littmann agreed. "Explore the wilds of Iowa. We'll take cameras. Make it a photo excursion. Perhaps we'll see Indians."

"Might we really?" Mr. Grey was enthusiastic.

"I was joking," Mr. Littmann said dryly.

"It's not likely, but it isn't impossible, either," Liddie said. "From time to time, small bands of Indians pass by our farm. You needn't worry. They're friendly," she teased. "Most of the time."

Mr. Grey laughed. Mr. Littmann didn't.

———

Mr. Grey seemed to enjoy the caves thoroughly. He carried a lantern and led the way as they squeezed through narrow passages, ducking fearlessly through archways where they all had to bend low to pass. They marveled at the stalactites dripping from the ceilings.

Liddie lagged behind from time to time, giving the men a chance to talk as she experimented with her camera. When she spotted Mr. Littmann with his arm resting on Mr. Grey's shoulder as the two men were silhouetted against the light of a cave entrance, she captured the scene.

"I took the perfect picture of the two of you," Liddie said as she joined them.

"What picture?" Mr. Littmann asked, his tone sharp.

"Just now. You with your arm on Mr. Grey's shoulder. You were in profile against the light."

He frowned. "You should have asked."

Bewildered by his sudden turn of mood, Liddie fumbled to explain. "It's creative. I thought you'd like a picture. You and Mr. Grey."

"I hope you'll make a print for me," Mr. Grey said. "I'd enjoy a remembrance of my time in Iowa."

His relaxed tone seemed to mollify Mr. Littmann. "Very well," he said. "Do you suppose you can find our way out of here, Jon?"

Mr. Littman was silent through the rest of the trek, and he emerged from the last underground passage with undeniable relief at their return to the late-afternoon light.

They spread a blanket on a hillside to watch the sunset. As a brilliant red sun streaked the sky with pewter, pink, and charcoal, Liddie commented, "We'll be having good weather."

"How do you know?" Mr. Grey asked.

"The red sun signals good weather. It's a sign that farmers know," Liddie explained.

"Did you know that, Tom?" Mr. Grey asked.

Mr. Littmann shrugged. "A myth. I can't imagine it's reliable."

"My father was seldom wrong," Liddie said.

Mr. Littmann gave her a sharp look, and she flushed. She hadn't spoken to contradict him, though apparently he'd taken it as such.

"I've heard the sailors watch the color of the sun," Mr. Grey said. "Now that I know farmers do, too, I'll pay closer attention."

Mr. Littmann relaxed. "Didn't I tell you, Liddie? A Renaissance man. Finding interest in the least of things." He brushed dust off his trousers as he stood. "Now, if we're ready to get back to town—what's for tomorrow? Something at the opera house?"

---

*October 29, 1915*
*Dear Joe,*

*I enjoyed hearing about the harvest in your last letter. In many ways, it sounds similar to when the thrashing crews move through here. Though yours seems to be on a much grander scale. I'm curious how you handle feeding all these men?*

*I don't like to think that you could already be deep in snow by the time you get my letter. I hope you have enough blankets.*

*The past days have had their ups and downs. Jonathan Grey, a friend of Mr. Littmann's, stopped on his way to California. He'd never been to Iowa, and he found everything so interesting. We went to the caves, took a rowboat on the river, toured the limestone kilns. The weather was perfect. It made me proud to show him things the likes of which he'd never seen, even in Europe. I had not realized Mr. Littmann had never seen any of it, either. I think if Mr. Grey had not been here, he would not have gone. Mr. Littmann is a curious man—so open in some ways and so closed in others.*

*It was a pleasure for me to talk with Mr. Grey. He spoke with me as though my opinions mattered. It reminded me of talking with Papa or you.*

*Those pleasant days put some distance on a horrible mistake I made. While I was ironing, I scorched the hem of an expensive dress. To my everlasting embarrassment, I didn't own up to it. Of course Mrs. Tinker noticed. I paid to remake the dress, but it is worse that I disappointed her. I thought not to tell you but knew I'd feel better if I did. I hope you do not think ill of me.*

*What do you hear about the war? More and more we hear of American men going to fight with their relatives. One of the Kaufmann boys wants to fight for the kaiser. Harley Ellers is going for England. I was taken aback. Is not America their home? Mr. Littmann shocked me when he said he would go as a photojournalist. Your parents came from Germany. Do you ever think of joining the fighting? When I thought of you or Vern going to war, I broke out in a sweat. I was so afraid for you. And you haven't even gone. Promise me you won't!*

*Thinking of you often.*

*Liddie*

*PS: I have almost finished Minnie's wedding dress. She is letting me take photos of their reception. I am as excited about that as making the dress. Then Christmas will be here.*

# Chapter 25

After Mr. Grey left for San Francisco, Mr. Littmann grew quiet. Once, Liddie walked past the room where they did sittings and saw him standing rock still in front of the camera. When she passed again ten minutes later, he hadn't moved. He printed the wrong images from marked proofs. He was short-tempered and snapped at a deliveryman for no reason. During a session with a fidgety little boy, instead of charming the child as she'd seen him do countless times, he was rough and brought the boy to tears.

She expected his bad humor to pass, but after two weeks with no improvement, she followed him into the studio one day.

"Mr. Littmann?"

"What?"

"I don't mean to pry, but I wondered if you aren't feeling well. You haven't been yourself lately."

"Oh? And what self would that be?"

The sarcasm in his voice pushed her back. "I'm sorry. I shouldn't have . . ." She turned to leave.

He groaned. "No. Come back. It isn't your fault." He sank into the ornate high-backed chair they used for portraits and rubbed his face and eyes with the heels of his hands. "It's mine. Seeing Jon. Hearing about the museums, the artists, the discussions. It reminded me of how much I'm missing."

She lowered herself onto a padded footstool. "I thought you were happy with your work here."

"I suppose the work's fine. But it's not the same as being in New York or Paris. Maquoketa isn't the center of anything."

Liddie had never felt embarrassed about where she lived, but when he said it in such a disdainful way, she felt foolish. She'd been so excited to get to Maquoketa, to experience life off the farm. Only a year ago, Maquoketa had been a big city to her.

"The worst was that he saw the Cassatt similarity in the photo."

"I thought that would please you."

He shook his head. "It showed me how far out of the artistic loop I am. Even if my effort wasn't intentional, I should have recognized what I had done."

"Then why do you stay here?"

"Why, indeed? I've been asking myself that since he left." He propped his elbows on his knees, his hands clasped tightly together.

"And why did you come to Iowa? I've never known."

"To find my style. Make my own way." He frowned. "It's not worth revisiting the details."

"You have done all that, haven't you? The studio is busy. Mr. Grey liked your work."

Mr. Littmann stood abruptly. "Leave me be," he said, and turned his back to her.

Nonplussed, Liddie left, her cheeks burning, embarrassed to be dismissed so abruptly. She was halfway down the hall before indignation replaced the embarrassment. She whirled on her heel and went back.

"Mr. Littmann," she said. "I realize I don't know everything about photography, but I'm learning as fast as I can. And I don't think I deserve your rudeness. I was only trying to help."

She did not wait for him to respond. She went to the desk, picked up her handbag, and left. She didn't care that it wasn't closing time.

That night, she lay awake for a long time, thinking. She loved photography with a passion. Working with and learning from Mr.

Littmann had been her gateway to a new world. But he was a puzzle she could not decipher. And frankly, she was tired of him making her feel inadequate.

———

Mr. Littmann was waiting for her when she arrived at the studio the next morning. "I want to apologize, Liddie." He spoke before she reached her desk. "I was boorish yesterday."

Liddie felt her mouth drop open. A slight breeze might have blown her over. Until now, he had never acknowledged a shortcoming in himself.

He exhaled deeply. "I snapped at you, and that was uncalled-for. You welcomed Jon as though he were your friend, and I never thanked you for that."

Still miffed, she went to her desk, put her handbag away, and took out the cashbook to begin work. "Anyone would have done the same," she said.

"May I take you to dinner to make up for my poor behavior?"

"It's not necessary."

"I want to. I don't know anyone else who would have been so kind."

This was the first personal kindness unrelated to photography that he'd offered her, and that was, she supposed, worth something. She accepted.

———

*December 15, 1915*
*Merry Christmas, Joe!*
*I hope you open my package right away. I made flannel shirts for you and Vern, and you should have it to wear as long as possible. See if you can find my secret message.*

*Thank you for worrying about me, but you needn't. Mrs. Tinker has forgiven me for my ironing fiasco. Mr. Littmann has recovered from his funk. In fact, since I blew up at him, he has actually been nicer.*

*We will celebrate the holiday on the farm as always. How different it will be with Minnie as the new Mrs. Treadway!*

*Will we see you in the new year?*

*With much affection.*

*Liddie*

# Chapter 26

"Oh, Liddie." Minnie's eyes lingered over each of the pictures spread on the dining room table. "I've never seen anything like them."

Tears welled in Minnie's eyes.

Liddie was aghast. "You don't like them?"

"Like them? I love them!" Minnie launched herself at Liddie and enveloped her in a crushing hug. No one has pictures like this of her wedding day. It's like living the day all over again."

"Oof!" Liddie gasped. She hadn't realized she'd practically held her breath from the moment she walked into the house where she grew up—the house that was Minnie's home now—until this moment.

Mr. Littmann had taken the formal wedding photographs at the studio. Vern wore his black suit for the first time since their father died. Minnie was radiant in the dress Liddie designed, an ivory silk with tiny pleats across the bodice and satin-covered buttons at each wrist and down the back.

In spite of Mr. Littmann's considerable talent, Liddie thought the studio photos stiff. The subjects were not the vibrant people she knew. She would not boast, but the couple she knew and loved showed themselves in the pictures she'd taken after the wedding.

The early-winter wedding day had been unusually mild, a boon for Liddie's efforts. For some photos, Liddie posed them against a tree trunk or on the porch. Other photos caught the couple unaware.

Liddie liked one in particular. She'd captured Vern gazing up at Minnie, who was standing two steps above him on the porch, with a look that was pure love. Vern was usually so contained, Liddie doubted he realized he'd let his guard down. It was, she thought, the most handsome her brother had ever appeared.

Over the past few months, she had realized that constructing photos was like designing a dress, but with a major difference. With dresses, she could work and rework tangible fabrics and colors. Meanwhile, photography was filled with variables out of her control—light, weather, people. Some of the pictures were taken without even a few moments of preparation. She finally, truly understood Mr. Littmann's point about film being cheap.

She had poured her heart into the wedding photos—her first big opportunity—and it meant everything to her to have Minnie happy with the results.

When Mr. Littmann offered to let her put her photographs in the studio window soon, she knew her work was good.

"Vern! Come look at what Liddie did." Minnie ran to take Vern's hand when he came in.

"Aw, Minnie. I'm all dirty."

Liddie ducked her head to contain a laugh. She did not remember her brother ever being concerned about bringing dirt into the house before.

"It's all right." Minnie tugged him toward the table. "Come see!"

Minnie snuggled up to Vern's side as she pointed from picture to picture. "Remember this one? Oh, and look at this one. I know what I was thinking when she took this."

When they came to the image of Vern looking up at Minnie, she rose up on tiptoe and kissed him on the cheek.

Vern cleared his throat. "These turned out real good, Liddie."

"Why, thank you, Vern. Mr. Littman will let me put some of them in his studio window. If you agree."

Vern looked puzzled. "Pictures of us?"

"Yes. Not all of them, of course, but one or two. This one of you and Minnie on the steps is perfect. And this one by the tree."

"Oh, Vern. Wouldn't that be fun?" Minnie clapped her hands lightly.

"No." Vern's answer was clipped, his tone hard.

"Vern, why not? They're good pictures," Liddie said. "You said they were."

"I said no." His jaw clenched.

"It would mean a lot to me."

"I got work to do." He turned abruptly and banged out the door.

A flush of anger shot through Liddie's temples as the slam of the door echoed in the silent dining room. "He can never support me in anything," she fumed. "It would break his back to do something for me." She gripped the chair in front of her, knowing even as she said it that she was being unfair.

"Oh, sweetie. That's not true. He liked the pictures, I know he did."

"Then why won't he let me show them?"

"You asked him out of the blue. And these pictures are so personal. He might have been embarrassed to think anyone else would see them."

"But other people will see them," Liddie said.

"I know they will. I'll show them to anyone who walks through the door. But that's not the same as strangers walking down Main Street. Let me talk to him. I'm sure he'll agree."

"Do you think so?"

"I do. Now let's have something to eat. I baked a cake this morning."

Liddie allowed herself to be coaxed into a chair while Minnie brought out cake and coffee.

"How are things in town?" Minnie asked as she set thick slices of chocolate-iced chocolate cake on the table.

"All is well. Mrs. Tinker is planning for us to go to Chicago this summer. And Mr. Littmann is letting me do more work in the darkroom, and even make some of the final prints."

"Ooh. In the *darkroom*." Minnie raised an eyebrow.

Liddie dismissed the implication with a laugh. "I'm working. I don't know how many ways to say it. I *work* there."

"But he does take you places."

"Yes, he accompanies me on occasion." Liddie slipped a forkful of the rich, moist cake into her mouth. "This cake is wonderful. Vern must think he died and went to heaven."

"He hasn't complained," Minnie said. "Now quit dodging the point. You know what I mean."

"There is nothing going on between him and me. He gets invited to an event and asks me along. I ask him when I'm invited. It's convenient."

"And how do you feel about that?"

Liddie knew she'd grown accustomed to a relationship most women, Minnie included, would at least find odd, if not completely unacceptable. "I think Mr. Littmann is an extraordinary man. What he knows about photography and art, everything he's teaching me. Sometimes, I feel like *I've* died and gone to heaven."

"So there could be something?"

"No." Liddie shook her head and took another bite of cake. As she chewed, she saw Minnie's skepticism and knew she would persist until Liddie answered directly.

"Really, Minnie. No. It's funny. At one point, I was ready to quit working for him, then he asked me out to dinner. If people didn't keep asking me what's going on or insinuating that something should be going on, it would never cross my mind. I like it this way."

Though he'd repeatedly asked her to call him Thomas, that level of familiarity never set comfortably in her mind. The furthest she'd gone was thinking of him as "Littmann." She still referred to him as "Mr. Littmann" in the studio and when they were together in public.

"Well, I'm not disappointed," Minnie said. "But are you really okay with it?"

"Yes, I am." She pushed a lone chocolate crumb around with a tine of her fork. "I don't like to admit it, but sometimes, I feel like I'm not good enough for him. No matter how much I try, he invariably brings up something I don't know, something he acts like I should have known all along." She glanced up from her plate but immediately returned her gaze to the cake crumb. "Sometimes, I feel so dumb. As an employee, I accept that. Otherwise?" She shrugged.

"Liddie. You're the smartest woman I know. There is no reason for you to feel dumb about anything."

Liddie smiled. "You always make me feel better."

"All right, then. It's odd, that's for sure, but to tell the truth, I'm glad there isn't anything between you."

"You are? Why?"

"I wish for you a man who makes you feel the way Vern makes me feel."

"And how is that?"

Moments passed before Minnie spoke. "I don't know if I can describe it. I just know that when he's not here, I wish he were. I know he'd do anything to make me happy." She studied a small mole on her left wrist, then whispered, "When he comes into the room, I tingle."

"You tingle?"

Minnie's face colored the brightest pink. She waved her napkin in front of her face. "Enough of that. Whew!"

Liddie finally captured the cake crumb and licked it off her fork. "Why did you say you weren't disappointed?"

"I did?" Minnie fanned her face again.

"You did. When I said Littmann is my boss and I am glad to be making pictures."

"Oh, I probably shouldn't say anything."

"You started, so keep going."

Minnie's face could not hide her conflicting thoughts. "I said I'd do anything for Vern and he'd do anything for me."

Liddie nodded.

"I think you'd do anything for Mr. Littmann—because you admire him and want to please him. I wonder if he'd do anything for you?"

"Go on."

"When he came for the barn dance, well, he didn't even try." Liddie had come to think of the barn dance as a fluke not worth dwelling on. When Minnie had told her about the Agners' barn dance, Liddie was excited at the prospect of seeing her old neighbors. Attending with an escort like Littmann was hard to resist.

The barn dance was everything she remembered and less. The problem was that she saw it simultaneously through the lens of her own memory and through Littmann's eyes.

Where she saw a buffet table laden with her favorite foods from her childhood, he saw boards and sawhorses holding mismatched dishes tended by women with chapped hands. Where she saw friendly people who'd do anything for a neighbor, he saw rough country folks who knew nothing about the finer things of life.

When they finished a rousing square dance, she was breathless from laughing. He muttered, "I can't imagine anyone wanting to learn that in New York." She swallowed her laughter.

Later on, when she saw him leave to stand alone outside the barn, she joined him.

"Are you all right?" she asked.

"I couldn't listen to one more discussion of corn harvests or settlin' a cow.'" He affected an irritating twang.

"I'm sorry. I thought you'd enjoy coming with me."

"I'm having a fine time," he insisted.

*You couldn't prove it by me,* she thought. She didn't say that, however, because he was her guest and she would not be rude. Even if she thought he was.

Littmann's boredom disappeared as soon as they'd returned to town. In fact, he'd later professed to have had a good time that weekend and seemed surprised when she questioned him about it. She had decided he had simply had an off night.

Liddie looked at her plate, then at Minnie. "I don't fault him for that. He didn't know the people or the dances. It was too different."

"If he cared for you, he'd at least have acted like he was enjoying himself."

"You're too hard on him."

"Maybe." Minnie shrugged. "But he could have tried."

Minnie studied her plate, and Liddie knew there was something else on her mind. "What else?" she prodded.

"Oh, Liddie. I don't want to be negative."

"I wouldn't ask if I didn't want to know."

Minnie looked doubtful. "I've mentioned this before. How he can't seem to say something nice without hanging crepe on it. Like when he said Mrs. Tinker could easily find someone else to do what you do. That anyone can run a sewing machine."

"That was one time."

"Well, it made me mad. Besides, it was more than once. He always has some comment about how New York or anywhere he's been or anyone he knows is better than anyone here. And it's not just what he says; it's how he says it. Don't you see that?"

"He has been places and seen things I can't even imagine. It's not bragging if it's the truth." Liddie felt defensive. It was true, wasn't it?

"I suppose that's right." Minnie smiled and reached over to take Liddie's plate and fork. "Look at that! You'd have thought we were starving the way we polished off that cake." She headed for the kitchen. "Are you going to stay for supper? I can easily set another plate."

"I really have to get back to town. When's Mama coming home? I wanted her to see that the world didn't come to an end because I came out to the farm by myself."

"She worries about you."

"I know, but I'm so glad she finally agreed to let me hire a buggy at the livery. Waiting for Vern every time I wanted to come home was truly inconvenient."

"The ladies must have gotten into a deep discussion at church. She said she'd only be an hour or so."

"The ladies can't get together for only an hour! Tell her I'm sorry I missed her, but I'll be home again soon. We'll catch up then."

"I wanted her to be here," Minnie said. "There's something I want to tell you both when you're together."

"What is it?"

"I wasn't going to say anything. I promised myself I wouldn't if you weren't both here. But I can't let you get away." Minnie grinned.

"What? Tell me."

"All right." Minnie lowered her voice, speaking like a child with a secret. "I'm in the family way!"

"Oh, Minnie! Are you sure?"

"It's still early. But I'm certain."

"Does Vern know?"

"He does," Minnie said.

"I'm so happy for you! You look wonderful."

"I feel wonderful."

"Now I really wish I could see Mama's face when you tell her. She will be so pleased. A grandchild right here for her to dote on."

"I know." Minnie glowed.

"I'm going to make a dress for the baby."

"You have plenty of time for that." Minnie laughed. "Now you better get going, the sun's already low. Vern says it's going to snow." She hugged Liddie. "The pictures are superb. I'll talk with Vern. I'm sure we'll work something out."

———

*April 23, 1916*

*Dear Amelia,*

*It is spring, yet I feel so low. I'm sure Mama told you Minnie lost the baby. Mama says it's better not to even talk about being pregnant until you start to show. No use getting hopes up. I made a dress for Minnie using fabric the colors of peonies. I hope it cheered her, even a little.*

*Aunt Kate took us by surprise. She is taking a position at a school in Columbus, Ohio. Mama is upset her sister is moving so far away. I know how she feels. I wish you were closer.*

*How are you getting along? Did Fred have time to till a garden plot for you? I'm sure you can do it yourself, but it seems like a little thing.*

*Mrs. Tinker is giving her annual May Day garden party. You should see the little girls in tissue-paper dresses dancing around the maypole! We'll hope for warmer days by then. Mr. Littmann will accompany me. It is easier to have an escort for these things, though we go our separate ways once we arrive. Not so different than the married couples, really.*

*The women want to talk about dresses and recipes; the men want to talk about war.*

*Be sure to tell me what the women are saying about the election this year. Some boys around here are going to Europe to fight. Are you seeing that? Joe says many Canadian men are volunteering. Of course, Canadians are British subjects. Write soon. I so enjoy your letters.*

*With much love, Liddie*

# Chapter 27

"Aunt Kate!" Liddie hugged her aunt after she stepped off the train in Maquoketa.

"It's so good to see you, Liddie." Kate held her niece at arm's length. "My, how grown up you are!"

"You say that every time!" Liddie laughed. "You're embarrassing me." She saw Littmann watching her, an amused look on his face.

Kate extended her hand to him. "Good day, Mr. Littmann. Thank you for coming with Liddie to meet me."

"Pleased to be of service, Miss Farrell." Littmann bowed. "May I take your bag?"

"I'm sorry to trouble you for such a short visit." Kate handed him her traveling case as she scanned the platform. "Your mother isn't here yet?"

"Mama and Vern will meet us at the Decker House." Liddie linked elbows with her aunt for the walk to the hotel. "I can't believe you're leaving Iowa. You and Mama have never lived more than twenty miles apart your entire lives."

"Never lived out of Iowa?" Littmann interjected. "How provincial."

Kate stopped abruptly. "Do you think so?"

Liddie's eyes darted between Littmann and her aunt. His comment was the type she'd come to overlook, but the shift in Kate's tone suggested her aunt would not let it pass.

"Someone as accomplished as you?" Littmann asked. "I would have expected more. The world is too large to waste it in one place."

"You make an assumption, sir, that is not accurate. Living one's life in one place does not show a lack of interest or involvement in the world, nor does it indicate that one has lived a less fulfilling life."

"But doing so means missing a great deal. Take Liddie, here. Think how she would benefit if she traveled to the great cities of the world."

Liddie tugged at her aunt's arm. The conversation wasn't going in a good direction. Kate ignored the tug.

"Mr. Littmann, you know a great deal about photography, but I fear you underestimate my niece. Recognizing an artist's name or seeing a painting does not guarantee that one will 'know' art. Visiting a city does not guarantee a broad-minded outlook. Having such experiences is wonderful, of course. But are they essential to Liddie's success as a human being? I cannot agree."

"I am simply saying that your niece could be more successful with the right opportunities. Most of them outside this rural area."

"And yet you stay," Kate said.

"And yet you're leaving," Littmann responded.

Liddie couldn't believe the two of them were talking as though she was not standing right there.

"Oh, look," she interrupted. "There's Mama."

———

June 25, 1916
Dear Joe,
    Aunt Kate left for Ohio, and I miss her already. I asked Littmann to join us at a good-bye lunch in Maquoketa. Afterward, I wished I had not. Aunt Kate took offense at his comment that if you live in one place you waste your

*life. They launched into one of those debates such as she and Papa used to have, except that it was about me. I wanted to crawl under a rock.*

*From his perspective, having seen so much, I'm sure his comment was true. However, Aunt Kate believed he was disparaging me. You've asked why I feel I need to keep chasing after every artist he mentions. I suppose sometimes it does seem as though he holds all he knows over me, but I'm so eager to take in everything the world has to offer.*

*How are your crops looking? I hope your wheat yields well again this year.*

*I think of you often. Wishing we could talk face to face.*

*Affectionately, Liddie*

———

Liddie sat under an oak tree, the letter she'd just received from Aunt Kate in her lap. The exchange with Littmann had embarrassed Liddie but apparently roused her aunt's spirit in quite a different way.

*The goal should not be a career*, Kate had written. *The goal ought to be a good life. Experiences may be wonderful, but only if they help you to be a better person.*

Leave it to her aunt to parse Littmann's comments so finely. Liddie wiped perspiration from her forehead. The July heat reached her even in the shade. As her father used to point out, Kate had her ideas, but what mattered was what Liddie thought. These ideas were no easier to tease apart than tangled thread.

Originally, her desire centered on escaping the monotony she visualized as the lot of a farmwife to pursue the far more exciting world of travel and adventure. Her love of sewing provided a vehicle for that move. Adventure for the sake of adventure. Travel for the sake of travel. Sewing as a way to support herself. She did not see any of these as bad things. How could she know what she'd find until she did it?

In truth, until Mrs. Tinker had encouraged her, she hadn't imagined that being a dressmaker, possibly even a designer, could be a reality, a true career.

Discovering photography had broadened how she thought about things. Another activity she loved to do. Another vehicle to carry her forward into an exciting future.

What she learned about sewing and photography helped her to be more, to do more. As far as she could see, a career was a means to a good life.

Kate wrote, *Where you live is not the issue. Who you are as a person is what matters.*

Liddie agreed that where she lived was not the issue. But if she could choose New York or Chicago instead of a farm, why wouldn't she? She thought she was a good person. She certainly hoped that to be true whether she lived on a farm, in Maquoketa, or someplace else.

As far as she could see, she was on a good path. She couldn't say whether Mr. Littmann valued things over people. But what if he did? He was her employer, not her husband.

# Chapter 28

Liddie settled into a forward-facing seat. As the train began to move, she looked out the window and waved one last time to her family standing on the platform. She could hardly believe her good fortune. Her long-held dream of traveling alone had come true.

When Mrs. Tinker twisted her ankle less than a week before the trip and the doctor said she'd be off her feet for weeks, Liddie saw the much-anticipated buying trip to Chicago slipping away. Joining Mrs. Tinker on her annual buying trips to Chicago had become a tradition she looked forward to all year. Even worse, if she couldn't go, she'd miss her opportunity to meet Janette Langston, a dressmaker and Mrs. Tinker's longtime acquaintance. When Liddie suggested that she could make the trip alone, she was not surprised that Mrs. Tinker's first response was no. Her concerns were many—from the dangers of a young girl traveling alone to the critical importance of buying fabric. Yet seeing no viable alternative, she finally agreed.

Liddie's mother was mollified once she understood that Mrs. Langston would chaperone Liddie in the city. Mrs. Langston would be waiting for her at Union Station, but for these hours on the train, Liddie was traveling on her own to a real city. A laugh swelled in her throat.

"May I join you?"

A familiar voice interrupted her thoughts, and as she looked up, shock punctured her bubble of laughter.

"Mr. Littmann!"

"I thought I might surprise you." He placed his hat and satchel in the overhead rack and took the seat facing her.

"What are you doing here?"

"Last-minute business. I'm seeing a photographer friend."

"You didn't tell me."

"You were so busy with your plans."

"But the studio?"

"I closed up. Bank holiday, you might say. Your trip to Chicago seemed the perfect opportunity to show you the sights."

"This isn't a vacation, Mr. Littmann." She scanned the car for familiar faces. The women in town couldn't stop speculating about the fact that Littmann escorted her to various events. The gossip that she was traveling unchaperoned to Chicago with him would spread like a wind-driven fire and could do greater damage.

"Oh, come now. Surely it won't require much time to buy a few sewing baubles. In any case, I was concerned about you traveling alone."

"Mr. Littmann . . ."

"Thomas."

"Mr. Littmann. I appreciate your concern for my safety, but I can manage." She tilted her chin at what she hoped was a confident angle.

"It seems I misgauged your reaction. Would you prefer I took another seat? Or shall I sit here while we pretend we don't know each other?"

"Joke if you wish." She turned her shoulder toward him, stared out the window, and fumed. This trip, her first big trip on her own, had been an idea as sweet as chocolate pie. Now he'd spoiled it.

He gave her less than ten minutes to think before he spoke. "Miss Treadway?"

She inclined her head, acknowledging him without speaking.

"Let me at least escort you safely to the Palmer House."

"It's not necessary. Mrs. Langston is meeting me at the station."
She fixed her gaze out the window, pretending serious interest in
the landscape. Then she looked at him. "How did you know I was
staying at the Palmer House?"

"You told me yourself. Almost a dozen times."

Recognizing the truth, she laughed. "I have been excited about
this trip."

"I know. And I hoped to make your experience even better.
The Art Institute is only a few blocks from the hotel. Do you think
you'd have time in your busy schedule to join me?"

She exhaled in resignation. "I've been rude. Do you really have
business in Chicago?"

"I do. At the *Tribune*." He spoke loudly enough for the couple
across the aisle to hear him, then leaned in close and lowered his
voice. "Appearances. Right, Miss Treadway? Even more, though, I
hoped to spend time with you."

"Oh." She blushed and quelled her disappointment at not having this experience to herself, for herself. This would simply be a
different adventure than she'd thought.

She told him the schedule she needed to keep to fulfill her
responsibilities for Mrs. Tinker and to meet with Mrs. Langston—
and the times she was free. She had already planned to visit the Art
Institute because he'd spoken so highly of it. Having him accompany her would be like having her own tour guide.

It seemed hardly any time at all had passed when the conduc-
tor came through the car alerting them that they were arriving at
Union Station.

"It was a pleasure talking with you," Littmann said, standing
to retrieve his hat and satchel as the train braked to a halt. "I hope
you enjoy a productive visit to the city." He leaned in close and
whispered in her ear, "I'll see you at dinner."

A butterfly flitted through Liddie's stomach.

———

"Miss Treadway." Littmann greeted her as the maître d'hôtel seated her at his table, which overlooked the Chicago streets. "I'd begun to think you would not join me after all."

"I apologize. Everything took longer than I anticipated." As she settled into her chair, Liddie relished the opulence of the ornate dining room: the candlelight reflecting in the cut-glass crystal, the bone china with its gold edging, the silver service with a multitude of pieces she always had to remind herself to use. "When I sit at a table like this, I half expect King George to be here, too."

"You won't see anything like it in Maquoketa," Littmann agreed.

"Will the lady be having wine?" the waiter asked.

"Yes," Littmann answered for her, gesturing for his own glass to be refilled.

"I seldom drink," she said. The glass of sherry she and Mrs. Tinker each enjoyed on these trips made her feel worldly; wine was even more cosmopolitan.

"This is a special occasion. We are celebrating." Littmann nodded at the waiter as he lifted his glass toward Liddie.

"We are?" she asked.

"To the wonders of the city!" He clinked his glass against hers. "And to us."

She took a sip. To us? She noticed a slur in his speech.

"Tell me about your day," he said once they'd ordered.

She struggled to answer. The day had been very different than she'd anticipated.

"I brought my portfolio to show Mrs. Langston."

"What did she think of the photographs?"

Liddie moved the soupspoon a fraction of an inch left and then back to the right. "She agreed it was a benefit to be able to show my work."

"You sound ambivalent."

"It wasn't quite what I expected."

"But what did she think of the photos?"

She looked at him, puzzled. "We didn't talk about photography specifically."

"You didn't tell her about your work with me?"

"Why, no. Did you expect me to?"

"There will be other times." Littmann lifted his wineglass, drank the remainder, and reached for the bottle. "For you?"

"I have enough. Thank you." She gestured to her still-full glass.

He poured another glass for himself and swallowed half of it at once.

The waiter came with their soup, providing a welcome interruption to the conversation and to Littmann's drinking. When Littmann turned the conversation to photography, she didn't mind. She felt she would really rather not try to explain feelings to him that she didn't understand herself.

Ever since she left Mrs. Langston, she'd tried to make sense of the woman's reaction to her portfolio. Mrs. Langston had been complimentary enough, but Liddie came away feeling less than positive.

When she boldly asked how someone like herself could become a designer, Mrs. Langston had snorted. "The real designers are in Paris. Or New York," she said. "Even here in Chicago, we follow their lead. Besides, most women don't want innovation in their clothing. Your work is appropriate, as I don't imagine the women in a town like Maquoketa are looking for too much. A difference in fabric or color. Something so the wearer feels special without standing out too much. Just as you've done." She concluded, "It's good."

Liddie didn't know how to respond to that assessment of her work. When the woman was suddenly called away, Liddie wasn't disappointed their time was cut short.

She went on to purchase the things on Mrs. Tinker's list. Her confidence shaken, she stood in front of the walls lined with bolts of fabric, intimidated by the reality of shopping on her own. She spent considerable time comparing bolts before finally selecting fabrics she hoped would satisfy Mrs. Tinker.

Throughout the afternoon, Mrs. Langston's comments returned to her mind. The dresses she designed were *appropriate, not too much*. There was no way Liddie could see those words in a positive light. An experience she'd been sure would be a highlight had only cast a pall on the day.

Littmann interrupted her thoughts. "You've gone away, Liddie."

"I'm sorry. It was a full day." She forced a smile. "This is the first time I've had a moment to think." She didn't want to admit to Littmann how disappointed she'd been. Instead, she asked, "How was your day?"

"I spoke with my photographer friend. He worked in New York before coming here. I'm certain now that my character photographs would be even more sought after in Paris."

"Do you *really* think that is something you'd want to do? With the war on?"

"The front is far from Paris. There'd be no danger there. I'm done talking, Liddie. It's time for action. That's why this trip with you is such perfect timing."

"It is?"

"Ever since this morning, I've been thinking about how I rely on you. I need you with me, Liddie."

"That is nice of you to say," she said.

"It's the truth. We make a good team."

He'd said they were a good team before, but the comments were typically spontaneous, based on some project completed in the darkroom. He'd never been quite so purposeful as this. She smiled and said nothing, aware that he did not expect her to speak.

"I'm sorry your conversation with Mrs. Langston wasn't what you wanted, but it's for the best."

"Why would you say that?" She frowned. "You know how much this meant to me."

"Sewing is fine, Liddie, but it's what every woman does. It sounds as though you saw that today. Photography is special. You have a talent I can help you develop. You can do so much more. *We* can do so much more."

His compliment about her ability with a camera almost made her overlook the slight to her sewing. Almost. She'd nearly gotten used to the backhanded comments he so often made. Nearly. Coming on top of Mrs. Langston's lukewarm praise, his words were a wasp sting. She bit the inside of her cheek hard.

Oblivious to her reaction, he continued. "I'd be lost if you weren't working by my side."

He reached for her hand and cradled it between his palms. The action was so astonishingly intimate that Liddie glanced at nearby tables to see if anyone was watching them. Her mouth was as dry as cotton when she forced her eyes back to his.

"I love you, Liddie. And I believe you love me."

She blinked rapidly. Had he actually said he loved her? Her heart raced.

"That's why I'm asking you. Will you marry me?"

Liddie's eyes widened. She'd imagined that when a man proposed to her, she would be thrilled by love, swept away by emotion. Like in a fairy tale. Now that the moment had arrived, she felt only shock.

"Oh, Mr. Littmann."

"I know this seems sudden. But it's the right thing to do. When I think of Europe, I see you there, too. Liddie, I want you as my wife."

Whenever he had talked about Europe—the art museums, the legendary cities, the grand balls—she had yearned—ached, actually—to see those sights herself. She had never imagined it would happen. Now she realized it really could. She could continue with photography . . . she could see the world . . . *and* she would be married.

He'd said he loved her. Should she say "I love you" in return? Liddie looked at her hand, held tightly between Littmann's long, slender fingers, as he continued to speak.

"As husband and wife, we can travel freely. Nothing else needs to change."

With effort she raised her eyes. "I am so . . . so . . . surprised." It was the only word that formed in her mind. She pulled her hand out of his. "Could we leave?"

"Our meal . . ." He gestured to the half-eaten steaks.

"I need some air." She stood, unable to get away fast enough. As she made her way out of the dining room, she heard him call the waiter. Out on Monroe Street, she stopped, lifted her face, and breathed in evening air heavy with the smells of horses, automobiles, and too many people.

Within moments he appeared beside her and took her arm. "Was my proposal so appalling?" he asked.

The injured look on his face touched her, and her thoughts turned to him for the first time. "Not appalling. I simply never imagined." She shrugged off his hand and started to walk. "Well, truthfully, I did imagine. Early on. But you never seemed . . ." Her words trailed off.

"This will work out, Liddie," he said, falling in beside her. He steered her toward the lake as he laid out his plan. "We'll have greater opportunities than we ever imagined." He was acting as though she'd already agreed to his proposal. "We'll find an apartment in Paris, set up a studio and a darkroom, and be back in business in no time."

Not once in the weeks he'd been talking about Europe had he even hinted that he considered her part of his future. Her thoughts in turmoil, she barely registered his voice as they crossed streets and railroad tracks. When the sidewalk ended, she took his arm to negotiate the rough ground. Finally, they stood at the water's edge where the air smelled moderately cleaner. Lake Michigan loomed ahead, dark and impenetrable, a vast emptiness lit by the last vestiges of the sunset and a halo of lights from the city. She shivered in the heat of the summer night. Littmann stood beside her, silent for the first time. Apparently, it was now her turn to speak.

"Going to Europe with you would be a dream come true. It's just . . . I hadn't even thought . . ." Was she a fool to hesitate? Marriage, travel, adventure. Why would an Iowa farm girl say no when handed everything she'd ever dreamed of?

"Tell me you will, Liddie."

He was waiting. She had to say something.

She turned to face him. "Yes," she said. "Yes."

She felt as though she'd stepped off solid ground and into quicksand as he pulled her toward him and kissed her.

That night, she lay in bed staring into the darkness, unable to sleep. Littmann had asked and she'd said yes. She'd always thought love and marriage went hand in hand. As she thought about the couples closest to her, it troubled her to realize that not only could she not define love, she couldn't see if or how love and marriage actually came together. With each thought, she flipped from side to side until the sheets were as tangled as her mind.

Her parents' relationship had always been reserved. She did not recall seeing them touch except when Papa held Mama's arm as she climbed into the buggy. Nor had they expressed affection for each other, at least not in public. Her mother wanted her to make a good match. Did a good match mean love? Or was it all about money, property, a man with a well-paying job?

She had never seen Amelia and Fred together. Without saying much, Amelia's letters portrayed lives lived increasingly apart.

Fred provided for Amelia and the children, but it was a lonely existence and he was gone most of the time.

She saw something different in Minnie and Vern. Taciturn Vern showed his affection more in actions than words—flowers he picked from the fencerows, a geode washed out of the creek bed—gifts of no real account, but ones that Minnie cherished. Liddie saw how Minnie's eyes brightened, how she checked her hair and pinched color into her cheeks whenever Vern came to the house.

Of course, all of this presumed love was something you could see. Even if she did not see outward displays of affection between her parents, she assumed they had loved each other. It might be the same with Amelia and Fred.

Perhaps love was simply a feeling you had. If love was a "tingle," as Minnie described it, Liddie knew the excitement she'd felt in the early days with Littmann did not hold the same enduring intensity she saw between Minnie and Vern.

Did she love Littmann? She whispered the words in the dark. "I love you. I love you, Thomas." It was exciting to say the words, even if they did not give rise to a specific feeling.

He said he loved her. He was older. He must know about love since he knew so many other things. Maybe the excitement she felt was love. Or could be. Perhaps it didn't matter if she wasn't in love with him, anyway. *Nothing else needs to change*, he'd said. They'd still be working together, just like always. What if that was all he really wanted? Did it matter? Still, he had said he loved her. If she could travel the world, see more places than she'd ever dreamed of, have grand adventures, might not love come?

———

Liddie looked at herself in the mirror the next morning. A woman who was soon to be married and traveling to Europe should appear . . . older . . . more sophisticated. More something. She inspected herself, peering straight into her own eyes, then peeking at herself in profile. She didn't see anything new. Even so, remembering his words, *I love you* caused her heart to pound.

She spent the morning purchasing the rest of the things on Mrs. Tinker's list, though she was so distracted she had to go back to one store twice. Finally, she stood waiting for him on the Art Institute steps, next to the lion statue, as they'd agreed. The bronze lion, its coat colored in a green patina, its mouth open in a roar, conveyed courage, confidence, conviction. Liddie felt none of that. What would Littmann say? What would she say? How would they be different with each other now that those words had been said? Surely saying "I love you" changed everything.

Throughout the morning, she'd run through a dozen conversations in her mind. How would they travel? When? Where? Which ship? Anxiety snaked from her stomach up through her chest as she thought about being on a ship, though the president had warned Germany against attacking civilian vessels. Before the anxiety curled around her heart, she pushed that fear aside to think of where they would live in Paris, how they would set up a studio. Getting chemicals for the darkroom had become increasingly difficult here. Would it not be more difficult, if not impossible, in Europe? What about their life together? They would live in Paris. But where? Would there be trees? Grass? Where would they buy food?

"Liddie, my Liddie. I am the happiest man alive." Littmann's euphoria broke through her anxiety when he finally materialized out of the crowd and came toward her.

*So it will be like this*, she thought. He would tell her again that he loved her. She smiled, timid in the presence of this handsome man who loved her and wanted to marry her.

"My meeting with the *Examiner* was top of the line."

"The *Examiner*? I thought it was the *Tribune*."

"I took a chance and stopped at the *Examiner*, too. I got lucky. The editor I talked with said if I shipped him pictures of Paris—the people and architecture—from time to time, he'd consider them." He grinned as he shifted his hat to a jaunty angle. "This is what we wanted, Liddie. Europe, here we come!"

He may have wanted that. She'd never even thought of it.

"That sounds . . . like a good idea."

"Let's go in, shall we?" He tucked her hand in his elbow.

She held back. Wasn't he going to say again that he loved her? She wanted to hear that, needed to hear that. She wanted to talk about the two of *them*. She wanted to discover how they would act toward each other as a couple, now and after they married. But she didn't know how to say that herself.

He looked back at her, puzzled that she hadn't moved. "Shall we go?"

She swallowed hard to force a lump of disappointment down her throat. "Yes. Let's go in."

Seeing the artwork was not as interesting as she thought it would be, not with the imminent trip to Europe on her mind. As they stood in a gallery of Dutch masters, in front of a portrait of a young girl who appeared as uncertain as she herself felt, Liddie screwed up her courage. "Mr.—Thomas?"

"Yes?"

Her palms were damp and she wound her fingers in the fabric of her skirt. "When would we leave?"

Littmann steered her to another painting before answering. "Before the winter weather sets in. I figure we'll be on a ship by early September."

Early September! Not even two months. What about a wedding? What about her mother and Minnie and Mrs. Tinker?

"When would we leave Iowa?"

"Probably mid-August. No need to worry. You can check into the train schedules. Find something that gives us good connections." He scanned the gallery. "I think we've seen everything here. Let's move on."

As they walked through yet another gallery with more paintings she couldn't find the energy to be interested in, she fixed her face in an expression of neutral contemplation to cover her dismay. Maybe this was the way it was supposed to be. Maybe she expected too much.

# Chapter 29

"He what?" Minnie took Liddie by the shoulders and asked again, adding a decibel to each word. *"He what?"*

"Shush." Liddie looked around. Out on the porch of the boardinghouse, they risked a neighbor overhearing. She kept her own voice low. "You heard me." It had been nearly a week since Littmann had proposed, and she had told no one. "I'm happy you came to town today. I was sure to burst if I couldn't tell you."

"I can't believe it. Were you surprised? What am I saying? Of course you were surprised. You said he'd never said anything about marriage before. Were you telling me the truth?" She looked at Liddie for a full second before concluding, "Of course you were. You must be in shock. *I'm* in shock. Tell me."

"We aren't telling anyone else until he talks to Mama. But I had to tell someone."

Minnie shook her head. "I never thought."

"Neither did I." Liddie told her how Littmann had surprised her by showing up on the train and then proposing over dinner at the Palmer House.

"It's so out of the blue," Minnie said. "What did you say?"

"I was so surprised. He said he'd been thinking about it for a long time, but now that he's going to Europe, he couldn't imagine being there without me."

"Hold on." Minnie gripped Liddie's wrist. "What do you mean, Europe?"

"He says it's time for him to do something big with his photography, and that we'll set up a studio in Paris. Minnie, all those places I've wanted to see, I'll be doing it!"

"You will, won't you? You'll be working as a team, like always." Minnie's expression sobered. "Do you love him?"

Liddie looked away. "He said he loves me. And I . . . I love so many things about him."

"Admiring him as a photographer is one thing. Throwing your lot in with him for the rest of your life . . ."

"He's successful. He's handsome. He can take me everyplace I've ever wanted to go. We'll be happy. I know we will." She pushed aside the feeling that she was trying to convince herself and changed the subject. "Now you have news, too. What is it?"

Minnie's cheeks colored. "I don't want you to leave. When you're married, I want you here, where we can raise our children together."

Liddie broke into a grin. "Really?"

"Really. The doctor said a miscarriage isn't all that uncommon, and that we should try again. So we did. And . . ." She spread her hands and laughed.

"Oh, Minnie!" Liddie hugged her. "I'm so happy for you. And Vern. And Mama. And me. I'm going to be an aunt."

"And I'm happy for you, too," Minnie said. "Truly, I am."

---

"I'll be glad to get this over with." Littmann was grim as he helped Liddie into his motorcar.

He was so easy in the company of women that Liddie hadn't thought he might dread talking with her mother. Only one other time—when Mr. Grey visited—had she seen him so unsettled.

He was silent during most of the drive, and she had no great desire to talk, either. As the fields flew by, she gripped the edge of the seat with both hands, as she did each time she rode in an auto. The speed was hard to comprehend. She felt as though her life were flying by equally as fast. She grasped the seat tighter. She didn't feel in control of anything.

Margretta and Minnie watched from the porch as Littmann maneuvered the vehicle to a stop near the front gate. Liddie was glad to see that while her mother had a cane, she wasn't leaning on it hard; her gout must not have been so bad just now.

Littmann opened Liddie's door and took her hand. "Don't get too far away," he whispered.

"They won't bite, you know."

He tucked her hand in his elbow as they walked to the porch. "One can never tell," he said.

Once they'd climbed the steps, he released Liddie to greet her mother. "Mrs. Treadway, it's a pleasure to see you." Littmann bowed over Margretta's hand.

"Mr. Littmann," Margretta said. "It's been too long."

"Liddie has invited me; I regret it has not worked out. I'm pleased you could find room for a guest at your table this evening."

"We always enjoy company," Minnie said. "Please come in."

Littmann sounded so polished in Maquoketa. Now his words seemed stilted, even mocking. Liddie wondered what her mother thought.

"Something has come up," Littmann said to Margretta as soon as they were inside. "I would like to talk with you in private, if I may?"

A small frown crossed Margretta's face, and she glanced at Liddie. In response, Liddie simply smiled.

"Of course, Mr. Littmann," Margretta said. "Will you join me in the parlor?"

More than half an hour passed before Littman found Liddie in the kitchen, where she and Minnie had been speculating about what was going on in the parlor. He was not smiling.

"Are you all right?" she asked. "Would you like a glass of water?"

"Yes." He wiped his forehead with a pristine white handkerchief, refolded it, and returned it to his pocket.

Liddie filled a glass and handed it to him.

He took a big swallow. "Your mother is one straightforward lady." He took another long drink. "She'd like to talk to you. She said she'd be in the garden."

Liddie raised her eyebrows. Minnie shrugged.

"Would you like to relax on the porch, Mr. Littmann? There's a nice breeze," Minnie suggested. "Or Vern's in the barn. You could join him."

"The porch is fine," Littmann said. "And more water, please." He handed the glass to Liddie before he went outside.

Liddie poked Minnie in the arm. "Please don't make it worse."

"Just having a little fun." Minnie smiled sweetly.

————

Margretta tossed a handful of lima beans into the dishpan. "You might have warned me," she said without looking up from the row of vines.

"Before he spoke with you?" Automatically, Liddie bent down and began to search the plants, pick chunky pods, and throw them into the pan. She was not surprised her mother was in the garden. When her mother wanted a peaceful moment, she took up her knitting. When she faced stress, Margretta headed for the rows of produce for physical labor.

"You thought the man should take the lead," Margretta said.

"Yes."

Margretta stood. She put her hands on her waist and arched her back. "Lord knows I wish G. W. were here now. This took me by surprise."

Liddie straightened up. "I was surprised, too."

"It makes me wonder."

Her mother's gaze implied that Liddie might have withheld the true nature of her relationship with Littmann. "He said he'd been thinking about it for a long time. And now that the assignments in Europe are certain, he couldn't imagine going without me."

"That's exactly what he said to me, too." Margretta picked up the dishpan. "Let's get out of the sun." She stepped over the bean rows and headed to the apple tree south of the garden, where she eased herself down on the grass.

Liddie sat, too, curled her legs up under her skirt, and waited for her mother to speak.

"I only want the best for you, Liddie. Do you love him?"

"I . . . do."

"I'd be happier if you said that with more conviction," Margretta said dryly. "When nothing happened all these months, I figured he had his eye on someone else." She flicked a ladybug off her apron. "I have to say, I don't like you going off to Europe with him."

"It's what I've always wanted, Mama. Travel. Adventure."

"You love the *idea* of travel. You've barely been outside Iowa. You can't speak French. When I asked him how you'll shop when you don't speak the language, he seemed surprised. Like it hadn't occurred to him how you'd manage."

"I figure things out. I'm good at it," Liddie said, at the same time wondering if she could learn French before they left. Although she didn't imagine the library had a book to teach her that.

"He may get you set up. Though how he'll do that when he doesn't speak the language, either, I don't know. But when he's away, you'll be on your own. How you'll get along will be up to you."

"I can take care of myself. Besides, look how many Germans come here and don't speak English. They get along. They learn."

"It takes them years to learn. And there's a large number of them. They help each other. And even then, it isn't easy. In France, you'll be alone."

"It won't be that way, Mama. Mr. Lit—he loves me."

"Hmm. So he says."

Margretta took Liddie's hand, stroking and then patting it as she'd done when Liddie was a little girl. Her mother's fingers were warm, gentle. She remembered her father's calloused hands. She blinked back the blur in her eyes. She wished her father were here, too.

"Liddie, there are many reasons to get married. You've had your heart set on getting off the farm and having some adventure. Whatever that means. But you need to be sure about the man you're hitching your wagon to. Do you care about the same things?"

Liddie would not admit the only topics she and Littmann ever discussed related to photography. Instead, she looked at her mother. "But you said yes?"

Margretta sighed. "I said yes."

Now that her dreams were in her grasp, Liddie was dismayed to feel confusion and uncertainty rather than the joy she'd expected.

———

"When I mentioned Paris, I didn't think you would go *now*. And I assumed it would be for clothing design. This! Well!" Liddie's normally unflappable employer threw up her hands. "I could use some tea." Mrs. Tinker gestured to her wrapped ankle, and Liddie headed for the kitchen.

"You cannot go to France without introductions," she said as Liddie poured tea for them both. When Liddie sat on the settee where clients usually relaxed, Mrs. Tinker continued. "Janette may have some connections. I'll contact her. Of course, that is the clothing business, but anyone is better than no one."

Again, Liddie found herself fighting conflicting emotions.

"Are those tears?" Mrs. Tinker asked.

Liddie searched for the hankie she kept tucked in her skirt pocket as she willed herself not to cry. "I'm . . . just . . . fine." She choked on a sob as the tears trickled down her cheeks.

Mrs. Tinker leaned forward and gently squeezed Liddie's forearm. "Take a breath and another sip of tea." When Liddie was breathing evenly, Mrs. Tinker repeated, "Tell me. Why the tears?"

Liddie hiccuped. "I just thought I would be happy."

"And you're not?"

"I feel foolish." Liddie blotted at the tears. "What girl wouldn't be happy to marry a man like Mr. Littmann and travel to Europe? It's everything, isn't it?"

"Have you talked to him about your concerns?"

"Until now, there was nothing to talk about. He's wanted to do more with his photography. Lately, he's talked about Europe. I never saw myself as part of it. It was only last week"—she hadn't told Mrs. Tinker that Littmann came to Chicago—"that he asked me."

"Hmm." Mrs. Tinker tapped the rim of her teacup with her index finger. "I thought you had simply decided to keep your relationship with him private. Not so?"

Liddie shook her head.

"So when he asked you to marry him, it was a *complete* surprise?"

Liddie nodded.

"Yet you said yes." Mrs. Tinker was quiet for several moments. When she spoke, her face was as serious as Liddie had ever seen it. "Liddie, a surprise might look like what we thought we wanted. And so we jump on the wagon. Afterward, we wonder how we got there. We might stay there because we think we can make it right. We might stay there because we're afraid of what others will say if we change our mind. Afraid to stand up and say what we want to. Afraid to go back on something we've committed to. Lots of reasons.

"Now, I can't tell you what to do. You have to decide for yourself. But just because you've gotten on a wagon doesn't mean you can't get off. Don't forget that."

Liddie knew every word Mrs. Tinker spoke could apply to her. She just wasn't certain which ones actually did. Peering into her half-empty teacup, she could almost see the bottom of the cup. But not quite. She felt as though trying to make sense of her life right now was like trying to see through the tea. She rubbed the back of her hand against her cheek, shook her head to clear it, and forced a smile.

"Better now?" Mrs. Tinker asked.

Liddie nodded.

"Well then," Mrs. Tinker said in a way that put a period on the conversation. "You may simply have normal bride jitters. August, you say? That's not much time." She smiled. "What say we get busy on your dress?"

"You're so good to me," Liddie said.

"We all want you to be happy, dear."

"Me too," Liddie said under her breath. "Me too."

# Chapter 30

As days passed, the awkwardness Liddie felt around Littmann sub-sided. In the studio, most of the time, the days passed as though the proposal had never happened. She did the work she'd always done. They interacted in front of customers as they always had. In all that, she was comfortable, confident. Then he'd catch her eye and smile. She would blush and drop her eyes. And the awkward-ness would return.

Where only a week ago she'd worked side by side with him in the darkroom without a second thought, now the fantasies of her first weeks returned. Every chance brush of their hands meant something. Or she thought it did.

Liddie searched out the few books about Paris the library had; one included a map with street names she could not imagine how to pronounce. Another book included plates of the most famous works of art in the Louvre Museum. She imagined standing in front of the Venus de Milo. Uncomfortable at even the idea of looking at a naked woman, she closed the book and put it back on the shelf.

Liddie grew bolder in conversations with Littmann. "What will we do for furniture? Will we take the darkroom equipment with us?" She opened the library book with the map of Paris. "Where will we live?"

"I haven't had time to think about that yet," he responded. "Now stop worrying, will you? It'll be fine."

A knot formed in her stomach as she came to suspect that he had no more knowledge of the city than she. All the thinking he'd been doing so far apparently concerned his photo assignments. And the more she reflected on his words regarding those assignments, the less certain she was that they were substantial, either.

The next day, she tried again. "Perhaps you could contact Jon Grey? Or maybe your photographer friend has recommendations for where we might live?"

"Good thinking," he said. "I'll send wires."

At his response, the knot in her stomach untangled a bit. "In the meantime, I'll make a list of the questions we need answered," she said. "We'll follow up the wire with a letter."

"Excellent. You're so good at this, Liddie."

She took out a notepad. In seconds, the list included apartment, groceries, transportation. Studio. Chemicals. Equipment. Clients. Crates. And prints for the *Examiner*. How in the world did one ship photographs from Europe to the United States?

At one point, she wondered if he had proposed to her only because he needed her to organize his life. Yet he'd said he loved her. Surely he did. She needed to believe he loved her, even if she wasn't sure she loved him.

"Has there been a response to your wires?" Liddie asked at the end of the week.

Littmann looked puzzled. "What wires?"

"To Jon. And your friend. About where we might live."

"I didn't send them. You were making a list of questions. No sense asking until we know what we need to know." He headed for the door. "I'll be back in an hour."

"But . . ."

The door closed behind him. Her questions filled two pages. Each time Littmann walked away, Liddie felt more helpless. More overwhelmed. More alone. He did not seem to notice.

Twice during that week, she sat down in the evening intending to write to Joe. Her hand hovered over the paper, but the words to tell him she was getting married did not come. She also thought about writing Amelia, but the notion of telling her sister that she was moving thousands of miles away, virtually assuring they would not see each other for years, maybe ever again, felt like a millstone on her chest.

Both times, she put her writing box back in the drawer.

# Chapter 31

"Where to first?" Liddie asked Littmann and Vern, who were finishing off the last remnants of the picnic lunch she and Minnie had packed for their day at the fair.

"A nap?" Vern offered.

"No, sir, mister." Minnie laughed, nudging him with her toe. "You can sleep when we get home."

"What do you think . . . Thomas?" Liddie asked. She still felt odd using his given name. "What do you want to see?"

"I don't want to tip my hand by telling you what I have my eye on," Littmann said. He handed her one of the two Brownie cameras he'd bought just for that day. "We'll see who takes the best photo, and neither of us will have an advantage."

She thought the cameras an extravagance, but they put him in a positive mood. Besides, she was eager to accept the photo challenge.

A month had passed since Littmann had asked her to marry him. Within two weeks of telling Mrs. Tinker, Liddie saw another girl sitting at the workstation she had come to think of as her own. Truthfully, Liddie was dismayed at how easily she had been replaced. She was even more dismayed when Littmann so quickly pointed out, "I told you so." Instead of working on client projects, she spent afternoons at Mrs. Tinker's house working on her own wedding dress.

She slowly grew more comfortable with the idea of marriage. It was not that she resolved the question of whether or not she loved Littmann. But she convinced herself that the opportunity to see the world was a sufficient trade-off for that ill-defined and elusive idea of love.

Upon waking the morning of the fair, she vowed that for one full day, even though the wedding was only three weeks away, she was not going to think about love or the mechanics of living in Paris.

Now, as Liddie helped Minnie pack up the picnic things, she resolved again to forget about the future.

"Thomas is in a good mood," Minnie whispered. "We weren't sure what to expect, the fair being farm business and all."

"Please." Liddie rolled her eyes. He really did have good qualities, and it annoyed her to have to constantly defend him. "I wish you saw in him all that I do."

Minnie shrugged. "Look at that." She pointed at Vern, who had stretched out on the blanket and was breathing heavily, his hat over his eyes. "Fifteen minutes of nap. Then we go." She claimed a corner of the blanket and sat, one hand resting on Vern's shoulder.

Liddie joined Littmann in loading the cameras with film. As soon as he had suggested the photo expedition, she began to think of possible images. The Wild West show later that afternoon held promise. Buffalo Bill's troupe performed all over the United States. Even in Europe. And now, right here in Maquoketa. Somehow that struck her as perfectly ironic. Before she could go to the world, the world had come to her.

Holding the camera steady, she looked through the viewfinder. She saw picnickers, horses and buggies, children playing. She turned the camera toward Minnie and Vern. Without hesitation, she pressed the lever and took her first frame: Minnie gazing down at her sleeping husband.

———

Throughout the afternoon, the four wandered through the livestock barns, looking at the blue ribbon–winning cows, horses, and pigs. They stopped at a booth decorated with red, white, and blue bunting and manned by the Council of National Defense. "Show your patriotism," urged a man who pinned buttons decorated with the American flag to their shoulders. He handed Liddie a flyer, which she put in her handbag and promptly forgot about.

Later, they took shelter from the sun in the tent where judges tasted, compared, and awarded ribbons to the best pies, pickles, and cookies.

"Minnie, you should enter your cake next year," Liddie suggested.

"It's not that good," Minnie said.

"It is," Liddie insisted. "You could call it your 'died and gone to heaven' cake."

"That's the truth." Vern nodded, and Liddie smiled at him.

"You could enter a loaf of your bread," Minnie said. "If you were going to be here."

"I haven't made bread in so long."

Vern asked Littmann, "Did you know she bakes the best bread in the county?"

"You are full of surprises," Littmann said to her. He gave a cursory glance at the tables, then sought the exit. "We haven't been down the midway yet. Shall we go?"

"Do we have time before the show?"

"Enough. I'm feeling lucky." He took her hand. "There might be a prize in it for you."

"For me?" She'd never had anyone try to win something for her.

"Of course for you." He squeezed her hand and let it go.

Minnie linked arms with Liddie, and the two walked ahead while the men compared strategies for outwitting the carnies. The carnival games offered enough hope to keep people playing without yielding enough reward to deplete the prizes hanging from the rafters. Today was no exception.

"That's enough, Thomas. You tried," Liddie said after Littmann rolled the balls five times without success, his frustration building with each loss. "Save your money."

"Once more." Littmann motioned to the carny.

"Give the man some space," Vern said. He'd won a string of beads in a shooting game. Minnie caressed the blue-glass strand hanging around her neck as though it were made of priceless sapphires.

"This is the time." Littmann eyed the pins for ten seconds before he released the first ball. Pins tottered, but none fell. Same with the second ball. He shook his head. "My luck is off. This is the last ball. Do you want to throw it, Liddie?"

She drew back, waving her hands. "No." She realized that whether she threw the ball and won or threw the ball and missed, she would damage his ego. "I know you can do it. You don't need me."

He shrugged. "This is it, then. All or nothing."

Liddie held her breath as the yellow wooden ball rattled up the alley. It connected with two pins, knocking them into the third, which tottered back and forth before all three finally fell. Flooded with relief, she breathed again. "Wonderful!"

"Good one." Vern slapped Littmann on the back.

The carny handed a stuffed bear to Littmann, who gave it to Liddie with a bow. "For you, my lady."

"Why, thank you, kind sir." Liddie executed a deep curtsy.

As she rose, her gaze was drawn past Littmann. Her mind could not conceive of what she was seeing. She looked away and then looked back. It was true. Joe was standing in front of the next midway booth, not twenty feet away, hands in his back pockets, grinning at her.

"Joe!" she shouted. She thrust the bear back into Littmann's hands, pushed past Vern and Minnie, and ran straight into his arms.

She hugged him and then stepped back, holding his hands as she peppered him with questions. "What are you doing here? I got your letter yesterday and you didn't say anything!" She looked to Vern. "Did you know he was coming? Why didn't you tell me? How could you keep this a secret?"

"Nobody tells me nothing," Vern said. He pumped Joe's hand. "It's good to see you, Joe."

"It was a spur-of-the-moment thing, had to wait till the threshers were done," Joe said. "Are you going to introduce me?" Joe looked past Vern and Liddie to Minnie, who stood watching them with clear delight. Meanwhile, Littmann's eyes moved between Liddie and Joe, the lines of a frown deepening into his forehead.

"Minnie. Come meet Joe," Vern said.

"You're even prettier than Vern told me," Joe said. "And that's saying something!"

Minnie blushed. "I feel like I've known you all along. Vern and Liddie talk about you all the time."

"Good, I hope?"

"We only had to polish the apple a little," Vern cracked. Then he introduced Littmann.

"Mr. Littmann." Joe extended his hand. "I feel I know you, too. Liddie's mentioned you in her letters."

"You have me at a disadvantage." Littmann shook Joe's hand, but he looked askance at Liddie.

Liddie realized she was still holding Joe's arm. She released it. "Joe's been a friend . . . of our family . . . for many years."

"I was a hired hand for the Treadways," Joe said.

"A friend." Vern cuffed Joe on the arm. "My hunting buddy and card-playing partner."

Littmann slipped an arm around Liddie's waist. "Is it possible your friend hasn't heard the good news?"

"News?" Joe asked.

Liddie felt her cheeks burn and knew the heat was not from the afternoon sun. "Oh. I expect he has not." She forced herself to meet Joe's eyes. "Thomas and I are getting married."

"Married?" The smile on Joe's face faded.

"That's right," Littmann affirmed. "Three weeks from today. Then we're off to Europe."

"Married," Joe repeated. "Europe?" He looked at Liddie.

"I've been meaning to write and tell you," she said.

"Sometimes, you have to act," Littmann added. "The opportunity arose for me, and I couldn't see going without her. Liddie's the best little assistant I've ever had."

Liddie held a tight smile on her lips.

Joe frowned. "Might your . . . *wife* to be . . . be more than an assistant?"

Liddie felt Littmann's arm tense against her waist. "Your meaning?" he asked, his voice stiff.

"From the pictures Liddie sends, I peg her as a fine photographer in her own right."

"She sends you pictures?" Littmann's cheek twitched as he looked at her. He fixed Joe with a superior look. "Even a novice can see her talent."

Joe met Littmann's eyes without wavering. "I expect there are different definitions of helpmate."

"How long are you going to be in Iowa, Joe?" Minnie interjected.

Liddie could have kissed her for changing the subject.

"A week or so. I want to check out that place Vern told me was for rent."

Liddie shot an accusing glare at her brother. "You did know he was coming."

"Nope. Sure didn't. Can't say as I'm disappointed, though." He grinned at Joe. "Suppose we'll get a game of cards in while you're here? Maybe go hunting?"

"I expect. But I want to see that farm. Got time to go over there with me?"

"I'll make time."

Littmann tugged Liddie's arm. "We must move on."

"B-but," Liddie stuttered. "Wait . . ."

"You're not forgetting the show, are you?" He urged her toward the grandstand. "Besides, they'll be wanting to talk farming."

Hearing some of the mocking twang Littman had adopted at the barn dance, she threw him a hard look. In fact, she'd forgotten the Wild West show. Taking photos was now the last thing on her mind.

"You coming to the farm tonight?" Vern asked Joe.

"Went right to the hotel when I got off the train," he said. "Didn't want to presume."

"Mama'll be upset if you don't stay with us. So will we," Minnie insisted.

"Time to go, Liddie." Littmann's fingers tightened on her elbow.

"Maybe Joe could join us?" she suggested.

Littmann didn't hide a scowl.

"You go," Joe said. "You have plans, and I want to look at the corn planters."

"If you're still in Iowa, I'm sure you'll want to come to the wedding," Littmann said. "Good friend that you are." The hard edge of sarcasm in his voice cut the air.

Liddie allowed Littmann to move her several steps down the midway. Shame crept up her back as she imagined Joe watching her be led away. She stopped. "No. This is not right, Thomas. He's a friend." She removed her arm from his hand. "I'll be right back." She ran the few steps to where Joe stood talking with Vern and Minnie.

"When will I see you again?" she asked, loud enough for Littmann to hear.

"I'll be at the farm in the morning. Will you come by?"

"I wouldn't . . . I couldn't . . . miss seeing you. It'll be like old times with all of us at the table." She smiled at Minnie. "I'm sorry. I invited myself to dinner. I'll help cook."

"You must come," Minnie said. "Bring Thomas, too. If he wants."

Joe lowered his voice. "He may have other ideas."

"Liddie," Littmann said. "Now."

When Liddie looked toward Littmann, the angle of the sun blinded her. She threw up her hand to block the glare, but she couldn't see his face. "I'll be right there," she called. She put a hand on Joe's arm. "I'm glad you're back."

"Just visiting."

"You know what I mean."

Joe's gaze shifted to Littmann and then back to Liddie. "I'll see you later on."

As Liddie turned to go, Joe winked at her. And when he did, her stomach tightened in a way that she could only describe as tingly.

# Chapter 32

Liddie relaxed in the darkness, lulled by the rhythmic clip-clop of the horse's hooves. On the seat in front of her, Minnie rested her head on Vern's shoulder, their forms silhouetted by the light of the waning third-quarter moon. Though Littmann had objected mightily, Liddie insisted on going out to the farm after the Wild West show. Littmann had refused Minnie's invitation to come along, acquiescing only to joining them for Sunday dinner, after which he'd bring Liddie back to town.

Wrapped in the quiet dark, Liddie let her mind drift to Joe. Nearly three years had passed since she'd last seen him. He looked the same and yet different in ways she couldn't name. Her fingers trailed along her arm. She could still feel his embrace.

Only when Minnie said, "Liddie, we're here," did she realize she'd fallen asleep. In the dark, she found her way to her old room and crawled into bed. Dreams that made no sense pestered her through the night, and she woke unsure at first where she was.

As she dressed in the shirtwaist and skirt she'd worn the day before, her gaze lingered on each piece of furniture, each crocheted doily, each small item that combined to create her childhood home. "I may never see any of this again," she whispered. By breakfast, she was almost frantic to revisit every bit of the farm before she went back to Maquoketa. She knew her anxiety was irrational—she'd be on the farm often before she left Iowa—but she could not quell the feeling of imminent loss.

———

After breakfast, Liddie walked the homestead, a journey that eventually led her to the grove where she'd spent so much time as a child. Weeds encroached. The roof on the lean-to had fallen through. Yet even in shambles, the grove gave Liddie a sense of calm she hadn't felt in a good long time. She set to picking up sticks, pulling weeds, restoring order to the disarray.

If only it were as easy to bring order to her mind, to answer the questions about her future that continued to plague her.

As she worked, the anxiety knotting her shoulders receded. When the area was tidy, she stood, breathing in the warm air. It felt so fine to be on the farm, to be home. She reached her arms above her head in a long stretch. Locking her knees, she bent over and put her palms flat on the ground. She held that position, enjoying the sense of muscles stretching along her legs, back, and arms.

"You can still do that."

Liddie jerked upright. "Joe!" She grabbed a sapling for support as the blood rushed from her head.

He stepped forward, taking her arm to steady her. "I didn't mean to scare you. Are you all right?"

"I'm fine." She shook her head to clear it. "I can't believe I'm seeing you; you should have told us you were coming."

"Didn't know I was for sure until I got on the train." He wedged his hands in his back pockets. Now she saw how he had changed. He was still slender, though he'd filled out; the muscles in his shoulders stretched against his shirt. His hazel eyes were the same, though. And his voice. The same voice she heard in his letters, though the words came slower than they used to, as if he now measured his thoughts more.

"Speaking of surprises, you put one on me." He rubbed his jaw. "Littmann's not what I expected."

"I forgot you'd never met him."

"You talked about him enough in your letters that I almost believed I had."

Liddie's cheeks flushed. What had she been thinking? Talking about one man to another. At the moment, it seemed wildly inappropriate.

"And you're getting married." He cocked an eyebrow.

"It came up suddenly. There hasn't been time to write." She shrank from the partial lie. "So. What do you think?"

Joe walked to the edge of the clearing and looked into the distance. She'd often imagined him standing that way on his porch in Canada, looking out over the fields.

"I don't expect I know Littmann well enough to make a judgment."

She knew he was hedging. "I value your opinion, Joe. Tell me."

"All right." He faced her. "I don't like it. 'The best assistant I've ever had.'" He mimicked Littmann.

"Well, I am a good assistant."

"Come on, Liddie. That's not how a man talks about the woman he loves. The first thing—the only thing—he says is what a great assistant you are?"

She flinched at the plain truth of his words. "You make him sound horrible. He's not like that all the time." Her back stiffened. "You know, you're right. You don't know him well enough to judge." She crossed her arms to hide her clenched fists.

"You asked."

"I never expected you to be mean."

"I wasn't trying to be mean. But you deserve better. I expect your pa would think so." He hesitated, then added, "I know I do."

Liddie took two deep breaths. How could they be fighting? This was not what she wanted. "I'm sorry," she offered. "I did ask. Can we start over?" She unclenched her hands, wiggling her fingers to release the tension, and smiled.

He snorted. "No, I'm sorry. Living by myself, I picked up rough edges. I was too direct." He sat down on a log, gesturing for her to sit, too, and she did. "You've grown up."

She looked at him wryly. "I guess it was bound to happen."

"I suppose." He chuckled. "It snuck up on me, though. Even the picture you sent didn't prepare me. I did appreciate those letters. I nearly wore the pages out reading them."

"I know what you mean." Liddie nodded. "It was as though you were right here talking to me."

"I came to count on getting something from you. I kept the pictures you sent on the table so I'd see you when I ate."

The image of Joe looking at her pictures during meals filled Liddie with tenderness. She hadn't known her letters meant so much to him. "I didn't show all of your letters to Mama," she admitted.

"Did I say something out of line?"

"You didn't. It's just . . . they felt like us talking, and I wouldn't tell anyone what we talked about if you were here. Why would I with you away?"

He looked off toward the fields. "Your ma kept telling me how I better get back here or all the girls would be married."

"She did?" Liddie was surprised. "Did you come back for someone?" Her stomach twisted at the idea.

"No." He stood abruptly and moved away. His shoulders rose and fell as though he were pulling something in with one breath and letting it go with the next. He turned back to her. "Forget what I said about Littmann. If you love him, then I'm happy for you, Liddie."

There it was again, the assumption of love. She pushed the thought aside. "How long will you be in Iowa?" she asked.

"A week. No more'n two." He averted his eyes and added in a tone that was flat and forced, "Sorry I'll miss the wedding."

She didn't think he sounded sorry.

"When do you go back to town?" he asked.

"Thomas is picking me up tomorrow afternoon."

"Humph."

Liddie couldn't decipher the meaning of that sound.

"We're riding over to the Gibson place this afternoon. Why don't you come along?"

Without waiting for a response, he headed for the house.

————

After dinner, Liddie helped Vern and Joe saddle the horses. She watched as Joe ran his hands over the gelding's chest, back, and flanks before saddling him. The skittish animal quieted under his touch.

An image of Joe running his hands over her arms, her back flashed in her mind. The image shocked her and she turned away, pressing her palms to her face, forcing herself to take even breaths until her heart slowed.

"It might be better if I stayed to help Minnie in the kitchen," she said when she felt calm enough to speak. "Besides, Joe, I bet Vern hoped to have some time with you."

"We'll have plenty of time," Joe said. "You're only here till tomorrow. Come with us. From what Vern's told me, this is the kind of place I've been looking for."

"Sure," Vern said. "Ride along."

Liddie agreed but wondered if it were really wise.

The farm was similar to the Treadway place—160 acres of rolling hills. Rich, black soil. Fifty acres under the plow. Fields planted to corn, oats, and alfalfa. The back forty included pasture and timber, with a creek running west to east. The renter had left without notice—not a common occurrence, but not unheard of, either.

"Gib said he'd meet us here," Vern said when they reined in their horses next to the house.

"You can see forever," Liddie exclaimed, looking in all directions before she dismounted.

"Any idea what kind of deal he wants?" Joe asked.

"I expect he'll be open to an offer. Gib's got his own farm. Can't do both."

"Looks like a fine barn. Think he'd mind if I checked it out?"

"Go ahead. I'll wait for him here."

"Come on, Liddie, let's explore," Joe said. He swung off down the hill, his strides long and purposeful.

Liddie matched his pace with ease. As they walked, Joe pointed out a fence to be mended, a pile of trash to be cleaned up. She found herself looking at a farmyard for the first time through adult eyes. This farm needed a lot of work, but she could see him warming to the task. She could imagine him walking down this hill every morning to do chores, making a mental list of tasks to be done in the coming day.

The barn looked to be sound, though it wanted care. A Dutch door opened onto an alleyway that ran the length of the barn. Bridles, the leather cracked from lack of oiling, hung by the tack room door. Past the tack room were horse stalls that hadn't been mucked out. Dust-covered pails hung from nails.

Liddie wrinkled her nose as she stepped over a pile of horse manure. "I'm used to how Papa kept our farm. How Vern still does."

Joe picked a rope up off the ground, coiling it before hanging it on a nail. "A good cleaning would take care of most of it."

At the other end of the barn, Joe opened the top of another Dutch door and leaned on the bottom half, arms folded, leaving room for her to join him. "You could see the livestock and most of the fields from right here."

Standing inches away, Liddie felt the heat from his body, smelled the soap he'd washed with that morning. She felt herself lean toward him and pulled back. Instead, she held out her hands, using her thumbs and index fingers to create a frame in front of her as though she were looking through a camera. "Don't you love the way the hills slope toward the lane? It makes me want to walk there."

"You think in pictures."

"Working with Littmann has made me more aware." She stopped. Talking about Littmann with Joe was awkward. "It would be an even better picture with cows grazing on the hills. Do you think there are cattle?"

"Probably down in the pasture. Let's check out the haymow." He headed to the ladder at the center of the barn. "You first," he offered.

"You go ahead." She demurred, embarrassed to think of him watching her from behind as she negotiated the ladder.

Joe went ahead and reached down to steady her up the last steps. It took several moments for her eyes to adjust to the dim light. Dust motes floated on shafts of sunlight streaming like golden arrows through cracks in the barn walls and piercing the darkened recesses of the loft. The mingled scents of hay and dust and livestock evoked a flood of pleasant memories.

"Watch your step." He held her arm firmly. "The boards are uneven."

"I'll be careful." Her skin pulsed where he touched her. "I haven't been in a haymow in years." She dusted her hands on her skirt. "I forgot how hot it gets."

"It is that." Joe rolled up his shirtsleeves. He picked up handfuls of hay, rubbed the stalks between his fingers, held them to his nose. "The hay he put up was good." He handed the dried alfalfa to Liddie.

She breathed in the dry, sweet smell. "I loved playing in haystacks when I was little." The idea was so appealing she plopped down in the hay and drew an armful to her face. "I can't think of anything that smells better than this."

He laughed. "It smells good, all right. But a loaf of your bread smells even better. Any chance you'll bake while I'm in Iowa?"

"Since I have to go back to town, I don't know when that would be. Besides, I haven't had much time for that since I've lived in town. Who knows how it would turn out?"

"A pity. Many's the time I thought about your bread. Cooking for myself . . ." He laughed again. "Let's just say I didn't overeat often."

"You could use some meat on those bones." She grinned, enjoying the familiar sound of his laughter. But she saw he was watching her look at him, and she flushed. She scrambled to her feet, brushing bits of hay off her skirt. "I'll try to make something for you."

"That alone would make the trip to Iowa worthwhile."

He walked to the other end of the mow and back, then pushed open a small door just big enough to throw hay out of.

Sunlight poured into the dark loft, silhouetting Joe as he stood with one hand braced on either side of the door frame. A halo of sun accentuated the leanness of his body, his strong shoulders, his slender hips.

"This is what I want," he said.

She came to stand beside him, taking in the fields laid out like a quilt top on the hillsides. "It is beautiful."

"You have hay in your hair," he said.

When she realized he was looking at her again, not at the fields, she self-consciously plucked at her hair.

"I'll get it." He stepped closer and began to untangle leaves and stalks.

As he worked, she found herself drawn to his eyes. In this light, they were more dark green than hazel. Standing so close, having him touch her with such care made it difficult for her to breathe. Littmann had never touched her so intimately.

"There. I think that's all of it," he said. After he tucked a strand of hair behind her ear, his finger lingered on her cheek.

"Thanks." That was all she could think to say.

He didn't step back and she couldn't make herself move, either. Nor, she realized, did she want to.

Voices carried up from the lower level of the barn. They both turned toward the hay chute as Vern's head poked up into the mow.

"You two up to no good?" Vern asked.

Liddie blushed and stepped back.

Joe looked at her steadily for another moment before turning his attention to Vern. "He put up some good hay," he said, and headed toward the ladder.

After they climbed down from the haymow, Liddie left the men to talk. What she'd felt when Joe touched her cheek was unlike anything she'd ever experienced before, and the sensation unsettled her. She only knew she needed to get away, so she rode home ahead of the men.

———

Back in the Treadway kitchen, Liddie threw herself into making a cobbler with blackberries Minnie had picked the week before. She brushed off Minnie's questions about why she'd come home alone with a light comment about making herself useful since the men were talking farming.

As Liddie worked, she reasoned that the feelings she had were nothing more than a foolish crush. A crush no more reciprocated now than when she was twelve. Besides, she was betrothed to Thomas. In less than three weeks, they'd be married and off to Paris.

At first, Liddie felt awkward when the men came in for supper, but the conversation was so easy her discomfort soon passed. They were all interested in hearing Joe's stories about life in Canada, and he was more than willing to share. Liddie encouraged him with questions based on things he'd told her in letters. They all stayed at the table long after they finished eating, the conversation full of jokes and interspersed with stories of life on the Canadian prairie.

"Has Canada been all you expected?" Margretta asked.

"Mostly. A man can make a living growing wheat if the weather's good."

"Mostly?"

"I miss having folks close. Talking with people every day like we're talking here." He looked around the table. "I go into town on weekends for the dances and potlucks. During the week, days go by when I don't see anyone. Just the other day, I was out in the field and scared up a flock of geese. If we saw game like that here, we'd be off hunting." He nodded to Vern.

"I figured you'd have a girl by now," Vern said.

"A few came courting me. None that struck my fancy. Never figured you'd be one to beat me to the altar, but I can see why you did." Joe turned to Minnie. "Now that was a fine meal, Mrs. Treadway," he said. "Thank you."

Minnie colored at the compliment. "Any time you're in the country, stop on by."

"The cobbler was a treat, too, Liddie." He smiled to her. "You haven't lost your touch. Now for the bread!"

"There's no time with me leaving tomorrow. I told you that."

"If you stayed for a few days, I'd be glad to turn baking over to you," Minnie offered.

"Could you?" Joe asked. "Stay?"

She hesitated. "Thomas will be here tomorrow morning. There's so much to get ready before we leave," Liddie said, though she was already mentally reworking her list to figure out how she could spend more time on the farm.

They moved to the porch and continued to talk until well past dark. It was the most relaxed, wide-ranging conversation Liddie could remember having in a long time. It was the kind of easy, give-and-take conversation she'd have with Mrs. Tinker or Minnie. It was not, she realized, the kind of conversation she ever had with Littmann.

———

The next day, Liddie found herself on edge from the moment Littmann stepped out of his auto. As they drove back to Maquoketa after dinner, she wondered if her inability to talk with Thomas was her problem or his.

He had spoken solicitously to her mother and to Minnie, engaged Joe in a discussion of the Canadian landscape, even recalled some of the points about livestock Vern had pointed out at the fair. It was she who had been uncomfortable, sitting on the edge of the conversation rather than participating. Imagining a slight. Anticipating a snide remark. Even when none came.

Now, on the drive back to Maquoketa, Littmann said, "I thought that went well."

"It did," she admitted. "Thank you."

He nodded. As though his good behavior was something she should thank him for.

"Now we can get back to business. We have the Schneider and Baker sittings tomorrow morning. I'll develop and print proofs in the afternoon." He glanced over at her. "What else is there?"

She searched in her bag for the list she'd taken to carrying with her everywhere. He relied on her to keep track of their work, and she knew he might question her at any time.

"We're waiting for proofs and orders from three families," she said. "I'll remind them they only have a couple weeks before the wedding." She peeked at him to see if he reacted to her mention of the wedding, but his face was impassive as he watched the road.

She turned to the next page. "We're caught up on billings." Just then they hit a particularly deep rut. She grabbed the seat with one hand, crumpling the list in her other hand as her stomach did a somersault. "I'm feeling a little queasy. Can we go over this when we're not moving?"

He glanced at her. "Close your eyes." They rode in silence for several minutes. He cleared his throat and she opened one eye. "You'll have to handle more motion than this on the boat," he said.

"I'm sure I'll be fine." She closed her eye again, willing her stomach to level out. As her queasiness abated, her thoughts returned to the farm. "I thought I might go home again on Wednesday and spend the rest of the week there."

"Not possible. We have too much to do."

"I need to look at the list again, but I believe I can get all caught up with two days in the studio. There's really nothing to keep me in town."

He was quiet for so long she opened her eyes again. "Please. I'm going to be away from my family for so long, I'd really like to spend time with them."

He threw her a black look. "Is this about that hired hand?"

"I have two days to get everything done, Thomas. Have I ever failed to complete an assignment?" She swiveled so she could look at him directly. "And his name is Joe Bauer."

"You are completely reliable. That's why I want you by my side. Now, if you're feeling better, let's get back to the list."

————

"It has everything you wrote about in your letters, but I thought it would be a lot bigger," Joe said when Liddie led him and Vern into the room where they did the photo sittings.

Liddie laughed. "All part of the magic." Proud to show off where she worked, Liddie pointed out the reflectors, the props, the way the windows slanted to let in the most light. "It's familiar now, but I still feel a thrill when I see photos we take in here being developed. Thomas is in the darkroom now, or I'd show you that, too."

Just as she'd predicted, she'd completed her work in two days. Littman had glowered when she said Vern and Joe were coming on Wednesday afternoon to pick her up. He'd gone into the darkroom early that afternoon and told her not to interrupt. Since he'd been out of sorts all morning, she wasn't disappointed not to have to deal with his mood.

Joe struck a distinguished pose in the high-backed chair as though he were having his photo made. "And you never came to see this?" he asked Vern.

Vern shrugged. "We had our wedding picture taken here."

"I suppose people who come for sittings don't think too much about how it all works," Liddie mused. "At first, I was afraid to get close. When Littmann let me look through the camera, it was like a different world." She went to the camera, leaned down, and peered through the viewfinder, remembering how hesitant she'd been that day.

"Come." She motioned to Joe. "Vern, you sit there, so Joe can see how it appears through the camera. Then we'll switch so you can see."

She posed Vern in the chair, positioning his head, arms, and hands. She stepped back to consider the effect, then had him cross his legs. "There. That's right," she said.

"We're not taking a photo, are we?" Vern asked.

"No. It's just for fun. Look now," she said to Joe.

"Is it supposed to be upside down?" he asked.

"It takes a little getting used to." She smiled.

"What are you doing?"

Liddie jerked at the strident tone of Littmann's voice. She stepped back from the camera as though she'd been caught doing something wrong. "Nothing," she said. "I mean, I was showing them the camera."

"This is expensive equipment. It's not a toy." Littmann glared at her. "You should know better."

Liddie was stunned by his tone, humiliated to be chastised in front of Vern and Joe. She struggled for a response. "I wanted them to see how we make the photos." She corrected herself. "How *you* make the photos."

"You don't even know what damage you could do." Littmann brushed past Joe and made a show of examining the camera.

"No one touched the camera," Liddie said. "I'm sorry if we interrupted you. I wanted them to see where I work."

He frowned. "I heard noise. You can understand why I'd be concerned."

His comment was disingenuous. He knew she was in the studio. She seethed at his rudeness but steeled herself to act as though everything were all right. "Would it be convenient to let them see the darkroom, too?"

"Since I've already had to stop, they may as well. Come this way." He headed down the hallway without waiting to see if they followed.

Liddie was grateful when they left the studio.

———

The first thing she did after breakfast Thursday morning was mix up a batch of bread. She easily fell back into the rhythm of kneading the dough. She found the feel of the dough taking shape under her hands deeply comforting. It surprised her how much she missed this simple task.

Vern and Joe had gone fishing that morning, and Minnie didn't expect them back until dinner. But as the yeasty smell of baking bread filled the air, the men showed up on the porch.

"I think he could smell bread a mile away," Vern said.

"I expect I could," Joe agreed, settling down at the kitchen table. "How soon until it comes out?"

"Another five minutes should do it," Liddie said. She set out a butter crock and a jam jar, then sat down across the table from him. "So what do you think about Gib's farm?"

"It's a good place, all right. Did you see what there was for equipment, Vern?"

"Didn't note it."

"That's another reason to go back over."

As they talked, Liddie took the bread out of the oven; the crust of each loaf was golden brown. When she tapped the pans on the breadboard, popping the loaves out on their sides to cool, Joe came to stand at her elbow.

"Smell that! I'm in heaven, Liddie." He licked his lips in anticipation.

She cut thick slices off each end of a loaf, then handed him both heels. She grinned as he bounced the hot slices in his hands.

"You going to leave any for me?" Vern asked.

"You men sure know how to make a woman feel good." Liddie laughed. She cut a half-dozen slices and brought them to the table.

Joe buttered both heels and spread them with jam. When Liddie sat down, he handed one heel back to her.

"Don't you want it?" she asked.

"I'll share the best with the girl who gave me the best." He winked at her.

Liddie ducked her head to hide the color she knew was rising on her cheeks.

——

"I thought Vern was coming with us," Liddie said as she and Joe rode over to Gib's farm on Friday.

"He's hunting down a sow that's ready to farrow. It's Gib I need to talk to, anyway."

Liddie accepted the explanation without another thought. When sows were ready to give birth, they often went off by themselves, and farmers had to search out their well-hidden nests.

"I don't see Gib yet," Joe said when they dismounted in the farmyard. He tied the reins of their horses to the hitching post.

"Look there." She pointed at two trees near the house with their branches drooping under the weight of mature pears. The ground beneath the trees was dotted with ripe yellow fruit. "It's a shame letting things go to waste. If Gib doesn't mind, I'll take some home with us."

"You can get them later. Let's go down to the barn. There's something I want to show you."

Liddie's heart beat faster as she recalled the last time they were in the barn. "What is it?"

"Something I found after you left."

"Don't we have to wait for Gib?"

"He'll find us." He strode toward the barn, his gait as assured as if this were already his place.

Curious, Liddie followed along. Once they were in the barn, Joe led her to the ladder and up to the haymow. Again, he steadied her as she stepped off the ladder. Again, her skin responded to his touch. He went to the small door on the south wall, opened it wide, and stood silently, looking out.

Stepping up next to him, she scanned the fields, but she couldn't see anything different. "What is it? What am I supposed to see?"

Finally, he spoke. "Liddie, could you live here?"

"What do you mean?"

"A farm like this is what I've always wanted. But it isn't just the land." He faced her and took her hands in his.

Immediately, her heart was in her throat.

"I didn't know it when I left Canada, but when I saw you at the fair, and being with you this week . . . I realized I came back to Iowa for you."

Her heart pounded. She looked down at their hands—his tanned and work toughened, hers white and soft. Her knees suddenly felt too weak to hold her upright.

"I love you, Liddie." His words drew her eyes up to his. "Could you be happy here? With me?"

His questions hung in the air. She knew what her answer was. She knew what she wanted. But she was engaged. She could not say yes to two men.

"Oh, Joe . . ." The loft air was too thick. "I . . . Littmann . . . Europe . . ."

"I can't give you Europe. But I love you, and I promise I will make you happy. Will you marry me?" Joe's tone conveyed humility and confidence, yearning and commitment.

Emotions flooded her mind—surprise, confusion, delight, dread—and her heart. "Joe, I . . ."

"Hello! Anybody here?" Gib's voice rose up to the mow.

"In the mow, Gib," Joe called. "On our way down." Joe looked at Liddie, waiting. When she didn't respond, disappointment flashed in his eyes. He squeezed her hands before letting them go.

———

The disappointment she'd seen in Joe's eyes distressed her. Had he seen the turmoil on her face and thought it to be rejection? She set to picking ripe pears from the tree and the least bruised ones off the ground. Picking pears had been a reasonable excuse for leaving the men to talk, and the effort gave her time to sort through her emotions. When the bucket was full, she sat on the slope north of the house, out of sight of the barn, looking to the familiar Iowa hills for an answer.

All her life, she'd wanted off the farm. All her life, she'd said she'd never marry a farmer. All her life, she'd wanted a career and adventure. And yet here she was, ready to throw away everything she'd ever thought she wanted to grab hold of something she'd been certain she didn't want. She looked up at the wide-open summer sky and laughed. The irony was inescapable.

Remembering the warmth of Joe's hands holding hers, the sound of him saying *I love you, Liddie* sent tremors of delight from her toes to her fingertips. At that moment, she knew without a doubt she wanted more than what Littmann offered.

She buried her face in her hands. Littmann. She'd said yes to his proposal. If she walked away, people would think she was a fool. Even worse, people would think she was like the woman who jilted Joe. While Liddie quailed at being compared to Catherine, she also felt empathy for her. Except Liddie was worse—Catherine had never said yes to Joe.

# Chapter 33

By the time they left the Gibson farm, Joe's decision to stay in Iowa was made. How he would dispose of his horses, equipment, and crops in Canada was yet to be worked out. But he and Gib had shaken hands.

During the ride back to the Treadway place, Joe repeatedly reined his horse close to Liddie's mare. Once, he drew her attention to a meadowlark on a fence; another time, he asked her opinion about the farmhouse kitchen.

She felt him looking at her, knew he waited on her answer. But as much as Liddie wanted to respond to Joe's attention, she avoided meeting his gaze. Each time she thought of looking into his hazel eyes, she felt Littmann's accusing brown eyes staring back.

When they were near the Treadway farm, Joe reached over and grabbed her horse's bridle, bringing both horses to a stop. "Liddie. Look at me. You can't ignore me."

"I'm sorry, Joe." She looked at him for only a moment before lowering her eyes to focus on the pail of pears hooked over her saddle horn. "I never expected you to propose, and I need time to think."

"You have feelings for me. I know you do."

"I don't deny it." She felt herself blushing.

"That's what I needed to hear." Joe released his grip on the bridle and reached over, grazing her cheek with his fingers.

She tilted her head, savoring the feel of his hand. Then she recovered her senses and shook her head. "But I'm engaged to Thomas. I can't deny that, either." She looked off into the distance. "I need to talk to him." She kicked her horse into a trot.

When they rode up to the Treadway farmstead, Littmann stood waiting in front of the house. Overcome by vertigo, Liddie gripped the saddle horn. Seeing him leaning with studied casualness against the fender of his motorcar, his tan fedora set at a confident angle, sent a wave of panic through her. She reined in her horse.

Joe followed her gaze, then turned again to look at her, uncertainty in his eyes.

She held his eyes for a long moment but didn't speak. Then she turned toward Littman, forced a smile to her lips, and nudged her horse forward with her heels.

"Thomas! You're here," she called out cheerfully, attempting to cover her discomfiture. "Look what I have." She handed him the bucket of pears. "Minnie asked me to make dessert." She spoke too brightly.

"I expected you to be here when I arrived. It's nearly dinnertime."

"Is it so late? I didn't realize."

He set the bucket on the ground and reached up, grasping her waist, then guided her as she stepped down from the stirrup.

Distressed at the thought of Joe watching them, Liddie slipped out of Littmann's hands and picked up the pears. "I've got to get a dessert in the oven. Thomas, will you put my horse up for me?"

"I'm not dressed for barn work," he said. "Joe will handle it."

Liddie sucked in her breath. He didn't ask; he assumed. It was the condescending way he spoke to waitresses and clerks. Shame sent blood pounding through her temples. "Never mind." She forced a stiff smile. "I should have realized. I'll do it myself."

Joe reached for the reins, letting his hand cover hers. "I'm happy to do it for you, Liddie."

"Thank you." Looking at Joe directly, she thanked him with her eyes as well as her words. She knew Joe felt her gratitude; she wished Littmann felt her shame.

It was unbearable. She could not stay with Joe and did not want to stay with Littmann. She sought refuge in the house. "I'll be making dessert," she said, and turned away.

"I won't be long in the barn. Want to come along?" Joe asked Littmann. "To watch." He spoke with thinly veiled mockery.

"I need to talk with Liddie," Littmann said. He called after her.

She glanced back. "Something's come up?" She kept her voice neutral, though her heart raced. She really didn't want to speak to him now. Maybe on the way to town. Or tomorrow. When she calmed down.

"I only said that to get some time alone with you." He took her elbow and steered her away from the house. "You've spent days with your family. I'd think you'd want to spend a little time with me."

"I can't right now. Minnie expects . . ." She stopped in the middle of her excuse. If she put him off, what would that solve?

The late-afternoon sun cast golden light through a nearby ash tree, creating a lacy web of shadows on the ground. A single bee buzzed past her shoulder and down by her hand, attracted by the ripening pears. She looked toward the barn. That's where she wanted to be, with Joe. She dropped her eyes to watch the bee. She fluttered her fingers gently, hoping to make it go away without angering it.

"All right. Over there." She gestured to a bench under the ash tree. This man had proposed, and she'd said yes. She owed him honesty. She owed herself that, too.

As they sat on the bench, she tried to think of what to say and how to say it. She felt as though she were balancing on the top rail of a fence, one man on either side, one life on either side.

"You're going to be glad to get out of here, aren't you?" Littmann's words broke into her thoughts. He removed his hat and set it beside him on the bench.

"What?"

"Think of where we'll be in another month. New York. Then Paris. You'll have left the sticks behind."

She stared at him. He was entirely serious. And she was appalled. He knew nothing about her. "No." She was getting off this wagon, here and now. "No, Thomas. I can't marry you." There. She'd said it.

Surprise registered on his face. "But Liddie, your mother will never let you go to Europe if we're not married."

She stifled a groan. "I'm not going to Europe, either."

A frown creased his forehead. "You said you wanted . . ."

She clasped her hands tightly in her lap, holding on to her resolve. "Until I came home this week, I thought so, too. I did. Working with you, learning about photography. When you laid out your plans for us to go to Europe, I saw everything I'd ever thought I wanted in life right there, waiting for me to say yes. And so I did. I said yes."

"You can have that. Even more," he said. "You said you loved me. Were you playing games?"

In fact, Liddie was not certain she had said she loved him. Those hours after he proposed were so fuzzy in her mind. But how could she argue? "When you said you loved me, I was swept away. I thought I should love you . . ." Her voice trailed off. She felt horrid.

"What do you propose to do instead? Go back to sewing? Go back to a farm?"

The disdain in Littmann's voice hit Liddie like a slap across the face.

"I'm giving you a chance to make something of yourself. Why throw that away? With me, you could be something. Here? You're wasted."

Wasted? Liddie fought back the angry words crowding her throat. She had never told him how much it bothered her that he dismissed her sewing, the farm, her family, even her. She had barely admitted it to herself. Instead, she made excuses. She could retaliate now, but she knew with absolute certainty that it would make no difference at all to him.

She set her shoulders. "We're different," she said. "I don't think I realized until now how different." She put her hand on his. She looked into the gold-flecked brown eyes she'd found so appealing. "You've been important to me, Thomas. You've taught me to see my own life—the farm, my family, the way I was raised—differently. Because of you, I value it more. I'm grateful to you for that."

"We're a good team, Liddie." He repeated the phrase she'd heard so often. "We've done good work here, and we can do more in Europe. Think about it. I know you'll change your mind."

"No." She shook her head. "I won't."

"You will." He stroked his chin with well-manicured fingers, looking at her, calculating. "You want to be with me; it's what you've wanted since the night we met."

He leaned in as though to kiss her. Liddie dipped away, but he caught her shoulders and forced his lips to hers in a rough kiss.

"Stop it, Thomas," she hissed, shoving hard against his chest. "Stop it." He let go and she jumped to her feet, glaring at him.

"You're making a big mistake, Liddie." Littmann made a show of picking up his hat as he stood, settling it on his head at the same confident angle. "You're throwing away your future."

"Going with you would be the mistake. I want more in my life." And this time, she knew what "more" meant.

———

Liddie met Vern on the porch when he came in from the barn. "Where's Joe?"

"Don't know." Vern shook his head. "It was the damnedest thing. He was all het up talking about the farm, coming back to Iowa. Took off for the house and not five minutes later was back, mood blacker'n a thundercloud."

"Why?"

"Didn't say. He took the horse and rode west. Didn't even saddle him up. Figured he mighta got into it with Littmann." Vern looked around. "Where is Mr. Littmann, anyway?"

"He's gone."

"Then what are you doing here? Thought you and him was gonna have supper and go back to town."

She wet her lips as she gathered courage to say the words. "I told him I couldn't marry him," she said. Then she braced for his criticism.

For some reason, telling her brother she'd called off her wedding was harder than telling Minnie and her mother. As soon as Littmann had left, Liddie had squared her shoulders and gone to the house. Upon hearing the news, both women stared at her for what felt like an eternity—but in reality was only a second or two. Minnie said, "You're making my head spin, Liddie." Then she added with concern, "Are you all right?" Her mother had hugged her and said, "I'm sure this is for the best."

Vern's reaction was immediate and unexpected.

"Well, hot damn," he said.

She drew back, surprised. "You're happy I'm not getting married?"

"I'm glad you're not marrying *him*."

"You never said anything before."

"When you get your head set on something, you're hard to talk to." Vern took out his pocketknife and scraped dirt from under his nails. "Nope. I didn't see you being happy with him."

"You were worried I wouldn't be happy?"

"You're my sister. Of course I care if you're happy."

Liddie thought she might cry.

"Why'd you change your mind?" he asked.

She looked off toward the barn. "I guess it was seeing Joe again."

"Huh. So that's it." Vern closed the pocketknife and put it back in his pocket.

"That's what?"

"Something Joe said when he rode off. Something about how a man shouldn't be so wrong twice."

With a sickening thud in her stomach, Liddie realized Joe must have seen her and Littmann. Seen them and totally misunderstood. Cords of anxiety tightened in her chest. "Oh, Vern. I have to talk with him."

"He'll come back once he's worked it out. He always does."

———

Liddie was surprised to feel such relief that Littmann and Europe were out of the picture. How could she so easily have done something that would have been so wrong? At the same time, anxiety flared up with each thought of Joe. When would he return?

After supper, they all sat on the porch chatting, as fireflies flickered in the growing darkness.

Before long, Margretta said, "I'll leave you young folk to talk." She took her cane and pushed up from the rocker, favoring her right foot.

"You need help, Ma?" Vern asked.

"I'll be fine," she said. "'Night, all."

"Her gout seems worse," Liddie said when her mother was out of earshot.

"It comes and goes. It flared up again last week," Minnie said. "I try to get her to take aspirin. She says chewing willow bark works as well."

Vern snorted.

"Now, Vern." Minnie shushed him.

"What?" Liddie asked.

"Ma liked to bit Minnie's head off for bringing up aspirin."

"But you get along so well," Liddie exclaimed.

"When you're home, yeah. When you're not here"—he nodded sharply toward the door—"Minnie can't do anything right."

"Enough of that," Minnie said. "Pain wears on anyone."

They lapsed into silence, but Liddie vowed to talk to Minnie later. Even though it was too dark to see, she looked out to the fields, wondering where Joe was, when he'd return.

Vern yawned. "Morning's gonna be here before you know it." He stood and stretched. "You coming?"

"I won't be much longer." Minnie touched his hand as he passed. "Are you all right, Liddie?" she asked when the two women were alone.

"Surprisingly so." Liddie nodded.

"Why did you change your mind?"

Liddie guessed that was the question of the day. "I think I finally saw some things clearly."

"I expect Joe coming back helped?"

Liddie peered into the darkness. "I wish he'd come home."

"I'm sure he will." Minnie looked up at the night sky, which was lit by a sliver of moon. "I'm going to bed. You?"

"No. I'll wait. It's nice here in the dark. Peaceful."

———

Even in the waning moonlight, Liddie saw Joe walking toward the house. She stood as he neared the porch.

"What are you doing here?" he asked, his voice weary.

"Waiting for you."

"I thought you'd be gone."

"He left. I stayed."

"I'll be going back to Canada in the morning."

"But Joe, what about the farm? What about . . . us?"

Joe's laugh was harsh "Us? There's no 'us.' I saw the two of you. I was a fool once. I can't believe I fell for it again."

"I was afraid that's why you left." She stepped down from the porch, wanting to be closer to him, wishing she could see his face. "That kiss meant nothing!"

"Kissing him was nothing? Is that what you learned living in town?"

"He kissed me, Joe. I didn't kiss him."

"It looked the same to me."

Liddie could have argued, but that wasn't the point. She said, "I told him I couldn't marry him."

"You told him that? Why?"

"Because I said yes for the wrong reasons."

"At least I kept you from one mistake. He wasn't right for you, and I'm not sorry you're not marrying him."

"Joe, stop being an idiot." She put her hands on his shoulders and stepped so close she could make out the contours of his face, feel his breath. "I told him those things because I made a mistake when I said I'd marry him. I told him no because you made me want more than a way to see the world. You made me want a life with someone I know I love. A life with you."

"You'd give up Europe for me?"

"I would. I have. If you still want me."

"You're sure you're not deciding too fast?"

Her tone registered disbelief as she backed a half step away. "Are you trying to talk me out of it?"

"I want you to be sure."

She stood her ground. "I'm sure."

Joe took her face between his hands, drew her close, and kissed her.

Tension drained away as she felt her body melt against his, and she kissed him back.

Yes. She was absolutely sure.

# Chapter 34

A rooster's crow woke Liddie from the most restful sleep she'd had in weeks. She opened one eye wide enough to see sunlight streaming in her bedroom window. The mingled smells of coffee and bacon hung in the air, overshadowed by the aroma of a pot roast. Her stomach growled. Breakfast had come and gone; dinner was in the making.

Stretching her arms above her head and flexing her ankles and toes, she eased herself fully awake. Memories of the previous night flooded in, bringing a smile to her face. She held up both hands and examined them. She could see nothing, yet she felt his touch as surely as if he were right there, right now.

She'd sat on the front steps with Joe until nearly midnight. After that first kiss, he'd kissed her again. On the cheek. On the back and palm of each hand. Again on the lips. Each kiss was soft and gentle; his lips lingered on her skin for precious seconds. Each of those kisses felt to Liddie like a promise fulfilled. They felt like certainty.

They talked and laughed. Even when they fell silent, it was as though they were still whispering to each other. By the time they parted—she to her childhood bedroom, he to the bedroom at the far end of the hall—they'd worked out a plan. After telling her family at dinner, they'd go to Maquoketa. While he wired a neighbor in Canada, she would tend to her responsibilities at the studio and visit Mrs. Tinker.

With a last luxuriating stretch, she threw back the sheet and got up. She dressed, wondering all the while what it would be like to see Joe in the light of day.

"Look who's finally up," Minnie said when Liddie made it to the kitchen. Minnie slid the Dutch oven back into the cookstove and closed the door. She wiped perspiration from her forehead with her apron.

"Morning, Minnie. Morning, Mama. How's your foot?"

"Not so bad. As long as I keep it up."

Liddie glanced at the stove. "Is there coffee?"

"Always." Minnie handed her a cup.

Liddie took her coffee to the table. "What are you making, Mama?"

"Pear crisp. Minnie thought since it's so hot we could have berry sauce for dessert. I said we have company, we'll do something special."

"Mama's right," Minnie said. The tight cheerfulness in her tone suggested she gave in regularly in discussions like this.

Liddie suspected this was the kind of tension Vern had mentioned. "Either is nice," she said neutrally.

Margretta scrutinized Liddie over the top of her glasses. "You were up late last night."

"Mmm. It was nice listening to the dark." She sipped at the coffee and changed the subject. "Minnie, you look flushed. Sit down a minute."

"I've got the last load of laundry to hang out," she replied. "Then I'll sit with you."

"You've already done laundry? If you had woken me, I'd have helped."

"I peeked in when we had breakfast on the table. You were dead to the world."

"At least I'll help you get it on the line." She followed Minnie out to the clothesline.

———

Joe came to the dinner table at noon in a white dress shirt with his long dark hair neatly combed. The sight of him sent blood rushing to Liddie's cheeks, and she longed to touch him.

"My, don't you look handsome," Minnie said as she set a platter heaped with roast beef and a bowl of boiled potatoes on the table.

Vern hooted. "That the way they dress for dinner up north?"

"I'm going into town this afternoon." He shrugged off Vern's jesting. "Liddie needs to go, so I'll take her."

Liddie caught Joe's eye. When he winked, she brushed her lips with her fingertips and smiled. It pleased her that he dressed up for this meal.

"It's good to have the table full. Like it used to be," Margretta said. "That reminds me. We got a letter from Ohio."

"Aunt Kate?" Liddie asked. "What did she have to say?"

"She still likes her job." Margretta tsked. "I suppose it's a foolish hope, but I keep thinking she'll change her mind and come back." She looked at Joe. "Glad you finally got some sense in your head!"

Joe looked at Liddie. She nodded. He cleared his throat. "I am happy to be at this table again," he began, his voice husky. "I've always felt welcome here." He paused. "I'm glad I had a chance to try Canada, but it feels right to be back in Iowa."

"'Bout time," Vern interrupted.

"Margretta, you campaigned for an Iowa girl," Joe said. "And an Iowa girl is the reason I'm here—and never leaving again." He stood and came to help Liddie slide her chair back. He took her hand as she stood beside him.

"I'm doing this backward, but this is how it worked." He looked from Margretta to Vern. "I asked Liddie to be my wife."

Liddie smiled at him. "And I said yes."

Margretta waggled a finger at Liddie. "I thought there was something."

Joe knelt by Margretta's chair. "I hope you'll give us your blessing."

"Of course. Of course." She held his face between her hands and kissed his forehead.

Minnie rushed to hug Liddie. "You sneak! You never said a word!"

"Well, all right." Vern shook Joe's hand like he was pumping water.

When Liddie bent to hug her mother, Margretta whispered, "You did good, honey."

Surrounded by her family, with Joe by her side, Liddie realized she did know what love was.

———

Liddie hummed as she laid out slices of bread, then spread butter and horseradish on each piece to put in the picnic basket for her and Joe to take to Maquoketa. Minnie hadn't stopped grinning at her since dinner. It felt good to have Minnie's approval. And with Minnie's baby coming, she had another reason to be happy she was staying in Iowa.

"Six cookies enough?" Minnie opened the tin.

"Plenty."

"Take a dozen. Joe could use some meat on his bones."

"You've picked up Mama's ways." Liddie chuckled as she piled slices of cold roast beef on the bread. "On that point . . ." She lowered her voice. "How are things with you two? Vern made it sound as though Mama pushes you pretty hard."

"He looks out for me, but Mama and I work it out. This has been her home for so long."

"It's your home, too."

"Yes. It is. She knows that, but it's hard to let go of what you've always done."

"I suppose." She set to wrapping the sandwiches in paper. "So what do you think, Minnie? Am I foolish to give up on what I said I always wanted?"

"It's more important what *you* think."

Liddie pursed her lips, collecting her thoughts. With the sandwiches stacked in the basket, she dusted off her hands. "I'd have had adventures in Europe. I expect I'll always wonder what that would have been like. But even before Joe showed up, I realized how often I made excuses for Littmann. I imagined making excuses the rest of my life." Liddie chewed on the side of her lip. "It made my mouth sour."

As she continued, her eyes twinkled. "When I saw Joe at the fair, when we talked, last night . . ." Liddie savored the memory. "When he kissed me . . . it was like we'd been together forever. And should be. Joe . . ." She stopped, rolling his name around in her mouth, enjoying the sound and the feel and the taste. *Yes*, she decided, it was possible to taste a name. "Joe loves me. I love him. Whatever we do together will be an adventure."

———

"I'm going in with you," Joe told Liddie when he brought the buggy to a stop across the street from the photography studio.

"I need to do this myself." She spoke evenly.

They'd been back and forth on this point throughout the ride into town. Joe saw no reason for her to go back to the studio at all. She disagreed. Though she did not look forward to seeing Littmann, she felt obligated to resign the job in person at the least, and beyond that, to finish out the job if he wanted her to.

In an odd twist of emotions, Liddie felt responsible for Littmann. She imagined he would be overwhelmed trying to close the studio and get things ready for Europe by himself. Joe didn't believe that was her responsibility.

"I don't trust him," Joe finally admitted.

"You don't trust him? Or you don't trust me?" She caught her breath at the boldness of the question.

Joe's voice cracked. "I wouldn't trust myself in his position. If he loves you even close to the way I do, he'll try to get you back."

"Oh, Joe," Liddie whispered. If they had not been sitting on Main Street in an open buggy in broad daylight, she would have kissed him. Instead, she put her hand on his. "You needn't worry. Mr. Littmann has never been anything but proper. I cannot imagine he will change today."

"He can make Paris and cars and travel damned appealing."

"None of that appeals to me as much as you do."

He searched her face. "All right, then." He jumped down from the buggy and helped her down. "I'll be waiting for you here in an hour."

———

Littmann sat tilted back in his chair, his feet on the desk, a newspaper open on his lap. When he saw her, a look of satisfaction crossed his face. "You changed your mind. I knew you couldn't leave this."

She flushed as she set her shoulders. "No." She gulped, her mouth as dry as stale bread. "No," she repeated more firmly. "I came back about my job."

He leaned forward, the chair legs hitting the floor with a thud. "You think you still have a job?"

She gripped her handbag with both hands. "I don't presume that I do. But you gave me . . ." She started to say how much the job had meant to her, but she'd said it before.

She started again. "I didn't want to just not show up. That wouldn't be right." Having said that, she relaxed a fraction. "Also, I need to get my things." She gestured toward her photos, including the two pictures she'd taken of Vern and Minnie's wedding that were displayed in the studio window.

Littmann pierced her with a look that erased the ease she'd begun to feel. With a mirthless laugh, he waved her toward the display window and went back to reading.

After she removed her pictures, Liddie rearranged the remaining photographs to create a finished display. "I'll check this from the sidewalk, but I think the arrangement . . ." Her words caught in her throat when she turned and bumped into Littmann, who was standing inches away.

"Was it marriage that threw you off?" he asked. "You have been both assistant and colleague to me. And still could be."

Liddie met his gaze and did not back away. She felt no ambiguity in her feelings toward him. "I'm here to finish up any work you need me to do."

He returned to the chair, picked up the newspaper, and spoke as he opened it. "You're done here. It will be easy enough to find a girl to take your place."

The comment was so reminiscent of his dismissal of her work for Mrs. Tinker. She felt her cheeks flush, but she swallowed and tilted her chin up. "I'll be going, then," she said.

She had opened the door and was halfway out when he said, "You have backbone, Liddie. I'll give you that."

"Good-bye, Mr. Littmann."

———

"I must say, I did not expect this!" Mrs. Tinker said.

"It was sudden," Liddie admitted.

"Indeed. A second very sudden decision about marriage. In an exceedingly short period of time." Mrs. Tinker looked thoughtful as she poured tea. "You've mentioned Joe from time to time but didn't really tell me anything about him. He shows up after being gone for three years and sweeps you off your feet. He must be quite the fellow!"

"He is." Liddie responded without hesitation. Her mind returned to how she'd thrilled to his touch as they sat on the porch in the dark, how her body melted into his when he wrapped her in his arms, how she'd known without doubt that he was her future. "We can talk about everything. I can see us talking together forever." She traced the handle of her teacup. "I had questions about Mr. Littmann even if I didn't admit them. I don't wonder about Joe. Not at all."

She paused, reveling in the exuberance that saying those words sent through her chest. "I expect many will think my choice is . . ." She searched again for a way to describe it.

"Outlandish?" Mrs. Tinker offered.

"Yes, *outlandish*." She laughed. "But they don't really know us. Joe and I talk the same language. When he looks at me. When he touches me. I know."

"Know?"

Liddie smiled. "That I've always loved him."

"Talking can get you through a lot," Mrs. Tinker acknowledged. "But I am curious. Why marriage at all? You were content with sewing and photography. Before Mr. Littmann brought it up, marriage seemed the furthest thing from your mind. Why not walk away from both man and marriage? Why jump right into another man's arms?"

Legitimate questions, Liddie knew. And she had no logical answers to give. "Did you ever just know something was right?" she asked.

"Sometimes, things do seem right. But there are often several right paths. Each one different, but each one right in its own way." Mrs. Tinker shook her head emphatically. "Tsk. I'm lecturing again. I must stop that. Your work as a seamstress will come in handy in your married life. And photography? You may find reasons to pick up a camera again, too."

"Oh, I hope so."

"Be determined, and it will happen. I guess you won't be needing introductions in Paris now, will you?"

There was humor in Mrs. Tinker's voice, but Liddie felt a pang of regret. "Oh, Mrs. Tinker. I feel as though I've let you down."

"My dear, you have not let *me* down. My life is mine to live. Your life is yours to live. I only worry that you're acting hastily in giving up both sewing and photography, work I know you love." She looked across the room to Liddie's almost-finished wedding dress, which hung on a form positioned between the sewing machines. The women had poured their combined creativity and love of craft into that dress.

"What do you think about it now?" Mrs. Tinker asked.

"I still love it." Liddie set her teacup in its saucer and went to the dress. "I wonder what Joe will think?"

"Joe will think you are beautiful no matter what you wear."

As they chatted, Liddie realized that she felt certain of many things. One was that she would miss her days with Mrs. Tinker.

# Chapter 35

Liddie stood hidden from sight in the hallway at the top of the stairs. She'd come down these same stairs all her life, as a child and young woman. This would be the last time she'd take these steps as Liddie Treadway. When Ida Mae played the wedding march, she would descend, but for now all she could do was wait. She could hear the voices of her family and friends filling the parlor, but she couldn't see anyone, not even Joe, who was supposed to be at the bottom of the stairs ready to meet her.

For perhaps the fifteenth time, she smoothed the ivory satin at the waist of her dress. A nervous gesture since the dress fit perfectly. This was the most beautiful dress she'd ever owned, the most beautiful dress she'd ever made.

For the past several weeks, ever since Littmann had left for Europe, her mind had focused completely on this new path she had chosen to walk. She never doubted her desire to be with Joe. But she knew she was leaving the track to a career and adventure to do so.

A frisson of fear pulsed in her neck. What if she did regret giving up photography? What if Joe wasn't at the bottom of the stairs? What if he didn't really love her?

Then the music began and the voices stilled. She took a deep, calming breath and smiled. She did not want to change her mind. She touched the banister and began to descend. After only two steps, she saw Joe looking up at her.

When her eyes met his, he held out his hand. She could see the love in his eyes and knew that all was well. She held out her hand and went to him.

———

Liddie observed that the happy moments in her life lingered in her memory, the details softened by time and illuminated with an afterglow of general pleasure. Traumatic moments, however, etched in her subconscious like wounds that heal but leave scars, ensuring she would never forget. She'd remember her wedding night that latter way.

Though she'd grown up on a farm, her father had shielded her from the business of animals mating, and her mother had told her nothing at all. As her wedding night had drawn near, Liddie was too embarrassed to ask. What she knew for certain was that whatever happened between men and women resulted in babies. Memories of the night Papa learned about Amelia's pregnancy returned. The speed with which her own wedding was happening would surely cause people to wonder if she, too, was pregnant. She remembered her vow never to repeat the hurt Amelia caused their family. Liddie had wanted to bring this up with Joe, but she had not figured out a way.

After the wedding guests were gone, Joe took Liddie's hand and led her toward the stairs. They would spend this night in her childhood home. The following day, they would board the train for a honeymoon trip to visit Amelia. When they returned, they would move into the house on the Gibson farm. But tonight, tonight was their wedding night.

Upstairs, he led her down the hall. With every step, her anxiety built.

Yet inside the room, when he reached for her, she went willingly into the warm circle of his arms. As they kissed, she smelled the musk of his sweat, tasted salt on his lips. Blood rushed to her stomach. Her knees quivered. Only when the back of her legs touched the edge of the bed did she realize they'd moved. She tensed. He drew back enough to see her face. In that moment, she slipped away from him.

"I can't do this," she said, one hand on the bureau to steady herself.

"Can't do what?"

She shifted her gaze from him to the bed. "I can't."

He stepped toward her. "I'd never hurt you, Liddie."

She inched away, her lower lip quivering, her face burning with embarrassment. "You know what people will say, don't you?"

"Who cares what people say? We're married."

"I do," Liddie whimpered. "I won't have anyone thinking I had to get married." In her mind, that explained it all.

"How in the world could anyone even think that?" Joe asked, bewildered. "I wasn't even in the st—" His face shaded red. He grabbed the footboard. "Did you?"

The anger in his voice jolted Liddie. "Did I what?" she asked.

"Did you?" The knuckles of Joe's hand were white. "With *him*?"

*With him?* Him! Liddie blanched. Did he really think she had done . . . *that* . . . with Littmann? "No! How could you think that?"

His eyes flashed. "Did you?"

"I said no. The answer is *no!*"

*"Gott im Himmel."* Joe glared at her, his voice filled with frustration. "Then I don't understand."

Liddie had barely thought of Littmann since he had left for Europe. It never crossed her mind that Joe might think she'd done something like that. She had been thinking only of Amelia. She stumbled to the rocker and sank down, doubling over, her arms wrapped around her waist.

"I don't want Mama to think I did what Amelia did. I never thought people might think . . . that you might think . . .

that . . . about me and him." She buried her face in her hands and sobbed, her tears creating ugly dark splotches on the satin dress.

Joe crouched in front of her and pulled her hands away from her face. "Liddie. Look at me," he said.

She refused to look up, knowing her blotchy, tear-streaked face was awful to look at.

"*Liebchen*. Darling, look at me." He used his thumb to wipe the tears from under her eyes. "I forgot about Amelia."

"You forgot?"

"It was a long time ago."

"Not to me." She hiccuped through another sob. "I've ruined our wedding night, haven't I?"

"It's not how I thought things would be." He lifted her from the rocker and sat with her on his lap. Holding her close, he rocked in silence until her body relaxed and she nestled her head on his shoulder, her forehead warm against his neck. "Now," he said. "Talk to me, *Liebchen*."

"I think we should wait six weeks."

"Six weeks!"

He tensed, and she thought he might dump her on the floor. She told him about what the neighbor women had said at one of the sewing bees, about babies taking nine months. Except the first one. The first one could come any time. They laughed, but their laughs sounded odd, even mean.

"I'll make it up to you," Liddie promised. "I'll make fresh bread or a pie. Every day."

"A pie?" He was astonished. "A *pie*? What the hell?"

Liddie recoiled, then caught the familiar twinkle in his eyes. She touched his lips with the tip of her finger. "You needn't swear."

"I may take it up." He began rocking again. "It better be a damned good pie."

Liddie heard a laugh concealed behind the gruff tone. She put her head back on his shoulder and brought her hand up to caress his cheek. "You'll love it."

———

As she stepped down from the train, Liddie searched the platform for her sister. The three years since Amelia had left Iowa felt like a lifetime.

"Maybe she didn't get our wire," she said. An anxious frown creased her forehead. "Maybe she won't be here."

For the third time since they had boarded the train in Cheyenne, Joe reassured her. "If she's not here, we'll hire a buggy."

"Liddie! Liddie! Over here!"

Liddie recognized the voice, but not the woman waving at her. A black wool coat did little to conceal the woman's advanced pregnancy; a faded blue bonnet shaded her face. Against her shoulder, she cradled a blanket-wrapped bundle; another child clung to the pocket of her coat.

"Liddie, it's me!" The woman waved vigorously. "I'm here!"

"Amelia?" Liddie couldn't believe this woman was her sister. She looked far too old. Liddie dropped Joe's hand and threaded her way through the crowd toward the woman, who, she realized as she drew closer, looked exactly like their mother. "Amelia!" Liddie threw her arms around her sister.

"Oh, Liddie. I'm so happy to see you." Amelia wiped at her face with a corner of the blanket. "Look at us both crying."

"I can't believe I didn't recognize you." Liddie laughed through her tears.

"Oh, come now. I haven't changed that much, have I?" Amelia laughed. "Don't answer that."

"I mean, I can't believe I'm seeing you. And your babies. This must be Melvin?" She touched the mound resting against Amelia's shoulder.

"He fell asleep as the train was pulling in. Once he's out, a stampede won't wake him." Amelia folded the blanket back.

Liddie willed herself not to react. She knew about the baby's harelip, but seeing the awful redness of the gaping lip was a shock. "He's a dear." She closed her eyes as she kissed the child's forehead. She would get used to the sight. Over time.

She crouched down in front of the girl hiding behind Amelia's coat. "You must be Hope. I'm Auntie Liddie."

Amelia put her free hand on the child's head and propelled her forward. "Say hi to your Aunt Liddie, Hope."

Sucking furiously on her thumb, the little girl retreated behind her mother.

Liddie laughed. "Don't you worry, Hope. We'll get to know each other."

"Are the tears over yet?" Joe asked as he set their grips on the platform.

"Joe. Good to see you again, too." Amelia greeted him with a one-armed hug. "Welcome to Wyoming. How was the trip?"

"Glad to be here." Joe kissed her cheek. "It's been a long time, Amelia. You're looking well."

"As are the both of you." She chuckled as she looked from Liddie to Joe. "The two of you together. Who would have thought?"

"Where's Fred?" Joe asked.

"Working at the Magnus place. He'll be home for supper."

"You came alone?" Liddie asked.

"One thing you learn quickly out west is how to do for yourself," Amelia said. "I've got the wagon at the end of the depot. Let's get you home; you must be tired from your trip." She switched the baby to her other arm and motioned to Joe to bring the bags.

"Hold on. I have to take a picture of this." Liddie fished in her large handbag for the box camera.

"She's been taking pictures at every stop," Joe explained.

"I only get one honeymoon." Liddie looked toward the sun.

The light looked different in Wyoming than it did in Iowa. Clearer, somehow. And the sky was impossibly blue. The color would be lost in the black-and-white film, but she took a mental picture to add to the store of memories she was creating. She arranged Joe and Amelia so they were facing only three-quarters into the bright morning light, the Lusk depot sign in the background.

"I've learned to go with what she wants," Joe said. "Gets it over faster."

"There's a good husband," Liddie said as she peered into the camera. "Now smile."

They did and she pressed the lever. *Click.*

———

Liddie's honeymoon trip printed in her mind as a series of snapshots, though she didn't always depress the camera lever and hear the *click*.

*Click.*

Wide-open plains. As soon as they had crossed the Missouri River, leaving Iowa behind, the landscape had changed. Fewer trees. Flatter land. Plains. As far as the eye could see.

She put her camera up to an open window, bracing herself with one hand on the window frame. Joe had steadied her with a hand on the small of her back. The landscape flew by.

When she sat down, her eyes gleamed. "It's beautiful."

"Did you take a picture?"

"It wouldn't have worked. It's all a blur."

*Click.*

She, Amelia, and Joe astride horses in front of the log cabin that had been Amelia and Fred's home when they first came to Wyoming.

The entire cabin was less than the size of the Treadway dining room and had been built into a hillock so the structure required fewer logs to build and had natural protection from the wind. A hole near the ceiling for the chimney pipe channeled smoke from the cookstove that served to both cook meals and provide heat for the entire living space. Abandoned now, the cabin was devoid of furniture. Amelia's letters had not said that the floor was dirt or that dried mud filled the cracks in the log walls.

"It was all an adventure," Amelia said after she showed how they put the bed against the hillside wall because it was warmer there. "We were just married. We could do anything."

The wistful sound of Amelia's voice caused Liddie to observe her sister more closely. When Amelia didn't say more, Liddie went to look out the small window. "You told me about the curtains you made," she said.

Amelia's smile returned. "They hang in my kitchen now."

"How long were you here?"

"Under a year. It wasn't so bad. Except for the winter. Gets a little windy. I was glad when we moved." Then the wistfulness was back. "Sometimes, I miss this. My neighbors were a blessing."

"This is twice as big as my place in Saskatchewan," Joe said.

"Really?" Liddie stared at him in disbelief. "Surely not that small."

He sized up the room. "Almost. A cot, a table to sit two, a woodstove. When I got my dog, I had to be careful not to step on him when I stood up."

Liddie stood in the middle of the cabin and turned around and around, trying to see things as she'd imagined them from Amelia's letters. She could not reconcile the pictures she'd made in her mind with the reality of cooking, eating, sleeping—let alone entertaining visitors—all in one room.

"I know what you mean about neighbors, Amelia," Joe said. "I was grateful for every face that came to my door."

Liddie had a hard time picturing the isolation her sister described. She nudged her shoulder against Joe. He put his arm around her.

*Click.*

Joe spun a top for Hope, who stood mesmerized, one little hand on his knee, her eyes darting between him and the whirling top. Each time Joe released the top, she cheered as though she'd never seen anything so delightful.

The two women stood watching from the kitchen doorway. Amelia had made the modestly decorated room that served as both parlor and dining room comfortable and homey. In addition to the pine table surrounded by six straight-backed chairs that served for all meals, an oak rocking chair and the upholstered chair where Joe sat now flanked a small pedestal table. A sewing basket and doll cradle by the rocking chair spoke of cozy family evenings. The Treadway family photograph Amelia packed when she left the farm held a prominent place on that table next to the Bible and a kerosene lamp.

"He'll make a good papa," Amelia whispered before turning to a wash pan of dishes.

Liddie enjoyed watching her husband with the little girl. Sensing her eyes on him, Joe looked up and smiled. She blew him a kiss, then picked up a dish towel and joined Amelia.

Throughout supper that evening, Fred had barely talked at all, his sullen silence darkening an otherwise happy reunion. The devil-may-care man Liddie remembered from Iowa had disappeared. Amelia's letters had not prepared her for the surly man Fred had become.

Fred left the table even though they were still eating, saying, "Gotta check on the horses."

"Can't you sit and visit even one night?" Amelia asked.

"Work don't get done with me sitting here yakking." Fred pulled on a heavy coat.

"Could you use some help?" Joe offered. "I could stand to work the kinks out from the train."

"Nope. One man kin handle it." He disappeared into the night.

Amelia stood to clear the table. "He works so hard. He has a lot on his mind." She held her head proud and met Liddie's eyes with an overly bright smile as she stacked the pale-blue plates, which were embellished with violets.

Embarrassment for her sister had rippled under Liddie's skin as she gathered serving bowls and headed for the kitchen. Except for how it had bothered Amelia, however, Liddie hadn't been disappointed when Fred left.

As the two women cleaned up after supper, Liddie kept up a stream of news from Iowa. She expected the two of them to talk like they used to, but Amelia was quiet. Eventually, Liddie let silence fill the kitchen.

"I'm not being a good hostess, am I?" Amelia said after they worked for some time without speaking.

"I'm glad we get to see you," Liddie said.

"It was seeing Joe with Hope that made me a little blue. I wish Fred played with her like that."

"He doesn't?"

"He wanted a boy. He likes Hope well enough, but to sit and play with her like Joe is doing? No." She scrubbed at the last pan, bearing down on the scratcher as though she could remove the hurt she felt along with the crusted meat juices.

"When Melvin was born, I thought he'd be happy. Then he saw the lip." Amelia's voice broke. "He still won't hold him."

"Oh, Amelia." Shame crept over her as she remembered her own reaction to the baby's harelip. "You said the doctor can fix it."

"When Melvin's a little older, they can sew it together."

Amelia returned to the dishes, working silently for several minutes before she spoke again. "I pray that this baby will be the one."

"The one?"

"The one Fred can love."

Amelia's words hung in the air. The one he could love? Did you get to choose which child you loved? Liddie ached for her sister and her children.

*Click.*

Amelia and Liddie packed a lunch for a trip to the river while Joe loaded the kids into the buckboard. That October, after a particularly dry year, a raging river was only the product of one's imagination. But the banks were dotted with trees, and Liddie found herself drawn to the greenery, so seemingly rare in Wyoming. While Joe and Hope went off to look for tadpoles, the women sat with Melvin crawling between them.

"I thought you might not marry. And a farmwife. I never." Amelia laughed.

"It came out of the blue." Liddie wrapped her arms around her knees. She looked out toward Joe. He and Hope were chucking rocks into a "river" narrow enough to step across in one stride.

She faced Amelia. "I didn't know Fred well before you married, but he seems different."

"He works so hard. He has a lot on his mind."

The comment reminded Liddie of how she'd made excuses for Littmann. "Are you happy, Amelia?" Liddie asked.

Amelia picked up Melvin and held him above her head, looking up at him and laughing. Even though Melvin was fifteen months old, the harelip made his attempts at words unintelligible. He flailed his arms and legs and gurgled in delight.

"I'm happy," Amelia said at last, her tone daring Liddie to say she wasn't.

*Click.*

Fred tossed the Cheyenne newspaper on the table. "Figured you'd want to see that," he said to Amelia. "Wilson Club of Women Formed," read a headline. "War or Peace the Issue This Year, Say Mothers," said the subheading.

"Thank you, Fred." Amelia dried her hands on her apron and picked up the paper. "He always picks up the paper for me," she announced, as though this were a great act of love.

"She can't get enough of the news," Fred said.

"Gertie's starting a Wilson Club here," Amelia explained. "I'll work with her."

Fred snorted. "It's a stretch to think women can change anything."

"We can try," Amelia countered. "I'll help if she gets it going."

Liddie was surprised to see her sister interested in politics. "Our paper has something on the war every week."

"Ours, too," Amelia murmured as she scanned the articles.

"What are people here saying?" Joe asked Fred.

"Some are ready to help take it to the kaiser. Most think it ain't our business."

"Even though they've been sinking American ships?" Joe asked.

"Damned Krauts," Fred spat.

Joe's shoulders tensed, though his face remained impassive.

"Fred!" Amelia's tone was sharp.

"I'll speak as I want in my own house," Fred growled. "Germans can't live in peace. They're always trying to take over something. Take a look at Franz Muller over by Laramie. He buys out every ranch he gets a chance. Man can't get enough. Somebody ought to do something about that."

"Franz pays a fair price, from what I've heard," Amelia said. "People don't have to sell to him if they don't want to."

"He's sneaky. Stands back until a man's a little short on cash, then buys 'em out."

"Everybody isn't the same. German or Italian or English," Joe said, managing neither to escalate the argument nor to back down.

"All I'm saying is if the Germans win over there, we could have the same trouble here."

This was the most Fred had spoken on any topic since they'd arrived, and Liddie was taken aback by his vehemence. It troubled her to hear someone speak against all Germans, yet she knew Iowans who felt the same. The state Council of National Defense said it would be patriotic for schools to teach classes only in English, and it had begun to urge ministers to perform services only in English.

Amelia handed the paper to Liddie. "Hopefully, we won't get in the war. Melvin would never have to go, but Gertie's boy Sean is old enough. President Wilson says he'll keep us out. I'd vote for anyone who can keep us safe."

"I can't believe you get to vote, Amelia! I'm jealous," Liddie said. "When you wrote about voting the first time, I tried to imagine myself holding a ballot and pencil."

"Hell, women vote the way their husbands do," Fred barked derisively.

"I suppose many do," Amelia placated him. "The women in the Wilson Club, though, they vote to protect their children. No matter how their husbands vote."

*Click.*

Their train crossed the Missouri River back into Iowa. It was mid-October, and the trees still held fall color but were rapidly dropping their leaves. They'd been gone only a week, but Liddie's eyes teared up.

"What's the matter?" Joe asked.

"I'm glad to be home." She laced her fingers into his.

# Chapter 36

"You've been busy!" Liddie exclaimed when her eyes adjusted to the dim light in the barn. "It's clean as a whistle." He nodded—looking pleased, she noticed.

It was the day after they returned from Wyoming, and Joe was taking her on a tour of their new home. He had lived on the farm since he had returned to Iowa, but when she'd come to the farm with Minnie and Margretta to take stock of the house and measure for curtains, she hadn't gone into the other buildings. This was their first day living on the farm as husband and wife.

A cow stuck its head through the slats of the pen, and Liddie stopped to scratch the tight whorl of hair on the animal's forehead.

"Bessie milks good," Joe commented. "You'll be able to churn plenty of butter. Maybe even sell some."

Liddie added milking the cow and making butter to the list of tasks that would fill her days. "Let's go up in the haymow," she said.

Joe climbed the ladder first, then helped her up. They walked hand in hand to the south end of the loft, where he swung open the small door so they could look out over the fields. The trees in the back forty had lost most of their leaves. The green of a few pines dotted mostly brown hillsides. Rows of corn stood ripe for picking.

"What a beautiful view." Liddie breathed in the landscape. "I could come here every day."

"I was right." Joe wrapped an arm around her waist. "Everything I ever wanted is here."

Liddie snuggled against his side, her heart full. "I'm so happy, Joe."

Joe gathered her to him, kissing her lightly and then with more intensity. A sound like rushing water pounded in her ears. She felt him against her, and her body flushed with desire. Then she remembered.

"Wait!" She gasped, putting her hands on his chest, pushing. "No."

Joe stiffened. "We're married, Liddie."

"We agreed." She pushed more firmly. Until now, living with her self-imposed rules had been manageable. At Amelia's, they had both been self-conscious. Doing anything on the train had not even been up for discussion. But now, in their own home, in their own bed, after days of touching him and smelling him and being so close, the want she felt was palpable. She could barely remember why she'd thought six weeks of celibacy were so important.

"Do you honestly think anyone will give us a second thought?"

"I will." She gulped.

He dropped his arms. "I'm a man. Your husband." His voice was husky. "You're asking too much."

As soon as his arms left her, she was bereft.

He latched the loft door shut, strode past without looking at her, and climbed down the ladder.

She scrambled after him. Outside the barn, she ran to catch up. "It's only a few weeks." She held on to his arm.

He stared at her, his eyes icy.

"Don't be mad," she pleaded. "Please."

"You need to see the garden." He strode toward the plot the renters had planted, now just a ragtag remnant of what it had been. She could see where there had been green beans. Someone had made an effort to dig the carrots, though they'd left a few behind. Pumpkins and squash were splashes of color against dried vines.

"Oh, look! There are still tomatoes!" Liddie exclaimed, overly enthusiastic, when they found a few fully ripe red fruits buried under a tangle of nearly dead vines, grass, and weeds. "I wish I had a basket."

"Use this." He stripped off his shirt and tied up the sleeves, fashioning a sling. "I've been eating them. Lucky we haven't had a hard freeze yet."

His bare arms, the muscles in his shoulders roused the same weakness in her legs she had felt when he kissed her in the haymow. Her desire was almost unbearable. She turned away as her cheeks turned crimson.

Joe erupted in laughter. "Would you rather I put the shirt back on?"

She shook her head without looking up. "No." She busied herself picking tomatoes. At least he didn't seem mad anymore.

He kicked at a dead vine, scuffed his boot at a mound of dirt. "I thought so." He bent down, dug out two potatoes, and held them up like trophies.

She smiled. "If I had my camera, I'd take a picture of you."

He stuffed the potatoes in his pocket. "We need to get these in the root cellar." He'd lost his humor. "Besides, you can't take a picture of everything."

"Maybe I can." She ignored his pique as she looked up at the sun. It wasn't yet noon. "Are you hungry?"

"Always." He put an acorn squash in the sling with the tomatoes. "What do we have to eat?"

"Minnie left enough meat and bread for another meal, along with lots of cookies. We'll eat that now, and I'll make something hot for supper."

"I'm going to like having you cook for me."

"I knew that was the reason you wanted to get married."

"One of the reasons," he agreed. Without warning, he pulled her to him and kissed her so deeply she felt faint.

When he released her, every muscle in her body quivered.

"I can do *that*, can't I?" he asked. Then he headed for the house. She licked her lips, longing for more of the taste and feel of him.

When they finished eating, Joe pushed back from the table and crossed his legs.

"More coffee?" She rose to get the pot without waiting for his answer.

He sat in silence while she filled his cup. He drank half of it before he said, "You can't take pictures of everything, you know."

It took a moment for her to remember he'd said something like that out in the garden. She laughed. "I didn't mean I really would. Only that I can think of so many pictures I want to take, to remember what we're doing all our lives." She dunked a cookie in her coffee. When she looked up, he was staring somberly into his cup.

"I'm serious." He looked at her. "We have to watch our money. Farming isn't like having a job in town. We don't get paid every week or two."

Liddie was mortified. She remembered the photos she'd taken on their honeymoon—how she'd said so flippantly to Amelia, *the film's the cheap part*. Since she didn't have access to a darkroom anymore, she'd mailed the exposed film to Kodak to be developed. It was the first time she'd had to pay for developing and the first time she'd had to ask her husband for money. Even working for both Mrs. Tinker and Mr. Littmann, she'd been able to save only a little. She had often used that extra money to buy material for gifts or photo paper for printing pictures. As a result, she came into the marriage as most women did, dependent on her husband for money to spend.

"All those pictures I took!" Her shoulders sank. "I didn't think."

"That was our honeymoon. I would never have told you no." Joe squeezed her hand. "I wish I could give you everything. Right now. Every day. But I can't."

He drained the last of his coffee and walked out.

Liddie sat at the table for a long time, thinking about their conversations on the train. Joe had talked about how it worked to farm on shares. He'd tend Gibson's livestock and they'd split the money made when pigs or cream sold. They could keep milk and cream to cook and make butter. A hog and half a steer was their share when it came time to butcher. They'd buy pigs of their own next year. She'd care for the chickens, milk the cow, make the butter, and make the most of the garden. Even as he'd said these things, it hadn't soaked in. Not really. She'd been so interested in the scenery.

It seemed ridiculous that she'd grown up on a farm without understanding the basic aspects of farm economy. This was the first time she realized that she would not have more than egg and butter money of her own.

She remembered the coffee can on top of the pie safe in the Treadway kitchen, where her mother put her egg and butter money. Margretta dipped into the can to buy a bottle of vanilla or liniment from the Watkins man when he stopped at the farm. When they went to town, she used to give Liddie two pennies from the can for candy. Because of the coffee can, her mother did not have to ask her husband for money every time she needed it. The can was a bit of independence.

Liddie rubbed her face hard with the palms of her hands. She wished she could rub away her naïveté. Then she retrieved her camera from the sideboard in the parlor. She looked through the lens, rotating slowly in every direction. Then she opened the bottom drawer of the sideboard, wrapped the camera in a napkin, and put it away. Her fingers rested on the napkin for several seconds before she closed the drawer.

She went out to the front porch and sat in the rocking chair, her hands quiet in her lap as she looked out at the fields. She'd chosen Joe. If that meant no photography, then that was simply the reality.

Each day on the farm came fast upon the one before. Her days were consumed by cooking meals, doing laundry, and, from time to time, working with Joe in the fields or barn. Mostly she worked alone as she cleaned the house, ironed clothes, or baked. When she didn't have anything else to do, she carried in wood to fill the box by the cookstove.

The end-of-the-season garden required both of their work. Joe dug the potatoes and helped gather squash and pumpkins to store in the root cellar. They worked fast to beat the first hard frost, gathering windfalls from under the apple tree, sorting out a bushel of the best ones for the root cellar. She would put the rest up.

She'd never canned anything herself start to finish, so she rang up her mother. They were fortunate Gibson had already run a phone line to the house.

"Hi, Minnie," she said into the receiver. "Can you spare Mama tomorrow? I have all these apples to put up, and I don't know where to start."

"Mama and I would love to help. We'll bring our pans and come over after breakfast."

"You're a lifesaver!"

At the end of the next day, Liddie stood surveying tidy rows of pint and quart jars filled with applesauce. Enough to last all winter. She was exhausted, but she felt the same sense of pride as when she saw Anna Caither wearing the dress she'd created. The jars were so pretty, they deserved to be photographed every bit as much as the dress.

It was at moments like these that she thought of Littmann. What would he say about the light? How would he think about the story these fruit jars told? On the one hand, she knew he would be intrigued by the photographic potential. On the other hand, she imagined he would dismiss the topic as too common to matter. She might miss talking about photography, but she did not miss being made to feel inadequate. Besides, these jars were worth a photograph. Still, she left the camera in the drawer.

———

"What are you going to do today?" Liddie asked Joe one crisp fall morning.

"Those trees in the fencerow east of the barn have been bothering me." He speared a bite of pancake to wipe up the last syrup on his plate. "Some have to go. Some trunks will make fence posts where they stand."

She'd heard her father call Osage orange trees a living barbed-wire fence. "I'll help."

"Weren't you going to iron today?"

She grimaced. Ironing was only the first of many tasks she'd planned for her day. The ironing, the cleaning, the mending, the milking would still be there when she returned, but a day with Joe was far more enticing. "I'd rather be out with you."

"It's mighty hard work."

"Better to have two of us at it, then."

As Joe chopped and sawed, Liddie dragged branches into a pile. By noon, she'd piled brush as high as her head. While Joe coaxed a fire to life, Liddie ran into the house and made a picnic. They sat upwind of the fire, devouring cheese sandwiches and molasses cookies. The fresh air and exercise made them ravenous.

After they brushed away the crumbs, Joe motioned her to slide over and sit between his legs. She scooted until her back was against his chest, his arms secure under her breasts. For the next half hour, they sat in silence, watching the flames lick at the sky. The fire warmed her face and he warmed her back. A more romantic moment she had never imagined.

By the end of the day, the fencerow was as neat as any, and they were too tired to do more than tend to the livestock and collapse into bed. Joe was under the covers when Liddie cuddled up next to him.

"Joe?" she said.

"Mmm."

"I was thinking." She hesitated. "Maybe I don't want to wait."

She held her breath, waiting for his answer.

He was already snoring.

———

The next day, after putting a soup pot on the cookstove to simmer, she took the clean laundry to their bedroom. As she put the stack of freshly ironed hankies in her dresser drawer, she saw amongst her things the arrowhead Joe had given her the day her father died. She took it out of the drawer and sat on the edge of the bed. Rubbing the arrowhead between her fingers, she recalled Joe's words—*from the land to Papa to Joe to her*. To Joe *and* her. When he came to the house at noon, she was still in the bedroom.

"Liddie! Where are you?" he called.

"In here."

He came to the bedroom, where she sat on the edge of the bed.

"Are you sick?"

She smoothed the bedspread beside her, inviting him to sit. "I found this today." She opened her hand to reveal the arrowhead in her palm.

"You still have it."

"I've kept it close. When I saw it today, it made me think about how you've always been here for me."

"I try to be."

"I want to be here for you, too."

"You are."

"I mean really here for you." When she tilted her head toward the pillows, her cheeks felt like they were on fire. She worked the arrowhead over and over in her fingers.

"Ah," Joe said. He took her hands and kissed their palms before folding her fingers over the arrowhead and putting her hands back in her lap. "Not for three more weeks, *Liebchen*. I don't think we want anyone to count." He stood.

Liddie's eyes widened. "I thought . . . I thought you would want . . ." Embarrassed, she turned so he could not see the shame on her face.

He crouched in front of her. "Look at me, Liddie." Touching her chin, Joe drew her face back toward him. "I do want to. You cannot imagine how much. But I know why you made this rule. I don't ever want you to regret it."

Liddie looked steadily into his eyes. She slid off the bed onto her knees, her face inches from his. "I love you, Joe."

He brushed her lips with his thumb.

"Oh." Liddie closed her eyes and sighed.

Then Joe kissed her. On the lips. In the soft place behind the lobe of her right ear. In the hollow at the base of her neck. He began to unbutton her dress. When his fingers grazed her breasts, the flesh between her legs felt as though it had been set on fire, and she gasped.

"Do you like how that felt?" he asked.

"I will never regret this," she breathed.

———

Midmorning a week later, her mother called.

"Oh no! What happened?" Liddie held the receiver tight to her ear as she pressed her forehead to the wall.

"The doctor came, but there wasn't anything he could do. He says she'll be fine."

"How is she really, Mama?"

"I told her she should rest, but she's making a cake. She said she'll feel better if she does something."

"I'll be over." Liddie put the receiver back on the hook and stood there without letting go. Poor Minnie. Pregnant twice. Twice she'd lost the baby.

The timing, right before Christmas, couldn't have been worse. Liddie stoked the firebox in the cookstove and checked on the roast. It would be ready when Joe came in at noon. She poured hot coffee into a quart jar, tied a scarf over her head, pulled a coat tight around herself, and went to the field where Joe was picking corn. As she stepped across the already-picked cornrows, she lowered her head, shielding her face against a biting north wind. The flat gray sky held the threat of snow. A bitter day to carry such bitter news.

"I'm sorry," Joe said. He pulled off his shucking gloves and wrapped both hands around the hot coffee jar. "Do you want me to come along?"

"No," she said, tucking her hands into her armpits. "Dinner's in the oven. I'll be back to fix supper."

"Stay as long as you need to."

She thought he looked relieved.

The cake was cooling on the counter when Liddie let herself in the kitchen door. Minnie was kneading bread.

"I'm so sorry," she said, hugging her friend tight.

A shudder ran through Minnie's body. Her voice trembled. "I get my hopes up and then . . . nothing. It's not fair."

"I know it's not." Liddie hugged her again. "What did the doctor say?"

"That it happens." Minnie picked up a dishcloth and wiped her hands calmly. Then her eyes flashed with anger. "It *happens*. I know that. But why?"

Liddie felt useless. "Why don't you sit with me for a while?"

"I can't." Minnie looked around absently as though she knew she should be doing something but couldn't figure out what. "Vern will be in to eat."

There was nothing on the stove. Aside from the cake, Liddie didn't see that Minnie had anything ready for dinner. "Where's Mama?"

"In her room." Minnie lifted her hands in a helpless gesture before letting them fall to her sides. "I . . . I snapped at her. I know she was trying to be helpful, but I wanted to be alone."

"Would you rather I left, too?"

"No." Minnie tried to smile. "I'm glad you came." She pushed her hair back from her face and looked blankly at the bread dough. "I feel bad about Mama. I think I upset her."

"I'm sure she understands." Liddie put on an apron. "Let me help. Do you have any leftovers?"

"A little roast from yesterday."

"I'll make a hash. You finish the bread."

Liddie set a cast-iron skillet on the stove to heat, added a scoop of bacon drippings, then set to chopping onions. They worked together in silence, taking solace from the dependable rhythm of labor.

———

Two weeks later, Vern showed up at their door after breakfast. "Morning, Joe. Liddie," he said.

"Vern! Come on in." Liddie looked past him. "Is Minnie along?"

"She stayed with Ma." Vern stood inside the door.

"Take a load off." Joe motioned him to the table.

"Yes. Have a cup of coffee," Liddie said. "We're done eating, but I can fix you a couple eggs."

"Coffee's fine."

Liddie poured a cup for her brother, then topped off Joe's cup and her own. She set a plate loaded with oatmeal cookies between the men.

"Get the last of your corn picked?" Joe asked.

"'Bout finished. Glad it ain't snowed yet." Vern pushed his chair back a few inches. "Looks like you're settled in." He leveled his pale-blue eyes at Liddie.

"Yes, we're settled in." Liddie returned his gaze. He wanted something. She dunked a cookie in her coffee. She knew to wait.

"I've been meaning to talk to you, once you was. We think Ma is better off living with you."

Liddie dropped the cookie in her coffee. "Is something wrong?"

"Ma's gout's making it hard for her to get up the stairs."

He couldn't have said anything that would have surprised her more. "Vern, Mama has lived on that place since she and Papa married. It will upset her to move someplace else."

When Vern and Minnie had married, Mama had given them her bedroom on the main floor and moved into Vern's old room upstairs. That was the way every farm family she knew did it. Liddie never imagined her mother living anywhere else.

Vern didn't take his eyes off her. "Minnie and me think Ma'd be better off living with you."

Liddie looked at Joe.

"If Mama wants to live with us, we'd be glad to have her," he said.

"Of course," Liddie said, though she wished she'd had time to think about it. "Of course she can live with us." She spoke with more enthusiasm. "I'll talk with Mama and Minnie. We'll get it figured out."

Vern relaxed visibly and took a cookie. "Got time to go huntin' this week?" he asked Joe.

"Always got time to hunt." Joe nodded.

While the men talked, Liddie washed the breakfast dishes and bided her time until her brother left.

"Well, that was something I didn't see coming," Liddie said after Vern was gone. "I wonder why Minnie didn't say anything to me?"

"You told me how Vern said Mama was hard on Minnie."

"I'd forgotten that. I thought it didn't amount to much because Minnie brushed it off."

"Must have been more than we knew."

"Hmm." Liddie raised her eyebrows as she looked around the kitchen. "I wonder what Mama will think of my housekeeping?"

"It'll be fine." Joe pulled her into his arms. "Think of this. Vern and Minnie didn't even get a couple of weeks alone after they got married. We've had two months."

Liddie blushed. "Do you have to go out right away?" She brought her lips to his.

# Chapter 37

Propped up against the headboard of their bed, Liddie stretched the fabric of her shift until it was smooth across her abdomen. She touched the tip of her little finger to her right hip bone and stretched her fingers wide. She imagined the palm of her hand resting directly over her baby's forehead.

Her baby. There'd been no nausea, no faintness, no food cravings. She wouldn't have known she was pregnant except that her monthly courses had stopped. Now there was this gentle mound to her stomach.

Liddie believed this baby was conceived on the very day she'd finally said yes to Joe. The day she'd said yes and they spent the entire afternoon in bed. The day she'd said yes and the soup burned on the stove. The day she'd said yes and discovered why Minnie blushed.

She'd told no one, holding this precious knowledge to herself until she was absolutely certain. A smile lifted the corners of her mouth.

In the kitchen, bread dough was in its second rise, ready to form into loaves. She stroked her stomach for another minute, then slipped into her wrapper and tied an apron around her waist. From these shapeless clothes, no one would know she was pregnant unless she told them. But it was time to tell the father, and she had an idea how to share the surprise.

She formed three tiny loaves with some of the dough. Then she rolled more dough into a thin rope and pinched off lengths to craft letters on the top of each loaf. When the three little loaves came out of the oven, she wrapped them in a towel, bundled up in a heavy coat, and followed the path Joe had shoveled through the snowdrifts from the house to the barn. The snow, sparkling in the sun, looked as though it were strewn with shards of cut glass.

"Whooo! It's cold!" she said, pulling the barn door closed behind her.

"Why'd you come out?" Joe was forking clean straw around the pens. "I'd have been in shortly."

"I have a surprise." She pushed the cat away and sat on the feedbox.

"Do I smell bread?" He propped the fork against the wall and joined her.

"You do." She unwrapped the towel and handed him a loaf.

"What's this?" He turned the loaf over and over.

She took the bread out of his hands and turned it upright. "See? It's an *L*—for Liddie." Before he could take a bite, she took another loaf out of the towel and gave it to him.

He considered it. "A *J* for Joe?"

"You're a quick learner." She laughed. "I have one more." She uncovered the last loaf and handed it to him.

He turned it around and looked at her, confused. *"B?"*

She ducked her head, shy, and whispered, "For baby."

"Baby?" He looked at the loaf in his hands and again at her, thunderstruck.

"Our baby." She kissed him on the cheek.

"Our baby," he whispered. "Our baby." His eyes glistened as he gathered her in his arms, the bread forgotten. "I love you, Liddie."

She felt as though her heart would burst.

# Chapter 38

"We'll head to town soon as I finish chores. Wouldn't want to miss the *festivities*," Joe said as he left to do chores. He'd been making light of signing up for the draft ever since they had read the announcement in the paper.

"I don't know how he can be so casual." The plates clattered as Liddie took out her anxiety on the breakfast dishes.

Once President Wilson had convinced Congress to declare war on Germany, talk shifted to manning the army. They needed men—American men, Iowan men, her husband, maybe—to fight. Today, June 5, men between twenty-one and thirty were required to register for military service.

Liddie dipped her hands into soapy water, washed two plates, and then whirled toward her mother, splashing water across the counter. "He promised to keep us out of the war. He promised!" She stamped her foot in frustration.

"Now don't get so het up," Margretta shushed. "You'll upset the baby."

Automatically, Liddie ran her hand over her stomach. She was sure her baby was fine, but with Minnie's history . . . she stopped that thought as fast as it came. Minnie was pregnant again, and there would be only positive thoughts. Healthy babies for them both. "Did I tell you Amelia helped get other Wyoming women to vote for Wilson to avoid this exact thing from happening?"

"You did." Margretta sat on a tall stool, taking the weight off her foot, while she dried the plates. "But the president's no better at predicting the future than the rest of us."

The war had seemed so far away for the past three years. The paper reported escalating tensions, but President Wilson stood strongly on nonintervention, even after the Germans sank the *Lusitania*. She had not been willing to believe the United States would put men on the front line. She had been content to believe that by being generally frugal and using less flour, they were doing their part.

"Surely Joe can't go," she said. "Not now." They were married. They were going to have a baby.

Margretta squeezed Liddie's elbow. "Nobody thinks married men will have to go."

Liddie straightened up. "I have to believe that." She wrung out the dishcloth and wiped off the counter. "I'm going to change clothes."

In the bedroom, Liddie slipped off her wrapper and stood in front of the mirror wearing only a shift. She stared at her body, circling a hand over the mound of her stomach. In the last few weeks, she'd begun to fill out, and she'd felt the baby move!

Daily, she was caught in the swirl of emotions that surrounded the feeling of this living being growing inside of her—the pride, the fierce protectiveness. Now she could imagine the devastation Minnie felt anticipating babies only to lose them.

All her growing-up years, Liddie had imagined adventure as living in a city, seeing spectacular sights. She had never thought her adventure would be this, to be married, to be with child. Then she remembered the war and shivers rippled up her back.

"Don't worry, little one. We'll take care of you." She patted her stomach.

*"Du bist so schön."*

She looked up, surprised. She'd been so lost in her own thoughts that she hadn't heard him come back into the house. She faced Joe and smiled, one hand still resting on her belly.

He came to her, putting his hands over hers. "So beautiful," he said.

"I never guessed how this would feel," she said.

When his lips touched hers, Liddie relaxed against him. She felt complete. He stepped away, and when she forced herself to open her eyes, she saw him grinning at her.

"Do you suppose you should dress before we leave?" he asked.

She laughed. "Walking down Main Street like this would be more than the ladies of Maquoketa could bear." Holding hairpins between her lips as she drew her hair into a bun, she spoke out of the side of her mouth. "Minnie said they'd be ready to leave as soon as we show up."

———

"Could be the Fourth of July," Vern said as Joe turned onto a street crowded with buggies and automobiles. American flags hung on the fronts of most buildings.

"I read some towns planned to close the schools—get the women to do registration—even close businesses so no one has an excuse not to show up," Joe said.

"Some of the guys at the feed store said they'd go to Canada before they'd get drug into a fight in Europe," Vern said. "I say we oughta be willing to fight for ourselves."

Minnie had been silent through most of the drive, but now she took Liddie's hand. Liddie could tell Minnie's nerves were getting the better of her.

"By the looks of this crowd, people are showing up." Joe reined the horse to a stop. "I guess having the sign-up in a pool hall will do it."

"I can't believe that was necessary," Liddie said.

Since the state had passed Prohibition, all the saloons along Main Street had installed pool tables and now called themselves billiard parlors. Jackson County and all the other river counties had voted against the law, and though the saloons didn't advertise it, most folks knew a drink could still be had at the right time of night for the right price.

"Men'll show up for a drink." Joe grinned as he jumped down and tied the lead rope to the rail. Apparently, the restrictions on alcohol would be totally overlooked today.

"Personally, I thought we were on the right road with mediation," Liddie said.

"The kaiser didn't leave room for talking. Not when he promised Mexico he'd give 'em half the American Southwest if they joined him," Vern said.

"Maybe not." Liddie held Vern's hand as she stepped down from the buggy. She whispered, "Try to talk about something besides the war. For Minnie's sake?"

Vern's eyes darted to Minnie, who stood waiting on the sidewalk. He turned to Joe. "How's the hay looking?"

Liddie patted his arm. She and Minnie strolled a few paces behind the men, stopping from time to time to look in the store windows.

"Sure would like to take one of these for a spin," Joe said, stepping into the street to take a closer look at a Model T.

"Never thought I'd hear you go for anything but a horse," Vern said.

Joe ran a hand along the fender. "I heard they go up to forty-five miles an hour. It'd be something to go that fast."

The dreamy quality in Joe's voice caused Liddie to glance his way. He liked fast horses; it made sense he'd like a fast car, too.

As the two men debated the relative merits of cars and horses, Liddie spoke softly to Minnie. "You seem well. How are you feeling?"

"Good." Minnie touched a hand to her abdomen. "I expect to feel the baby any day. This is the time. I know it." She turned toward Vern. He saw her looking and tipped his hat. In response, she touched her fingertips to her lips.

"You'll never guess what he did yesterday," she said. "He picked irises and put a bloom in each room of the house!" Tears sprang up in Minnie's eyes. She turned her back to the men, dried the tears with a hankie, and forced a smile. "We're both ready for this baby!" A frown settled between her eyes. "If it weren't for this draft."

"Try not to let it worry you. I'm sure we'll be fine." Liddie wished for a distraction, and her eyes fell on Minnie's favorite bakery. "After the men register, let's get a pastry at Becker's."

"Didn't you hear? They found glass in his flour."

"No! How did that happen?"

"Some on the county Council of National Defense say he did it himself in support of Germany. Anyway, everybody's afraid to go there now."

Liddie was speechless. Mr. Becker had never been anything but friendly. Even though Mrs. Becker spoke only a few words of English, she greeted everyone who came into the bakery with a cheerful smile. Her fruit tortes were famous. Why would they destroy their own products? It made no sense.

Joe joined them on the sidewalk. "Let's get this done." He steered her toward the pool hall, where groups of people congregated outside. The smell of stale beer reached them from twenty feet away.

"Oh." Minnie put her hand to her nose.

"Are you okay?" Liddie asked.

"The smell. I don't know if I can go in."

"You can stay out here," Vern said.

"We won't be long, *Liebchen*." Joe touched Liddie's arm.

A man who'd been leaning against the building straightened up and spoke loudly. "Do you smell sauerkraut?" He scanned the crowd, then moved forward, planting himself squarely in front of Joe. "That'd make any American sick, wouldn't you say, boys?"

"Sure would, Mac," another man agreed as he stepped up next to the first man. "Damned sick."

Other men standing nearby laughed as they moved in around the two couples.

"What are you getting at?" Joe frowned.

"You forget where you live?" A sneer curled the first man's lip.

"What?" Joe asked.

"This is the United States of *America*." The man's clothes and breath reeked of alcohol. "We speak English here." He thumped a finger against the American flag pin on his chest.

"No offense intended," Joe said. He moved toward the steps. The man braced his arm across the door and angled a knee out, blocking the path.

"You got a problem?" Vern stepped up beside Joe.

"Not me." The man poked a finger in Vern's chest. "You oughta think about who your friends really are." He nailed Joe with a malicious glare. "Kraut." He spat, then swung his gaze to his buddies. "What do you think, boys? Maybe our Kraut friend here needs help with his English."

Hair rose on Liddie's arms as a bead of sweat trickled between her breasts. She scanned the crowd for any friendly face. There was not one.

"You don't even know me." Joe pushed the man's arm aside.

"We're signing up. Like you," Vern said.

The circle of men tightened.

"Don't know's how I'd want to serve next to a Kraut. Stinks." He laughed, though his eyes were flat with hate. "And you might wake up dead."

"Joe. Please." Liddie tugged at his arm.

The man's voice filled with scorn when he turned to Liddie. "You're English. You coulda done better." He poked a finger in Joe's chest. "And you. You better remember where you live."

She moved closer to Joe. The man's words raised her ire. "I'm American," she said, her eyes never leaving the man. "Joe's American. A pin doesn't make you anything."

"Stay back, Liddie," Joe said. He grabbed the man's hand, twisting his wrist hard, shouldering in so his face was inches from his accuser. "You leave my wife alone."

For the baby's sake, Liddie knew she should step away, but she wouldn't leave her husband.

"Let it go, Joe." Vern put a hand on Joe's shoulder. "He's not worth it."

"Everything all right here?" a man interrupted.

When Liddie saw the county sheriff, his two deputies behind him, she gasped in relief.

"Going in to register, Sheriff." Joe released the man's hand. "Just like everyone."

The man rubbed his wrist. "Making sure these folks know the rules for signing up."

As quickly as it had formed, the threatening circle of men dissolved.

Joe took Liddie's elbow. "Let's go."

The women stayed within arm's reach of their husbands while the men registered. Later, they rode back to the farm in silence.

After that day, Joe confined his German words to their home.

———

In mid-July, Minnie suffered her third miscarriage. In mid-August, Liddie gave birth to a healthy baby girl who looked just like Joe. They named her Rose. At the end of August, Joe and Vern received certificates from the draft board discharging them from military service on the grounds that they were married men, the sole support of their wives and children. For Vern and Minnie, the wording was cruel.

# Chapter 39

Liddie reveled in being a new mother. Seeing her daughter grow and develop every single day reminded her of watching an image emerge in a darkroom developing tray, though this was tenfold better. And the process never ended. Almost daily, Rose found a new way to delight, from her first smile to finding her toes.

Whenever Joe came into the house, he peeked in the cradle. If Rose wasn't sleeping, and even sometimes if she was, he picked her up, supporting her in the crook of his arm, and told her stories about his day.

Some evenings, Liddie cuddled next to Joe on the sofa or in their bed as he held Rose, singing German lullabies to her until it was time to nurse again. Sometimes, both Liddie and Rose fell asleep to Joe's singing. Then, with luck, Joe could slip Rose into the cradle without waking her and they all got to sleep.

On other nights, after Liddie had crawled out of bed for the third time in response to her baby's hunger, she wondered if she'd ever know a fully restful night again. Even the beauty she found in the dark quiet with her daughter at her breast was lost as her eyes drooped and she jerked awake again and again.

On the days following those sleepless nights, Liddie was particularly grateful her mother lived with them. In addition to calming whatever worries Liddie may have felt about caring for a new baby, Margretta yearned to hold Rose as much as Joe did. If Liddie so much as yawned during the day, Margretta sent her off to rest for a few minutes while she took care of Rose.

While Liddie thrived in new motherhood, the strain of three lost pregnancies drained the life from Minnie. She lost weight, and her already-small frame shrank in on itself. She spoke less, smiled less. After Rose was born, Minnie feigned happiness when they visited, but Liddie saw her smile fade when she thought no one was looking. More and more often, Minnie begged off when Vern came to Joe and Liddie's farm.

She understood how conflicted Minnie felt seeing Liddie's healthy baby. But she missed her friend and wanted to help.

Earlier that summer, Liddie had read an article in the newspaper about adoption. She hesitated to bring it up lest Minnie think she was suggesting giving up on a child of her own. But when Minnie's malaise persisted, Liddie thought she had to try. She called Minnie and asked her to come help in the garden. Minnie could not ignore someone asking for help. Margretta found an excuse to be at work in the house and kept Rose there with her.

As they searched the dying vines for green beans, Liddie kept glancing at Minnie. "That's the end of that row," she said as she threw a last handful into the dishpan. She lifted her face to the warm September sun. "Isn't it beautiful today? Let's sit on the grass, okay?"

"I guess." Minnie didn't bother to look up.

She'd been like that all day. There, but not there. Liddie drew a breath. "I'm concerned about you, Minnie. How are you doing?"

"Oh, fine." Minnie picked at the hem of her apron. "A little tired, I guess."

Liddie felt intrusive but plowed on. "I wondered. Have you and Vern ever talked about adopting a child?"

Minnie's eyes filled with tears. "I tried. He stomped out of the house. He's so angry all the time. He goes out in the morning and stays out all day. He comes in to eat and leaves as fast as he can."

"I'm sure he's not mad at you."

"Really? Why not?" She thrust out her chin, looking directly at Liddie for the first time. "If he had a cow that couldn't have calves, he'd get rid of it."

"Minnie Treadway!" Liddie was shocked. "You are not a cow. You're his wife. Don't you ever think that way."

"I feel so guilty."

"Why, Minnie? You didn't do anything to cause yourself to lose those babies." Liddie put an arm around Minnie's shoulders. "So why feel guilty?"

Tears streamed down Minnie's cheeks. She shook her head, the defiance gone. "Having children is my job. He wants a baby, too. So badly." Minnie coughed a sob. "The doctor doesn't think I can have any."

"Oh, Minnie." Liddie pulled her close. "Does Vern know this?" Minnie nodded.

Liddie wanted to shake her brother. How could he turn away when his wife was hurting so badly? "He loves you."

"I thought he did. But three times, Liddie. I've lost three babies. How can he love me now?"

"No one wanted those babies more than you, Minnie. He knows that. Would *you* adopt?"

"I would. But he said if he couldn't have his own, he didn't want any children at all."

Minnie crumpled, waves of grief racking her body. Liddie could do nothing but hold her, rocking as she rocked Rose when she was upset, wishing she could make things better for Minnie as easily as she could for her daughter.

Two weeks later, Minnie visited again, holding a newspaper article about a train bringing orphaned children from New York to Iowa. "Look at this." She pointed to the headline: "Make a Choice of an Orphan—Fourteen Bright-Faced Children Craving a Mother and Father's Love."

"Has Vern changed his mind?" Liddie asked.

"No. I thought you and I could go. Just to see some children get homes. That's all."

Liddie was skeptical. Why would Minnie taunt herself by going to see children she couldn't have?

"Please? We'll get a soda after."

For the first time in weeks, Liddie saw light in Minnie's eyes, and agreed.

A week later, standing in front of the Congregational church, Liddie stopped Minnie with a hand on her forearm. "Are you sure you want to go in?"

"Why not?"

*Because it's perverse, that's why,* Liddie thought as she looked down at her own baby sleeping soundly in her arms. For Minnie to see so many children who wanted homes and know none of them could ever be hers.

"Why don't we skip this and go to the drugstore now?" Liddie turned to walk away.

Minnie gripped her arm. "I may never be lucky like you, but it will be a comfort to know those children are finding homes."

Minnie's overly bright smile did not fool Liddie, but she resigned herself to the day.

The sanctuary was crowded. From what they'd read in the paper, thousands of children—orphaned or abandoned, reduced to begging or stealing or actions too horrific to even contemplate—ranging in age from infant to teenage were being rescued from New York streets by the Children's Aid Society and sent on trains to rural areas to be adopted. Mrs. Wilstock, an agent traveling with the children, would be supervising the adoptions.

As they entered, they overheard two farmers, who were standing inside the door, talking.

"You get some good work out of these boys if you know how to handle 'em," said a wiry, dark-haired man.

"Amos Larkin took one," related a burly, ruddy-faced farmer. "Said the boy was worthless. Couldn't get a cent of work outta him. Kept runnin' off."

"If Larkin handled that boy like he handles his horses, don't know as how I'd work for him, either," the smaller man responded.

Liddie and Minnie exchanged glances. Minnie's eyebrows were arched in horror. As Liddie steered her toward a pew, she thought of Joe. She'd never thought about how hard it might have been for him to come live with them after his parents died.

"I've heard that Mrs. Wilstock takes good care of the children," said a woman sitting in the pew behind them.

"I heard it's not as up-and-up as they like to say." Another woman sniffed. "I heard she'll place the children wherever she can so she doesn't have to take them back to New York."

Liddie saw color rise in Minnie's cheeks as she twisted her hankie in a knot. "Don't pay them any mind," she whispered.

Minnie shook her head. She wrenched the hankie harder.

"Probably can't have children of her own," the skeptic added with a brittle laugh.

Minnie's cheeks flamed. She swung around in the pew and glared at the woman. "How dare you talk. You don't know any-thing. Mrs. Wilstock is an angel. These children have no prospects, and she makes sure they have homes. Whether she has children or not is none of your business . . . you . . . old . . . biddies!"

The mouths of the two women formed circles; their intake of breath was audible. Collecting their handbags and umbrellas, they made a show of moving to the other side of the church.

"Good for you, Minnie. That's telling them." Liddie muffled her laughter behind her hand. "I'm sure Mrs. Wilstock would be happy she has a defender."

"How could they?" Minnie raged.

"Nothing better to do than talk, I'm sure." Seeing such spunk in Minnie was an honest relief. "Look. Look." She grasped Minnie's hand. "Here they are."

The room fell silent as a woman Liddie presumed was Mrs. Wilstock led thirteen children—each child holding the hand of the next one in line—to stand in front of the altar. Each boy was dressed in a wool suit, white shirt, and black shoes. Each girl—her hair bobbed and adorned with a ribbon—wore a plain dress. The agent held a fourteenth child, a baby, in her arms.

"Oh, aren't they sweet!" breathed Minnie.

"Look at the boy on the left." Liddie gestured toward a lad with a shock of unruly oat-colored hair. Maybe ten years old, the boy stood stiff as a soldier, his eyes focused above and behind the congregation. "He's trying to seem so strong."

The agent had each child step forward to sing a song, recite a poem, or say what they hoped for in a home or family. After the older children were introduced, the agent folded back the blanket in her arms to reveal a sleeping baby whose coal-black hair and translucent skin made her look like a china doll. "Her name is Pearl," she said. "She's six months old."

"She's so tiny," Minnie whispered. "How can she be six months old?"

Liddie shook her head. "I wonder if she's had enough to eat." Liddie looked down at Rose's plump face. Though Rose was less than two months old, judging from their sizes, the two babies could have been the same age. She touched Rose's lips with a fingertip, triggering the little sucking motions she made even in her sleep.

With all the children presented, the agent invited those interested in adopting to meet the children individually.

A rough-looking farmer took the oat-haired boy aside, felt his arms, slapped him on the back, and checked out his teeth.

Liddie's mouth dropped open. "It's like he's buying a horse. I can't stay for this." She took Minnie's hand to pull her from the pew.

Minnie didn't budge. "Look there." She pointed to a couple talking to a brown-haired, brown-eyed girl of about six who barely raised her head. "I know them. Their daughter died of the influenza. It nearly broke their hearts."

The couple talked with the child for several minutes. Liddie heard the woman ask, "Do you want to be our daughter?" When the girl broke into a smile that revealed missing teeth and leaped into the woman's arms, tears welled in Liddie's eyes.

But Minnie was now focused on Mrs. Wilstock. "I'm going to see the baby," she said.

"Don't." Liddie put a hand on Minnie's arm. "Don't make it harder for yourself."

Minnie shook off her hand. "One look won't hurt. Before someone takes her." She approached Mrs. Wilstock before Liddie could protest again.

"May I hold her?" she asked, her voice firm.

"Of course," the agent said. "She's a precious one. Very alert."

Cradling the bundle in her arms, Minnie gently folded the blanket back from the baby's face. When she trailed her index finger along the infant's cheek, the little girl woke.

"Why, Pearl. Aren't you the most beautiful thing," Minnie cooed. A smile formed on the infant's tiny bow-shaped mouth. She reached up as though she had wakened to see Minnie's face every day of her life.

"She's perfect, isn't she?" Minnie looked at Liddie.

The happiness in Minnie's eyes made Liddie's heart ache. "She is pretty." She touched Minnie's elbow. "Remember. You were just going to look."

Minnie hummed an Irish lullaby as she moved to a quiet corner.

Liddie followed, speaking urgently. "Minnie. You're only hurting yourself."

Minnie ignored her.

After a short time, Mrs. Wilstock joined them. "She's beautiful, isn't she? With her black hair, she looks very like you," she said to Minnie. The agent's comments were no doubt intended to present the baby in the best possible way, but it was unnecessary. Minnie was smitten.

"How does this work?" Minnie asked. "Surely people simply don't walk out of here with a child."

"Some do." The agent nodded. "If the husband and wife agree. Others go home to talk it over. We're here for several days, so people have time to think it through. We want the best for the children and the adoptive families." Mrs. Wilstock glanced around. "Is your husband here?"

Minnie sat at the end of a pew and bounced Pearl lightly on her lap, causing the baby to giggle. She ignored Mrs. Wilstock's question. "What happens if a child isn't adopted?" Minnie asked.

"We take them to another town."

The idea of children put on display time after time horrified Liddie. To lose their parents, to get their hopes up for a new family, and then to be passed over. The feeling of rejection weighed like a boulder on her heart. Unconsciously, she tightened her grip on Rose.

"We do our best to place the children in the right homes," the agent said.

Liddie touched Mrs. Wilstock's arm. "Would you give us a moment, please?"

The woman nodded, stepping away as Liddie sat down.

Before Liddie spoke, Minnie whispered, "I can't let her go."

"They will be here for a few days," Liddie reasoned. "You can talk with Vern tonight and come back tomorrow."

"Vern won't come to see her. He'll say no." Minnie counted on her fingers. "If Pearl is six months old, she must have been born around April. Won't it be nice? The girls can grow up together!"

Liddie would not be distracted. "You can't adopt a baby without talking to your husband."

"He'll love her once he sees her. How could he not?" Minnie planted kisses on top of Pearl's head.

Liddie opened her mouth, then closed it. The idea that Minnie would take a baby without Vern's agreement was astounding.

"Besides, I can't leave Pearl here." Minnie pronounced "here" as though the Congregational church were the gates of hell.

"You need to at least try to talk to Vern. Mrs. Wilstock will take care of the baby." She nodded to the agent, who stood a few feet away, watching. Liddie did not call the infant by name. A name made the child real, and she wasn't going to encourage Minnie in any way.

Minnie stood up, the glint in her eyes fierce. "Pearl is coming home. With me."

"Can she do that?" Liddie asked the agent.

Mrs. Wilstock studied Minnie with Pearl.

"My husband wasn't able to be here today." Minnie smiled innocently. "You can see how happy Pearl is in our home when you visit us."

The agent considered for a bit longer and then nodded.

Liddie could not imagine how Vern would react.

Minnie didn't seem to care.

# Chapter 40

Breakfast was over. The remnants of fried eggs and bacon grease congealed on empty plates as they lingered over a last cup of coffee. Margretta pulled a piece of paper out of her apron pocket, smoothed it out, and slid it across the table. Her hand trembled as she lifted her arthritis-bent fingers, leaving the paper beside Liddie's plate.

"What's this?" Liddie picked up the slip. It took several seconds before the reality of what she was looking at sank in—a bank draft made out to her. For five thousand dollars.

"Mama?" Liddie didn't know what to make of it.

"It's from G. W., too." Margretta nodded with a satisfied smile.

An image of her father standing with his hand on her mother's shoulder flashed into Liddie's mind as vividly as though he were still alive. Her eyes burned, and she blinked back an urge to cry. "Joe, look." She handed him the check.

"It's what's fair," Margretta said. "Vern has the farm. I was waiting for you to settle down to give you your share." She nodded to Joe. "You want to buy this place. Now you can. Or at least start to."

Liddie wondered if the check was her mother's way of saying she approved of the choices she'd made. She and Joe had so much happy news this summer. Their beautiful baby. Joe's draft deferment. Now this money. "Thank you, Mama." She smiled. "Thank you."

Joe stared intently at the check. His voice was husky when he spoke. "Thank you, Margretta." He handed the check back to

Liddie and went to look out the window, his hands stuffed in his back pockets.

Liddie looked at him, puzzled. He always called Margretta "Mama." She didn't know what was wrong, but she didn't want her mother to think they were ungrateful. "This is cause for a celebration," she said. "I'm going to make something special for dessert." She checked on Rose, who slept soundly after her morning feeding, then went to the cupboard and pulled out the mixing bowl, flour, and sugar.

Later that afternoon, Liddie sought out Joe in the barn, their private place since Mama had come to live with them. When he saw her, he stopped cleaning out the calf pen.

She leaned against the feedbox. "I've never seen that much money at once."

"Me either." Joe took off his hat and wiped his forehead with the back of his arm. "What are you going to do with it?"

"What am *I* going to do with it? Mama gave it to us."

"It's your inheritance."

His tone confirmed her fear. He had taken offense.

"Mama wants us to use it to buy the farm. That's what she said. Papa would have wanted that, too." She traced a fingertip along the smooth edge of a crescent-shaped groove in the top of the feedbox. "I don't understand. I thought you'd be happy."

He pulled the pitchfork out of the straw, then jammed it back again. "She doesn't think I can take care of you and Rose."

"Oh, Joe! That's not true. Why would you think that?"

He didn't respond.

"This is because the check was made out to me and not to the both of us."

He jabbed the pitchfork into the straw again. "At first sight, it hurt."

Liddie left the feedbox, took the pitchfork out of his hand, and propped it against the wall. She put her hands on his cheeks. "She didn't mean that." He tried to turn his face away, but she didn't let go. "Look at me. I know she didn't mean to insult you."

"Liddie, I want to be able to give you everything."

"We have everything already, without this money. With the money, we can own the farm sooner. Like she said."

"Because she said it doesn't mean that's what you have to do. You could save it. Or spend it on something you want. We can keep on renting and buy when we get enough money together. Like we planned." Joe strode to the barn door.

Liddie watched him stand looking out at the fields, but didn't follow. He needed time to think; so did she. Unexpectedly, she felt sad; right now the money seemed more a curse than a blessing. When she saw Joe run his fingers through his hair, she knew he'd come to a conclusion.

"I expect your ma and pa talked about this before he died," he said when he returned to her. "Your ma is doing what she and G. W. agreed. No reason for me to take offense."

"So you're not upset?"

"I don't take it personal." Joe reached down and scratched the neck of a yellow tabby cat winding between his legs. "But if we didn't put it down on the farm, what would you buy? If you could buy anything?"

She searched her memory. The only material thing she'd ever wanted badly in her whole life had been a doll, and like a miracle, the doll she'd desired had appeared under the tree at Christmas. She'd grown up having what she needed, blessed with a wealth of love and contentment. Because her family provided her every-thing, she'd never imagined otherwise. She laughed. "It's hard!"

Joe looked skeptical. "Didn't you ever imagine having all the money in the world?" He took her hand. "Let's walk." He led her through the barnyard out to the hay field.

She racked her brain for things she wanted. Did it signal a dearth of imagination that nothing grand came to mind?

Until she lived in town, she'd never thought about the cost of things at all. As a child, she seldom saw money change hands. Her room and board in Maquoketa was her first inkling, and though Mama and Vern had managed that until she could cover her own expenses, she had been proud to pay for things with her own earnings. Working and earning enough to fend for herself had been rewarding in their own right.

Now the cost of running a farm was abundantly clear. Her experience at the studio prepared her to keep the farm's books, and she was proud Joe trusted her with that responsibility. Because she was the one to add the numbers at the end of the month, the cost of things was always in her mind, and many nights, she sat up totaling the monthly expenses.

They talked often about buying the farm, but it was difficult to see how they'd ever have enough to make it happen. To even think of spending this money on anything other than the farm felt wrong.

"It's a game," Joe persisted when they stood at the top of the rise. "Come on. What's one thing you'd like?"

She recalled her days with Mrs. Tinker. "Maybe a new sewing machine. I could make new clothes for all of us."

"Something bigger. Just for fun."

"That would be fun! You know I love to sew," she insisted. "Okay. How about a new cookstove?"

"You are so practical."

A breeze blew strands of hair across her face, and she snagged them, tucking the wayward locks behind her ear. Closing her eyes, she breathed in the dusty warm smell of autumn. She opened her eyes to see Joe watching her, smiling.

"All right," she said. "A darkroom." She hastened to add, "But that's a really big thing. I know it's too much."

"Now you're talking!" he said with such enthusiasm it surprised her. "That's something to dream about."

"What about you?" She threw the challenge back to him. "What would you spend it on if you could have anything?"

"Another trip like our honeymoon. A horse I could race and stand at stud. A car. A home where you and I and our babies can be happy. And this farm."

He rattled off the list so fast, Liddie laughed. "You've already been thinking." Then his comments caught up with her. "You'd build us a new house?" she asked.

"I want to give you things." He planted a kiss on her cheek. "I want you to be happy."

"I am happy. You make me happy. This place makes me happy."

She looked across the fields. With that much money, she could have anything she could think of: new furniture, new clothes, a new cookstove. But the cradle Joe had built for Rose was perfect. There was nothing wrong with the cookstove they had now, nothing that a little persistence didn't manage. The dresses she had were fine. She had what she needed right in front of her.

She looked intently into Joe's eyes. "You're serious? I can do anything I want with this money?"

"It's your money, *Liebchen*."

"All right, then." She laid the palm of her hand on his cheek. "I want this farm."

Joe wrapped his arms around her waist, lifted her up, and twirled her in a circle until they collapsed on the ground laughing.

"*Mein Liebchen*," he said, and kissed her in the way that made her forget about everything but him. "I'll talk to Gib."

# Chapter 41

Liddie watched the buckboard come up the lane. Vern was bringing Minnie and Pearl to spend the day while he and Joe went into town. Joe planned to talk with the banker about a mortgage on the farm. The money was in the bank, waiting for the details to be worked out.

"I wonder what the temperature will be like today?" she muttered. The late-October weather had been warm of late, but as far as Liddie could see, the Treadway household had been decidedly chilly ever since Minnie had brought Pearl home from the church. Minnie was back to her old self, color back in her cheeks and as lively as ever. But since that day—four solid weeks ago—according to Minnie, Vern hadn't spoken a single word to his wife.

As Minnie told it, she'd finessed his silence during Mrs. Wilstock's visit with coffee, cake, and a tour of their well-kept home. She laughed off Liddie's concerns. "I talk with Pearl about everything from laundry to the cooking, and she babbles right along. I also talk to Vern. I don't pay any mind that he doesn't talk back. He'll come around."

It was a contest of wills in the Treadway house, that was for sure. As Vern tied up the horses, Minnie called out, "Hi, Liddie. Beautiful day, isn't it?" The cheerfulness of her words matched the tone of her voice.

Liddie went to help with Pearl, but Minnie warned her off with a little shake of her head. To Liddie's surprise, Vern reached up to take the baby and held Minnie's hand as she stepped down.

Vern did not hand the baby back to Minnie. Instead, he held Pearl in his arms as though he'd been doing it since she was born. "Morning, Liddie," he said.

"Look how happy you are today." Liddie tickled Pearl under the chin. Her comment could just as easily have been addressed to Vern.

"How's Ma?" he asked.

"She's good. She's in the kitchen." Liddie stared after him as he went to the house.

Minnie lifted her sewing basket out of the buckboard. "I told you," she said.

"And it only took a month," Liddie observed with dry humor as they followed Vern into the house.

As soon as the men left for town, the women settled down around the kitchen table with knitting needles and balls of yarn. The neighborhood women had committed to knitting two pairs of socks to send with every county man going to the war. The knitting pattern was so familiar by now, the women barely looked as their needles clicked away.

"Tell us how you did it," Liddie urged.

"It was all you, wasn't it, sweetie?" Minnie kissed the top of Pearl's head as the baby pawed at her mother's yarn. "A couple of days ago, we were having breakfast. I put the high chair between Vern and me so he could help her with her food. Which he never did." Minnie glanced at Margretta, then continued. "He can be such a mule. He never even looked in her direction.

"Anyway, I went to get something in the living room. I heard a spoon hit the floor, and I sneaked close enough to peek back in.

"There was Pearl straining over the arm of her chair toward her spoon. At first she babbled. Pretty soon, she screwed up her little face, and big tears started to run down her cheeks. He tried not to look at her, but he never could ignore a woman in distress. He picked up the spoon and went to put it on her tray, but she grabbed his finger and held on. As soon as she had hold of him, she stopped crying. Then he wiped a tear off her cheek with his finger. It was the first time he touched her."

Minnie nuzzled Pearl. "By the time I came back into the kitchen, he was feeding her cereal." She smiled triumphantly.

"What did he say?" Liddie asked.

"Not a thing. And neither did I. We acted like him feeding her was as natural as the sun coming up in the morning. Didn't we, Pearl?" Minnie turned the baby to face her. "Now your daddy can't wait to have a meal with you, can he?" Pearl tried to put the brooch on Minnie's dress in her mouth.

"I'm happy for you all," Margretta said. "Vern will be a good father."

"I knew he would. Once he let himself."

Liddie stuck the ends of her knitting needles into the ball and squeezed Minnie's hand. "I know I'm happy Rose has an older sister to play with." She went to the cupboard for plates and forks. "Let's have a piece of crumb cake to celebrate."

"I hope you'll take a picture of our family," Minnie said.

"Pardon?"

"We'd like a picture of our family," Minnie repeated. "And we'd like you to take it."

Liddie felt a twinge in her chest. She hadn't used her camera since the day she had put it away almost a year ago. What had once been so important to her and had sparked her imagination now lay buried in the sideboard drawer. Joe never said anything about the camera and neither did she. She expected he was happy she wasn't wasting money on a hobby.

Liddie busied herself with the cake, keeping her back to Minnie lest her distress show on her face. "Oh, you should go to a studio. You'd want someone good to do it," she said.

"Why, Liddie, I can't believe you said that. Your photos are wonderful."

"Were. Maybe. I haven't picked up a camera in ages."

"It can't be more than a few months. And I seriously doubt you've forgotten how." Minnie frowned at her. "What's going on? What happened to the woman who was going to travel the world with her photography?"

Liddie laughed. "I'm a farmwife now. Not a photographer."

Margretta stopped knitting and looked at her. "Can't you be both?"

"It surprises me to hear you say that, Mama. As I recall, you were not particularly happy when I went to work for Mr. Littmann."

"You have me there," Margretta said.

"I don't care how long it's been," Minnie said. "I want you to take our family pictures. We'll pay you. And I want a picture of all of us with Margretta. We could even do it today."

"No. We can't." Overwhelmed by the rush of emotions the conversation roused, Liddie was curt. "I don't have film."

"Oh." Minnie's enthusiasm deflated. "I wish we'd thought of that. Vern might have bought some while they're in town. Or does it have to be ordered?" Her spark returned. "Could we get film and do it soon? Please say you'll do it. Promise me. Okay?"

Liddie couldn't help but smile at Minnie's enthusiasm. In fact, the idea of having a camera in her hands made her feel unexpectedly buoyant. "Okay. But you don't need to pay me." She hesitated. "Maybe for the developing."

"I wish I had a photo of Amelia's family, too." Margretta's voice sounded ragged.

Minnie patted her hand. "What have you heard from them?"

"We got a letter last week. It's in the desk. Liddie, get it so Minnie can read it."

Liddie retrieved the letter, glad to let Minnie carry the conversation.

"How's she doing with the twins?" Minnie asked. "She sure has her hands full."

"She didn't say. I hope she still has that neighbor girl staying with her."

"I wonder what Fred's doing now?"

"She hasn't mentioned in the last few letters." Liddie put cake on the table and poured coffee. "Maybe still working for that neighbor."

"I don't expect she sits down often," Minnie said. "Who's this Sean she mentions?"

"Her neighbor Gertie's boy," Liddie said. "He was among the first American troops to go to France. He hadn't been there two weeks and was killed."

"Oh, how sad!"

Liddie caught Minnie's gaze. The two were thankful their husbands had been deferred from service. But it was hard knowing so many men who had gone.

"With winter coming on, I expect the men will welcome warm feet." Minnie picked up her needles.

Between knitting and babies and talking, the day passed pleasantly. Liddie was putting a fresh pot of coffee on the stove when they heard the sound of a motorcar driving up the lane.

"Who could that be?" Liddie wondered aloud.

"Someone must be lost," Minnie suggested.

"I hope it's nothing serious," Margretta said.

All three women were out on the porch in time to see Joe steer a car into the yard. Vern followed in the buckboard, some distance back.

# Chapter 42

Joe swept an arm dramatically toward the automobile. "Isn't she a beauty?"

"What in the world?" Liddie ran down the steps.

"Look at it, Liddie." Joe took her by the arm and walked her around, pointing out the leather seats, the retractable top, the running lights.

Liddie stepped back to observe the motorcar. "When do you have to take it back?"

"We have plenty of time. Let's take a ride." He ran up the steps to get Margretta.

"You go ahead." Margretta waved him off. "Someone has to mind the babies."

He pecked her on the cheek. "You can go next time." He led Liddie to the front seat. "Come sit up here with me. Vern, you and Minnie get the backseat."

As they bumped along on the rutted road, she asked, "Whose car is this? I can't believe someone would let you keep a car overnight. When do you have to give it back?"

Joe drove with his eyes fixed on the road, both hands on the steering wheel. "I don't. It's ours."

"What do you mean, ours?"

"Augie Mathis was getting a new car. He gave us a deal on it." Joe finally glanced over at Liddie, a grin on his face. "We're automobile owners, Liddie!"

"What?" she gasped.

"The first in the neighborhood!"

"Oh my," Minnie said in a very small voice.

The car was theirs? She bit down on her cheek.

"No need to harness up the horse and buggy when you want to go someplace. Besides, it's economical. We don't have to feed it. Or water it."

"Or shovel shit," Vern interjected.

"That's a fact," Joe said. "You can drive it, too, Liddie. I'll teach you."

The more Joe talked, the less Liddie heard and the harder she bit on her cheek. Only the coppery taste of blood caused her to unclench her teeth.

When they got back to the house, Vern and Minnie left at once. As Liddie and Joe watched Vern's wagon disappear down the lane, he draped an arm around her shoulders.

She swatted at his hand and whirled to glare at him, anger pulsing under her skin. "How could you do this without talking to me?"

"We have been talking about how to spend the money."

"To buy this farm. That's what we talked about."

"And we will. It's taken care of. We sign the papers this week."

Without warning, the pressures of the past months—another flare-up of her mother's gout, a new baby, lack of sleep, the war—all came crashing together.

"What did it cost? How did you pay for it? How could you do this?" She peppered him with questions as hot tears streamed down her cheeks.

Joe stared at her. "We'll talk when you calm down." He swung toward the barn. "I'm going to do chores."

"Don't walk away from me!" she yelled, the shrillness of her voice shattering the still afternoon air.

He kept walking as she bored holes in his back with her eyes. Just then, Rose's cries pierced the air. It was feeding time. Again.

As Liddie turned toward the house, confusion, shock, embarrassment, and anger raged through her. She walked over and kicked the motorcar's fender, stepped back, and kicked it again. She wiped her eyes with the back of her hand and headed up the steps. She wished she did not have to see her mother.

In the kitchen, Margretta held the squalling baby on her shoulder, patting her back.

Liddie avoided her mother's eyes as she reached for Rose.

"Everything all right?"

"Everything's fine." Liddie spoke through clenched teeth. She had no privacy. None.

"Hmm." Margretta picked up her knitting needles. "She's not going to nurse if you're upset."

"I'm not upset." Liddie fumbled with the front of her dress, the buttons defying her words and her fingers.

"If you say so."

The baby latched on to her breast with a vigor that vindicated Liddie. At least Rose was with her.

"That's quite a surprise." Margretta nodded toward the door.

"He bought it." Liddie struggled to keep her voice even.

"So I gather."

As Rose suckled, Liddie stroked the baby's cheek and relaxed in the pleasure of being with her baby. Gradually, the pressure in her breast eased, and she felt a little of the anger she'd been holding drain out, too.

Then her mother said, "I thought you'd put the money on the farm. Getting started on a farm is costly."

Liddie felt her hackles rise. That was exactly what she had thought, but coming from her mother, the comment felt critical of her as well as of Joe.

"I know getting started on a farm is hard," Margretta said. "Especially renting. At least with the mortgage you can make your own decisions."

"Mama." Liddie held up a hand. "We're doing fine."

"I never said you weren't. Joe works as hard as any man, but he didn't have anything to start with."

Liddie looked up sharply. "That's what's always mattered, hasn't it?" she accused her mother. "Not just finding a man, but the right man." An ache grew in Liddie's chest. Had Joe heard her mother's true thoughts the day she gave them the check? If they didn't have everything right away, did that make him a poor husband? The idea made her mad.

"All G. W. and I ever wanted was for you to be happy. Then I saw how you loved your pictures. I was glad for you."

"You wanted me to get married. Now I am, and honestly— between cooking and laundry and taking care of the baby—who has time to make pictures?" She switched Rose to her other breast.

Margretta lowered her voice. "I won't be here forever."

"Oh, Mama, where did that come from? And what does that even mean? You have years ahead of you."

"That's what I always said to my mother."

Liddie frowned. "Are you trying to tell me something?"

"Of course not. No one knows the day or the hour." Margretta brushed Liddie's question aside. "It's important, Liddie. You both have to be happy."

"I am happy." Liddie prickled.

"All right, then." Margretta was silent for only a few moments. "Why did he buy the car?"

"I have no idea."

"Men have their reasons."

"What reason is there to buy something like that and not talk to me first?"

"You need to talk to him."

The memory of her standing there in tears, yelling at Joe's back, made her cringe.

"When the baby's done, go find him. Talk to him. Take something to eat. Make up."

Liddie bristled. "I didn't do anything to make up for!" The baby scrunched up her face and began to cry. "Oh, Rosie, no," Liddie crooned. "It's okay. Mommy's sorry." She caressed the baby's cheek and brought her breast back to Rose's mouth.

"You keep peace whether it's your fault or not."

Liddie chewed her lower lip. Was this always to be her role?

After Rose finished nursing, Liddie laid her in the cradle. Though it galled her, she wrapped two pieces of crumb cake in a checkered towel and headed to the barn.

She found him sitting on the feedbox, one hand resting on the back of the yellow tomcat. Joe looked up when he heard the barn door open and then turned away.

A calf stuck its head through the slats of the pen and stretched to lick her hand. She scratched its head. The silence in the barn was thick. "I'm sorry I yelled," she said.

Joe rubbed his neck, then nudged the cat off the feedbox and slid over to make room. "Sit with me."

Anger flared under her skin, but she swallowed her pride and edged up onto the feedbox, holding the napkin on her lap, keeping several inches of space between them.

"Why, Joe?"

"Truthfully, I thought you'd like it. A car will make things easier. You want to visit Minnie? You need to get into town? You crank up the car and go."

"That's not the point. We agreed my money would go to the farm." The moment "my money" slipped out of her mouth, she regretted it. "You went to town to buy this farm. You came home with a car."

"I wanted to do something for you. A surprise."

"It was that," she said dryly.

"I ran into Augie at the bank. The car's used but in fine shape. It'll last for years. The banker agreed we can roll the cost of the car into the farm mortgage. We'll only have the one payment, and the payment won't be much different than what we pay in rent. This will get us almost a quarter of the way to owning the place outright. We'll hold some of your money back in the account. A cushion."

His emphasis on "your money" told her she'd wounded him.

"I still don't understand. This farm is what we've been working for. When we finally get the money, you buy a car?" Liddie's voice rose.

She stopped, lowered her voice, willed her anger to subside. She straightened the edges of the towel in her lap. "Do you know what we were talking about before you and Vern came back from town?"

He shook his head.

"Taking pictures. Minnie wanted me to take their family picture, and I couldn't say yes. Because we've been saving every cent for the farm, so I don't have money to buy film, let alone pay for the developing."

"What made you think you couldn't take pictures?"

"When we came back from Wyoming, you said I couldn't take pictures because of the cost."

"God, Liddie, I didn't mean you couldn't take *any*." He looked at her, dumbfounded. "Is that why you don't take pictures anymore?" He shook his head. "I figured you were too busy with the house and the baby."

Joe bent forward, his elbows on his knees. When he spoke, his voice was so low she strained to hear.

"When I was in Canada, it was just me. If there wasn't food in the cupboard, I could get another job or bum a meal or go hungry. But now there's you. And the baby."

She waited.

"Every day I go out and do the chores, take care of the pigs, the crops, the fences, the barn. It's what I wanted, what I still want. But then I thought, what if it isn't enough? What if a day came when I couldn't take care of you? Then this money drops right into our hands."

"How does buying a car make any of what you're saying right?"

"I want you to have everything. *I* want to give you everything."

"Oh, Joe." Liddie nudged him with her shoulder. "I have you. We have Rose. There isn't anything else to want." She remembered the crumb cake and unwrapped the napkin. "I brought a peace offering. But I'm afraid it's smashed."

"We'll make peace from the pieces." Joe didn't smile. "Do you forgive me?"

Liddie nodded. "Might Augie take his car back?"

———

Liddie kicked the fender each time she walked by the car on the way to collect eggs or milk the cow. However, the intensity of her kick eased after a week or so. Eventually, she only gave the hood a firm slap with the flat of her hand as she passed.

As much as his buying the car irked her, she had to admit she enjoyed the jaunts they took on nice afternoons. Picnic lunches by the river reminded her of when she lived in Maquoketa. Plus, the pleasure he took in driving that car was so evident she could not stay angry.

Even so, the cost of what he had bought (and she hadn't) continued to surface in her mind. She compared the cost of gas—sixteen cents a gallon—and the cost of film—fifteen cents for six exposures. Though Joe maintained the car himself; she had to pay to develop film and print pictures. But if he wasn't concerned about cost, why was she?

Each time he started the car, he talked through the steps out loud. Pull the sparker lever down. Hold the right tire with your right hand; turn the crank with your left. "Don't ever want to forget that." He smiled. "Too many fellas get their arms broke when it kicks back."

Though he offered to let her drive, she refused, content to let him take the driver's seat. But one day, when Mama and Rose were napping and Joe was working in the field farthest from the house, she walked out to the car.

"You and I, we have to get along," she said. To her delight, the car started the first time she pulled the crank.

"There!" she said. "That wasn't so hard." She almost wished Joe were here to see her success. She climbed into the driver's seat and put her hands on the wheel. The car vibrated; she tightened her grip. Looking down at the pedals, she reminded herself. Left: go; right: brake; center: reverse.

She released the hand brake and stepped on the left pedal. The car shot forward. Panicking, she yanked the hand brake. The car jolted to a stop. Only then did she think of the brake pedal. Sweat broke out on her palms.

"Don't be an idiot!" she chided herself. Drying her palms on her skirt, she gripped the wheel again. She released the brake and stepped on the pedal.

Steering in a big circle, she guided the car around the walnut tree, past the barn, past the house. Around and around. She stopped and started until she could do it and still breathe evenly. Then she stopped and looked at the pedals. "You're going to have to go backward sometime," she muttered.

Holding the steering wheel in a death grip, she stepped on the reverse pedal. The car lurched back. She stomped on the brake pedal and gasped for breath. She tried again. And again. It took most of an hour, but by then she felt she had a pretty good handle on this driving business.

She steered the car back to where Joe parked it. Though her legs quivered when she finally stood with both feet on solid ground, she gave the fender a friendly pat and strode to the house. She felt as though the world were hers.

———

"You better take the buggy," Joe said. "The road's still soft after that rain."

"I'll be fine," Liddie insisted.

"I could drive you," he said.

"You have work to get done. You said so." Liddie buttoned her coat and bundled Rose in a blanket. "Minnie is waiting for us. Ready to go, Mama?"

"She's a stubborn one, isn't she?" Margretta whispered to Joe as he helped her to the car.

"I heard that," Liddie said.

"Get in," Joe said. "I'll start her for you."

She nestled Rose in her mother's arms. "Honestly, Mama. He wanted me to drive, and then he resists."

"He wants to take care of you. It's what husbands do," Margretta said. "A smart wife lets him."

"Hmm." She reached over and adjusted Rose's blanket.

It took Joe three tries to get the car running.

"I didn't expect it to be so hard," Liddie said.

"She was a little cold. If she's that way in town, get someone to help you."

She kissed his cheek. "I couldn't have got her going without you, Joe. Thank you."

———

Rose gurgled and waved her arms. "She's lovely, Liddie," Mrs. Tinker said with a smile. "I'm so glad you came to visit."

"I wanted you to see my greatest creation." While Minnie and her mother shopped, Liddie had come to show off her baby. Sitting in Mrs. Tinker's front room felt so familiar. "I see you have a new girl."

"Yes." Mrs. Tinker lowered her voice. "She does well with the work we have now."

"Now?"

"With the war on, most women make do rather than making new. Even in the cities, it is considered unseemly to wear fancy new things. It's more appropriate to tell how you remade one of last season's dresses." She poured more tea. "Someday, this war will be over, and women will want new dresses again. Everything comes around."

"I expect it does." Liddie nodded. "By the way, when Minnie and I stopped at Becker's today for a pastry, we found the shop empty."

"That is a sad situation. It started when they found glass in their flour."

"We'd heard about that. Did they ever learn who did it?"

"If anyone knew, they didn't say," Mrs. Tinker said. "Poor Mrs. Becker was so distressed she was sick in bed for a week."

"Surely people didn't really think they'd done it themselves?"

"Some believed it. Some didn't. But that's not the worst of it. That same week, Mrs. Becker called a cousin who lives near Davenport. Of course they spoke in German. Well, someone on the line reported it to the state Council of National Defense. Both women were thrown in jail on charges of sedition."

"Oh, Mrs. Tinker. Surely no one could believe those two old ladies were plotting against the country."

A darkness clouded Mrs. Tinker's eyes. When she spoke, her voice was tight with barely concealed anger. "I like to think the governor didn't have people like Mrs. Becker in mind when he passed the law making it illegal to speak anything other than English in Iowa."

After a pause, during which more thoughts crossed her face, she took a careful sip of tea and continued in a more relaxed tone. "Fortunately, cooler heads prevailed, and they were only in jail overnight. But the damage was done. Mrs. Becker was too embarrassed to wait on customers anymore. One morning, the shop didn't open, and we learned they'd left town."

"Maquoketa without Becker's Bakery." Liddie sighed. "It was always such a treat to go there. And what will Mrs. Caither do? The Beckers made those pastries for her parties. Or with the war on, is she even having her party this year?"

"Oh yes, Anna is of an age to be interested in young men. Though I expect the party will be more subdued."

"Can she be so old already?"

"Time passes. The party is an opportunity. With so many young men gone to fight, the mothers are anxious for their daughters' chances." Mrs. Tinker's voice faltered.

"Has something happened?"

Mrs. Tinker shook her head. "No. No. I just worry about my sister's son."

"What do you hear from him?"

"Precious little. His last letter came from France. He said he and the other fellows have been training since they arrived. He can't say more." Mrs. Tinker squared her shoulders. "We are proud of him."

"We all are." Liddie put her hand on Mrs. Tinker's. "He'll be fine."

Mrs. Tinker smiled resolutely. "I know he will."

# Chapter 43

"Where did you . . . ?" Liddie looked at Joe and then back at the camera nestled in her lap amidst wrinkled wrapping paper. A red velvet bow lay on the floor at her feet. "How did you . . . ?"

She looked at the Kodak folding camera from all angles. She extended the bellows, shifting it to frame images horizontally and vertically. Her palms warmed to the touch of the leather case.

"It's the latest model. With the best lens." Joe hovered by her side, pointing out the features as though he'd made the camera himself. "You can use dry plates or roll film."

She hadn't realized he even knew the difference. "How did you know to buy this one?"

"I wanted you to have the best," he said. "And I had a little help." He gestured around the living room where the family had gathered to open presents, waiting for Christmas dinner to settle before they returned to the table for mincemeat pie.

"I remembered you said a Kodak dealer used to come to Mr. Littmann's studio," Mama said.

"I tracked him down at Cundill's Studio when I was in town," Joe explained.

"He had it shipped to our house." Minnie clapped in delight.

"A group of conspirators." Liddie shook her head.

"We still want you to take our family photograph," Minnie said. "Don't we, Vern?"

"Long as we don't have to show it to everybody in town."

Minnie cuffed him on the arm.

"As soon as I get film, I'll do it," Liddie said.

"Maybe we could use this." Joe reached into the branches of the Christmas tree and pulled out another package. "I got two rolls. Remember, you said the cheapest thing is film."

She gazed up at him, recognizing this camera for the make-up gift that it was, knowing it made all the difference that he'd decided the timing, loving him for loving her.

"Could we do it today?" Minnie asked. "We're dressed up. The girls are being good. Please say yes."

Liddie looked around the parlor, gauging the light, thinking about composition. "We'll need to move some chairs."

"Vern and I are at your service," Joe said. "Tell us what to do."

"No time to sleep off the ham?" Vern asked.

"You can do that later," Minnie said.

They spent the afternoon rearranging furniture and composing family groupings. Liddie piled up books as a makeshift camera stand. She drew back curtains to bring more light into the parlor. In a moment of inspiration, she used cookie sheets to fill in the light. Holding a camera again made her float with joy.

At one point, Liddie looked up before taking a picture of her mother with Vern's family. She noticed Joe leaning against a door frame, watching her. "Thank you." She smiled. He nodded. She was home in so many ways, and it felt so good.

# Chapter 44

"What are you up to today?" Joe asked. He cradled Rose in his arms as he did most mornings while Liddie fixed breakfast.

Liddie stirred the pot of oatmeal and put the lid back on. "It's the day to clean the lamp chimneys. Mama never lets me forget that." She sliced a loaf of bread and put it on the table with butter and jam, then stuck her head in the living room and called to her mother. "Mama! Breakfast is almost ready." She returned and finished setting the table. "How about you?"

Joe settled Rose in the cradle they kept by the table while they ate, then buttered a piece of bread and chewed as he talked. "I want to check out the planter. Make sure the check chain is working right. We'll be planting soon enough."

Liddie enjoyed these morning chats she and Joe had. Her mother had taken to staying in her room until breakfast was ready. At first, Liddie had thought she did it to give them some time alone. Finally, Margretta had admitted she enjoyed sleeping in and having a little extra time to herself in the morning to read her Bible.

Liddie lifted the lid on the oatmeal again. "Looks like it's ready," she said. "I'll see if Mama's ready to eat."

She knocked gently on her mother's door. Generally, Margretta was up, dressed, and reading by the time Liddie called her for breakfast. This morning, she didn't hear movement, so she knocked again and opened the door wide enough to peek in. Her mother was still fast asleep, one arm under the covers, the other flung up on her pillow, her fingertips resting against her temple.

"Mama?" she whispered. She didn't want to startle her mother awake, so she stepped softly up to the bed. "Mama?" She touched her mother's shoulder. "Are you going to have breakfast with us?" She shook her mother gently. Her mother did not respond.

Liddie snatched her hand back as though she'd been burned. She stepped backward, a lump growing in her throat. "Joe!" she called. "Joe, come here. Something's wrong with Mama!"

Joe rushed in. "What?" He stopped short when he saw Margretta's face. He went to the bedside, leaned down, and touched his hand to Margretta's neck.

A coldness crept over Liddie's shoulders as she watched him, and she folded her arms tight against her chest. Without realizing it, she stepped away until her back touched the wall.

Joe took Margretta's hand and held it for a minute before tucking it gently under the covers. Then he straightened up and held out his hand to Liddie.

Liddie shook her head, her eyes fixed on her mother's face. "She was fine last night."

"I'm sorry," he said.

She stared at him in disbelief. "She can't be gone." She shook her head again. "She can't."

He held out his arms to her. Her eyes filled with tears, and she buried her face in his chest.

———

*January 10, 1918*
*Dear Amelia,*

*It was good to hear your voice. I'm glad you live close enough to Lusk for the man at the mercantile to get you to the phone. Mama really did go peacefully. I think I told you the last thing she said before she went to bed the night before was, "I'll see you children in the morning." I wish you could have been here for the funeral. There was a crowd at the cemetery and at the house after. She'd be happy we had the funeral back at the home place. Even though she settled in with Joe and me just fine, I know she missed the farm.*

*Aunt Kate went back to Ohio after only a week. It was good to see her. I remember when Papa died, she said crying wouldn't bring him back. At the time, I thought she meant it was wrong for me to cry for him. Now I think she meant we grieve, but we have to keep on living. Really, what other choice is there?*

*There were times I felt differently, but now I realize I was lucky to have Mama living with us this past year. We cooked and sewed and talked. I walk into the kitchen now and still expect to see her there holding Rose. She often said she wished she could rock your babies for you.*

*Seems like we hear every day about more boys gone off to the war. You'd remember Harold Dirks, Morris Blake, and Carl Mason. Last week, they went to Camp Dodge for training. From there, they head to Europe. I don't know how their mothers sleep at night. The Shiflers' son, Angus, was killed in action.*

*Rose is growing up fast. She sits up on her own. She and Pearl play so nice together. Pearl can pull herself up using chairs. The four-month age difference shows how much they change in a short time.*

*I will close and get this in tomorrow's mail. Joe and I send our love.*

*Liddie*

Finished with the letter, Liddie leaned back in the chair and pulled her shawl more tightly around her shoulders. Outside the amber circle of lamplight, Joe slept in his chair, a newspaper crumpled in his lap. As much as she liked to end her day talking with him, she let him rest. Seeing him sleep reminded her of her father, who'd often fall asleep after a hard day of work.

If she weren't such a night owl, she'd be asleep herself. She lifted her chair as she slid back from the table so as not to make a sound and went to the window. The moon was rising and the reflection off the snow was so bright she could see almost as clear as day. Nights like this were so peaceful, Mama always said.

Liddie was grateful the images that came to her most readily at moments like this were of her mother alive—peeling potatoes, writing letters, holding Rose. Her reaction to her mother's death haunted her. She had struggled to touch the body, and irrational fear had gripped her each time she went close. Only with Joe there had she been able to do it. Now she wished she could hold her mother's hand again.

Snippets of comments her mother had made in her last weeks came to Liddie's mind often, and she wondered if Margretta had sensed she didn't have much time left. Regardless of what she'd said about not knowing the day or the hour, it appeared her mother had been tying up loose ends.

She left the window, moved the lamp closer to her rocking chair, and turned up the wick for a brighter flame to sew by. As she searched in her basket for the darning egg, she spotted the quilt square with the oak leaf and reel appliqué and smoothed the square out on her lap. She so rarely found time for that kind of fancy work anymore. When she'd started the project, she surely hadn't imagined this was where she'd be five years later. She chuckled to herself as she put the appliqué square back in her basket and pulled out a sock.

With the threaded needle in one hand and the sock pulled tight over the darning egg, Liddie made the stitches to get months of additional wear. The tiny stitches she had perfected under Mrs.

Tinker's tutelage worked as well for darning a sock as they did for sewing a fancy dress. Joe wouldn't feel the patch.

Sewing was, indeed, a skill she could always use. Looping the thread around the needle twice and then sending the needle back through the first loop, she tied off the yarn. This was one of her special "love knots" that caused little bulk and never came loose.

"There." She touched her lips to the knot and blew a kiss toward her sleeping husband. "You'll have my love with you every step of the way."

————

Liddie left her mother's bedroom untouched. After the funeral, she had laundered and ironed her mother's apron, dress, and stockings and returned them to the bedroom as though they would be worn again. The old family photo, the one taken before Liddie was born, sat on the dresser. Her mother's shoes were under the straight-backed chair, where she put them when she undressed at night. Letting go of the things in her mother's room felt like letting go of her mother. And she just couldn't.

One day Joe came upon Liddie standing motionless, staring at the bedroom door as though her mother might walk out. "I miss her, too," he said.

She blinked back tears as she rested her head against his shoulder.

When the photos they'd taken on Christmas Day came in the mail, the Kodak insignia evoked both excitement and dread. She didn't open the envelope. Instead, she propped it against the salt-shaker and set to making bread.

Throughout the day, her eyes landed on the envelope. Finally, she picked it up and slid a fingernail under the flap. When she saw the photos, she gasped a breathy "Oh."

She hadn't been prepared to see her mother looking back at her. So real. So alive. Scooping up the photos, she ran to her mother's bedroom, threw herself onto the bed, pressed the photos flat to her stomach, and sobbed.

———

When Joe came to the house for supper, he found her sitting on the bed, legs curled up under her. She held Rose against her shoulder as she looked at the photos spread out before her.

"The Christmas pictures were in today's mail. Take a look." She scooted over so he could sit.

"There's a good one." He picked up the picture of Margretta holding both her granddaughters. Liddie and Minnie knelt on either side.

"Of course." Liddie laughed, nudging him with her elbow. "The one you took."

"I only pushed the lever." He lifted Rose from Liddie's arms. "It is a good picture, don't you think, little girl?" Rose giggled. "See? She agrees with me." He settled the baby in the crook of his arm.

She picked up the photo of Minnie standing at the window holding Pearl. Vern faced them, his hand resting lightly on Pearl's head. "I like this one. But it could be printed better."

"It looks fine to me."

"Fine, yes. But when I had the darkroom, I would have worked to get more gradations."

Joe laughed. "I don't even know what you're talking about."

"Hmm." Liddie picked up another picture of her mother. "If I could have printed these myself, Mama could have seen them."

"Mama was happy holding her grandchildren. A picture wasn't going to make her happier than she was right then."

"I know you're right. Still, I'm glad the girls will see her holding them." She placed the picture on the bed. "She asked me once why I couldn't do both."

"Do both what?"

"Be a farmwife and a photographer."

"You're already that."

"Yes. But I could do more. Set up a darkroom and print our pictures. Take pictures for neighbors."

"Whoa! Where did that come from?"

"You don't think I could?" she bridled, recalling how Littmann had challenged her when she suggested something similar.

"I didn't say that. You took me by surprise, is all."

Liddie scrambled off the bed. "Are you willing to let me try?" She tugged his hand. "Come to the kitchen. I baked bread today. We can talk."

"Have you ever noticed that you always bake bread when you want something?"

Liddie pulled plates out of the cupboard. "Here are some potatoes. Mash them up and see if Rose will take a nibble while I get supper on. I was so caught up in the photos, I let myself get behind."

"What do you think, Rosie?" Joe asked as he spooned a bit of potato into the baby's mouth. "If your mama had a darkroom, would we always wonder if we were going to eat?"

"With a darkroom right here in the house, I could work while Rose sleeps. Or at night. Besides, it's just our photos, so it wouldn't take long. With a black cloth over the window and door, Mama's room could be a darkroom."

"You'd take your mother's things out?"

Liddie worked silently at the stove. The pictures had jarred loose the grief she'd held inside, made her remember her mother's words as well as her own joy in making pictures. "She put the idea in my mind," she said at last. "I think she'd be happy with it."

"What about equipment?"

"So you're not saying no?"

"I'm not saying no. But we can't spend money willy-nilly."

"I understand." Liddie bent as she passed the table and kissed his forehead. "No willy-nilly."

After supper, she got out the catalog that came with the camera. Together they made a list of materials that would equip the most basic darkroom. Even that added up. She had nowhere near enough in her egg-money jar. Her shoulders slumped. "I guess we can't do it."

Joe studied the list. "Maybe we can. We kept back money from your inheritance."

"That was for emergencies. A darkroom is hardly that."

"This is your dream, Liddie. We'll make up the money somehow."

"Really?"

"We're having a good year with the pigs."

"You are a wonderful man, Joe Bauer." She leaned over and hugged him. "If I did something for neighbors from time to time, I would make some of it back sooner."

"Stop worrying so much." He pulled her onto his lap. "And kiss me, *Liebchen.*

———

*April 13, 1918*
*Dear Amelia,*

*I cannot tell you how concerned we were when we received your letter saying that Fred had disappeared. We were beside ourselves wondering if he'd been in an accident and couldn't let you know, or if something worse had happened. You must have been so frightened. How relieved we were when the telegram arrived. Your latest letter was even more reassuring. We are happy you are well and a family again.*

*My friend Mrs. Tinker was down with influenza in February. She was so sick with fever and chills her sister called the doctor to come twice. He administered salts of quinine and recommended what we already know—bed rest, liquids, and aspirin. He also suggested Vicks VapoRub. She got a jar and said it did help her breathe better. Fortunately, she is now right as rain again.*

*Joe is helping me set up a little darkroom in Mama's old room so I can make pictures. Ever since the idea came into my head, I've been so excited I can barely sit still.*

*Pearl has taken steps on her own. Rose gets around by flipping over and over. She's so funny to watch. Are the twins walking yet?*

*The war fills the news here, and the battles aren't all in Europe. The body of a soldier who died in battle was returned to Iowa for burial. The minister preached part of the funeral service in Swedish so the dead man's grandparents could understand. For that, the minister was put in jail. I don't know what we are coming to when human kindnesses are made to seem unpatriotic.*

*I must get supper on. Amelia, we truly are so thankful things turned out well. If you need anything, you will let us know, won't you? Write soon.*

*Your loving sister, Liddie*

Liddie did not want to read trouble where there was none, but she wondered how Fred could have been "detained on business" for three weeks without getting word to his wife.

The whole thing did not feel right. Still, it might be as Amelia explained. And it was not her business to question.

# Chapter 45

"Oh, don't you love days like today?" Liddie stretched her arms up to the sky and then lay back on the blanket, her hands clasped behind her head, her eyes closed as she soaked in the sunshine.

"June is my favorite month," Minnie said. "No more cold, but it's not so hot yet." She turned onto her knees and crawled to the picnic basket. "How about a pumpkin biscuit? I'm trying recipes that don't use wheat flour." The Food Administration list of ways women could contribute to the war effort by conserving, preserving, and flat-out eliminating food was impressive.

Liddie propped herself on an elbow and held out a hand to accept the biscuit. "Did you make them with lard?"

"Bacon drippings. I'm making butter tomorrow."

"We have some advantages living on a farm, don't we?" She broke the biscuit in half and took a bite.

"I do try to conserve at every turn, even though we raise so much we hardly lack anything," said Minnie. She looked toward the river. "I wonder if Joe and Vern are having any luck?"

"I bet they're having a lot of luck getting a nap in. Just like their daughters." Liddie glanced at the blanket in the shade of the oak tree where their daughters were curled together like kittens. She smiled. They hadn't moved in half an hour. She turned back to Minnie. "Thanks for recommending Edna to me. I never expected a paying client."

"Really, I never said a word. They stopped by the other day, and when Edna saw the pictures, she wanted one of her and her grandsons. She didn't know you could take nice photos like that right in her house."

"I hope she's not disappointed. I haven't taken pictures in so long."

"Stop that, now. You took our pictures and we love them." Minnie shook her head. "I don't know how you find time."

"I can find time for photography." Liddie smiled. "Besides, so far I've only done pictures for you and us. Edna is my first real client."

"I've no doubt you'll do well. But wait until Rose is walking. Then we'll see. I spend all my time running after Pearl. She gets into everything."

"Rose pulls up on things. I expect her to take steps on her own soon." She brushed crumbs off her lap. "Joe may have gotten more than he expected when he gave me that camera. I almost feel as though I must take on clients to justify the costs."

"After what he spent on the car?" Minnie giggled.

"What?"

"I swear, Liddie. I thought I saw steam coming out of your ears that day."

Liddie buried her face in her hands. "I'm still embarrassed by how I acted. Besides, he was right. We both use the car."

"He should have been ashamed. Springing that on you. Your darkroom helps make it up." She pulled the picnic basket closer and began to dig through the contents. "I brought something I thought you might like to see."

"What?"

Minnie handed over a folded-up newspaper.

Liddie unfolded it and saw it was a page from the *Chicago Examiner*. She looked up, puzzled.

"There." Minnie pointed.

When Liddie found the item, her heart pounded. The article reported that Thomas Littmann, a photographer whose photos of French soldiers had appeared periodically in the *Examiner*, had been injured in a motorcar accident. He was expected to survive. Liddie searched for more, but there was nothing else.

"How did you get this?" she asked.

"Mr. Caither picked it up on a trip. He recognized Littmann's name and knew his wife would be interested. She passed it along. I held on to it for a while. I wasn't sure I should show it to you."

"I'm glad you did. I've wondered if he made it to Paris."

She read the item again. He'd done what he wanted to do. And apparently achieved some success. She was glad for him for that. She shivered. "I hope he's all right."

"The article didn't give us much. I've wondered. Do you ever regret not marrying him?"

Liddie smiled. "Not in the least." She folded the newspaper and handed it back.

"You don't want to keep it?"

"No. I'm glad to know what happened to him, but knowing is enough. Do you have another biscuit?"

As Minnie reached in the basket, she asked, "Do you suppose you could take another picture for us?"

"Another?" Liddie frowned. "Didn't you like what I did?"

"Oh, don't worry. I love them. Vern does, too. I had the one of the three of us in the parlor, and he took it to our room and set it on the dresser so he can see it more often."

"That's sweet. So why do you want another?"

"When we have a baby . . ." Minnie let her words trail off.

"A baby?" Liddie looked at her blankly.

Minnie ran a hand over her midriff, a coy smile on her face.

"You're pregnant? But the doctor said . . ."

Minnie raised her eyebrows. "I guess doctors don't know everything."

"Oh, Minnie!" Liddie hugged her. "I'm happy for you." Then she searched Minnie's face. "Are you okay? Really okay?"

"I'm fine. I'm not getting my hopes up this time. Maybe a little. I can't help it. I'm going as easy as I can. And I'm praying."

"What does Vern say?"

"I know he's trying not to hope too much, either. But he's excited. He's the one who wanted to tell the two of you today."

Liddie hugged Minnie again. "This is wonderful news. I can't wait to take a picture of the four of you. My gift to the new baby."

———

"Let's sit on the porch," Joe said as they finished up supper.

"I planned to make the Fergusons' pictures tonight." Liddie spoke over her shoulder as she washed the dishes. Who'd have imagined the Miller photos would have led to two more clients? Liddie was euphoric that people wanted her to take their pictures.

"Couldn't they wait? The moon is full."

"How about this: I'll only develop the film. That doesn't take long. I'll join you in plenty of time for the moonrise."

"Honest to God, Liddie. I think you'd rather be in the darkroom than anywhere else."

"Not true. I won't be long. Half an hour at most."

She wiped her hands and scurried into the darkroom. Several nights in recent weeks, as soon as she'd put Rose to bed, Liddie had lowered the black cloth over the door and slipped into her other world. Once she started, she usually became so enthralled with the process that by the time she hung the last prints to dry and cleaned up the chemicals, it was often near midnight.

The last time she'd gone into the darkroom, she had been sure she hadn't been in there more than a half hour when Joe had knocked on the door.

"Coming out soon, Liddie?" he asked.

"In a bit. I have prints in the trays."

"I had something more fun in mind for us to do," he teased.

A familiar ripple raced through her groin, but inexplicably, impatience edged her voice when she replied, "Only a little longer."

He left without another word.

*Honestly*, she thought. Didn't he know she couldn't quit in the middle of printing? But niggling guilt snaked through her gut, and she finished as fast as she could. When she came out of the darkroom, he was in bed, his back toward her. She crawled in, wrapped her arm around his chest, and blew kisses against his neck. She knew he wasn't asleep, but he wouldn't be enticed. Lying there, Liddie had almost heard her mother's voice admonishing her that the wife's job is to keep her man happy.

Joe had been chilly for days after. Even fresh bread hadn't been able to bring him around. Liddie had vowed not to let the darkroom come between them again.

In under an hour, she developed the Ferguson film, cleaned up, and joined Joe on the porch. They held hands as they watched the moon rise over the barn. Even as they talked, she listed in her mind all the things she had to do tomorrow. It would be a full day.

———

"You gonna be gone all morning?" Joe asked over breakfast.

"Morning is the best light in Edith's parlor. We only have a couple hours to get the photos taken." Liddie put the breakfast plates in the dishpan to soak and went back for the breadbasket.

"Hey, I'm not done." He snatched another slice of bread and reached for the jar of strawberry preserves before she took that away, too.

"Sorry. I don't want to be late." She whisked the table clean, leaving Joe holding bread in one hand and a coffee cup in the other. "I'll drop Rose off with Minnie on the way." She'd tried taking Rose along to photo sittings, but it wasn't practical now that the child had started walking.

Joe grunted.

She looked at him. "What?"

"Nothing."

"Something." She smiled, hoping to bring him out of his pique.

He ignored her smile and drained his coffee. "Will you be here for dinner?"

"Of course." She expected a kiss good-bye, but he was out the door. "Joe?" She ran out onto the porch. "Joe, please."

He kept walking. She wanted to go after him, but there wasn't time. Everything was ready to go; she had only to put it all in the car. She wrestled the heavy camera stand into the backseat along with three reflector sheets. She wished she had tripods, but Joe had been none too pleased with the cost of the reflectors.

On her last trip into the house, she gathered up Rose and a bag of diapers. A dishpan of tomatoes and the bushel of yellow apples sitting by the door were the latest reminder of work she hadn't done. Maybe tomorrow. Or the next day.

She'd talk it out with Joe over dinner, she promised herself as she cranked the car to life, though the cold roast beef sandwiches she had planned weren't all that conducive to a warm conversation. She'd make him something special for supper.

When she drove into Minnie's yard, Liddie didn't even turn the car off. She set the hand brake and rushed Rose up to the porch and into Minnie's arms.

"You're a lifesaver, Minnie." Liddie gave her a quick hug. "I hope Rose isn't too much trouble. I wish we had time to talk. Maybe when I pick Rose up." She brushed her lips against Rose's forehead. "I'll see you soon, sweetie. I love you."

"The girls will have fun." Minnie adjusted Rose on her hip. "She won't even notice you're gone."

Back behind the steering wheel, she waved to Minnie, released the brake, and set the car in motion. Minnie's last words echoed in her ears. Would Rose really not notice she was gone? It was an offhand comment, she decided. It didn't mean anything.

Once she was in the Gaftons' parlor, creative energy swept away those thoughts as Liddie shared her ideas for a photo of the Gaftons' daughter, Nessie, an attractive and accomplished pianist.

By the time they were finished, it was nearly noon, and Liddie's anxiety resurfaced. There was no way she'd be home in time for dinner. Joe would come in to eat and find nothing. He would be angry. And with good reason.

As she drove into Minnie's yard, Minnie came out, Rose in her arms.

Liddie reached for her daughter. "Hi, sweet Rosie. I told you I'd be right back." The lighthearted tone she used with her baby gave way to contrition when she spoke to her friend. "Minnie, I'm so sorry. I didn't realize it was so late."

"It was no problem. Rose ate when Pearl did. I was about to put her down for a nap."

Vern stood at Minnie's side, arms crossed, displeasure in the set of his jaw.

"Thank you, Minnie. You too, Vern." She offered an apologetic smile. "I'll make it up to you, but I have to run. Joe . . . I think he'll be upset."

"Worried, maybe." Minnie spoke evenly. "I was beginning to worry, myself."

"I'm sorry. So sorry."

"Go."

"You're a blessing."

As she drove, Liddie rehearsed an apology, every version sounding inadequate. By the time she pulled into the yard, Rose was asleep and her own stomach was a tangle of nerves. She scooped up the toddler and ran to the house. She expected Joe to be there and steeled herself for the anger that would surely be on his face, for the harsh words that would follow.

Silence greeted her when she opened the kitchen door. A silence that elicited relief in Liddie's stomach and apprehension in her heart.

"Joe?" she called softly, so as not to wake the baby. "Joe?" There was no answer. She looked around. If he had eaten dinner, there was no sign of it. No dirty dishes. No crumbs. She lightly touched the stove. It had not been lit. And what did she think? That he would fire up the stove and cook a meal for himself? That was her job. Guilt weighed heavy on her heart.

She settled Rose in the crib with a kiss, covered her with a light blanket, and stood at the door for a full minute to be sure the baby didn't wake. Then she went in search of her husband. He could be anywhere, but she took a chance and climbed up to the haymow. Sure enough, he sat looking out the south door.

"I thought I might find you here." She tried to sound cheerful as she picked her way between the mounds of hay.

He did not speak.

"I'm sorry I'm late." She rested a hand lightly on his shoulder.

He shrugged her off.

"Please, Joe."

"This was a mistake." He stared into the distance.

"A mistake?"

"Asking you to live on a farm."

"What are you talking about?"

"You love photography. A farm isn't what you want."

As his words soaked in, Liddie almost stopped breathing. "I do want this."

"The farm was my dream, not yours."

"Joe, stop." She crouched, taking his hands in hers. "I love the farm. I love our life together."

"You're gone during the day to shoot photos. You disappear in the darkroom at night." He looked beyond her. "What am I to think?"

Liddie pried open his hands so hers could rest in his palms. She knelt there, feeling his warmth soak into her skin. She looked up at him. "I never meant to neglect you. Please believe me. I do like photography. But I love our life here. Have I not told you that I love you?"

"You have."

"Do you believe me?"

"I do. But you love photography more."

"I don't, Joe. Truly."

"I miss you, Liddie. I want you to be my *wife*."

"I really thought I could do both. Do you want me to stop?"

Finally, he looked at her. "You'd quit photography if I asked you?"

She ached for his forgiveness. She nodded and immediately ached for the loss of her beloved photography, too. When she'd worked in Maquoketa, she'd found ways to do both sewing and photography. Wasn't it possible to be married and still do the other things she loved?

"I would not ask it of you. But Minnie shouldn't be working so hard. Not now. She's got her own family." He brushed her hair back behind her ear, then brought his hand to rest against her neck. "And Liddie, I want time for us to talk like we used to."

The heat of his hand radiated through her skin, melting her reticence. He was what she loved. "These photos for the Gaftons are the last. I only have to finish printing them." He frowned. "Three hours at most," she added. Maybe she could do it faster.

"I didn't say never. You know that, right?"

"I know."

Liddie remembered how Mrs. Tinker had told her she would clear off the worktable when her husband came home. Liddie had to go away from their house to take photos. If she made pictures in the future, she could not let time with Joe and Rose suffer.

"I wonder if other farm wives ever think about needing a maid? Having someone to cook and clean while I did photography would surely help."

"But not to replace you in any other way." Joe pulled her into his arms.

"Definitely not." She cuddled against the familiar warmth of his chest.

# Chapter 46

When the phone jangled, Liddie was cleaning oatmeal off Rose's face. "That does it, honey. All clean." She looked up at Joe as the phone rang again.

"I'll get it," he said.

Liddie set the toddler on the floor. "You play quiet now." She held a finger to her lips as she waggled a sock doll in front of the little girl. "Daddy's on the phone."

"I'm real sorry to hear that," Joe said. "When did it happen?"

His sober tone sparked anxiety. Liddie arched her eyebrows in question. *Who?* He shook his head. Dread formed in her chest. *Who?* She gripped the back of the chair.

"Of course. I'll be there." He hung the receiver on the hook and faced her. "Minerva Ward died last night."

"Oh no! I saw her a week ago. She was fine." Liddie shuddered. "What happened?"

"Flu. Henry said she came down with it two days ago. She died last night."

"So fast! She was my age." Liddie clenched the sleeves of her dress in her fists. "We went to school together."

"They asked me to be a pallbearer."

"You can't," she blurted.

Joe looked at her with surprise. "Of course I will. Minerva was our friend."

"No, Joe. Once was enough. You were just a pallbearer for Nessie. Why does it have to be you?" Her voice broke.

She'd taken those photos of Nessie a little over a month ago, delivered the prints only a week ago. The images of the young girl, the light from the window illuminating her face as she sat with one hand on the piano keys, were etched in Liddie's mind. The family had been so happy with the photos. And now she was dead.

Her reaction to Joe was not logical. She knew it. Friends were supposed to help each other in times of need. But not now. Not when death was crowding on all sides.

Every week, the paper detailed battles, advances, defeats. One story touted that the first US soldier killed in combat in the war was from Iowa. The article made it sound as though that were a badge of honor. So many soldiers dying in battle. Now, the influenza.

"It isn't safe anymore. They've canceled public gatherings in New York, Boston, and Des Moines because of this influenza. There's talk of doing that in Maquoketa, too. It's dangerous to even attend the funeral."

Joe didn't relent. "Hank and Minerva are our friends. I won't turn my back on him."

"But what about us? What about Rose? How can we risk putting her in a crowd?"

Joe pointed to the article they had cut out of the newspaper. "They say this flu is no different than other years. If we do what we've done before, we'll be all right."

Liddie frowned as she ran a finger down the article. "If this is like other years, why are they canceling meetings? Some people at Nessie's funeral wore masks." She rubbed her left temple. "Even thinking about it gives me a headache."

"We talked about this. In the cities, people crowd together. Not like here. Besides, they say it's winding down." Joe shook his head. "Look. If you'd rather not go, Hank will understand. A funeral is no place for a baby, anyway."

Liddie lowered her eyes. Now that she'd gotten him to agree, she was ashamed of herself. How could she not be there for their friends? They would be there for her and Joe.

She went to the kitchen window and looked out over the fields, her arms crossed tight at her waist. The maple and oak trees flamed red and yellow under the October sun. She loved the color and smell and temperatures of fall, but sometimes, October left like a tease. A last bit of good weather before the harsh cold of winter.

When she turned around, Joe had not moved. He waited. This was her decision. She could go or not. She managed a weak smile. "If you're going, I'm going with you."

"You're sure?"

She nodded.

Joe kissed her on the cheek. "Thank you, *Liebchen.*"

Liddie nodded. No doubt Joe was right. She was worried for nothing.

———

"Let's surprise Daddy with a little lunch." Liddie spoke as though fifteen-month-old Rose understood. "Won't that be fun?" She raised her eyebrows and screwed up her face in a way that made Rose crow with delight. "That's my girl." Liddie hugged her.

Liddie still felt guilty for being so selfish that morning. Of course they'd go to Minerva's funeral. Of course Joe would be a pallbearer. It was an honor to be asked.

She put the camera in the basket along with the cornbread. With the onset of the flu, people had stopped asking for pictures, which was just as well. She took her own pictures, developing the film after she put Rose down for naps. She checked with Joe before working in the darkroom at night.

Now, hoisting Rose onto her hip, she got a grip on the basket and headed to the field.

"Hello, Joe!" She picked her way over the uneven ground, kicking her skirt out of the way when it snagged on downed cornstalks. "Do you have time for lunch?"

"I always have time for food. And for my girls." He tossed an ear of corn into the wagon, peeled off his gloves, and reached for Rose.

Liddie set the basket on the ground by the wagon and fished out the camera. "First, a picture of the two of you."

"I'm not so clean."

She laughed. His protests at being photographed had become a game between them. She'd taken pictures of him with holes in his trousers, with a brace of rabbits dangling from his hand, with sweat soaked through his shirt as he chopped wood.

"How do you want us?"

"Sit up there." She gestured to the end of the wagon. "Hold Rose by your side."

Joe swung up on the wagon and held his daughter securely under her arms as she tottered on the pile of corn.

Watching through the viewfinder, Liddie framed the picture and waited. When Joe hugged Rose to him, his head and hers side by side, Liddie depressed the lever.

"Oh, that will be a good one," she exclaimed. She put the camera aside and began to pull food out of the basket.

"If you're happy, I'm happy." Joe hopped off the wagon and set Rose in the middle of two rows, handing her an ear of corn that went right into her mouth. Joe took a square of cornbread and crouched down, his back braced against the wagon wheel.

"You know, I always wished I had a picture of me and Papa," Liddie said.

"I thought you did," Joe said.

"There's only the family portrait taken before I was born."

"I have a picture of me and my Pa with a horse."

"You do? Let's find it. When Rose is older, she can know both her grandpas."

"Our little girl is never going to want for pictures of her and me, is she?"

"Not if I have anything to say about it." Liddie tilted her head back, her eyes closed. The warmth of the afternoon sun radiated through her chest, melting away her earlier anxieties. "This is a perfect day, don't you think?"

"Yup," Joe said.

"Yup," Rose mimicked her father.

Liddie laughed.

# Chapter 47

"Here now, sweetie." Liddie scooped Rose up off the floor. "It's not so bad as all that. You took a little fall. You'll be fine." She kissed away the baby tears. "How about we have a cookie?"

At the mention of cookies, the child stopped crying. Liddie rubbed her temple as she sat with Rose on her lap, watching her baby stuff bits of cookie into her mouth. The headache simmering behind her eyes when she woke that morning had worked itself to a full boil. She had hoped that by cleaning and cooking she could distract herself. But the pain did not go away.

Propping her elbow on the table, she rested her head in her hand. She ran a finger across Rose's forehead and along her hairline, then paused with her fingertip in the indentation behind her daughter's ear. *The softest place in the world*, she thought as she closed her eyes.

She was sure she'd closed her eyes for only a second, but when she opened them, she did so with a jerk. The late October sun cast golden streaks on the kitchen floor. Rose played with her blocks on the rug. How long had she been sitting there? How had her daughter gotten down from her lap?

Liddie folded her arms on the table and laid her head down. When she opened her eyes again, it was nearly dark. She had to make supper. When she tried to stand up, her legs went rubbery, and she fell back in the chair.

Rubbing her eyes and temples, she realized her skin felt hot. Sweat beaded on her forehead. Yet she saw the fire in the stove was nearly out.

"Rosie, are you cold? Come here by Mama." Liddie reached out her hand. The child's tiny fingers curling around her own felt like ice. "Oh, honey! You're freezing!" She ran her hands along the baby's arms, only then realizing Rose's skin felt cold because her own was so warm.

Liddie gripped the edge of the table, steadying herself as she stood. *I'm fine*, she told herself. It was only a headache. Maybe a little fever. She wiped her face with her sleeve. The wooziness passed as she threw corncobs into the stove to stoke the fire.

"You feeling okay?" Joe asked later as he mopped up gravy with a slice of bread. "You didn't eat much."

"A bit of a headache." Liddie eked out a smile, though her head was throbbing so fiercely she could barely focus her eyes.

Joe put his hand on her forehead. "You're hot. You should be in bed."

"It's only a headache. It'll pass. Besides, who would take care of Rose and get meals ready?"

"Did you forget that I spent two years on my own in Canada? And lived to tell?"

"I have wondered. Were you really on your own?" Liddie attempted to joke as she let him guide her to the bedroom, where she sank weakly to the edge of the bed.

He helped her out of her housedress and slipped her nightshift over her head. "You sleep. I'll get Rose to bed." He brushed Liddie's hair back from her forehead and planted a kiss above her left eyebrow.

The next morning, Joe woke her. "How are you feeling?"

"Not perfect." She threw back the covers and swung her legs over the side of the bed. "Where's Rose?"

"In her crib. She's had breakfast."

Liddie pulled a shawl around her shoulders and forced herself to stand. She willed herself to feel better in spite of a pan-banging headache. She kissed him on the cheek. "I love you, you know."

He put his hand against her forehead. "You're still hot."

"I'm fine."

"I only woke you because I have to feed the hogs."

"Go." She nudged him toward the door.

As soon as Joe left, Liddie sank back on the bed. Yesterday's headache was joined by an ache in her bones. When she had been sick as a little girl, Mama had brought her glasses of water and kept cool cloths on her forehead. She wished her mother could do the same for her now.

By late morning, Liddie had put Rose back in the crib and propped herself on a stool to peel apples. Then the phone rang. She stared at it but made no move to answer it. It would be bad news. What was the point of walking all that way for bad news? The phone jangled again, a harsh, metallic sound that made her ears hurt.

Pinpricks of white flashed in her vision as she finally laid the apple and paring knife on the counter and pushed herself off the stool. She picked up the receiver, braced a shoulder against the kitchen wall, and closed her eyes.

"Hello?" she said.

Then she slid toward the floor in a dead faint.

———

When Liddie woke, she was confused to find herself in bed. Dim light seeped in at the edges of the curtains, but she couldn't tell what time it was. Joe sat in the rocker pulled close to the bed, his eyes closed. Rose slept in his arms.

"Joe," she whispered.

He opened his eyes.

"What happened?" She struggled to focus.

"You fainted. I caught you." Joe laid Rose in the cradle he'd brought to the bedside, then held Liddie up so she could sip water from a glass. "You had the phone in your hand, and you collapsed."

"I'm going to get up," she said, though she made no move to do so.

He put his palm on her forehead. "You're still sweating. Lie still." He sat back in the rocker. "I've been thinking Vern and Minnie might take Rose until you're back on your feet."

"Rosie's never been away from us overnight. She'd be scared."

Joe stopped rocking. "I'm sorry, Liddie. I wanted you to go to that funeral. And you got sick. It's my fault."

"It's not your fault." She covered her mouth against a barking cough. "I expect I'd have gotten it anyway."

"We have to do something. I'm afraid to leave you alone with Rose. If she was with a neighbor, you could stay in bed."

Liddie forced herself upright. "I'm fine, Joe. I'm fine." She managed a weak smile. "Put Rose in the crib. I've had the fever two days now. It has to be over soon."

When Joe returned to the house, Liddie was doubled over beside the kitchen table, her hands over her ears to block the sound of Rose's crying. He took Liddie's face in his hands.

"God, Liddie. You're burning up."

"I'm so cold," she whimpered. "I hurt all over." She let him take her back to bed. "I can't stop shaking," she mumbled as he pulled blankets around her shoulders. Joe's hand felt cool against her forehead, and she put her hand over his to hold it there. She was so hot and so cold.

He tucked the quilt in tight. "You sleep. I'm calling the doctor."

"What about Rose?"

"I'll take care of everything."

Teeth chattering, Liddie closed her eyes and tried to lie still. "I'm so sorry, Joe," she whispered through gritted teeth.

He kissed her forehead. *"Schlaf, Liebchen. Schlaf."*

———

The next time Liddie woke, she didn't open her eyes immediately. The memory of how it hurt to see light was too strong. From behind closed eyelids, she assessed her body. Her skin no longer felt on fire. The deep ache in her bones was gone, though her ribs hurt. A sour smell rose from the clammy bedclothes. She slowly opened her eyes. It was dark.

Realizing how very stiff she was, Liddie attempted to roll over and bumped up against Joe. She brought a hand out from under the covers and sought his face. In his sleep, he covered her hand with his and brought it to his lips.

"Joe," she whispered.

"Liddie," he mumbled. "Liddie?"

"I'm fine, Joe," she said.

He propped up on one elbow and put his palm on her forehead, her cheek, the back of her neck.

"I'm really fine."

He pulled her into his arms, and she felt his tears on her cheek.

The next morning, Liddie tried to get up, but her legs barely supported her.

"No wonder," Joe said, helping her to a chair. "You haven't eaten anything but a few spoonfuls of soup for five days. Sit there. I'll bring you something."

"Five days? What do you mean?"

"You've been out of your head with fever. It's November second."

"How can that be?" Bewildered, Liddie looked around. "Where's Rose?"

A muscle twitched in his cheek. "You were so sick."

Even though the lamp was turned low, she saw how haggard his face had become.

"I couldn't take care of Rose and you and the farm," he said. "I had to give her to Vern and Minnie."

"She's all right?"

"She's fine." Joe raked his hands through his hair. "I guess you may as well have all the news right away."

The hair on Liddie's arms stood up. "What?"

"Fred's gone. He's not coming back."

"Oh no."

"Amelia sent a telegram. He left a note. Said he was going to California, that she'd be better off without him."

Liddie was speechless.

"Vern said he'd go get her. She said he didn't need to. Said she'd been living on her own for a long time, and she'd get herself and the kids back to Iowa if Vern wired money for the train. Bastard didn't even leave her money for that."

"Poor Amelia." Liddie pulled the blankets closer. "When will she be here? Where will she live?"

"She should be here in a week, maybe less. They'll live with Vern and Minnie until we get it figured out."

A cough erupted from deep in Liddie's chest. Now she knew what caused the ache in her ribs.

Joe held her until the coughing fit passed. "I had the doctor here. He said it had to run its course." His voice was heavy with weariness.

"I'm better now. The fever is gone, or mostly gone. Feel my face." She lifted his hand to her cheek. "See? My skin isn't burning. My bones don't ache like they did." She choked on another cough.

"That cough is bad. I could go to the doctor and see if he has anything to help it."

"Let's give it a few days. It should clear up on its own. And bring Rose home? My arms ache to hold my little girl."

"I'll get you something to eat first."

"I am hungry." She ran a hand across her shrunken stomach.

"Now, that's good to hear." His face lightened. "How about pancakes?"

"Sounds perfect. Bring me a pan of water. I'll clean up. I must smell like I've been spending time with the pigs."

"Not so bad as all that. But . . ." He wrinkled his nose and went for water.

By the time Liddie made it to the kitchen, Joe was pouring batter on the griddle.

"You look exhausted," she said.

"Nothing sleep won't take care of."

Through the kitchen window, she saw the sun rising, a big copper ball in the cloudless sky. She pulled her shawl up around her neck. Today would be grand. She was weak, but she was well. She would eat breakfast with Joe. He would bring Rose home. She was happy her sister was coming back, whatever the reason. And she felt only a little bit guilty for her happiness.

# Chapter 48

Though she was better in most respects, her dry cough persisted over the next week. She put meals on the table. She tended to Rose's most basic needs. At least once a day, she retreated to bed after putting Rose in the crib to play. Her cough kept Joe and her both from sleeping, but she did her best to get their lives back to normal. One night, after the supper dishes were done and Rose was asleep, she suggested to Joe that they spend a few moments in the parlor.

"Sit with me." Liddie patted the cushion next to her.

"Don't you think you should be in bed?"

"Soon enough." She patted the cushion again. Joe sat, his shoulder touching hers. "Tell me what's going on with the farm," she said. "I haven't been outside in so long."

Stretching out, Joe leaned back and closed his eyes as he talked. "The corn's in. Vern's going to help us butcher. When you feel up to it, we'll look at the records. We should be able to pay ahead on the mortgage." He opened one eye to look at her. "You were right about the photos. What you sold made a good dent in what we spent for the darkroom." His eyes closed again.

She squeezed his hand. It meant a lot that he acknowledged the photos. She chewed the inside of her lip as she watched him. Ever since he'd told her that Fred left, she hadn't been able to shake an uneasy feeling. She finally asked, "You're glad you came back to Iowa?"

He opened his eyes. "Why are you asking me that?"

"I can't help it. I think about Amelia all the time. How could Fred leave her and the children? Was he always unhappy? Was she?"

"And you wonder if I would leave you?"

Liddie didn't answer.

"You and Rose are my life. I will never leave you. Never. This is our home for the rest of our lives." He leaned over and kissed her squarely on the mouth.

Liddie pulled his arm around her shoulder. "I can't hear you say it enough. I look forward to seeing my sister, but I'm sad for her. How will she manage?"

"She'll live one day at a time. Like everyone does. She won't be alone. We'll help."

Joe handed her the paper. "Why don't you read? I'm going to close my eyes."

"Don't you feel well?"

"Just tired."

Liddie searched the headlines. "The war news sounds positive. This article says it could be over soon. Wouldn't that be wonderful?" A cough tickled her throat, and as she sipped some water, the cough broke through, and she splashed water on them both.

Joe sat up. "That settles it. I'm going to town in the morning. Doc Milburn must have something for that."

"I'm fine, Joe. Really."

"I don't want to risk you getting the fever back. Let's go to bed. Now." He took Liddie's hands and pulled her to her feet. "You don't know how sick you were."

"You're right," she acquiesced.

———

"I'll take Rose with me. You sleep while we're gone," Joe said at breakfast. He drained the last of his coffee. "We'll take the auto."

She went to get Rose's coat. "Come here, honey; let's get your coat on. You're going to town with Papa."

"Go town! Go town!" Rose parroted.

"Oh, Rosie, not so loud," Joe said. "You're hurting Daddy's head."

"You do have a headache." Liddie scanned his face.

"A little one. Maybe the doc will have something for me, too." Joe buttoned his coat and scooped up Rose. "We'll be back before you know it."

Liddie stood at the door, watching until he had the car started and was out of sight. When she cleared the breakfast table, she saw half an egg congealed on his plate beside most of a slice of bread. It was not like him to leave food.

She was beside herself by the time Joe returned three hours later from a trip that should have taken half the time. "Finally. I thought you were stuck somewhere."

She took Rose from him, slipped off her coat and scarf, and put her in the high chair. "Are you hungry, Rosie?" she asked as she set about getting food from the cupboard. "I bet you and Daddy didn't eat, did you?"

"Oh, that was noth—" Joe coughed harshly and sat without taking off his coat.

The raspy sound focused her attention on him. "When did that start?"

"In town. Got worse on the drive home. Probably caught it from you." His attempt at a grin was erased by another cough. He pulled out a kerchief and covered his mouth as he hacked, then wadded it up when the cough subsided. He pulled a packet out of his other pocket. "Doc gave me this. Quinine. Mix it in some tea with honey. He says it should help."

Liddie took the packet and reached for the kettle on the stove. "It sounds like you need it more than I do."

When she looked at him again, a chill shot up her back. Joe sat with his arms wrapped around his chest, forehead resting on the table. Putting her hand on his cheek, she was shocked at how clammy his skin felt to her touch. The same fever chill she'd had.

Liddie pulled out a chair and sat close enough that their knees touched. "Oh, Joe, you've got the flu." She pushed back hair that was plastered to his forehead by sweat. "What did the doctor say?"

"Said we both need to get more rest." He doubled over coughing.

When the spasms stopped, Joe's hand dropped to his knee, and Liddie stared in disbelief at his kerchief, which was covered with bloody mucus.

"Come. Let's get you to bed." His normally taut muscles felt flaccid under her fingers when she took his arm to help him stand. She gripped his arm tighter, alarmed by the sudden thought that he might slip away if she did not hold on to him.

As she helped him into his nightshirt, she talked. "There now. That's better. I'm going to make Doc's tea. We'll both have some." She tucked in the blankets. "I'll be right back with a cool cloth for your forehead."

When she returned, Joe's eyes were glassy; sweat beaded on his forehead. She slid her arm under his shoulders, lifting him so he could drink. He swallowed a few sips and fell back on the pillow. She wiped his face and neck.

"Feels good," he whispered.

"I'll get fresh water and be right back." Liddie stood to leave but couldn't stop staring at him. His face was so slack. He looked like an old man.

Throughout the afternoon, Liddie spent as much time at Joe's side as she could while still taking care of Rose. Joe's cough grew deeper, more ragged. Whenever he woke, she tried to get him to drink more of the tea, but he didn't wake often.

By midafternoon, she called Vern, trying in vain to quell the anxiety in her chest as she asked for help with the chores. When she hung up, Liddie realized she hadn't coughed even once in the last couple of hours. She put wood in the firebox and brewed more tea.

When she returned to the bedroom, she thought her eyes were deceiving her. Joe's skin looked blue. She lit the lamp and held it closer to the bed. She'd heard neighbor women talk about babies born blue, but she'd never seen it herself. She ran to call the doctor. Fear clawed at her chest as she waited to be connected.

"His skin is blue!" she exclaimed. "He was coughing badly when he got home from seeing you. And there was blood. And now he's blue."

Liddie clutched the receiver tight to her ear, willing the doctor to tell her something to help. "Are you there?" she asked when he didn't answer right away. "Can you come out? You need to see him. I don't know what to do."

"Are you giving him the quinine?"

"Yes. But he isn't drinking much. I gave him aspirin, too."

"Good. Give him what tea you can. The fever has to run its course."

Joe's coughing caused Liddie to race back to the bedroom as soon as she hung up. He'd thrown the covers back and sat upright. Blood dribbled down his chin. Sprays of blood dotted the sheets.

"Oh, Joe." She wiped away the blood that ran from his nose and threw the bloody handkerchiefs and towels into a bucket. She stripped off the bloody sheet and replaced it.

No sooner had she got Joe cleaned up than she heard Rose crying. She'd totally forgotten about her daughter! She had no appetite herself, but she had to feed Rose. As she heated green beans, Vern called to her from the porch.

"Come on in," she called.

"Only wanted you to know I was here," he said through the closed door.

"Wait. I'll come out." She threw on a coat and stepped out into the damp November air.

When she came out, Vern backed off the porch. "How is he?"

"As sick as I was," she said. "Maybe worse." She didn't say anything about the blood or his blue skin. She was trying not to think about it herself. "It came on so fast. He was fine this morning."

"I'll get goin' on the chores."

She noticed that Vern kept backing away from her. Regardless, seeing her brother calmed her, and she was reluctant for him to leave. "How's Minnie?"

"Getting along fine."

"What will Amelia do?"

"We'll figure that out when she gets here. I gotta get goin.'"

"Thanks for coming over, Vern."

He nodded.

Liddie fed Rose and put the child in her crib long before her normal bedtime. Then she pulled the rocking chair close to sit by Joe. The color of his skin caused her stomach to clench with fear. From time to time, she wiped his face and straightened the blankets, talking as she did to still her fears.

"I've been thinking about the garden. You could plow up a bigger area next spring. We'd plant enough vegetables for Amelia's family, too."

As the evening wore on, she also talked to God, even though prayer was not her habit.

"I love him so. For Rose. For me. Please make him well. Please." Eventually, her prayer came down to one word. *"Please."*

By eleven, Joe was resting more easily. She slipped into bed beside him, laying one hand on his shoulder.

*"Schlaf schön, Liebchen."* She whispered his German words. "I love you, you know." A low moan passed Joe's lips, and Liddie felt

him relax a little under her hand. She kissed him on the forehead and closed her eyes.

When she woke the next morning, light filtered in at the edges of the window shades, and it took several seconds for her to recollect where she was. She had slept soundly and felt better than she had in days. She had not been wakened even once by Joe's coughing. The doctor was right. Rest was exactly what they both needed.

Propping herself up on her elbow, she laid her fingers against Joe's cheek. It was stone cold.

# Chapter 49

Liddie knelt at Joe's side. She put her fingers to his throat, searching for a pulse. She pressed her palm against his chest, willing herself to feel his heart beating. There was nothing, and she felt the fabric of her heart tear.

She laid her palm against his cheek. *He's so cold*, Liddie thought. *He shouldn't be so cold*. She stretched out beside her husband, pulled the quilt up over them, slipped her arm over his chest, and nestled her head against his shoulder. She knew he was dead. But she couldn't leave him. Later, when tears erupted at every thought, she would wonder that she didn't cry then.

An hour later, she heard Rose calling from her crib. She forced herself out of bed and tucked the quilt back around Joe. She lit the lamp on the nightstand and looked at him for another long moment. "*Schlaf schön, Liebchen*," she whispered. "*Schlaf schön.*" Then she kissed his cheek and went to get Rose and call Vern.

The rest of the day, the phone rang relentlessly as news of Joe's death and the signing of the armistice spread along the party line.

The war was over. Liddie felt her life was over, too.

———

Three days later, she stood in her front yard waiting for the funeral service to start. A mist so light she wasn't conscious of it collected on her wool coat. Pulling the coat up around her neck, she saw the beads of moisture and wondered if they were her tears. She shivered, a quaking that came from inside her bones and set her whole body trembling.

"Do you want to sit down?" Amelia asked.

Liddie stared dumbly at her sister and returned her eyes to the casket. Amelia had arrived in Iowa the day after Joe died. Leaving her older children with Minnie, she brought the twins and moved in with Liddie to help prepare for the funeral.

Liddie had scarcely taken her eyes off the casket since the undertaker and minister moved it from the porch to where it rested now atop two sawhorses some fifty feet from the house. She wanted to rip off the coffin lid, shake Joe awake, look into his eyes, and remind him that he had just told her they would live here for the rest of their lives. She wanted to ask him why he hadn't told her their time together wouldn't last more than forty-eight hours.

Her mind barely registered the handful of neighbors forming a ring around the casket, white masks covering their noses and mouths. People who'd come in buggies and wagons a few minutes before the service, arriving so they wouldn't be there much more than the time it took for the minister's words.

Her heart was with Joe. Joe who called her *Liebchen*. Joe who made her laugh. The father of her daughter, her friend, her husband, her lover. At the thought of Joe making love to her, Liddie felt pain rip through her gut, and she doubled over so fast Amelia barely caught her in time to ease her into a chair.

Liddie buried her face in her hands and wept.

When the minister finished, all the people who endured the bleak day and muddy roads, who faced their fears of the influenza because they could not face themselves if they did not, passed by Liddie murmuring condolences. None of them touched her.

There was no luncheon after the funeral, no reminiscing with family and friends, no comfort for the widow. All her life, she would remember that only Dr. Milburn, the undertaker, and

Amelia came into the house when Joe died. Though she herself had insisted Minnie not come over while she was pregnant, for years after, Liddie felt disappointment tinged with anger that Minnie had not been there when she needed her most.

———

"Feed Rose." Amelia slid a bowl in front of Liddie. "Here's her peas."

Liddie looked up. Seeing Amelia in her kitchen was as unbelievable as having Joe gone. She still could not grasp that her husband had been alive one morning and dead the next. How did that happen?

Liddie put the spoon in Rose's hand. "You can feed yourself. Can't you, sweetie?"

Using her hands more than the spoon, the toddler scooped up peas, hitting her mouth with a few, smashing many on her cheeks, dropping most in her lap.

Amelia put a dishrag in Liddie's hands. Liddie dabbed at Rose's face. "If you didn't keep making me do something, I doubt I'd ever move."

"It's hard."

"Here's what I don't understand. Everyone asked Joe for help. He never turned them away. Minerva's funeral. Nessie's. He never said no. Where were they when Joe died? Where are they now?"

"They call," Amelia said. "And seems like every time I go out on the porch, there's a hot dish or a pie or a loaf of bread. I expect they're afraid. If someone strong like Joe can die of the flu, who is safe?"

"You aren't afraid."

"I survived losing my husband. I'll survive this, too."

Liddie blinked. She'd been in a fog. Amelia had lost her husband, too. Maybe he wasn't dead, but he was gone just the same.

"I'm sorry about Fred, Amelia. I haven't said that before, have I? I am sorry."

Amelia sniffed. "He's been gone a long time, as far as the children and I were concerned." She swiped a dishrag over the table and shrugged in resignation. "Some men aren't meant to be married."

"Aren't you angry?"

"More hurt than angry. I thought we could make a life for the babies. But even that . . ." She roughly wiped her nose on a handkerchief and stuffed the wadded cotton in her apron pocket.

Liddie rose, wrapped her arms around Amelia's waist, and rested her head on her sister's shoulder. "I'm so sorry, Amelia."

"I know." Amelia turned and pulled Liddie into the circle of her arms. "I know."

Her sister's embrace sent grief sweeping through Liddie, and she trembled as tears soaked her cheeks.

Amelia rocked her gently. "It'll be all right, honey. It will."

"How will it be all right, Amelia?"

Amelia stepped away from her sister, poured coffee for herself and Liddie, then sat down. She scooped sugar into her own cup and stirred it for a good while before speaking. "I'll stay with Minnie when her baby comes. Any day now. Then as long after as she needs me."

"I'm happy for her. After all this time." Liddie's voice was flat. "Have you thought about after that?"

"Vern's looking into getting me a place in town. I expect he'll be glad to have my brood out of his hair."

"What will you do? How will you get along?" Liddie pulled her chair closer to the table, cradling the hot coffee mug to warm her hands.

"A widow woman in Lusk took in laundry and sewing." Amelia tapped a spoon against the rim of her cup, then drank deeply. "What about you?"

"I don't know. I can't string two thoughts together anymore." The discussion made her tired. It made her think of Joe. She swallowed the lump in her throat. "I can't . . ."

Amelia squeezed Liddie's hand. "You're going to have to. You're responsible for yourself and Rose. Vern said you and I could share a house in town. Help each other out with the children. Between the two of us, we could find enough work sewing and taking in laundry to pay the bills. With what you'd get from selling the farm, we'd make out okay."

Liddie stared at her sister. "Sell the farm?"

"You can't farm this place on your own."

"But . . ."

"Vern's been asking around. Looking for a buyer."

"I can't sell this place. Joe and I . . . it's our place."

Amelia shook her head. "I don't mean to be harsh, Liddie, but you need to wake up. You can't farm this place on your own, and you can't expect Vern to take care of it."

"What if it was you and me? Couldn't we do it together?"

"Some of it we could do. But not the crops. Not without a man."

"I suppose not." Liddie propped an elbow on the table, leaning her cheek on her fist. She felt so tired. Every movement took so much effort.

"Together in town might be the best way," Amelia said.

Liddie looked at her sister. "Does that sound good to you? Really?"

"Things don't always turn out like you want. Besides, in town you might find another man."

Until that moment, Liddie had felt vaguely disconnected, as though the outcome of the conversation had no real effect on her, but Amelia's last comment sliced through her lethargy. "Another man?"

"You're young, with only one child. You'd make some man a good wife yet. You'd have more suitors in town."

Anger burned color into Liddie's cheeks. "My God, Amelia!" She shoved back from the table. "Joe is barely dead. Can't you give me even a few days? And why are you so set on fixing things for me? What about you? Why don't you get married?"

Amelia's face contorted in a bitter grimace. "Don't you remember? I am married."

"Fred's gone."

"A small detail as far as the law is concerned."

"But you could get a divorce, couldn't you? Or have him declared dead?" Liddie choked on her words. Her own husband was dead, and she was suggesting her sister would want the same. She stood up. "I can't talk about this now."

She grabbed her coat and ran to the barn. Up in the haymow, she threw herself into a stack of hay. Sell the farm? She clenched fists full of hay. Marry someone else? She burrowed her fists against her chest. Life without the farm? Life without Joe? She curled on her side, wrapped her arms around her head, and sobbed.

It was a full half hour before she rolled onto her back, wiped the remaining tears from her cheeks, and stared at the rafters. Amelia was right. She had to get a hold of herself. This was her life. She was responsible. No one else.

# Chapter 50

Over the next week, Liddie pulled herself together. When she thought she'd cry, she bit her cheek hard, forced a smile to her lips, and did something. Everyday needs were a constant—pigs and cattle to feed, the cow to milk, meals to cook, laundry to do. All of it—the chores inside and out, the physical activity—helped.

With all four of Amelia's children living there now, the house also teemed with activity. At nearly five, Hope was capable of helping with the twins. Melvin's lip had been sewn up, and though he'd always have a scar, his face looked almost normal. The twin girls, Faith and Grace, were mirror images of each other. Overwhelmed at first by so much noise, Rose soon joined her cousins and they all tumbled around like a litter of puppies.

Between the two of them, Liddie and Amelia were able to take care of most things and tackled the chores with minimal fuss. An early riser, Amelia checked on the livestock and milked the cow before Liddie was out of bed. By the time Amelia was back in the house, Liddie had the children dressed and breakfast on the table. If there was a good thing at all about the timing of Joe's death, it was that there was no fieldwork to be done.

"We could do it, don't you think?" Liddie asked one Tuesday morning as she washed the breakfast dishes and Amelia set up the ironing board. "Take care of the farm?"

Amelia took her time answering. "Why are you so set on staying here? You liked living in town, didn't you?"

"At the time, I did. Then when I came here with Joe, I don't know how to explain it, but I knew I was home."

"Couldn't that have been about Joe?"

Liddie smiled. "Some of it, I suppose. But once we were settled, I realized how independent we were living on a farm. What we did, when we did it, how we managed. It was up to us."

Amelia laughed without humor. "Are you joking? 'What' is taking care of the livestock and putting meals on the table and doing the laundry and minding the children. 'When' is every minute of every day."

"That's true. But everything we did was for us, for our future. I laugh at myself when I think of how I viewed farming as a child. When I would look out the windows, my view felt blocked by the trees and hills. I saw fences that held me in as much as they did the cattle. I wanted to see what was beyond the fences, beyond the hills. Now I look out the windows, and I see fields that are mine to walk, trees that shade my family when we picnic, and open space that lets me breathe. Not neighbor women looking out their windows at me."

The more she talked, the more Liddie realized how much the idea of staying on the farm with Amelia appealed to her.

"There was a little more aloneness than I liked," Amelia said.

"Wyoming was different. Here, we'd be together. Family and neighbors are close. You're home now, Amelia. We're together."

Only a week later, Amelia and her children moved in with Minnie to help when she delivered her baby—a healthy boy they named Joseph George.

When it was only her and Rose on the farm, Liddie understood better the aloneness Amelia had talked about. Though a few neighbors stopped by from time to time, they shared news from their buggy seats and left, still wary of the flu.

Most days went by without the sound of another adult voice. So it was with surprise and gratitude that she opened the door one day to see Mrs. Tinker.

"My sympathy," Mrs. Tinker said as she hugged Liddie.

Liddie gulped down the grief that surged into her throat. "Thank you. Come in. I'll make some tea."

It felt odd to be serving tea to Mrs. Tinker on the farm. In Liddie's mind, they were always together in her former employer's front room.

"It's nice of you to come," she said.

"I heard you were ill, but I had no idea it was so severe. I didn't know of Joe's passing until I read the obituary in the *Sentinel*."

Liddie dipped her head. "It was sudden."

"I am so sorry." Mrs. Tinker squeezed Liddie's hand.

The tenderness in Mrs. Tinker's voice caused Liddie's eyes to blur. Blinking rapidly, she forced a smile, reached for the teapot, and changed the subject. "I've been meaning to ask, what have you heard from your nephew?"

"There is some good news," Mrs. Tinker said. "Thad will be home by the end of the year."

"That is wonderful news. Will he work with his father on the farm?"

"For now. I imagine he'll want to start a life of his own." She sipped at the tea. "We are so grateful, so relieved he will be safe at home."

Liddie had thought Joe was safe at home when he had not been drafted. Yet he hadn't been safe. Mrs. Tinker's nephew went to war and would return home alive and well. It was so unfair. She dug her fingernails into her wrist, refocusing on the pain to push the tears back. She was horrible to think another man's living was unfair.

"You have a lovely home, Liddie. Look at these photos." Mrs. Tinker set her teacup down and went to the sideboard, where Liddie displayed pictures. "These are wonderful. You took them?"

"I did." She joined Mrs. Tinker. "Joe gave me a camera last Christmas. We had such fun taking pictures that day."

"Have you been taking many photos?"

"Until . . . recently." She hadn't gone into the darkroom since Joe's death. The thought of going there reminded her of the hours spent in isolation when she could have been with him. How foolish she'd been. "I took photos for a few neighbors."

"Are you going to continue? Taking photos for others, I mean?"

"With the war and the flu, people are less interested." Liddie traced her finger along the edge of the photograph of her mother holding Rose and Pearl. "It was a hobby." Liddie felt nothing for the photos. It all felt so meaningless.

"Hobbies can become businesses, as mine did." Mrs. Tinker returned to her chair. "Liddie, I came as a friend but also with a proposition."

"A proposition?"

"Have you given thought to taking up sewing again? My business is not anywhere near the level it was, but now that the war is over, many of my women are beginning to freshen their wardrobes. It's more than I can manage alone. I would welcome working with you."

"You're gracious to offer, Mrs. Tinker. But I'm not leaving the farm. Besides, my sewing . . ." Embarrassment flashed through her. She shook it off and squared her shoulders. "I've been mending socks and trousers."

"One does not lose the skill." Mrs. Tinker sipped at her tea.

"It's odd, isn't it?" Liddie tried to smile. "At one time, I couldn't wait to leave the farm behind. Now I would do anything to stay here."

"Don't give up on your dreams, Liddie. Where there's a will, there's a way."

"Aunt Kate said that to me."

"It's an old saw." Mrs. Tinker smiled. "I enjoyed Kate's determination. You have much of her in you."

"I wish I was as strong as her."

"You're stronger than you realize."

Liddie was uncomfortable with the praise, and thinking of Aunt Kate opened a chasm of loneliness. Kate's career had advanced since she had moved to Ohio; she was superintendent of a large district. She'd found like-minded women among the suffragettes. But letters did not fill the gap Liddie knew existed between the reality of someone's life and what they chose to share on paper. After Aunt Kate left, Mrs. Tinker was the person Liddie turned to for counsel. Now she did so again.

"How did you do it?"

"Do what?"

"Go on. After Mr. Tinker passed? I'm trying to put on a good face, but I feel as though I can barely think."

Mrs. Tinker sat quietly, her thimble finger tapping her cheek. "One day at a time," she said at last. "It sounds too simple, and I'm not saying it's easy. But that's it. One day at a time. You have your daughter, and you must keep going for her. I did not have children, but I did have my sewing. The ladies kept coming to my door." She smiled. "I honestly believe they gave me projects they didn't need doing to keep me working. I was grateful for each of them."

"Does it ever stop hurting?"

"Over time. Which is not to say you forget. Goodness knows, you will never forget. Don't let the pain make you forget how lucky you are to have had Joe."

After Mrs. Tinker left, Liddie wandered from room to room, smoothing doilies on tabletops, straightening chairs that didn't need it. She appreciated Mrs. Tinker's offer, but did she really want to return to sewing? She found herself in front of the darkroom, and for the first time since Joe's death, she opened the door.

She and Joe had talked over the cost of each piece of equipment, each sheet of photo paper, each bottle of chemicals. She'd convinced him there was potential. Now that she was on her own, did she believe it? Was she a fool to think she could stay on the farm? How could she take care of this place herself? Without a man? Maybe Vern was right. Maybe she would have to sell.

That night, after she milked the cow, fed the pigs, and collected the eggs, after she fed Rose and tucked her in bed, Liddie sat down with her sewing basket. The feel of the cloth and the needle was reassuring. She made a few stitches, then tilted her head back and let her eyes close.

She knew she should go to bed, but sleep was not easy to come by. The act of lying down in their bed brought Joe's death back fresh each night.

"You know what to do." Joe spoke to her from a chair by the window.

A bubble of happiness filled Liddie's chest. "I thought you were gone."

"What are you waiting for? You know what to do."

"Not without you."

"I trust you. Now you trust you."

Me trust me. She smiled. "I love you."

"I know. Now figure it out."

She opened her eyes, the smile still on her lips. She could hear his voice. She could see his face. Yet he was not there. Her heart twisted and the smile faded. How could he leave her again?

Joe's words echoed in her head. *Figure it out.* The memory of his smile brought a smile back to her face. "I can do that," she said out loud.

She put the sewing down, brought out the ledger, and took it to the kitchen table, where they had worked together on the farm records. As she wrote figures on a new sheet of paper, she imagined Joe sitting there, watching her. Sometimes, she asked him questions out loud and waited until the answers came. She wrote them down and went on.

She drew columns and labeled them *farm*, *photography*, and *Mrs. Tinker*.

The need for a man kept coming up, and Mrs. Tinker's nephew came to mind. She jotted *Thad*, *Amelia*, and *rent* in the margin. The more she wrote down, the more her anxiety receded.

By the time she extinguished the lamp, she had a page with neat columns of items and numbers. She was ready to talk with her brother.

# Chapter 51

"Mornin', Liddie." Vern wiped his boots on the rag rug by the kitchen door and shrugged out of a heavy coat splotched with drops of rain. Early December had brought a week of weather extremes, from warmer days that felt more like spring to bitter cold, sleet, and snow.

"Good morning, Vern." Liddie motioned her brother to a chair as she poured two cups of coffee and set out a plate of cookies. "Thanks for coming over."

She took the chair that had been Joe's. As she sat down, a breath of air wheezed past her lips. The influenza was completely gone, but sometimes—like the moment before her hips met the chair—movements still generated an ache in her joints.

Ever since Mrs. Tinker's visit, her plan to keep the farm had grown in her mind, and she'd worked the numbers over and over. She needed her brother's support, but talking to him about the farm—about business—was new territory. She'd put the farm ledger and her lists on the table, ready for when she needed them.

"How's that baby boy?" she asked, easing into the discussion.

The frown lines on Vern's face relaxed a little. "He's got a set of lungs."

"You won't be getting much sleep now. How does Pearl like her brother?"

Vern grinned. "She thinks she's got a new baby doll."

"They'll be good playmates. I'm so pleased for you and Minnie."

"Minnie said to be sure to remind you to come over Sunday for dinner. She and Amelia are doing it up big for the christening."

"I wouldn't miss it. I was only waiting until I was sure my cough was gone."

He drained his coffee cup. "You wanted to talk."

"I do. About the farm." She attempted a confident smile. "I want to thank you, Vern. You've been a blessing all these weeks. Helping Joe and me while we were sick and still helping now. I understand you can't keep doing that, and I know you think I should sell the farm."

"I talked to a couple fellas who might be interested."

She gripped her cup with both hands. "I appreciate your effort. But I've been thinking there might be a way to stay on the farm."

He eyed her suspiciously. "You can't farm it yourself."

"I know I can't. But I'm thinking we could stay here anyway. I worked it out." She reached for the ledger and worksheets.

"What about the fieldwork? What about when something breaks down? A farm ain't no place for a woman alone." Vern's jaw set tight.

"I know that, Vern." She struggled to soften her voice.

He cut her off. "You think I can come over here every time you need something? I can't. I'm gonna say it one more time. You have to sell." Vern slapped the table with the flat of his hand. "I swear to God, Liddie. I don't think you listen to me at all."

His abrupt anger raised the hackles on Liddie's neck. She stood to compose herself and made a show of getting more coffee. When she came back to the table, she faced him squarely. "This farm belongs to Joe and to me. Now that he's gone, it's mine. Don't be telling me a woman can't do it. Don't tell me *I* can't do it."

Vern shook his head. "Now you're sounding like Aunt Kate."

"I hope I learned something from her. You can help me or not, Vern. It's your choice. I know we need a man. I had a thought about that, if you'd let me tell you." He didn't interrupt. "What if we had a hired hand? Someone who lived here and took care of the crops and livestock?"

The cords in his neck flexed, but he didn't speak.

"I know someone who might be perfect," she continued. "Mrs. Tinker's nephew, Thad. He was in the war, but he'll be back real soon. She says he'll be looking for a place."

"You'd take the first man to walk by? He mightn't know a damned thing about farming."

"I know what Mrs. Tinker says. He's worth talking to."

"If he's looking for a place of his own, why would he come here?"

"Help me think it through, Vern. Could we make it right for him? Work out shares for the crops and livestock? Give him a start the way Joe got his start. He'd take his meals with us."

"People'd talk."

"They'll get over it."

"Liddie, it's gonna be hard enough for you. Why don't you get shed of this place?"

"Joe loved this farm, Vern. No one knows that better than you." She opened the ledger. "I worked out the numbers. Please look at them." She nudged the ledger toward him. She kept her eyes on him, her jaw set. She could be as strong willed as he. Finally, he grunted in resignation.

"Thank you." She slid the ledger in front of him, placing the sheet with income and expenses on top. "Let me show you how I thought of it. Amelia and her children can move in here with Rose and me. That would be money saved. We'd take care of the cows and chickens, the garden, the house. We can take in sewing. Mrs. Tinker was here, and she asked me to work with her."

"I expect she meant in town."

"Whatever I'd do there, I can do here. Amelia and I can both sew. Besides, no matter where Amelia and I are, you'll be looking in on us. Won't you?"

He screwed up his mouth. He knew that was the truth.

"Wouldn't it be easier if we were close by?"

She watched him think, then took another breath and added, "Plus, I have my darkroom. I can take photos for neighbors."

He couldn't contain his skepticism. "Pictures of two or three neighbors ain't gonna make no money. What'll you do when they've all had their pictures took?"

"There will always be pictures to take. Weddings, graduations, funerals. Now that the war's over, people will get back to living. Mrs. Tinker says she sees it in her business. Look at this."

Over the next hour, Liddie shared the records she'd kept on the farm and the darkroom. At one point, Vern looked up from the numbers. "You make that from taking pictures?"

She nodded. "I gave you the family discount."

By the time he left, they'd agreed he would talk with Thad. If Thad passed muster with Vern, then they'd all get together.

"Don't forget about Sunday," he said as he mounted his horse.

"I wouldn't miss it. Should I bring my camera?"

"Don't know's how I can afford it."

She slapped at his leg. "Family discount, remember?"

# Chapter 52

Liddie dreamed about baking bread. As she kneaded the dough, Joe said, "See? Doing something is better than doing nothing." The smell was so vivid, his voice so clear, she woke up. It took several moments lying there to realize neither the voice nor the smell was real. She drifted off to sleep. When she woke again, she was hungry.

After breakfast, Liddie brought Rose's rocking chair into the kitchen. "You can rock your baby while I bake bread."

"Me bake, too." Rose ran to the cupboard.

The enthusiasm on Rose's face made the little girl look so much like Joe that Liddie caught her breath. With Rose, she knew she'd always have Joe close by.

"Not this time, Rosie. Sometime I'll teach you to make bread just like your daddy liked." She handed the child a wooden spoon and pan. "Today, you make something with your baby, okay?"

That satisfied the child, and Liddie threw herself into the familiar task. Mixing the bread made her feel better than she had in weeks. She relaxed into the rhythm of kneading the dough, the first batch she had made since she came down with the flu. Outside to inside. Outside to inside. The more she worked at it, the stronger she felt, the clearer she thought.

Outside to inside. She could still sew and make photographs. Outside to inside. She could manage the farm, with Amelia or on her own. Outside to inside. She had lost Joe, but she had not lost everything.

By the time Rose was ready to go down for her nap, the yeasty warm smell of baking bread filled the kitchen. Joe had loved that smell. She remembered how often he'd come walking in the door the moment she pulled loaves out of the oven. They'd laugh about how he could smell bread baking from anywhere on the farm. Then they'd sit together and eat the heels off a hot loaf. Liddie rubbed tears away with the back of her hand.

After she tipped the loaves out of the pans to cool, she cut both heels off one loaf, slathered a thick layer of butter on each crusty slice, and wrapped them in a towel. Assured Rose was still asleep, Liddie put on her coat, slid the towel and bread into her pocket, and walked down the hill to the barn. Inside the barn, she stopped to breathe in the familiar warmth of the animals in their stalls. Then she climbed up to the haymow.

Ice crystals glittered on the rafters like stars in the night sky. Liddie could see her breath as she picked her way to the south end of the haymow. She swung open the door that afforded their favorite view of the farm.

She sat down in a mound of hay, surrounded by the smell of alfalfa, as she surveyed the length and breadth of the farm. This was where Joe had asked her to marry him. This was where they came to make up after spats. This was where he liked to talk about his plans for the farm. This was where he drew her down onto his lap and they talked about the children they would have and the parties they would throw. Where they talked about their future. Together.

The December scene offered no green pasture, no lush crops, no leaves on the trees. And Joe was not there by her side drawing the future with his fingertips and his words. Liddie's gut twisted as she thought of him, feeling the hands that would not touch her again, looking into the hazel eyes she would never see again, listening for the laugh she would never hear again.

# Acknowledgments

A novel is born as the result of the efforts of a great many people. I am indebted to all those who supported me in writing *Go Away Home*.

Many served as historical resources for information about life in the early twentieth century. I owe a debt of gratitude to Donald Wentworth, who was as close as I came to having a research assistant to dig out historical details about Jackson County; to Roger Kilberg, who shared rich stories of party line telephones and their importance to farm families; and to my uncle, Mahlon Denter, who confirmed the realities of growing up on a farm pre-electricity.

The manuscript benefited immeasurably from the input of workshop leaders and participants at the Iowa Summer Writing Festival, beta readers in my own book club and the Crows Reading Prose book club; fellow writers of historical fiction, and Jenny Toney Quinlan.

Special thanks to my writing partner, Mary Gottschalk, whose dedication to writing and insightful reading and indefatigable ability to stay at the keyboard inspired me.

It was an indescribable joy to hear from Jodi Warshaw, senior acquisition editor for Lake Union Publishing, who wanted to bring *Go Away Home* into the Amazon Publishing fold and to help ensure the story reached the widest possible audience. Many thanks to Amara Holstein and Kirsten Colton, who edited these pages with insight and a desire to help me make the story shine.

Finally, thanks to my son, Lance, who never stops believing in me, and to my husband, David, who served as consultant on all things farm-related, helped me noodle out male reactions, and constantly cheered me on. I love you both.

# Author's Note

*Go Away Home* was inspired by my maternal grandparents. Even as a young child, I knew that my grandfather died of the Spanish Influenza in 1918, and I was always fascinated by my connection to that major world event. Yet even though my grandmother lived until I was in my twenties, I never asked her a single question about him or their lives together.

In the course of family history discussions, my mother provided names, dates, and places of some events and passed along family lore, yet I had no sense of the truth of these stories or the motivation for any particular event. As a result, the novel is entirely fiction. But fiction based on facts.

When Kodak introduced the Brownie box camera in 1900, making photography available to the masses, my grandmother acquired one. I was fortunate to have the many pictures she took of life in the early 1900s to inspire my thinking and stories.

Research was an integral part of my writing process, leading me to story lines about photography, the attitudes and actions on the home front during the war, and the impact of the influenza pandemic.

Since I grew up on a family farm in the 1950s, I have a good sense of farm life, though I enjoyed the benefits of tractors, cars, and electricity. I was aided in my understanding of farming and life for farm women before those conveniences by the interpreters at Living History Farms in Des Moines and through conversations with my uncle, who has vivid memories of farm life pre-electricity.

Since I chose to set much of the action in Maquoketa, the county seat of Jackson County, Iowa, I felt a particular obligation to be true to the geography of the area and layout of the town. The Jackson County Historical Society provided a fire department plat map of the city, which was useful not only in locating businesses but also in understanding the vitality of the town at that time.

The Des Moines Public Library offered up copies of *Ladies' Home Journal* from the period for information about women's fashions and how women were encouraged to support the war effort. President Woodrow Wilson enlisted Iowan and future president Herbert Hoover to head the Food Administration, which developed guidelines encouraging Americans to demonstrate their patriotism by voluntarily observing "wheatless" Mondays and Wednesdays, "meatless Tuesdays," and "sweetless Saturdays." Issues of *Studio Light*, a Kodak publication for professional photographers in the early 1900s, was an invaluable resource about studios and darkrooms of that time.

The population of Iowa draws heavily from Germany and other northern European countries. Until the Great War, those native languages were still widely spoken throughout the state. The effect of Iowa governor William L. Harding's "law" on moving the state to speak only English is documented by Nancy Rugh Derr in her article "The Babel Proclamation" published in the *Palimpsest* in 1979. Iowa Public Television offers a wealth of information on Iowa in World War I through "Iowa Pathways" on the IPTV website (www.iptv.org/iowapathways/mypath.cfm?ounid=ob_000259).

Information about the Spanish Influenza in Iowa, including symptoms, remedies, and deaths, was gleaned from reports of the Iowa State Board of Health and the *Des Moines Register*. A valuable resource for understanding the influenza pandemic on a broader scale was *The Great Influenza* by John M. Barry.

I value research and have attempted to treat the historical record with respect. Any errors are solely my responsibility.

# Go Away Home

## Reader Discussion Guide

1. As a teenager in the early twentieth century, Liddie sees very few career options available for women. Housewife. Teacher. Seamstress. How do these differ from the options you saw when you were sixteen? What factors contributed to her having such a narrow view?

2. One theme of the book is women's ability to make their own choices. Two women—Aunt Kate and Mrs. Tinker—have careers they arrived at via different routes. What limitations did Kate's choice never to marry and Mrs. Tinker's position as a widow place on them? Would either woman have had the same success if she'd been married? How did you react to the advice these women give Liddie?

3. Liddie found a passion for photography. What do you think about her chances to be happy on the farm if she did not take up photography again?

4. Places hold special significance for Liddie—the grove, the hay-mow. Discuss the importance of place in your life.

5. Liddie struggles to balance jobs, family, and personal interests. Women today struggle with the same issues. What made this balancing act more or less of a challenge in 1918 than it is today?

6. What challenges will Liddie face in keeping a farm? How realistic is it for her to try to run a farm? How willing would you be to try such a course of action?

7. Honesty and openness can be critical to all relationships. Why does Liddie feel more free to share with some people than others? What prevents her from sharing openly?

8. What did you think about Liddie's two different decisions about marriage? Did they make sense to you? Why or why not?

9. Liddie initially resists familial and societal expectations to marry, yet ultimately decides to marry. How much of her decision was a function of the times and how much was a function of the relationship itself?

10. At one point, Liddie considers what constitutes love and how important it is to a marriage. Have you reflected on the importance of love in marriage, and if so, what was your conclusion?

11. What was the relationship between Margretta and G. W.? Both daughters appear to reject their parents' wishes and attitudes about marriage. Why do you think they did?

12. After Liddie decides to marry, Mrs. Tinker questions her making two very rapid decisions. Have you ever made a

spur-of-the-moment decision about a serious topic? What was the outcome?

13. Death strikes three times. Liddie deals with the loss differently each time. What contributes to these different reactions? If you've faced the death of a loved one, what helped you through the grief? How might the deaths of three people so close to Liddie affect her future?

14. In the lead-up to World War I, Americans were urged to be patriotic, to "Buy American." How are things different from or similar to that now?

15. During World War I, the patriotism of German immigrants was questioned. Japanese immigrants were targeted during World War II. Middle Eastern immigrants have been questioned during the wars in Iraq and Afghanistan. Why do we repeat this pattern?

# About the Author

Carol Bodensteiner grew up in the heartland of the United States, and she continues to draw writing inspiration from the people, places, culture, and history of the area. She is the author of *Growing Up Country: Memories of an Iowa Farm Girl*, a memoir about growing up in the middle of the United States in the middle of the twentieth century. Her essays have been published in several anthologies. *Go Away Home* is her first novel.

She enjoys hearing from readers, so don't hesitate to be in touch. You can reach her via:

Her website: www.carolbodensteiner.com
Twitter: @CABodensteiner
Facebook: www.facebook.com/CarolBodensteinerAuthor
Goodreads:www.goodreads.com/author/show/1323422.Carol
   _Bodensteiner

F Bodenstei Carol
Bodensteiner, Carol.
Go away home /
22960001053700

4 - 16    IAFI